THE IMMORTALS OF LIGHT

THE RAPTURE

BOOK 2

K.P. BOUDREAUX

For Veronica, Jessica, Michael, and Emily.
Thank you for being there.

Table of Contents

PROLOGUE

Research Labs, Colony of Atlantis

"Destroy the biped. The creature will never be useful."

The dutiful assistant turned away from his superior and stepped toward the reinforced glass—the wall to the creature's caged habitat and the thin protective barrier between him and certain death. He approached methodically, studying the animal's hairy, muscular frame. Its broad shoulders and developed forearms communicated a savage dominance. The beast snarled, its brown eyes creasing as it exposed its long, fang-like canines. "Are you sure? I say we give it more time, Marou. It's showing some promise."

Marou stood at the computer console in the near corner of the antiseptic white marbled room. His wide-set Atlantan eyes were focused on the console's electronic screens, not bothering with so much as a glance at his assistant. "Really, Prometheus? Is that your professional judgment? You seem to have become overly fond of this particular creation. Why?"

Prometheus hesitated, thinking about the question. "I don't know, there's something in its eyes, the way it watches me." He put his hand to the glass, palm open, fingers spread. The creature just stared, watching his every move. The thick metallic collar around its neck now clearly evident. The animal took a small step toward the glass, eyes locked on his.

"Unless it follows our commands, it's of no use," Marou insisted. "In fact, it's an overly aggressive danger. Watch again." Lowering his head, he spoke into a mesh square in the center of the console. "Sit." The word echoed through a speaker behind the glass.

The beast reacted. It turned and scurried toward a fallen tree dividing its habitat. Using both arms and legs, it propelled its hominoid body over the wood and into the tall grass that provided a comfortable, savannah-like home for the animal. A moment later, the creature popped its head above the bladed tops and snarled again, before dropping below the grass line, out of sight.

Clearly frustrated, Marou shook his head. "Okay, now let's use a little incentive, see if that helps." He said, "Sit," and waited a moment. With no response from the beast, he pressed a button on the console.

The creature exploded out of its hiding spot and into the open, screeching and pulling at the collar around its neck. It dropped and started rolling, all the while tearing at the device. Then, as if recognizing it couldn't be removed and the pain wouldn't stop, the animal stepped forward and pounded the glass barrier with its fists. The wall's strength was tested to its limit, threatening to explode as the animal raged against it.

No longer sure of his security, Prometheus took a step away from the barrier.

Breathing hard, eyes on fire, the creature stepped back and picked up the downed tree like a small branch. It slammed the timber against the ground, fracturing the thick wood. The building's floor shook from the impact, the jolt resonating through Prometheus's body.

Marou lifted his finger from the button, and the beast's thrashing halted. It dropped to the ground, whimpering, lying still for a few seconds as if collecting itself. The creature turned its semi-furred head toward Prometheus, its moist brown eyes studying him, then slunk back into the high grass.

"Don't do it again. He won't sit for you," Prometheus said.

Marou stepped from behind his console toward the enclosure, his iridescent suit now visible to his young associate. "As I said, useless. It's tolerable for the creature to be fierce, but it has to have discipline and must follow commands. You saw its strength, temper, and lack of intelligence. That's a dangerous combination." He glared at his assistant, "Destroy the biped. We have other, more promising creations." Marou turned and walked away, not waiting for an acknowledgement of his order.

Prometheus stepped forward again. He reengaged his open hand, spreading it on the glass. He watched, patiently waiting, as the blades twitched where the creature hid.

With Marou now out of sight, the biped crept from its hiding spot and into the open area. It moved past the shattered tree, pausing a few feet from the glass wall, studying the vacated area behind the assistant. As if sensing all was safe, it stepped next to the glass, eyes focused on him.

"What's going on in that head of yours? What are you thinking?" Prometheus asked rhetorically. He tapped his long index finger on the glass.

The creature watched and listened, then raised its oversized hand, pressing it against the glass barrier, mirroring the placement of Prometheus's. Its dirty, claw-like fingers aligned perfectly with the assistant's green digits. The animal held its gaze, eyes never straying from his. It answered, tapping its black nail against the glass.

For a moment, Prometheus wondered who was studying whom. He whispered, "Sit."

The animal bent its knees and lowered its bottom flush onto the ground. A guttural noise came from its mouth, sounding like the word, "Sit."

CHAPTER 1

September 14, 2014
Sunday
West Bengal, India

The midday sun peaked in the sky as the heat of the day sweltered down on them. Austin was hiking through a tangle of brush, just a few steps away from entering camp, when he heard Gabriel say, "Break's over. Where are Austin and Rebecca?"

"I'm betting he's curled up napping under some bush," Maya joked.

Austin strolled into the camp. "Hey, hey, hey, I'm right here, and can hear you." He shot her a playful look. "And contrary to popular opinion, I was just checking out the area. This place is unreal, there are old—and I mean ancient—Hindu ruins about three minutes that way."

A wide-eyed Rebecca followed just behind Austin. "Was Guatemala like this? I've never seen a forest so beautiful; it's a perfect habitat for Bigfoot." She laughed at her own joke. "I'm sorry, they're called yetis over here."

Gabriel answered, his voice gentle, "Yes, similar to Guatemala as far as the wilderness, but I doubt a Chupacabra is stalking this place." He grinned at Rebecca. "And you can find actual yetis just north of here, in the mountains of Nepal. They aren't as friendly as their North American cousins."

Austin shuddered at the memory of the demon they'd encountered in Guatemala. "I hope there's no Chupacabra. You said this trip was going to be easy, just research, right? No rescue, no retrieval—and most important—no demons."

Maya removed her Sig from its holster, seated the cartridge, then fed the first bullet into the chamber. "Let's not take any chances; plenty of nasty stuff in the jungle besides monsters."

Austin and Rebecca did the same with their weapons, while Gabriel adjusted the pouch holding his pen-like antimatter laser.

"Let's go." Gabriel said.

With his pack in place, Gabriel waited for the others to ready before plunging into the wall of brush. Rebecca followed close behind him, Austin and Maya trailing. As demonstrated in Guatemala, Gabriel was fluid in his navigation, adjusting the path as the landscape dictated, but always heading north and up the rising terrain.

They hiked this way for over an hour. As Austin walked, he was deep in thought, remembering their travels in the Guatemala jungle and his first impressions of Gabriel. The guide was knowledgeable on all things, not to mention brave. He saved Austin a few times in their foray into Ixlu's chamber to save Michael, who was held captive by the Chupacabra, and to retrieve the Star Crystal. With that said, Maya more than repaid the debt at the shootout with Mack's henchmen in the jungle, saving Gabriel, but sadly ending with the death of Michael's guide, Tomas. Maya's face was etched in grief after the ordeal—a pain she still carried with her today.

Choosing to remember better times, he smiled at the memory of Rebecca's stunning entrance at the Sedona fundraiser. After Maya said no to attending the event with him, he'd invited Rebecca with the promise of a great evening. But the weekend brought two kidnappings, a shootout, a near death experience, the killing of the deviant Atlantan Bernael, and an implausible escape from an exploding warehouse. As far as first dates go it was, without a doubt, the worst in history. As he stepped over a fallen branch, his energy stone popped through his shirt collar. It glowed a purplish-yellow. Twisting it in his fingers, he recalled the vision quest, the beauty of the Well of Souls, and the confirmation that we are all part of a larger existence beyond that which our five senses deliver.

Maya glanced over, eyes sparkling, giving that look that only she could, reminding him of the unexpected kiss he shared with her in Sedona. She was beautiful in her black dress, her hair down. He could still taste her lip gloss and smell her sweet perfume. It was a moment he'd always remember.

She kept her gaze, interrupting his thoughts. "What are you smiling about?"

"Just thinking," Austin said, trying to hide his feelings.

"About?"

He held her stare, "What a long, strange trip it's been." He paused, letting the words sink in. "Ever reflect about how this all started, all we've been through, and where we are now? If I hadn't lived through it, I'd say we're crazy."

She glanced away, her eyes set on the path. "I have thought about that, a lot. It is way out there. Six months ago, we worried about usual things, like college grades or future jobs. But today we're wondering if we'll run into a class four demon, or if we'll find the wormhole-opening crystal." She paused. "But in a way, I'm glad it's all happened. I prefer to know the reality, even if it's a dangerous one. Oh, and nice Grateful Dead reference. You're not going to start singing, are you?"

"Very funny, and no, that'd be cruel and unusual to you guys," he quipped.

She caught his eye, smiling back.

Austin felt good seeing her happy, a rare event as of late.

They returned to silence for a few moments before Austin commented, "Gabriel, I know we're trying to find a lost Hindu temple, but what are you searching for now?"

Gabriel stopped walking. He pulled out his water bottle and took a sip. "Do you remember the whole story of Indra and Vritra? We talked about it while trekking in the Maya Biosphere Reserve on the return from Qitaxa."

"Yes, I do," Austin said.

"I read the brief, but tell me. And start at the beginning. I wasn't with you in Guatemala and I don't want to miss anything," Rebecca interjected.

"Sounds good, it'll help pass the time." Gabriel placed the bottle back in his bag and continued walking. "As background, we have three of the six crystals. We think Lucifer has one, based on a couple of old Hindu myths. There are two versions of the story. The short one has Indra battling the demon serpent, Vritra, in northeast India. The actual location of the struggle isn't revealed. However, the bulk of the myth refers to Vritra as being the hoarder of waters. On the surface, I think much of the story is symbolic. Vritra represents a drought in the South, and his death signified the end of the dry period. What likely happened is that a warming trend occurred, the glaciers in the north country melted, and water flowed to the villages in need. Vritra the drought was dead. With that said, if we read between the lines, we can find the thread of truth to the myth. There is a more detailed version of the story that tells of a great battle that took place in this area during this warming period, where a serpent demon died by a thunderbolt from Indra's hand. Does that sound familiar?"

"Sounds like the battle at Tikal between Yax and Kukulkan all over again," Maya said.

Gabriel swatted at a fly buzzing his head. "Correct Maya. An Atlantan weapon, the same that killed Yax. That myth details the battle took place in a great cavern underneath the house of Shiva, the destroyer god. Michael and I read that as a cave below a Hindu temple dedicated to Shiva. I've suspected for some time that the battle took place in this huge jungle area, but had no idea where."

"I read that on the flight over. Do you think their destroyer god was really Lucifer?" Rebecca asked.

Austin answered, "Makes sense. We know that on Lucifer's orders, the Immortals of Darkness hid the pieces of the Star Crystal in caverns and pyramids. We also know ancient man worshipped the Atlantans as gods. Seems reasonable the IOD would hide a crystal below a temple dedicated to the leader."

"You mean psychopathic leader," Maya added.

"I believe you're both correct. That was my conclusion as well." Gabriel paused, studying the landscape in front of him. "So, back to your question, what are we searching for today? In your prep material, there are a few paragraphs about an encounter someone in our group had in 2013 when he came across a man at a bazaar in Kolkata selling a rock carving."

"I read that section; the figure depicted what appeared to be a Gray," Maya said.

Austin recalled the footnote in that portion of the text that described the foundation's inquiries on where the man had found the statue. All the traveler could remember was that it came from a mountain temple he had stumbled across in the area. He described the shrine as hidden by the forest with a narrow path in, its entrance partially destroyed, and the inside sacked clean. Only rock carvings were left on the walls, which he thought may have value; thus, he removed a few. The man recalled a river running below and on his right as he'd hiked in on an overgrown trail.

"So, I gather we're looking for a river, but there are multiple rivers in this area. Why this one?" Austin asked.

Gabriel stopped. "Correct Maya, maybe it turns out the statue was just bad art, but it's a lead. And Austin, recall the satellite photos. Although there are a few rivers, this branch flows way up-country, providing the link to the myth where Vritra captured the waters in the North. I'm guessing when we find the river, we follow it into the mountains and find that trail. It's in this forest somewhere, but it's probably overgrown; foot traffic is not what it used to be around here." He laughed at his own joke.

"So, we find the river to locate the path, which will lead us to the temple," Rebecca said.

"Exactly. We're heading north now; we'll run into the river soon." Gabriel started walking again.

Maya adjusted her pack. "Well, at a minimum, we get a nice hike in a beautiful country."

The group continued their trek deeper into the jungle. A muggy hour later, Austin heard the low roar of rushing water surging through a rocky channel.

Austin noted the West Bengal jungle canopy of hardwood trees growing tall and wide, intertwined with large-leaf vines. The forest floor was littered with ferns and green brush of all types. It was the landscape described so vividly by Kipling.

For the most part, the animals could be heard around them, but not seen. The hikers were inundated with squawks from birds and trumpets from distant elephants, but were fortunate to avoid the man-eaters that in all likelihood prowled the darker shadows.

Gabriel began heading toward the river sounds, choosing the circuitous route in order to avoid the densest underbrush. A few minutes later, the group stood on the broken stones that edged a fast-flowing river.

Austin reached down, touching the waters. He pulled his hand back at once. "Wow, that's cold."

Gabriel dipped his hand in, letting the water run down his fingers. "It flows from the mountain glaciers. It's pristine, and yes, still cold."

Rebecca crouched down, immersed her hand, and wiped her face, cleaning off some of the day's grime, appearing to find the cold refreshing.

Gabriel stepped forward, searching for the best path. The rocky terrain along the shore was difficult, at best. They walked this way for some time, studying the surrounding ground and brush. Austin was about to suggest they stop to rest, when Gabriel pointed forward. "Ah, there it is. It's overgrown, but the ground underneath still appears trodden."

Maya stepped to the area and crouched to better examine the jungle floor. "You've got a great eye, Gabriel. It could be a path; no doubt it's worn." She stood. "No harm in seeing where it takes us."

The team mobilized, breaking through the covering growth along what they hoped was a narrow path. After five minutes of paralleling the river, Austin was sure they had found something.

Although branches and leaves crossed the trail, just as Gabriel predicted there was a narrow area of compacted dirt, no more than twelve inches wide, beaten down from travel long ago. The trail eventually broke from the riverbank and headed up the mountain. The farther they moved from the water and the higher the terrain rose, the sparser the trees and ground foliage became. The path became easier to follow.

They took a short rest; Austin sipped water while Maya and Rebecca scanned the cliffs above. The late afternoon sun still blazed in the sky. A mountain breeze swept across them, providing some relief from the unending humidity.

Rebecca pointed up to the cliffs. "Do you see the rock fall up there?"

Maya squinted against the glare. "Yeah, I do, a few hundred yards up?"

"I can see columns against the cliffs, to the left of the fall," Rebecca said.

Gabriel stood, peering at the mountainside, his hand blocking the sun from his eyes. "You're right!"

"What are we waiting for?" Maya said. "Let's get up there and investigate."

As the group traveled higher, the view cleared, and the more certain Austin became that the rock formation was man-made. When they neared the fall, the trail they walked transitioned to a wide path lined by smooth black river stones—an obvious guide that this was some place important. The path was soon interrupted by a large section of broken granite that had fallen off the mountain cliffs high above. The boulder's slide had destroyed the bulk of the intricate rock carvings that adorned the outside of the temple, with the exception of two columns to the right of a gaping door. The fall had also cleared much of the tree line that would have previously hidden the cave from any travelers trekking below, making the temple visible to would-be looters and thieves. A small, worn path between the jumble of broken stone guided the four sweaty travelers to the front door.

Austin stopped to observe the area. The two standing stone columns were crafted by skilled tradesmen. He viewed his energy stone, and the crystal revealed a soft purplish glow shaded by yellows and blues. Over the last few weeks, he had become accustomed to this color combination, which reflected the four travelers' auras. They were still alone.

"All clear; nothing but our energies in the area," Austin said.

Gabriel patted Austin's shoulder. "Excellent, glad you checked. You've come a long way since Ixlu's chamber." He paused, "I'll lead. Maya, take the rear. Stay armed and stay close, I'm not sure what we'll find."

"If this is the location where Lucifer killed Vritra," Maya said, "it's probably where they hid the Star Crystal, meaning there may be traps. So be careful, and search for evidence of a struggle."

"And if it's not the location, we shouldn't expect any surprises from the monks who built it; it should just be a temple," Austin said.

"If you're all ready?" Gabriel asked.

One by one, they squeezed past the fallen stones into the mouth of the temple cave. The outside tumble of rocks fractured the light in the hallway, creating an alternating pattern of shadows and sunshine, until the sunlight faded and darkness took hold. The entryway's width spanned enough to accommodate two people side by side and high enough for Austin—at over six feet tall— to walk without stooping. Gabriel was soon forced to pull out his flashlight, scanning the entire area at first, but ultimately focusing the beam on the ground. Austin followed his lead.

The group came to the temple's main hall, and Austin flashed his light around the darkened room. The area was rectangular with high, vaulted ceilings carved into the rock. The smooth stone walls had intricate columns chiseled every few feet, distributing support to the upper weight of the room. A beam centered in the ceiling ran the length of the cavern, with curved weight-bearing support struts every few feet. This brace was held aloft by the lower wall columns. The structure's appearance reminded Austin of the arched ribs of a giant spine.

In the middle of the room, a tall, thick boulder with a knobby top had its front half sculpted to portray a man-like creature sitting in the lotus position under a full moon. Each of the creature's hands held a coiled snake. On either side of the being, two smaller men stood with hands raised in worship. His eyes wide, Gabriel approached the huge stone carving, his light focused on the creature. It was the face of his people—Atlantan. An oval skull with an extended forehead, two large eyes, and a small mouth. The two men carved at its sides were traditional Hindu monks. Gabriel squatted down to illuminate the inscription below the creature.

He turned to his three companions, "It reads: 'Beware of Shiva the Destroyer.'"

"You read Hindi?" Rebecca asked.

"Among other things, right Gabriel?" Maya answered for him.

"Correct . . , a little." Gabriel paused, studying the sculpture. "Bears a striking resemblance to an Atlantan in our Gray form, don't you think?"

"Yes, it does," Austin answered. On reflex he grabbed Demon Slayer, lifting it from its sheath.

Maya continued, "Okay, so this is the place. What's next?"

"The briefing paper said there is likely a sub cavern where the battle took place," Rebecca said. "This would be consistent with how they hid the Roswell crystal, not in the main cave but in a smaller, more protected area."

Gabriel answered, "Correct. So we find the entrance to the sub cavern, then we head down."

Rebecca and Maya flashed on their lights.

While Austin and Maya examined the walls, peering into each nook and corner for anything unusual, Rebecca studied the center carving of Shiva. Gabriel inspected the ceiling and rib area of the upper walls. They searched the entire temple end to end with no luck, finding only a few small stone carvings resembling the Atlantans.

Austin asked, "Could there be a trigger, like in Ixlu's chamber?"

Gabriel said, "Maybe, but unlikely; the walls appear to be natural rock." He knocked his closed fist on the stone. "It'd be difficult to construct behind them. I'm betting it's a door or just an opening."

"Could it be outside, you know, separate from the temple?" Maya asked.

"That's possible."

Rebecca climbed onto the center stone, scaling to its large top. She stood on the knobby area, then bent over and heaved at the capstone. It gave way and crashed to the floor.

Rebecca studied the newly exposed area. "This could be it. There is a hole in the center of the rock. It seems large enough for a person to squeeze down." She bent down, examining the opening. "It's man-made. I thought that capstone looked out of place."

Austin started walking toward the center statue. "Hold on there! That's a good find, but don't go into any dark places; let me go first," he said.

He scrambled to the top of the rock as she descended. Once there, he saw the circular opening. "You're right; it's ingenious, a portal hidden in plain sight." He peered down into the blackness. "Can somebody grab me a stone?"

Gabriel tossed him a rock from the floor. Austin shined his flashlight into the hole and dropped it. A solid clacking noise came back at once. "It's not that deep."

Austin checked his energy stone again and noticed a slight change from its earlier color, but nothing too radical. "We're still clear. I'm going down. Can somebody hold a flashlight in here while I climb?"

Maya hopped up. Her eyes scanned Austin's face. "You sure about this?"

His eyes met hers. "Yeah, I'll be fine. If this is the cave of the myth, the demon died a long time ago. Besides, the energy stone is clear. Just stay close."

Maya raised an eyebrow, making it clear she didn't like him being first. "Don't be a hero."

Gabriel climbed on top of the structure, shifting in close to Maya, preparing himself for a rapid entrance in case he needed to follow Austin down.

Austin slid feet first into the circular opening. Rebecca was right—it was a tight fit—but he managed to squeeze his torso through. Once in, his hands and feet found the rungs of a stone ladder.

Maya continued to shine her light from above, but his body blocked most of the beam, and he couldn't see below his feet.

Twenty or so rungs later, Austin's foot hit solid ground. "I'm here," he called. He shined his light around the space. "It's an entryway. There's a narrow tunnel carved through the rock. Hold tight, let me check it out."

"Don't go too far!" Maya called back.

Austin flashed his beam up. "I won't. Be right back."

He slid through the narrow corridor, his light illuminating the black, jagged stone walls. It appeared that whoever crafted the tunnel connected the hole in the temple above to a natural fissure, creating an uneven, almost broken flow to the passage. A few yards in, he shivered when cooler air hit his face. The passage turned twice more before he came to an opening, where the walls expanded out and the ceiling graded up. He flashed his beam into the blackness. The area was large; his light only illuminated a short way out, then faded into darkness. Squatting to shine his beam on the floor, he reached with his fingers to touch the soft ground. The covering appeared to be a mix of sand, small rocks, and a mossy substance that was sticky to the touch. He took one more step in while glancing at his yellowish energy stone. He was alone. It was safe for the group to come down.

He returned to the shaft and peered up into the portal. "Come on down. This is an entryway to a larger cave. This has got to be the place."

One by one, the three lowered themselves into the hole. Together, they navigated into the larger cavern.

Once assembled, Austin whispered, "This is as far as I went. The path leads down into the mountain." He flashed his light to the ground again, illuminating the area. "Be careful walking, the floor is weird. It's mostly sand and rocks, but has this sticky stuff on top; I've never seen it before."

The others shined their lights to the ground.

"I'll go first," Gabriel said. "Maya, you're last. Keep your weapons ready." Gabriel stepped away from the entry toward what appeared to be the back of the cave. At one point he crouched, studying the ground. He touched the sticky substance, then smelled his fingers.

Rebecca asked, "What is it?"

"I'm guessing moss or a mold," Austin answered.

"Couple of things," Gabriel chimed in. "Austin's right: there is a path here, it's lined with rocks. So, we're heading in the right direction. The builders must've constructed this, meaning they intended travelers to go this way. I'm not sure if that's a good or bad thing." He paused. "Second, be careful. This sticky stuff is everywhere."

They crept forward through the darkness. The passage was unusual: the walls would close in only to expand out and up, rendering their lights useless, as they couldn't see beyond the end of their beams. It felt to Austin as though they were traveling through a series of connected caverns deep into the heart of the mountain.

The path turned damp with a hint of a colder breeze hitting his face. Moments later, the sound of flowing water echoed on the walls around them.

Gabriel stopped and shined his beam on a small open doorway chiseled through the rock, its corners precise, as if constructed by man. With their beams on, Austin couldn't be sure, but a dusky light seemed to emanate from the opening.

Gabriel approached; he shined his beam on markings on the door's mantle while rubbing his hand on the smooth rock. "This is the place. I've seen an entryway like this before. These words inscribed above the opening are in the language of my people. It reads: 'Death to all who enter this chamber.'" Gabriel paused, turning to face them. "Remember: there may well be hidden traps."

One by one, they stooped through the doorway and entered the next chamber. Once inside, Gabriel turned off his beam, confirming Austin's earlier observation. High, near the ceiling, the last vestiges of daylight shined through a crease in the rock, providing a natural light in the area and revealing its forgotten contents.

The cavern was the largest they'd seen yet, and in the center, the frothing waters of a dark river rushed through and drained into a black hole in the corner nearest them. They had found the source of the chilly, damp breeze.

Gabriel moved toward the water. He stopped halfway there, motioning for the others to follow. Switching his flashlight back on, he illuminated the floor in front of him. An unusual rock formation sprawled at least thirty feet in length, while rising waist-high in a broken pattern. The formation appeared ridge-like, splitting the floor in two.

Maya and Austin walked around its edges, circling to the other side.

Rebecca stepped in, flashing her beam up close on the unusual ridge. "There's something underneath the layer of moss."

Maya studied the object. "Agreed. If it's been here for a thousand years, I'm not surprised it's overgrown." She started to reach for the covering substance.

"Let me." Austin pulled out Demon Slayer while striding over to Maya. Using its razor edge, he cut, then lifted the sticky material away, exposing a hard, white stone underneath. With his free hand, he peeled a huge section of the sticky layer back, revealing not rock, but a bleached skull bone of a dragon-like creature. The head, as big as a horse's body, lay intact, its dagger teeth sitting secure in the jawbone with two horns projecting off its brow. Gabriel and Maya moved closer as Austin wiped his blade clean of the sticky substance.

Gabriel's eyes gleamed. "This must have been the demon Vritra. So, the myths are true." He bent to study the creature's bones. "Ha! Vritra was a blue dragon. I haven't seen one of these in a thousand years. Their skin had a bluish hue. They were majestic and beautiful when flying in the sunlight, but also known for their bad temper."

Maya held up a thread of the sticky material, twisting it in her fingers. "What is this stuff? It's almost web-like. It's everywhere in here and deep." She flung the strand from her fingers. "I wouldn't touch it anymore; we can't be sure it's not poisonous."

Gabriel stooped next to the creature, examining its bones under his light. "Agreed, I can't recall ever seeing anything like it and that worries me." He paused, shifting his focus to the covering layer on the bones. "Let's keep moving."

He circled the remains one last time before continuing toward the echoing rush of water. The group followed. The riverbanks were lined by large blocks of carved rock, creating an immovable channel that guided the ice-cold water neatly through. On each side of the riverbank lay a heap of rubble, tumbled rocks piled high on top of old buttresses: the remnants of a collapsed bridge. Despite the shadows, Austin could see more boulders scattered just below the roiling water.

"It appears the ceiling collapsed," Rebecca said, "and took out the bridge. I'm betting it's what created that hole in the cave's roof."

"You're right, and unfortunately the river's not passable; the current is too fast. We'd need equipment to cross it." As Maya spoke, she shined her flashlight toward the far bank, hoping to glimpse its secrets.

Austin also stared into the shadows of the far side, noting the light was almost gone from the cave. He could barely make out the shape of a pedestal on a rocky rise, but there was no luminescent glow, confirming no piece of the Star Crystal was in the area.

"I'm not sure we have to get over. Even if we could cross, it's doubtful we'd find anything." Gabriel paused, scanning their faces. "We're here to confirm that Lucifer retrieved a crystal. We know this place was an Atlantan cavern from the writing on the door. We've seen Vritra's body. And, I've seen something similar to this roof collapse in Roswell, New Mexico."

"I know that story. Once the crystal was removed, the cave roof came down on Austin's grandfather. He made it out safe, but . . ." Rebecca trailed off, not describing his grisly death at the hands of the Pitkus demon.

Gabriel continued, "I suspect the same traps were laid here, and there are no remains of the IOD's team evident, which tells us they removed the crystal and got out. I doubt Lucifer would leave without it. Meaning . . ." He stopped without saying more.

So now, not only did they have to recover two more sections of the Star Crystal from still-to-be-identified locations, but to finish their quest, they'd have to retrieve one from Lucifer himself.

"Nothing we can do about that here. What now?" Austin asked.

"Austin, your energy stone—it's glowing through your shirt!" Rebecca interrupted.

He pulled out the crystal; it glowed a dark red.

Gabriel hissed, "Demon!"

"Back to back. Lights on. Weapons ready," Maya ordered.

The group converged in a tight circle, each holding their flashlight out, their weapons drawn. Austin felt the approaching evil energy radiate in his body but couldn't see it. He waited, a morbid anticipation gnawing in his chest, and stared into the darkness just beyond their lights' reach.

"I can sense it; the demon is here," Rebecca whispered.

"Another dragon? Is this a nest?" Austin said.

"Shh," Maya hissed.

The four beams darted back and forth, cutting into the darkness surrounding them, but nothing came into view. Austin listened, but only heard the water roaring through its stone channel and plunging into the chamber's black hole.

An all too familiar stench hit them.

Rebecca's voice cracked, "That smell is getting worse."

"The creature is close," Gabriel whispered.

Austin waved his beam up and down, back and forth on the space in front of him, watching for the unseen creature. Suddenly, a wet, sticky substance dripped onto his arm. He instinctively screamed, "Up!"

The group raised their weapons, firing at will. The blasts from the gunshots rumbled through the cavern as Gabriel's blue light pulsed through the darkness.

A hideous screech came in reply, just before a massive thud. The giant creature roared as it battered the group with black stick-like appendages, scattering them from their tight circle. Austin was knocked to the ground but recovered quickly to see an armored head and giant belly raking over a fallen Gabriel, the unlucky target of its initial assault. Maya and Rebecca were both on their feet. Rebecca was standing directly in front of its head, blasting her pistol. Maya emptied her full cartridge into its abdomen. Both had little effect in slowing the demon's attack.

Austin holstered his gun and withdrew Demon Slayer. He took two steps then leapt, impaling the pointed blade into the back of its massive body. With adrenaline-fueled strength, he stabbed the beast again and again, finally ripping through its armored hide. A black ooze seeped from the wound.

The demon shuddered and screeched in pain before swatting him off with a targeted swing. Forgetting Gabriel, it spun, turning its attention to Austin and his biting blade. As it stepped forward, Austin could see the black bulbous body covered in scaled barbs. It had eight spindly legs coated with short, wiry hairs and ending in three dagger-like toes. The small but lethal head had multiple eyes with armored horn-like protrusions protecting the front that could easily spike anything that got too close. A foul-smelling slit in its face held fanged teeth just visible through the foaming sticky substance oozing to the ground. As it crept toward him, Austin absorbed its evil energy. He fought the hopelessness penetrating his body and braced for its next attack.

He sheathed Demon Slayer and drew his Sig, stepping back in retreat toward his three companions. Raising the weapon, he held it firm as the spider-demon clicked its way closer. Rebecca came from the shadows, standing to defend him; she raised her gun in anticipation of the onslaught. She lifted her flashlight's beam into the creature's black eyes, forcing it to recoil under the light's glare.

Maya used this time to help a stunned Gabriel to his feet. With him leaning on her shoulder, she ordered, "Back to the river."

Austin did as instructed, glancing to Rebecca to confirm her retreat. They backstepped together, slow and sure, never taking their eyes off the advancing demon. With their escape through the caverns blocked by the creature, the four stood trapped on the boulders channeling the water over the collapsed bridge. The light of the day was all but gone, and the cave stood cloaked in complete darkness. Austin knew their options were fading.

The creature gnashed its deformed mouth. Its foul reek was filling his senses, its evil overwhelming his energy.

Maya screamed directions. "On three, fire your weapons then jump into the river!"

Austin and Rebecca replied in unison, "Got it."

Gabriel was unsteady and only standing due to Maya's support.

Maya pushed Gabriel into the water; he landed with a splash and was quickly swept away. "One, two, three!"

The blasts were deafening as the three companions unleashed

their full complement of ammunition into the spidery beast. It screeched in agony as the armor-piercing bullets hammered it again and again. Enraged, the screams reached a crescendo before it responded in a ferocious charge. Rebecca dove into the water first, followed by Austin. Maya finished her second clip before jumping. Austin glimpsed the creature's spiky leg thrusting toward her as the cold hit him.

The frigid water struck hard, stealing his breath. He bobbed for a second in the roaring current before falling into the black hole. Down he plummeted. For a bleak minute, he churned in the torrent, twisting and turning while fully immersed. With his lungs searing, he fell, twisting into the night air, the cascade of water beating down on him. A breath later, he crashed with a cracking splash deep into a pool of black water. He made a disoriented turn before righting himself. Swimming up, he exploded at the surface, gasping for air, choking the river from his lungs. As the coughing subsided, he sucked in a few deep breaths.

Rebecca called to him, "Austin, over here!" She waved her arms from the beach.

Swimming to her voice, he reached for her hand as he hit the shoreline. "Are you okay? Where's Maya, Gabriel?"

Rebecca answered, "Gabriel's here, Maya's right behind you."

Austin rose, standing on the shore, then reached down, helping Maya out of the water.

Once her foot hit dry ground, she ordered, "If everybody's okay, we need to keep moving. That thing can leave that cave; you saw the opening in the roof."

"Which way?" Rebecca asked.

"Follow this flow to the main river, then parallel the river's edge. It'll bring us out." Gabriel's reply was weak.

Austin put his hand on Gabriel's shoulder. "Are you alright?"

The Atlantan winced. "I will be. But Maya is right, we need to move quickly, far away from here."

Austin helped Gabriel to his feet, allowing him to lean on his shoulder.

Maya adjusted her pack. "Ah, damn it!" She hissed, her face wincing in pain. She stumbled, almost falling in the process.

Rebecca reached over, helping her up. "What happened?"

She answered by pulling the top of her shirt back. "I'm fine, but my shoulder burns. I think the demon's claw stabbed me as I jumped."

Rebecca's hasty scan revealed a pencil-sized puncture wound on her upper left arm near the shoulder. The sting already appeared inflamed and discolored with weeping red lines radiating out from the entry point.

Gabriel's face went ashen. "Maya, this is serious. Demon venom will attack your nervous system—it can literally drive you insane."

Maya answered in a casual, almost indifferent tone. "Is there an antidote?"

"Possibly, but I've never seen that demon before, and the medicine is hours, if not days away."

"Then there's nothing we can do here. We'd better get started," she said calmly.

CHAPTER 2

September 14, 2014
Sunday
New Orleans, Louisiana

"I'm telling you: Drew Brees is all washed up. The A'ints are zero-and-two and they lost to the Browns. I mean, the *Cleveland Browns*! Man, nobody loses to them. I think my son's high school team can beat 'em. And Brees's pick-six lost the game!"

The larger man shook his head. "I don't know what you're smoking Bobby, but save me some. Drew Brees is still the best QB in the league—done. He had one bad play today! That's it. Just bad luck, that's all it was. They'll be back. And by the way, the Browns will be too. I think they're way better than the talking heads say they are."

Bobby laughed. "Come on Big John, we need to do the rounds. I hear the boss is coming in tonight and we don't want to piss him off." The two guards started walking down the darkened sidewalk.

Michael stood in the shadows, watching them finish their inane conversation; they were oblivious to his presence. As they passed, he pressed a small button on his left bracelet. A short click came in response, then silence. The man's image was captured.

He remained still, safely hidden by the Hannibal Industries sign, watching as Big John turned right into a small alley between two brick buildings. The lead guard, Bobby, continued the length of the larger structure before entering a side door and vanishing from sight. Once clear, Michael emerged. He motioned to his companion, signaling his readiness, then pressed two small symbols on his bracelet. His transformation began, morphing first into his Gray form, then into the likeness of the larger guard. Once complete, the only discernible difference was the backpack he carried and the silver bracelet around his wrist.

He motioned to his Atlantan associate and used telepathy to communicate, "I'm going in. Give me fifteen minutes, then execute the plan. Anan: no exceptions. Make sure the devices are placed in the designated locations; they won't know what hit them."

Anan unzipped his pack and removed a small, wired bundle. "Will do, and be careful. You heard them—the boss may be in tonight."

Michael clenched his jaw. "I would love to see my old friend Lucifer. I have a couple of things I'd like to address with him one-on-one."

"As would I. But remember, we're here for another pretty important reason as well. Let's take care of that first."

"Let's hope this key card is worth the money we paid." Michael started to step away, then stopped. "If we get separated, go to the meet site. But don't wait; I expect there'll be a lot of police buzz in the area."

Following the path of the smaller guard, Michael made his way to the side door, then raised the just-acquired white plastic key card and swiped it in the electronic reader. A short beep was soon followed by a green flashing light, then the loud click of a door lock releasing. Michael twisted the handle and eased Big John's hulking frame into the building.

The door opened into a dim hallway with worn tile floors. The faded gray walls were painted cement blocks, producing a neglected appearance, not unlike most of the buildings and inhabitants in this part of the city. Passing two closed side doors, he made his way to the far end of the hall, where a reinforced steel door protected the warehouse contents. Once again, he flashed his key card, only this time, he also placed his right eye in front of a sophisticated retina scanner. A second later, a double beep ensued, followed by a small red blinking light, denying his access.

Michael hesitated, wondering if this was a trap after all.

He stood in silence, allowing the system to reset, then flashed the card once more. This time, he leaned in tight to the eye scanner. He inhaled a deep cleansing breath when a single beep and green light flashed. The door lock clicked opened, allowing him to slip into the warehouse.

Once inside, he stood studying his surroundings. The entrance led into a large, open storage area with a mezzanine of offices overlooking the warehouse floor. The main room's lights were off, and small efficient nightlights set high on the walls provided an eerie ambience to the cavernous room.

The building space was not only new, but almost antiseptic, in stark contrast to the worn hallway he just exited. There was no wear, no vintage building material, and not a shred of paper lying about. The ground floor was meticulously organized. Lines of various pieces of equipment sat equally spaced, side-by-side, most of which were covered by thin white sheets. On one larger piece, Michael could see the form of electrical insulators contained within. He guessed it was more equipment salvaged from Atlantis.

At the far end of the floor, he found what he was searching for: the Atlantan transporter used on the fateful night in Sedona when Bernael's energy was destroyed, ending the deviant Atlantan's killing spree of young women. This finding confirmed that this was the place where Lucifer and Abaddon had transported from to make their explosive appearance.

He shivered. The room temperature was cool, the antithesis to the steamy New Orleans night, but designed to offset the heat generated by the abundant operating equipment. Turning right, he found what he required: a bank of computer servers racked together, humming and flashing in unison.

Stepping over to a group of laptops neatly organized on a table next to the server racks, he pulled up a chair, then removed a small silver box from his backpack and placed it on the table next to him. He clicked the laptop's keyboard and, as expected, a password prompt appeared. In response, he pressed the first of three buttons on the small silver box. The laptop computer's hard drive hummed in response, and multiple asterisks soon filled the password area. Michael hit return, and the computer sprang to life.

He pressed the second button on the box, this time the laptop screen flashed, "Negotiating with host." It remained this way for a few moments, then the screen started a rapid scroll through directories and files. The computer would pause every few seconds, then reengage with relentless efficiency. As the machine processed, Michael heard a door open and footsteps approaching from across the warehouse. He placed the silver box deep into his backpack, allowing the data download to continue under cover.

The Atlantan leaned back in his chair and put Big John's huge feet on the desk, pretending to relax.

The smaller guard walked to him, scowling in agitation. "Big John, what are you doing? Are you trying to get us fired? You're supposed to be patrolling the back warehouse now."

Michael replied, "I'm sorry Bobby, just taking a little break. I've had a long day; you know, a couple beers watching the game. I'm tired."

Bobby glared at his friend, "I don't give a shit if you drank a case today, get your butt back to your area and do your job. If you can't, first I'll kick your ass, then I'll find your replacement."

Michael put his hands out in a gesture to calm down. "Hey man, relax! I'm sorry. I didn't think it'd be a big deal. Every night we patrol, patrol, patrol. And nothing ever happens. I figured five minutes to recharge my battery was no big thing. I'm going."

As Michael finished his statement, a second warehouse door opened, then slammed shut.

Bobby shot Michael an angry look. "Who's that? Nobody checked in with me from the front gate."

"You said the boss was coming in. Maybe it's a surprise visit," Michael replied as he stood up. As Bobby turned toward the noise, Michael lifted his backpack from the floor.

Bobby turned back, pointing at him. "Don't you move. If this is the bossman, you're going to explain why you're here. I need this job; I'm not taking the heat for this."

Michael watched the hallway, anticipating the visitor's arrival. "I already said okay, Bobby. Again, I'm sorry." As he said this, he edged toward the side door.

He didn't get far before Abaddon stepped into the room. The Immortals of Darkness's second-in-command paused for a moment, scanning the area and the two men. "Bobby, what's going on here? Why aren't you guys outside doing the rounds? This is a dangerous part of town and we have valuable inventory to protect."

"I'm sorry, sir. I was doing the rounds when I came across Big John here with his feet up on the desk. I was just sending him back out. Tell him, John." Bobby motioned to Michael.

Michael glanced down, reluctant to make eye contact with his former subordinate. "I'm sorry, sir, it was my fault. I came in here to cool off. I'm going back to my post right now. It won't happen again."

A side door to the warehouse clicked open again before slamming shut. A slow progression of heavy footsteps echoed toward them.

Bobby eyed Abaddon. "What's going on?"

Abaddon grinned as Big John stepped in view.

Bobby stood wide-eyed, stunned into silence, his confusion evident. "What the hell . . . I mean, what is this? Two Big Johns?"

Abaddon asked, "Do you want to tell him, Michael, or should I?"

Michael answered by swinging his backpack, connecting cleanly with Bobby's face, thumping him back. He made a quick move toward the side door when the real Big John clipped him with a right-hand punch. The blow glanced into Michael's shoulder, spinning him to the side.

Bobby was already up, racing toward him. He jumped Michael from behind, tackling him to the floor. Big John took one step and kicked Michael in the gut. The blow was crushing; Michael groaned in response as the pain shot through him. He rolled to his side, hoping to provide cover for his damaged abdomen.

The second kick came with equal devastation. Just missing his face, it pounded square in his chest. Gasping for air, Michael swung an elbow at Bobby. It landed with a vicious crack, knocking the guard off of him. Michael jumped to his feet and rushed his kicking assailant. The giant Big John counterattacked, swinging wildly at his head. Michael blocked the right punch by the huge man, countering with two short body blows before sweeping his legs. Like the oak he was, Big John fell with a crash.

As the two guards tried to recover, Abaddon stepped toward Michael. "My turn. I've waited a long time for this." Abaddon came at him. Michael dodged his first swing, countering with a short right to his jaw then following with an uppercut into his gut; Abaddon grunted.

Abaddon stepped back, using his sleeve to wipe a drop of blood from his mouth. He smirked at Michael before attacking again. Moving forward like a buzz saw, he unleashed a series of coordinated blows into Michael's face and body. At the end of the combination, Abaddon spun into a bent-legged kick that sent Michael flying off his feet. He landed with a thud against the wall before slumping to the ground, stunned.

Bobby and John had recovered enough to grab Michael off the floor. They held him firm as Abaddon approached to finish the job. His first punch blasted into Michael's stomach. The second punch to his head knocked the Atlantan down. Bobby and John lifted the bloodied man up again. Michael's head slumped to one side; things were going gray.

Abaddon stepped in for the next shot but halted when a stranger in black stepped from the shadows.

"Three on one doesn't seem fair. Even if it is Michael."

Abaddon turned toward the voice with a grimace. "Ah, Anan, I hoped you would be here. I wasn't satisfied with our last meeting."

Anan smirked. "I was."

Infuriated, Abaddon charged the new entrant, unleashing a barrage of kicks, punches, and elbows. Anan stepped back and away from the onslaught, his martial arts skills blocking every move with little effort.

Abaddon stopped, sweat streaming down his flush face.

"What did you say earlier . . . My turn?" Anan mocked him.

Michael watched through blurry eyes as his friend countered with a lethal combination of spinning kicks and straight-armed punches, all landing with destructive force on Abaddon's head and chest. With his opponent faltering, Anan kneed him in the jaw. Abaddon collapsed, unconscious, hitting the floor with a crack.

Big John did not hesitate; he launched at Anan with reckless abandon. The big man swung, but missed as Anan ducked under the blow. He countered with a single debilitating punch to John's throat. The giant dropped, face first, as he gasped in desperation for air.

Bobby avoided the fray, choosing instead to remove his concealed Glock. "I don't know who you are, Mr. Karate man, but say goodbye." He raised the weapon, ready to fire.

With lightning speed, Anan closed the gap between himself and Bobby. As the shot fired, he sidestepped, then launched a single chest punch that connected into Bobby's heart. There'd be no second shot.

At first, Bobby appeared merely stunned. Then he dropped the gun, his body trembling. The shakes progressed to violent tremors, the result of his heart refusing to pump life-giving blood. He collapsed a few seconds later.

They watched as the black mist of the reaper enclosed the man's brown transient before flashing away with a growl.

Anan glared at Abaddon and Big John, confirming both were

neutralized. He took two quick steps to Michael, grabbing his injured friend under the arm while picking up the backpack. "Come on, we need to go, and fast. This place is coming down."

They stumbled through the nearest door and into the hallway. Anan helped Michael walk down the corridor to the exit. Moments later, they stood in the humid night air.

Michael pushed Anan away. "I'm fine. Run for it."

Anan's brow furrowed. "I'm not falling for that line again." He glanced at his watch. "We have forty-five seconds. Move it, old man!"

The two Atlantans ran as best they could, exiting the property by the hole they cut in the fence during their entry. They dashed across the street and down the next block. They were in a full sprint when the warehouse exploded. Four successive blasts rocked the structure's corners, leveling the building and all those in it. The concussive force of the blast blew out nearby windows and knocked Michael down.

Running behind him, Anan bent down, scooping his friend back to his feet. "Come on, we're not out of this."

They continued running south to Lafayette Cemetery, where they paused to catch their breath. The sirens of police and fire crews wailed in the background. Anan spoke to a gasping Michael, "Are you okay? Can you continue?"

"Yes, I'm okay. Thought I told you fifteen minutes and to follow the plan, with no exceptions," Michael answered through heaving breaths.

"Sorry, I saw the big guy talking with Abaddon outside, and I thought it may be a trap for you. He was so focused on getting into the fight, he didn't realize I was behind him the whole way," Anan replied.

Michael rubbed the back of his neck, his head pounding. "Well, you were right: it was a trap. Which raises a whole new set of questions."

He grabbed the backpack from Anan. Reaching inside, he took out the silver box. "Get this to Charles at our Atlanta location, and wait for me there. He'll know what to do with it. Follow Sixth Street south for ten blocks, cross Tchoupitoulas, and get to the river. There's a red boat tied up there. You can't miss it. The keys are under the cooler."

"What about you?"

Michael's face was strained. "I have something I need to check out."

"You sure? You took a few hard blows back there. Your face is pretty beaten up," Anan said.

Michael gave a bloody grin then pressed his wristband twice. Slowly, he transformed from Big John back to Michael's human form. "Better? I was not that attractive to start."

"Much better."

"Thanks for your help. I'll be fine. I'll see you in two days. With a little luck, Gabriel will be there as well. Don't let that box out of your sight."

"Got it." Anan stepped to leave, but paused. "Do you think Abaddon made it out?"

Michael hesitated while contemplating the question. "We'll know soon enough. There will be a reaction, one way or another. Count on it."

CHAPTER 3

September 15, 2014
Monday
New Orleans, Louisiana

Cloaked in the street's shadowy recesses, Michael glanced at his watch. It was 12:30 a.m.—time to call on an old friend. He stayed off the main drags to avoid the drunken revelers in the French Quarter who were just hitting their stride at this hour. Turning on Chartres Street, he passed the open door of a seedy bar, and a hardened woman stepped out to greet him.

"Hi there, handsome. Care to join me for a drink? You seem like you can use one, and I'm good company."

Michael paused, staring deep into the woman's transient energy, observing the amber glow of her pain and suffering. Taking pity on her, he reached in his pocket. Removing a fifty-dollar bill, he placed it into her palm. As their fingers met, he held her hand for a moment before whispering, "I'm sorry, I wish I had more time and more money. I can feel your suffering. Take this and get something to eat, then go home. Not here, your real home. Your life and transient are in danger in the Quarter."

The woman stared at Michael, her eyes welling with sadness. She held his gentle gaze for a few tranquil seconds, absorbing his peace of spirit. The moment embarrassed her; she glanced down in shame while taking the money. "Thank you. I didn't want this life. I'm not even sure how I ended up here—it all happened so fast."

Michael sensed the woman's gentle heart. "It's never too late to change, to do good. Most times the right path is the harder journey. But at your end, you'll be glad you took it." He released her hand and gave her a gentle smile before continuing on his way.

He kept to the darkened areas, avoiding the lamplight as he followed Chartres Street north, pausing in a doorway alcove at the corner of Dumaine. He waited there, watching and listening to ensure he still traveled alone. Once convinced no one was following, he walked west on Dumaine until he came to the green two-story building. Run-down in appearance, the traditional French Quarter establishment had large windows framed by craggy wooden shutters and a worn double door, adorned by an ornate iron grated opening at its top. The entrance sat on the sidewalk, a few feet from the street, nestled below a weathered metal balcony. The lower floor housed a sordid drinking establishment, frequented by the locals who sought refuge from the throng of tourists visiting the Crescent City. Michael had never seen it, but sensed the upper floor contained rooms used for illicit dealings of flesh and drugs.

He entered through the large doors and into a dim hallway, where he was met by a heavy man in a black biker vest perched on a barstool. The man grumbled, "You again. What do you want?"

Michael's eyes locked on his menacing acquaintance. "I need to talk with her, and I want to do it now."

The man stood with an ominous glare before stepping toward Michael, his tattoo sleeves now visible from the light streaming in from the street. "If you don't have an appointment, you don't go in."

Michael returned the stare, never wavering. "We can do this the hard way or the easy way, but I'm going back there. And something tells me, when she finds out we even had this conversation, you're going to be a dead man. You tell her Michael is back and demands to talk—or else."

The thug hesitated at the threat, mumbling something under his breath before turning and motioning to an unseen associate. Michael heard a rear door unlock, open, then close. A few tenuous moments later, the door reopened and closed again. A gravelly voice floated in from the back room. "Nick, she said to send him back."

Nick gestured for the Atlantan to continue down the hall. As he passed, Michael paused for a second. "I was hoping we could do it the hard way."

"Be careful what you wish for, old man," Nick shot back.

Michael leaned in to whisper, "Pretty sure I'll be seeing you later."

He continued through the hidden door and passed a bear-like man standing guard, his eyes fixed on Michael. This man didn't say or do anything as the Atlantan walked by. Michael felt a goodness in his energy, and he gave the giant a reassuring nod.

Michael walked the hallway that continued the length of the house, passing several rooms on either side. A large open area on the right held the dank bar where a handful of drunken customers sat zombie-like on beer-stained stools in a smoky fog. Not having the time or inclination to probe there, Michael proceeded straight to the back of the house that opened into a quaint, unlit courtyard. He crossed the open area to a small building.

Once inside, Michael stood in a small, dimly lit waiting area with two comfortable chairs. The room's decor was vintage Haitian voodoo. Candles burned in each of the room's four corners, highlighting the carved wooden masks hanging on the walls. On a black dresser, a burning stick of incense protruded from a bleached white human skull, its patchouli fragrance filling the room. The skull sat next to a bowl holding crow's feet that supported a propped-up doll with pins sticking out of it. A stick figurine bundled by a black string hung over the doorway leading to the next room.

Michael started for this door, but stopped when it clicked open, and a priestess entered the room. The woman's hair was braided up, and her face powdered white with black makeup around her eyes and over her nose. Her lips were crimson with black ink marks made to look like they were stitched around her mouth; her face resembled the walking dead.

She spoke English in a thick island accent. "Why are you back? Our business concluded when I gave you the key card."

Michael started to answer when the door he had entered through reopened. Nick came in with a scowl on his face and positioned himself a step inside the door, then crossed his arms.

Michael's focus turned back to the woman. "Surprised to see me, Delphine?" He stared into her dark transient, her evil transparent to his view.

"To be honest, yes. The access card I provided worked. I received news of the explosion and thought you were leaving town after the job," she said.

"Leaving town? Not until our business is finished. You set me up." Michael raised his voice. "I was lucky to escape. You didn't realize I was bringing an associate, so neither did they." He paused while glancing over at Nick, then back to Delphine. "I'm going to ask you just once: Who do you work for?"

Nick didn't wait for her response. He rushed Michael, who couldn't avoid his attacker's iron grasp in the confined space. The heavy man locked his left hand on Michael's shirt collar, and swung his right fist at the Atlantan's head.

Michael ducked, dodging the blow, then counterattacked. Using an upward maneuver, he broke the man's grip on his shirt, then spun, throwing a left elbow that landed with a thud in the startled man's chest. In a seamless motion, he continued with a right cross that caught Nick's chin, sending him into the wall. As Nick struggled to keep his feet, Michael finished by throwing a knee, cracking the middle of his chest. The tattooed man slumped to the ground, blood drooling from his mouth. Michael couldn't be sure if he was dead, or just unconscious. He didn't care.

Michael lurched at Delphine and grabbed the voodoo priestess by the throat.

She recoiled, squealing, "They'll kill me, I swear to you! I had to do it. They made me!"

Michael's words were slow and threatening. "Who made you?"

"Who do you think?" She coughed while tugging at his hand, "Abaddon, he threatened me, my family, all I own. And the one thing I'm sure of: I'm more afraid of him than you." As she answered, her painted face contorted, appearing even more like a human skull.

Michael glared into her eyes. "That was a mistake on your part." His right hand squeezed tighter, and her eyes bulged from the pressure. "What's he planning?"

She gagged trying to speak. Michael eased his grip.

"I don't know. Please Michael, I didn't ask. He just showed up, like you did." Tears filled her eyes.

"Wrong answer, witch," he answered, reapplying the suffocating pressure.

Delphine panicked as the lack of oxygen and loss of control washed through her. She slapped his arm again and again.

Michael maintained his resolve.

With her remaining strength, the voodoo priestess mouthed two very distinct words.

Michael eased up on her throat. "What did you say?"

Gasping for breath, she whispered, "Star Crystal."

"What about it?" Michael demanded as he released his grip.

Delphine's eyes dropped to the floor. "I don't know what it is, only that Abaddon took a phone call from the main house. My eyes and ears there listened to him talk about the Star Crystal being under a temple of ice, in the Sea of Trees in Japan. He used some Japanese words, but they couldn't remember them."

Michael responded, "Was it *Aokigahara*?"

Delphine's lips quivered, tears now rolling over her cheeks. "Maybe, I don't know. I swear on my mother's grave." Her bloodshot eyes raised, locking on Michael's. "Abaddon will kill me for this. You and I both know I just signed my death warrant."

Michael gave a callous response, "We all die sometime." He gestured around the room. "Leave this place. Give this up. Do something good with what's left of your life. If you don't, you'll reap the evil that you've sown."

He turned to exit but stopped when Nick groaned. He squatted down to eye level with the injured man. He pulled the thug's eyelid down and checked his pulse. "Start now. Get this man to a doctor, or he's going to die."

CHAPTER 4

September 16, 2014
Tuesday
Frankfurt, Germany

The bearded man in his expensive tailored suit reached to his right and pressed the black button empaneled in the wooden table. In response, a long length of frosted glass adorning the room cleared, revealing a beautiful jungle landscape enclosure, built adjacent to and below the viewing room. The walled compound overflowed with fern-like plants; tall flowering bamboo stalks; and thin, blade-like grass standing shoulder-high. The sizable area was enclosed by impenetrable walls of reinforced concrete blocks, designed to house an array of large predatory animals such as lions or tigers. The open-air area was covered by a thick wire mesh that loomed high above the floor with razor wire hanging ominously on its underside. This was a fortress, or better yet, an inescapable jail.

Five occupants conversed around the polished wooden table, safe above the enclosure in an air-conditioned room. The individuals rested comfortably in oversized dining chairs facing the window, a pair of dark sunglasses placed in front of each, along with sparkling water and foie gras appetizers. Their show was about to begin.

As the observers peered down, a solid metal door leading into the overgrown enclosure clanged opened. Two men stepped with caution into the grassy field. Both appeared haggard, their clothes worn and dirty. Their long, matted beards framed their gaunt faces. Each man carried a long knife secured to his belt. Once inside, the door slammed behind them. They spun in unison, in evident surprise to see their exit blocked. With no clear way out, they turned forward to investigate their new outdoor accommodations.

The taller of the men stood upright to see over the grass, peering around in an attempt to comprehend their plight. He spotted a container in the center of the cavernous area: a crate perched on a small square platform, which sat on a single columned stand. The raised table was chest level and sat just over the bladed grass. The tall man sprinted to the box and tore open the lid. Reaching deep inside, he pulled out a loaf of bread and a bottle of water. As his companion arrived, he tore off a hefty chunk of the loaf and shoved it at him. The men devoured the food, then guzzled the drink to wash it down, seemingly unaware of the spectators sitting comfortably above.

A loud squealing arose from the unseen rear of their prison. A short bang followed, as a grated cage door had slammed shut. A guttural snarl roared from the area.

Although nothing obvious raced forward, the observers from above followed the moving fern leaves and parting grass as the creature stalked away from its holding pen. The two captives froze, fear lining their faces as they listened to the grunts of the newest guest. The shorter man dropped the remaining piece of uneaten bread and sprinted back toward the metal door that had just provided them entry. The tall man followed, racing close behind. Both arrived to find the door handle locked. It was clear to the viewers: this was the moment the captives realized they were bait for the unseen creature.

The smaller of the two men panicked, pounding on the door before collapsing to his hands and knees, shaking in fear. The taller man grabbed his friend's torn shirt, jerking him up. He screamed something into the small man's face before pushing him against the concrete wall. The brave one removed the smaller man's knife from his belt, thrusting it into his shaking right hand, forcing him to hold it. He then turned to stand alongside his scared companion, his back protected by the concrete wall, knife held high in defiance to the unknown beast.

The group sitting in air-conditioning above, watched as the faces of the two men grimaced at the same time. Abaddon laughed, "They smell the creature's foul stench. But they still can't see it."

Lucifer gave a malevolent grin. "They will soon. Daughter, which one gets it first?"

"I'm guessing the small man; he's weak of spirit. You?" Ojater answered, not breaking her gaze of the men below.

"I'm betting the big one. The brave always die first," Lucifer said.

The group fell silent as the still unseen creature stalked through the bladed grass to within feet of its frightened prey. The brave man waved his knife back and forth, waiting for the camouflaged demon. Lucifer noticed a light shimmer as the creature struck. With a snarl, it launched at the tall man and buried its fanged jaws deep within his neck. The decapitation was complete in a frightening second as the iron jaws and razor teeth closed with an audible snap. Blood splattered over the timid man, who ran from the frenzy.

The demon turned in pursuit. With two quick bounds the shimmer buried its long claws deep in the fleeing man's back, pinning him to the ground. With ruthless efficiency, it plunged the talons from its free arm into the screaming man's shoulder. In a display of sheer brute power, the beast tore the body apart. As the victim took his last breath, the demon released a guttural howl over its kill.

"Very impressive. I assume it's suitable for our other plans?" Lucifer asked.

Marou stroked his beard. "Yes, it is. It can survive a desert environment, eats almost anything, and as you can see, blends into its surrounding. It also follows a few basic commands, like, 'kill.'"

"What is it, and why can't we view it clearly?" Ojater asked.

Marou turned to her, a gleam in his eye. "It is my latest version of the Chimera. It has the reflexes of a cat, the intelligence of a Chupacabra, morphs to blend into its surroundings like a chameleon, and as you observed, the sunny disposition of all my demons."

Abaddon stood, walked to a glass door and peered down on the enclosure. He slid the door open, walking onto the narrow balcony. "It's amazing; it blends into the grass. I can only see a shadow of it. What does it look like?"

Marou tossed Abaddon a pair of the sunglasses that were sitting on the table. Each person followed the lead by putting a set on. In unison, they peered down into the enclosure. The glasses filtered the majority of white light, allowing the group to view the monster.

The creature was pacing back and forth around the dead man's torn body. Its fur was short and silver, covering a tall, muscled frame. It walked on two sinewy legs, similar to a man's, with two long arms that ended in massive hands and dagger claws. Its head appeared abnormal: bony, with a dragon-like elongated snout lined with pointed dagger teeth, ending in four large canine fangs. On top of its armored skull were two small pointed horns. As it turned, the group observed its long muscular tail with a spiked club appendage at the tip. The creature bent down, clamping its jaws on the body before twisting its head. The ripping motion tore flesh off the bone. The creature raised its head, gobbling it down.

Ojater pressed the black button once more. The glass refrosted, concealing the feeding from the group. "You know how the rest of this goes."

Lucifer removed his glasses before scanning the faces around the table. "I do. And it is time to get down to business. What's the status of our acquisition?"

Abaddon closed the balcony door and returned to his seat. He put his elbows on the table, then created a triangle with his fingers in front of his face. "Dr. Petrov, can you meet the specifications of our desired acquisition?"

The angular doctor shifted in his seat. He replied in English with a thick Ukrainian accent, "Yes, I can. There will be an opportunity in the near future to acquire the desired commodity. The acquisition has to be done with extreme care and may require force. It will cost one million US dollars to buy the codes that provide access to the material."

Ojater interrupted, "A million dollars? That's double what you quoted before."

Dr. Petrov had a smirk on his face. "I'm sorry, but that is the going rate today. If you wait another week, it may double again." He paused to let them take in the bad news. "If you think you can get a better deal, by all means, go to my competitors."

An uneasy silence hit the room. Lucifer glared at Petrov. Abaddon stood from the table, stepped toward the entry door to the conference room, then made a gesture toward the door. "Please, Doctor, we'd like to discuss your latest proposal in private."

Petrov pushed out his chair and stood. "I understand. I'll wait outside."

The doctor took two steps toward the door, then Abaddon grabbed him by the coat and neck. With all his strength, he pushed the thin man through the closed balcony door. The glass shattered on impact, and the doctor tumbled into the enclosure below. This startled the demon into a frenzy. Using its long claws, it speared the moaning scientist in the calf before dragging him into the nearest stand of bamboo. The group watched with pleasure as the brush jerked over and over while agonizing screams of pain echoed through the room. Then silence.

Lucifer turned to Marou. "Make sure the creature is safe and securely stowed. Bring it to the departure location as soon as it's practical. Take care of any medical issues—we need it to be in perfect health." He gave a malevolent smile. "I know it's been well fed." He glanced to Abaddon. "Contact Petrov's competitors. Let them know what happened here today. The same fate will await any who betray us. Also, find out who knows he was here and take care of them as well, as a warning to the others."

"This may set back our schedule, but I didn't trust the man," Abaddon said.

"I'm sure we can still be ready for the eleventh of October," Ojater interjected.

Lucifer faced Abaddon. "Nor did I. This task requires confidentiality by people who value their lives." He paused again. "And what of New Orleans? Did the world's savior take the bait?"

Abaddon grimaced. "The good news is that he did. The bad news is, he leveled the building and killed two of my men in the process. I was lucky; I got out just in time." He ran his fingers through his blond hair. "Anan was with him; I didn't foresee that. I knew Gabriel was chasing ghosts in India, but wasn't aware he brought

Anan to the States. I'll send a stern reminder to our insider about that missed information."

Lucifer smirked. "Don't be too harsh; Michael is unpredictable. What did he get from the computer?"

Abaddon met Lucifer's eyes. "He had more time than I planned to scan our servers, but it's unlikely he got anything unexpected or of merit. We're confirming every file downloaded right now so we're not surprised later."

Ojater interjected, "I don't understand, why give him access to anything?"

Lucifer flashed her a menacing glance. "You go with Abaddon. Find out who can provide the nuclear material. Let me worry about Michael and what he has access to. Make sure there are no more mistakes."

CHAPTER 5

September 16, 2014
Tuesday
Flying West Over the Atlantic Ocean

Austin sat across the aisle from Maya. The constant drone of the jet's engines hummed in the background of his anxious thoughts. He glanced at his friend. She was either asleep or unconscious—he couldn't be sure. Austin had reclined her seat as far as it would go and put blankets over her, trying to keep her warm. Reaching over, he touched her forehead, feeling the fever's burn. He grabbed the wet hand towel and wiped her face again, hoping to soothe her pain. Her body shivered in response.

Feeling unsettled, he leaned back into his chair and replayed the events that led to this. The trek out of the jungle was arduous; Maya struggled, but walked on her own most of the way. In the end, the demon's poison took its toll. She had to be helped by him first, then Gabriel as well. When they arrived at the Jeep, her breathing was shallow and barely rhythmic. Gabriel cleaned the wound before injecting her with a cocktail of antibiotics, morphine, and adrenaline. The drug combination worked to stabilize her, but was a far cry from actual healing.

The drive out of the mountains to the airport was draining as he watched her condition deteriorate. The only good news was their private plane was waiting for them on the runway, gassed and ready to depart. The pilot put down in Amsterdam just long enough for more fuel, then was back in the air again for Atlanta. Austin hoped that when they arrived, Michael and Charles would be able to help get her the medicine she required. Gabriel barely left her side for the duration of the trip, and Rebecca did all she could to assist him.

Gabriel stood from his seat and walked back to Maya and Austin. "How is she doing, any change?"

"Same. No better, but I don't think any worse."

Gabriel felt her forehead then checked her pulse, concern lining his brow. "That's good. She's strong, her body is fighting the creature's venom."

Rebecca rotated in her seat to face them. "How long will she stay like this?"

Gabriel shrugged. "I can't be sure. Each person has a different reaction, and each demon's venom is unique."

"What was that thing? Have you encountered one before?" Austin asked.

Gabriel remained silent as he pulled her eyelid up. After studying her response, he answered, "No, I've never encountered a demon like that. It reminded me of a spider, but armored and fanged—

that worries me. My gut tells me it's something new and different. And if we're dealing with a new, more powerful derivation of a monster, the serums we've developed over the years to heal demon wounds may be useless." Gabriel patted Maya's good arm.

"She's a fighter; I know she'll be okay." Rebecca's frown countered the optimism in her voice.

Austin considered Gabriel's words. "New creature? You make it sound like demons are still being created."

Gabriel pursed his lips. "I suspect they are. Oh, not in the same volume as they were in the past. Over the years, we've destroyed most of the IOD's production capabilities. You need a secure biolab to create them, and in today's world, they're not easy to hide. But every now and again, we encounter something new, more horrible. Something like this creature. It makes me think Marou is still at it."

"Marou, who is he? I've read the name before but don't know a lot about him," Rebecca asked.

"Same. I know he's an Atlantan," Austin said.

"Yes, an Atlantan, a loyal follower of Lucifer, and a fanatical hater of the human species. He makes Bernael seem like a Boy Scout."

"That's hard to believe. Why?" Rebecca asked.

"He's done more evil to the human species than anyone but Lucifer himself. There's not enough time for me to give you all of his dark résumé. But we have a few hours; I'll share some indicative stories."

Austin and Rebecca settled in while Gabriel took his seat and started. Austin continued to glance over to Maya's face and chest, ensuring she was breathing.

"I'll start at the beginning. You recall our history on this planet: We came by spaceship, but opened the wormhole about twenty thousand years ago. Over two hundred of our kind found their way here, by one of those two ways."

Rebecca replied, "Yes, and if I'm not mistaken, you and Michael came via the wormhole."

Gabriel continued, "Correct. Before the journey, every Atlantan selected for the mission was vetted to ensure he or she would fit into and contribute to the society we were building. We were first and foremost trained soldiers who knew weapons, survival training, hand-to-hand combat, and most important, when to kill, if needed." He paused, taking a deep breath after those words. "We also each had our expertise in varying professional fields required to build a civilization. For instance, I was both a medical doctor and a bioscientist. I studied the diversity of the flora and fauna of this planet while also treating my fellow Atlantans' injuries and illnesses. A few were skilled agriculturists for farming, while others still were civil engineers for building, or mechanical engineers to maintain our ships and equipment. You get the idea."

Rebecca interrupted, "That explains your care of Maya's wounds. You were so precise in your actions."

Gabriel appeared thoughtful, "Thank you, but I wish I could do more. It's unfortunate that I don't have the tools with me to heal her."

Austin took Maya's hand. "You've bought us time, time to get the right medicine. That's all we could ask for."

"What was Marou's expertise?" Rebecca asked.

"Marou is brilliant. He worked with another Atlantan in the biolab, a man named Prometheus. Together, they cataloged the animals on this planet, which included developing genomes for many of the species. They used these to domesticate livestock, canines, felines—you name it. Many of the farm animals still working today were developed during this time, and all by those two in response to the Atlantan need for developing a sustainable civilization."

"That doesn't sound bad at all—in fact, it sounds good," she said.

"But I suspect the bad part comes next," Austin said.

Gabriel nodded. "It does. You recall the fracture in our society. It's something we don't speak of, but I know Michael shared a little of the story with you in Guatemala," Gabriel said.

"Yes, but he didn't share a lot though," Austin said.

Gabriel continued, "When the group split, Marou was at the heart of the issue. He went with Lucifer and fought against us in the great war. Many of my friends were slaughtered by him. Worse still, he used his knowledge of living energy and the animals of the planet to bioengineer the monsters—we call them demons. At first, they were novelties that were easy to find and destroy. But Marou worked tirelessly to produce a slew of creatures you've heard of, like the Minotaur, Medusa, and the Midgard Serpent, and released them into the world. Real monsters with a focused evil energy that killed thousands of people. I can't tell you the number of times I've sat—just as I am here with Maya—and watched, helpless, while someone I care about . . ." Gabriel's voice trailed off.

Austin said, "What caused the fracture in the colony?"

Gabriel's face tightened. "I can't—I mean won't—answer that. If Michael wants to share that, it's his call. Feel free to ask him."

Rebecca changed the question. "If not what, then why? Why would he do it?"

Gabriel thought for a second. "I suspect there are a couple of answers to that question. But I know for a fact a big part of his motivation is that he despises the humans and has a blood lust for killing them. He considers you an inferior life-form, like a mule, nothing more than a work animal for the Atlantans to use. As does Lucifer. They wanted to enslave your ancestors; I'm guessing they still do. Following Lucifer was a natural fit for Marou. His legacy—the demons—still serve their purpose: killing people and protecting the crystal pieces."

Maya thrashed and gave a soft moan.

"So, what happens to Maya?" Rebecca asked.

Gabriel glanced over to Maya's ashen face, a clear attempt to avoid Rebecca's eyes. "I'm not sure. If I can get her to a lab, I may be able to synthesize something to help her. I just don't know what the toxin is."

"And if you can't?" Austin stared at Gabriel, watching for his reaction.

"I don't know. She shows a remarkable strength in fighting the poison; most humans would have succumbed by now. But I do fear the worst."

CHAPTER 6

September 17, 2014
Wednesday
Buckhead Heights, Atlanta, Georgia

Austin was supporting Maya upright. She was barely conscious and hanging like a rag doll as he carried her down the stairway of the plane. Her once glowing face had lost all color, and dark circles now lined her eyes.

An idling black Escalade waited for them just feet from the plane, its rear hatch open. Rebecca and Gabriel loaded their bags into the vehicle, and Gabriel greeted a young Asian man who had exited the driver's seat. Their warm embrace suggested they were well acquainted. Rebecca opened the rear door and climbed into the back row, and reached over to help Austin guide Maya into the reclined middle seat. Austin then met the youthful driver extending his hand.

Gabriel spoke, "Austin, this is an old friend, Anan, an Atlantan. Anan, please meet Dr. Austin Denton."

Austin shook his hand. "Nice to meet you. Sorry it couldn't be under better circumstances."

"I heard about your work in Guatemala. That was impressive," Anan answered.

Gabriel sat in the passenger seat, and Austin sat next to Maya. "Anan, Rebecca Davis, in the way back. Rebecca, my friend Anan."

Rebecca waved to the driver, who returned the gesture while adding, "Nice to meet you."

Gabriel continued, "Last but not least, Amaya Luna; she was also in Guatemala with us."

Anan's smile evaporated, revealing his inner concerns. "How's she doing?"

"Not good, we need to get her someplace where I can treat her, and soon. Hopefully I can stabilize her," Gabriel answered.

Anan threw the car into drive. "We're all set up. We have a five-bedroom house nearby, including a triage area." Anan's eyes met Austin's, "Your uncle, Charles, flew in from Tucson, he brought the supplies Gabriel requested. We're only a few miles away."

"Excellent, thank you. And what of Michael?"

"He got in an hour ago. He was on a call when I left, but is waiting to see you all," Anan answered as he sped out of the parking lot.

"Good, we have a lot to discuss," Gabriel said.

The group rode in silence to Buckhead Heights, Anan easily navigating the winding streets and bustling shopping district. Minutes later, he pulled into the driveway, its long entrance twisting between towering oaks before splitting the ornate iron gate protecting the stone-faced mansion. As the barrier closed behind them, Austin could see security cameras situated around the compound nestled behind the fortified walls. The car stopped in front of the three-story home.

As the team exited, Austin again supported Maya out of the car. He was walking with her to the front of the house when Charles swung open the front door. He quickly inserted himself under Maya's open arm.

The two men carried her up the curved wooden stairway to the second-floor landing with Charles guiding them into the first bedroom off the hall.

As they laid Maya on the bed, Rebecca walked in behind them. "Let me get her cleaned up and out of these clothes, then Gabriel can take over."

"Thanks, Rebecca. Washcloths are in the bathroom, and fresh clothes are on the bed. Call if you need any help," Charles answered.

Austin touched Rebecca's arm, holding it. "Thank you, I know she'd appreciate you doing this."

Charles left the room but stopped in the hall, turning back to Austin. "You okay? You look like you haven't slept in a while."

"Good, but tired," Austin sighed. "Long trip back. Didn't sleep a lot, between turbulence and trying to keep an eye on Maya."

"I figured as much. Why don't you get cleaned up and take a nap? We have some downtime. Gabriel will see what he can do for her now with the medicine we brought in. Assuming it helps, we're going to debrief a little later. So, best you recharge the batteries now."

"That sounds good. But make sure you get me if there are any changes with her."

"Of course, but rest knowing she's in great hands. Gabriel is her best chance."

Austin hoped Gabriel's expertise would be enough. He made his way to the third floor, taking the first open bedroom. After a quick shower, he climbed into bed, mentally and physically exhausted.

He woke to a gentle shake of his shoulder. Creasing an eye, he saw Rebecca standing over him.

She whispered, "Sleepyhead, you need to wake up; we're all meeting in fifteen minutes." She offered him a cup and saucer. "I made you some coffee, just like old times," her face beaming as she finished.

"I miss those times at the coffeehouse; things were a lot simpler back then." He sat up, accepting her offering, then sipping from the cup. "That's good stuff." He took a longer drink, almost finishing the coffee, then placed the cup and saucer down on the nightstand. "How's Maya?"

Rebecca sat on the bed next to him, her thigh comfortably touching his blanket-covered leg. "Not sure. Gabriel has been with her the whole time, but they haven't said a whole lot. I suspect we'll learn more in a few minutes." She paused, her face somber while staring into his eyes. "I get you like her. What's not to like? She's smart, she's strong, she's beautiful—I mean, I kind of have a crush on her myself." She hesitated as if choosing her next words. "And, I see the way you watch her, the pain in your eyes as she lies there.

I want you to know, it's okay." Shaking her head as if confused, she stammered, "That's not what I mean. I understand you have feelings for her, and I don't want you to be uncomfortable around me. You know, to hide them. I value our friendship, even if there is no chance for something more."

Austin reached over, clasping his hand into hers. "Our friendship means everything to me. I can't tell you how much I enjoy being with you, the moments we've shared, the strength you've given me in some pretty dark times. And . . ." He paused, glancing down.

"And what?" she asked.

He met her eyes. "And I guess I'm confused. It's not like that with Maya, and I doubt it ever will be." He caressed her hand. "I admit I do have feelings for her and to see her lying in there, not knowing... it's tough. But she's kept me at arm's length for a long time. I used to think she was uncertain on what she wanted, so I gave her space. But now, I'm starting to believe she knows what she wants, and it's just not me." He gave a small shrug. "Oh well, that's life."

She squeezed his hand back. "She'll come around. She's been through a lot."

Eyes locked with hers, his head tilted to the side. "I guess that's part of my confusion. I'm not so sure I want her to come around now."

A puzzled expression crossed Rebecca's face. "What do you mean?"

"I mean, I don't know what I want. To be 100 percent honest, I think of her, a lot. We've been through so much between school,

Guatemala, and Sedona. And all of it has been good, if not great." He paused, touching her hand again. "But lately, I also find myself thinking of you, and the time we've spent together. The laughs; the crazy conspiracy theories; that night you walked into the fundraiser in Sedona and kissed my cheek. The way you walked in—your perfume, everything—that night will be blazed forever in my mind." He shook his head. "I can't believe I'm telling you this."

She blushed, eyes darting away, his words clearly filling the right spot in her soul.

Austin continued, "I don't want to lead you on, and I don't want to hurt Maya, especially now. So, I'm kind of stepping back, and while all this craziness is going on, I've decided to just let things be, knowing eventually it'll all be okay, one way or the other." He paused, placing his hand on her knee. "I promise you, if Maya and I ever become something more than friends, I'll tell you first." He smiled at her. "And as far as something more for us—"

She leaned over, giving a tender kiss to his lips, holding it for a moment. She pulled slowly away, her eyes locked on his. "I'm sorry, what were you saying?"

He didn't answer right away. "That was nice, and that exact thought has occurred to me more than a few times, but I can't, not with these circumstances." He brushed her face with his fingers as he finished.

Rebecca glanced down, first to break the tender connection, but held his hand a moment longer. She cautiously reengaged her blue eyes with his. "I agree, we need to focus on getting Maya better.

And then things will be what they are." She brushed her long hair away from her face. "We'd better get downstairs." She stood and started toward the door, turning at the last second. "You coming?"

Austin grinned at her. "Yep, was going to wait until you left to put my pants on. But if you insist." He pretended to pull the covers back.

Rebecca's eyes softened. "Got it. How about we save the pants thing for the right moment. Let me get the door for you." She smiled as she left and closed the door behind her.

Austin dressed, then headed down the stairs. He stopped at Maya's room, peering in. She looked comfortable, resting on her back, head turned to the far wall, her damaged shoulder exposed. An IV flowed into her good arm. He stepped over to better view the wound, and noted dark red lines radiating out from the puncture's lesion, the poison methodically working its way through her body. He reached down, touching her arm. He was surprised when she responded, turning her head, giving a weak smile before dozing off. The morphine was doing its job.

Time to meet the others.

He entered the dining room to join the group sitting at the table. Gabriel's face appeared tense and rigid with concern. Austin greeted Michael before taking the chair next to his uncle, Charles.

Charles spoke first, "Alright, we're all here and have a few things to cover, so let's get to it. Why don't we start with Maya. How is she doing?"

All eyes turned to Gabriel.

He bit his lower lip. "In short, not good. Right now, she is resting, but getting weaker. The poison is shutting down her organs. I've been able to determine this is a new toxin. The wound is different, the discoloration unique, and none of the previous antidotes we've developed are stopping its progression, albeit, they have slowed it. To state the obvious, the odds are against her."

Austin jumped in, a noticeable throb in his right temple. "What do we do? We can't just sit here, hoping she fights through it."

Gabriel continued, "It means we need to identify the toxin, then synthesize an antidote. I can do this if I can get to a suitable lab—a very advanced lab—within the next forty-eight hours. If not, I fear we'll lose her."

Michael spoke, his words not reflecting the concern in his face, "New toxin? Is it slow-activating? I mean, how is she still alive? I would imagine the newer venoms would be stronger, more lethal than the older ones."

"From all I can tell the venom is stronger, but there's something different about Maya. Her system is unusually strong." Gabriel motioned to Charles, Rebecca, and Austin. "Any of you would be dead by now, but she's in there, still alive and fighting. I have a theory, but again, I need to be at an advanced medical lab to confirm it."

"Understood. Let's table that for now. Tell me about the trip and the creature. What did you find?" Michael asked.

Gabriel stood. "Austin, why don't you debrief. Rebecca, please add anything he misses. I'll be right back. I'm going to check on her."

Austin recounted their hike in, finding the cave entrance, and navigating through the temple's etched center stone. It was routine until they got into the main cavern and discovered the remains of Vritra.

At that point in the story, Gabriel rejoined the dining room meeting. Taking his seat, he interjected, "She's stable, fever is still high but at least not increasing. He paused. "Austin, did you mention yet how we found the remains of the demon?"

"I just did," Austin said. "The bones were at least thirty feet in length, the skull at least six feet long. It was as the legend told. There was an underground river, and on the other side of the river was a pedestal that could easily have held the crystal. But we couldn't cross over. The bridge had been destroyed by a rock fall from the cave roof. From what I know of the story, it appeared to be very similar to the Roswell, New Mexico, retrieval."

Charles interjected, "So, we think it was found, taken, and Lucifer has a piece of the Star Crystal?"

"Yes. As far as we could tell, there was nothing left in the cave but the ruins. With that said, we couldn't cross the river to confirm it," Rebecca answered.

"I could just make out the pedestal in the shadows, and there was no glow from the Star Crystal. I'm confident it wasn't there," Austin's voice trailed off.

"I suspected as much. That makes our task somewhat harder. Go on," Michael said.

Austin spoke of the change in the energy stone, the creature's wafting stench, the ensuing fight with the demon, and their escape into the frigid black water.

Michael asked, "Gabriel, you've never seen anything resembling this creature?"

"No, I have not. It was spider-like, but bigger, faster, and more aggressive than anything we've encountered before. And again, the venom is new to me."

"If this is a new demon, that means Marou is still alive and still creating the evil that has plagued this planet," Anan said flatly.

"Agreed. But why would Lucifer release it there? If the Star Crystal was retrieved as we suspect, it's in the middle of nowhere—there is nothing to protect?" Charles asked.

Rebecca answered. "Because Lucifer knew you—the IOL—would eventually come searching for the crystal there. He set it as a trap and maybe also to try out one of Marou's new creations."

"I think you're right. He figured one day we'd get there. So he set a trap and waited patiently for us, knowing we'd eventually solve the puzzle that would lead us there," Austin said.

Gabriel turned to Michael. "Knowing Lucifer, that's probable. We can speculate on why all we want; but it doesn't help now. And time is short. Let's continue with you, Michael. What of your and Anan's trip?"

"Successful," Michael said.

"Very," Anan added.

"In what way?" Austin probed.

Michael said, "If you recall when we were in Bernael's Sedona warehouse, there was an old Atlantan transporter. Before Lucifer came and the explosions occurred, I pulled the coordinates from the location Lucifer and Abaddon transported from. It led us to a warehouse in New Orleans where Anan and I found a military contractor building full of equipment either direct from or developed through Atlantis technology. We destroyed the building and the equipment, but not before extracting a series of files from within their main computer. I'm hoping the data will tell us the IOD's plans, or better yet, lead us to Lucifer himself." Michael paused, scanning the faces around the table. "And as a bonus, we may have gotten insight to the location of a new section of the Star Crystal."

"Another piece? That's great news. Where is it?" Austin asked.

"Its potential location is a place called the Sea of Trees in Japan," Michael said. "I wasn't too surprised to hear this; we've investigated the area before. Hidden somewhere in that forest is an ancient ice temple within a cavern that runs deep into the mountain among lava tubes. Sound familiar?" Michael paused, letting the news sink in.

"In legend, the crystal resides there, guarded in the darkness by a fire-breathing dragon. We've searched but have never been able to find the temple or the dragon," Gabriel added.

"I know the place well, Aokigahara," Anan said. "I've trekked through the forest before. It's a huge expanse, very remote on the northwestern side of Mount Fuji. There is dark energy present for sure—the locals now call it the Suicide Forest. Lost souls go there to exit their mortal life and enter the spirit world. In theory, it all fits."

"How did you find out this piece of information, Michael? Are you sure it's not one of Lucifer's traps?" Charles asked.

"I can't be sure it's not a trap. Let's just say the person who relayed the information believed what they told me; their life depended on it." Michael glanced around the room. "I think it's worth another trip in."

Charles reached into his pocket and removed the silver hard drive Anan had brought him from New Orleans. "We've analyzed the files you downloaded. They are in fact valuable; we have financial documents, emails, contacts. It'll take a while to get through them all, but we will." He paused. "There are two large files which we couldn't open. They're unlike the others, either encrypted, or a different language base, not hexadecimal. We haven't been able to crack those yet."

Gabriel glanced to Michael. "You think it's an Atlantan-based language?"

"It wouldn't surprise me. They've been salvaging the old equipment, maybe they're using our programming as well."

"The only place I know where we can still decipher information like that was destroyed nine thousand years ago. And I hear it's dangerous traveling there these days," Anan interjected.

"Lucifer has made the trip; we can too," Michael said.

Gabriel's voice turned serious. "I'll go. I need to get to my lab. It's Maya's best chance."

"Are you saying what I think you are? That trip is way too dangerous." Charles's face flushed.

"I am," said Gabriel. "I need to go Atlantis, and so does Maya. We don't have time for me to go in, then get back out. It's her best chance to survive."

Austin jumped in, "I'll go with Gabriel. We have to do everything we can for her."

"I'll go too. I can help," Anan added.

It appeared Rebecca was also about to volunteer when Michael raised his hands. "I appreciate everybody's willingness to risk their lives, but we can't all go. I suggest that Austin, Gabriel, and I take Maya to Atlantis. Anan and Rebecca, you head to the Sea of Trees and do whatever prep work we'll need to send an exploratory team into the forest. Connie can help with that. She's in the Tucson office waiting to hear from us. Plan on three people, and trust no one." He turned to Charles. "You head back to Tucson and work on those files that we could open. There has to be something in there we can use to find Lucifer. Now that we know he has a section of the Star Crystal, we need to find his location more than ever."

Charles nodded and scanned the faces in the room. "Are there any concerns?"

The group was silent.

"I'm assuming silence means none," Charles said. He turned to Rebecca and continued, "Connie uploaded our material on Aokigahara earlier. You'll want to review it on your way over. Read it, prepare yourself, see what we've missed. Anan can fill in any questions on the data."

The room again went quiet, and Austin raised a tentative hand. "Can somebody tell me where Atlantis is and how we're getting there?"

CHAPTER 7

September 18, 2014
Thursday
Palm Beach, Florida

Austin tossed the last case into the back of the AgustaWestland 109, completing the baggage transfer from the private jet they flew out of Atlanta earlier that morning. He leaned forward to see Gabriel studying the helicopter's controls in the cockpit. Gabriel peered back at him, giving him a thumbs-up. Austin replied with the same gesture. He glanced to Rebecca, who was busy strapping Maya into a gurney on the floor at the rear of the copter. Rebecca met his gaze; her beautiful smile wasn't enough to hide the fear he saw in her eyes. Maya's condition had continued to deteriorate. She appeared weaker and more frail than at the house, and her breathing was shallow.

Stepping away from the aircraft, he headed back toward the car. Charles, Anan, and Michael walked away from the helicopter's cranking noises, conversing in hushed tones.

Rebecca approached Austin from behind. "All set. I think they're ready for you."

"Thanks." He paused. "Think about it: I'm about to fly to the lost city of Atlantis while you go to Tokyo to hunt a mystical dragon demon. It's a far cry from sitting in the coffeehouse talking about aliens and Bigfoot."

"I've said this a few times, but the truth is crazier than anything I could ever have imagined." Rebecca's face turned serious. "You remember what I told you that day at the coffee shop, when Mr. Smith was watching you?"

He stepped close to her. "I do. I told you the same thing in the parking lot: be careful, there are a lot of crazy people out there."

She returned his gaze and joked, "Impressive. You do pay attention." She stepped even closer, her chest almost touching his. "I'm going to say it again, but change it a little. Be careful, there are a lot of crazy *things* out there. I want to hear all about Atlantis when I see you again. And most important, take care of Maya."

Austin leaned down, giving her a tight hug. "Will do. And you be careful too." He stepped back, adding, "With any luck, I'll get to Tokyo one day behind you, two at the most. Try not to slay any dragons without me."

"No promises," she said, waving as he walked to the helicopter.

As he approached, his uncle leaned in, shouting over the now whooping blades, "You have your three gifts?"

"Yes sir, the gun and Demon Slayer are in my pack. And . . ." He lifted the energy crystal out of his shirt, showing Charles. "I never leave home without them."

"Excellent. Here are your arrangements for Japan. Be careful and hurry back," Charles said, handing Austin a slip of paper.

Austin glanced at the document. Seeing the travel details, he shoved it in his pocket. "Got it." He placed his hand on his uncle's shoulder and gave a reassuring smile, then climbed into the rear seat next to Maya.

The interior of the craft was a comfortable six-seater with a small cargo area. Two of the rear seats had been removed to accommodate Maya in her gurney. Michael and Gabriel sat belted into the pilot chairs. Austin put on a headset.

Speaking into the microphone he said, "Testing, one, two, three, testing. Can you hear me?"

"Loud and clear," Michael said.

Austin was surprised at the clarity of the sound in his headphones; there was little hint of the background chopper noise in Michael's message.

Austin bent down and adjusted Maya's ear protection before touching her face; it was cold and death-like in appearance. He grabbed a blanket, covering her. The realization she may not survive another day hit him like a blow to the gut.

The pull of the helicopter lifting off interrupted his thoughts. He peered through the window as the airborne craft crossed West Palm Beach and headed due east over open ocean toward Grand Bahama Island. The crystal-blue water transitioned to a dark, almost black, ocean, highlighting the large container ships steaming through it.

They sat in silence, cruising high above the water for some time, until Austin asked, "Okay to talk now?"

"Sure," Michael said.

Austin leaned forward, touching Gabriel's shoulder to get his attention. "I didn't know you could fly helicopters."

Gabriel turned to better see him. "Oh yes, I can fly . . . among other things."

Austin wondered if there was anything the Atlantan couldn't do. "Can one of you tell me where we're going?"

"Yes. Sorry for all the secrecy, but we thought it better to not discuss it in front of the others. Only a few people in the world have the information we're about to share with you. You need to ensure it's kept safe at all costs. The revelation of Atlantis would give concrete proof to the existence of our kind and our history, which could lead to chaos in the world order. Got it?"

"I understand. I'll keep it safe."

Michael continued, "Good. We're heading approximately three hundred miles southeast of West Palm Beach. We're flying a little slower, as we're carrying extra fuel weight to extend the range of the copter, so, present cruising speed will get us there in a little over two hours."

Austin asked, "How is it possible with today's technology your destroyed city is out there, and no one knows about it? Is it under water like the legends say?"

"That's a complicated question." Michael said, "I guess there are three parts to the answer. So, it's not under water. It's still sitting out there, but it's cloaked. Part of the city is submerged, but most remains intact above sea level. When we traveled to Earth, part of our craft's technology was a cloaking device. Once on the island, our engineers adapted the ship's equipment to cloak the city. It's remained this way for over ten thousand years, from before the great war."

"Makes sense from the air, but this is one of the busiest shipping lanes in the world. If it's not under water, how do ships not see it?" Austin asked.

"That is part two and three of the answer," Gabriel said.

Michael continued, "There's a mist associated with the cloaking device. So, unless you're right on it, the island appears like a storm in the distance. When ships or low-flying aircraft get close, the electromagnetic radiation from the device wreaks havoc with their electronics. Navigation goes awry, crafts get lost, and unfortunately, people die. Ships have crashed and planes have vanished."

Gabriel added, "I'm sure you've heard stories of the Bermuda Triangle. The cloaking device is the source of that phenomenon."

Austin's eyes went wide. "I know I should never say this to you anymore, but you have got to be kidding me. The Bermuda Triangle is real?"

Gabriel said, "Oh yes, it's a real phenomenon. With the help of some key people in the US government and Wikipedia, over the years we have created the public impression that it's a myth only crazy conspiracists believe. What better way to keep inquiring minds from searching for answers?"

Michael continued, "The general media can be a helpful ally—they worry more about clicks than investigating the truth these days."

"Funny, but sad. And yes, I've learned to take anything in the news with a grain of salt." Austin glanced out the window and saw Grand Bahama Island in the distance. "So there were three answers? I've only heard two."

"The third piece is," Michael continued, "there's a natural reef and a force field within the cloaking device. If on the remote chance a freighter does steer into the area, it has to navigate a pretty complex reef first, and if it makes it through that, it hits a protective electro-gravitational field. It is like hitting rocks. A few unfortunate ships have done this and sunk, and all on board were lost. Over time, as shipping has grown, the fleets have learned to avoid the area. Therefore, less exposure for us now than when integrated trade took off after World War II."

"If there is a force field protecting the city, how will we get in?" Austin sat forward in his chair.

Michael turned toward him. "Good question. Are you familiar with generating alternating current?"

"I mean, I know it's used in the electric grids around the world, but not how," Austin said.

Michael continued, "The simplest way to think about the process is a magnet that rotates around a coil of wire inducing three phases of voltage that alternate back and forth between a negative and positive peak energy, sixty times per second here in the States. During each cycle, for a fraction of a second, the voltage is zero. The same general process is applied here on a much larger scale using gravitational waves originating in the Earth for the force field. The waves alternate back and forth between positive and negative fields, creating the impenetrable barrier; but for two minutes every three hours, it goes to zero. It's during this time we have a window to enter the center portal from above. If we're too early or too late, or choose the wrong location, we crash a fiery death into the sea. Sound like fun to you?"

Austin chuckled. "I'll pass on the fiery death and really hope you guys have it synchronized."

Gabriel glanced back. "Did he mention I'll be flying blind? All electronics will be out, and it'll be stormy weather. I'll just be winging it in by hand."

Michael patted his friend's shoulder. "If Lucifer's men can do it, then I have confidence you can." Michael reached into his pocket and opened a small bottle. Turning to Austin, he continued, "I forgot, you need to take this. It's a potassium iodide tablet. It'll protect your thyroid from the radiation we'll be exposed to."

Austin took the pill. "Radiation? From what? And what about Maya?"

"Maya's all set; Gabriel took care of it before we left." As Michael spoke, Austin glanced left to see a loaded container ship passing below. "During the battle for the city, one of our plasma reactors was sabotaged. It released a lethal amount of radiation. It's one of the main reasons we abandoned the city—it wasn't safe to live there. That was over nine thousand years ago, but I'm sure levels are still too high."

Austin put the pill in his mouth and swallowed. "So after the war, what happened to those who were living there?"

"Well actually, most died here," Michael said. "But, due to the efforts of an Atlantan named Uriel, a sizable group did make it out. Those that escaped scattered around the globe. Most landed in Egypt where they helped build that civilization."

A jarring blow bounced the helicopter down.

Gabriel held steady; there was no concern in his face. "The first of the many air pockets we'll be hitting. The force field creates them. Strap in tight; it's going to get bumpy."

Michael pointed to the horizon where, off in the distance, lightning flashed in black clouds. "There, you see the storm, beyond that wall is Atlantis. Buckled up tight, then check Maya."

The next thirty minutes were harrowing as heavy turbulence rocked the helicopter again and again. To make matters worse, the weather deteriorated. Heavy rains lashed the windshield as gale force headwinds howled into the craft, creating an extreme roller coaster feel to the ride. Lightning flashed and thunder clapped all around them. The only measure of assurance was Gabriel's slight grin; Austin guessed the Atlantan was enjoying the ride.

The electronic readouts on the dash were jumping everywhere, and the elevation dials were spinning back and forth. Two bubble gauges communicated to Gabriel the level plane on which to hold the craft.

Then, as quickly as the turbulence started, it stopped. The copter emerged from the foul weather into clear air, as if entering the eye of a hurricane. Austin could see the storm clouds behind them and far off in the distance, but the space directly in front was sunny and clear. Below them, waves of blue ocean rolled as far as the eye could see.

Michael glanced at his watch. "If my calculations are right, we have less than five minutes until the portal opens. Get above the center and drop it."

Gabriel pulled back on the stick. The copter rose, moving to the center of the clear circular eye, still high in the sky. While hovering in position, Gabriel waited for the unknown signal, his hands relaxed on the steering rod. A loud hum soon came, then a snap, followed by a yellowish light filling the cabin.

Michael urged, "Now Gabriel, drop it!"

His friend was in motion before he finished the statement, pushing down the control lever with all his strength. The machine responded to perfection. Austin almost lost his breakfast as they sped downward toward the blue ocean. The controlled fall continued for almost a minute before Gabriel pulled back on the control stick, initiating a gradual slowing of the helicopter's descent until it came to a full hovering stop. Relieved, Austin peered out of the window. The endless waves of the dark blue ocean had vanished. Instead, the lost city of Atlantis sprawled below them.

Michael grinned. "Nice flying; well done my friend. You good back there, Austin?"

"Never better. This is unbelievable."

"Yes, it is." Michael turned to Gabriel. "Take us lower, let Austin see what he can before we set down on the third band. Let's not waste time."

"Agreed, those headwinds were stronger than I thought. We'll be cutting it close on fuel for the trip home."

Gabriel broke hard right, flying low toward the main island. "The city was at least seven miles in diameter and made up of five concentric circles around the central island. As you can see, the first circle is water, then the narrow circular strip of land. The larger third band is water again, surrounded by an even larger band of land. All of this is enclosed by a final circular expanse of water protected by a natural rock barrier."

Austin noted that the three land masses were connected to each other by long, ornate bridges, many of which had partially collapsed into the water with the ravages of time.

"The central land mass was formed when a meteor hit the shallow ocean floor and formed a giant impact crater. You can see the main island is the elevated center of the impact, and the outer rock fence is the outer edge of the resultant bowl. The two concentric land circles surrounding the main island are natural ripples of rock that formed by the shock waves of the collision. We worked them to be uniform in appearance, but the underlying land was all Mother Nature. The circles of water were also byproducts of the crash, creating the bands you're seeing."

Gabriel cruised above the city on the main island. The dry land was covered with some form of a building or structure in a state of quasi-ruin.

Michael said, "This is the oldest section, where the government sat and the Atlantans made their homes. It housed our living quarters, laboratories, schools, gardens, theaters—the general infrastructure required to run a city this size. As you can see, much of it collapsed by fire and earthquake. The rest is rotting in place. It's here we need to get to; I'm hopeful our labs are still usable."

"What about the land rings, what were they used for?" Austin asked.

Michael pointed as he spoke. "The ring closest to the main island provided housing, stores, and schools for the humans that lived here."

Austin interrupted, "Humans were here? On Atlantis? How?"

"There were about half a million people at its peak. The outer ring had two purposes. Foremost, it was the waterfront area where our fleet of ships would come with the spoils of their trade or our harvesting of the planet's natural resources. Given it was also open land, there was some farming done here. It was designed to provide a walled protection to the city. We never had to use it, as humans had not perfected long voyages in that era, but its design was preparing for the future."

Gabriel made a quick turn so the copter faced the back side of the city and what should have been the western half of the island. The outer third of the concentric rings were gone, and open ocean flowed over the walls of the second land circle.

Michael continued, "This part of the island collapsed into the ocean. This was the Great Plains Plato described, where the bulk of our crops grew and many of the domesticated animals roamed. The plasma reactors operated in an underground bunker there, feeding the city with electricity and fresh water. When our main reactor exploded, it triggered a massive earthquake that took the plains and the outer portion of the city into the ocean—the self-induced cataclysm that doomed Atlantis."

Michael motioned for Gabriel to put the copter down.

Gabriel turned the control shaft left, making for the outer land ring.

They flew over a band of decrepit buildings and put the copter down in a wide-open field on the second strip of solid ground.

After shutting everything down, Gabriel spoke as the group unbuckled. "I'm sorry for landing so far away from our destination, but there's a lot of debris on the main island and inner circle." He patted the shell of the copter with his hand. "This is our only way out, and we need to keep it far away from anything that could damage it. Atlantis is a nice place to visit, but I don't want to live here again." He winked at Austin as he finished.

"After that ride, firm ground under my feet feels good," Austin said.

They unbuckled Maya's stretcher and removed her from the passenger area. She appeared even weaker, her face more drawn, the circles around her sunken eyes darker. Gabriel spent a few moments checking her vitals before administering an injection.

She responded with a soft moan as the needle entered her arm.

Gabriel frowned. "I fear she doesn't have more than twelve hours. We need to hurry; I have no idea how long it will take to solve the toxin."

"Let's get moving," Austin said, taking a quick step toward Maya.

"You want Gabriel and I to carry her?" Michael asked.

"No, I want to do it. I'll take one end. You grab the pack."

Michael strapped on a loaded backpack while Austin grabbed the front end of Maya's stretcher. Built for travel, he attached its two front straps over his shoulders like a pack, freeing his hands for the walk. Gabriel did the same with the stretcher's back end. Once situated, they moved toward the nearby bridge to cross to the inner band. The terrain was flat but overgrown. Stones still lined the walkways.

Austin noticed a distinct lack of any animal life. It was unusual for a tropical setting: no lizards, no butterflies, not even a seabird in the air. The residual radiation must be worse than Michael thought.

Once at the bridge's entrance, they slowed. The white marble structure appeared dirty and weatherworn—a stark contrast to its original grandeur. Despite the wear, the bulk of the bridge remained intact and still appeared somewhat sound. Michael walked to the edge, peering forward. A center section of the supporting lower arch had collapsed, disappearing into the water. He motioned at them to follow, then continued moving across.

As they arrived at the damaged section, he again peered over the side to the under structure. Austin and Gabriel joined him near the edge and peered at the supports spanning the blue water. Something stirred the lapping waves.

Austin pointed. "What's that, a fish?"

A greenish creature, the size of a young boy, emerged from the buttress's shadows into the open turquoise water. Appearing curious, it stared back at the three men. Its oval head had large, yellow eyes and a small, thin mouth. Its lean shoulders and arms were human-like, but its hands had webbing between spindly fingers that ended with sharpened claws for nails. There were no legs, only a long flipper-like tail. Its body was covered in hardened scales. With its head out of the water, it hissed at them, exposing its jagged, pointy teeth before diving deep, disappearing from sight with a flip of its fish tail.

Gabriel replied while moving, "That's an adaro—a pesky little creature with a bad temper. Harmless to humans for the most part, but they can give you a nasty bite. They're an early creation of Marou, before he started designing demons. They're scavengers—they'll eat just about anything—designed to keep the waterways clear of algae, dead fish, you name it. Haven't seen one of those in thousands of years."

"The adaro is the basis for the modern-day myth of mermen and mermaids," Michael added.

Austin watched for the creature's return. "You're telling me there is no mer-kingdom under the oceans where mer-kids frolic and sing with starfish and seagulls? Say it isn't so!"

Michael rolled his eyes. "I'm afraid not. Let's pick up the pace."

With Michael leading, they crossed the weakened area of the bridge. This center section looked like it had collapsed long ago into the water with just the edge frames still intact. They traversed the area with care, staying to the extreme outside of the span. As they passed, Austin observed the rolling water just covering the white rubble underneath them.

Austin and Gabriel synchronized their steps to minimize the stretcher's jostling. Once safe on the other side, they double-timed to the edge of the first land mass. Despite being in good shape, Austin had difficulty keeping up with the stronger Atlantans.

Austin now had a better view of the retaining wall that held the ocean at bay. The protective barrier was made of thick, white marble blocks, milled smooth with a slight curve that supported the circular design. The wall provided a grand visual appearance and was still effective in holding the blue waters at bay, even after nine thousand years of neglect.

Gabriel commented, "At one time, each wall was protected by a different metal. This was tin, the outer band used brass. It was a beautiful site when the first rays of sunlight reflected off these covers."

The land before them rose into the skeletal remains of an ancient city. Broken buildings sat one after the other in a jumble of tumbled rock interlaced with beautiful architecture. A green flowering plant grew wild, covering much of the dull white stone the Atlantans used for construction. Despite being in ruin, the city was still humbling in size and design.

Michael said, "This section of the city was the warehousing district. We stored much of the goods brought in here as well as the minerals we exported. This road will take us straight through to the bridge connecting this area to the main island."

As he walked the cobbled stone, it was easy for Austin to imagine the streets thronging with people: merchants selling their wares, academics pondering their latest theories, and families feasting on the harvest.

"What is the green plant? It's growing like an ivy. Seems to have taken over the island," Austin said.

Gabriel bent as he walked, picking a leaf off. He smelled it. "Believe it or not, this is a popular medicinal tea called euphrasia. You dry the leaves and steep it. It invigorates and clears the mind. We farmed it at one time; I guess it took over after we abandoned the city." He broke off a small vine, sticking it in his pack, still moving. "I'll test it for radioactivity. If it's safe, I'll make some tea for you when we get back."

As they approached the second bridge, Michael paused to examine some old debris on the side of the road. He reached down to pull a tattered jacket from under a fresh covering vine of euphrasia. With the cloth came a human skull. Even more surprising, next to the human bones was the small skeletal head of an adaro.

"You guys see this?" Michael asked.

Gabriel and Austin stepped over together to get a better view,

Maya's stretcher swinging between them.

Gabriel peered in at the find. "That's odd; the clothing is modern and the skull human."

Michael pulled the ivy vine back a little more. "And what is an adaro doing so far from the water?"

"That's a puzzle. They never leave the ocean. Maybe one of Lucifer's salvage teams tried to take a souvenir with them," Gabriel said.

"Maybe. It's definitely a puzzle . . . and possibly a concern," Michael replied.

CHAPTER 8

September 18, 2014
Thursday
Miami, Florida

As the chopper flew away, Rebecca stepped over to Charles, who was engaged in quiet conversation with Anan.

Charles gave a reassuring smile as she approached. "You ready to go? Your flight leaves Miami in a few hours."

"I'm ready. I've uploaded the files on the previous trip summaries and will review them on the flight."

"Good. Anan will also take you through his research; he's been out there several times."

"Too many times—with no luck I might add," Anan said. "Why don't we get going and we'll start our debrief at the airport."

They drove to Miami International in silence. Rebecca worried how Maya was just clinging to life, and hoped her lasting memory wasn't that of Maya struggling to breathe. She couldn't help but wonder if she'd ever see her beautiful face again. As she went through airport security, she forced those thoughts to retreat and resolved to stay optimistic, focusing on Japan and what lay ahead, believing in her heart that Maya would recover to her old self.

Rebecca and Anan settled in the terminal waiting area. This was the first occasion they were alone since they met, and Rebecca knew little about the Atlantan. Much like Gabriel, when engaged in dialogue Anan presented himself as friendly and easy to talk with, but during other times he was more reserved. The strong silent persona was reenforced by his intense brown eyes and chiseled jaw. Rebecca found his broad shoulders and cut physique both striking and reassuring, given their impending travels into the Suicide Forest.

"What materials have you uploaded?" Anan asked.

Rebecca replied, "I've got six—I'm sorry, seven files. One appears to be a compilation of old stories that reference either the crystal, a demon, or the area. The others are summaries of expeditions that traveled there: what the travelers saw, found, etcetera."

"At least three of the summaries would be mine," Anan smiled, "the others would be from Michael and Gabriel; they've trekked through there a few times."

"Why don't you tell me what you know and think is important? Then I'll read the files in flight and overlay the two."

"How about we start with the legends?" Anan replied.

"That works for me."

"Over a thousand years ago, we received reports of dragons on the main island of Japan. The IOL knew Lucifer and Marou were releasing demons everywhere, so we weren't too surprised. We took the reports as truths and went there in pursuit of the creatures with hopes of finding the crystal they protected. Over time, we traveled the country, speaking with the locals and searching for a solid lead. It was a tedious task as most of the stories included the typical human embellishments. Some people reported forty- and fifty-foot demons, a few animals that could be seen a hundred miles away, others were invisible. We listened to all of the tales, following each one with on-site research. The only thing we ever found was a Ka-Rui, a nasty class three demon in a remote section of Mount Fuji. We surprised the creature in a clearing, while it was feeding on a bear. It was about eight feet long, narrow in build, but powerful and definitely a fire-breather. It seemed to like the warmth of the summer sun." Anan paused to sip from his water bottle.

"Don't leave me hanging, what happened next?"

He set the bottle on the table. "We destroyed the creature, but never found its cave nor any leads. I wasn't too surprised. The Ka-Rui is a smaller demon, not likely used to guard something as important as the Star Crystal. After that, we thought the stories would end. But they didn't. The sightings of something in the wilds continue to this day. In all likelihood these creatures are benign, something akin to Indonesia's Komodo dragon. With that said, the stories are still frequent and descriptive enough that maybe there's a Ka-Rui nest out there, or a different type of dragon that's actually protecting the crystal. We don't know, so we keep searching."

"What about the Star Crystal—what are the legends or myths in Japan?" Rebecca asked, and then was hit with an uncomfortable feeling that she was being watched. She glanced toward the sitting area of the next boarding gate to Caracas, where a young man staring at her snapped his head away in an awkward attempt to hide his gawking.

"We have little on its location," Anan said. "That was and still is the problem. The most solid thing we learned was a reference to a 'tunnel of fire.' You'll see it in one of those documents. One of the IOL picked this up long ago, and the tip had a lot of credibility. But Mount Fuji is an ancient volcano, and the forest we're heading into is set on its western slope. There are old lava tubes everywhere; it's literally a maze and the perfect spot to hide the crystal. Michael, Gabriel, and I have searched a number of them, but again, with no luck."

"You mentioned Michael and Gabriel a few times. Have you gone on a lot of these missions with them?"

He glanced around to see if anyone was watching. "More than you can imagine."

She countered, "Like?" Working up the courage, she continued. "I don't mean to pry, but I'm about to travel into the wilds of the Suicide Forest in your company. We should know each other better."

Anan recognized what the question was really about. "Got it. How about I tell you a little about me?"

She grinned.

He laughed. "Michael, Gabriel, and I were among the first group through the wormhole. Michael was the appointed leader of the colony, and Lucifer and Gabriel were his seconds-in-command. I reported to Gabriel. While everybody else had one or two roles in the settlement, my sole job was head of security. I was trained as a soldier on Atla, and while here I trained all the Atlantans on Earth survival. My primary responsibility was to understand the risks to the colony, then develop and execute mitigation plans for them. In doing that task, I foresaw all of the security issues but one. I never considered I should worry about our own people. And make no mistake, betrayal was our downfall. When the war came, I fought alongside Michael, Uriel, and the rest of the IOL, and have ever since. I won't rest until the traitors responsible are held accountable."

"Uriel, I've never heard his name before. Who is he?" As she asked, she again glanced at the sitting area for the next gate. This time her admirer didn't bother averting his gaze, giving her a sheepish grin instead.

"Was. He was my friend and Michael's nephew. Uriel died long ago by the hand of Abaddon. He was a good man, brilliant, loyal, and a fierce soldier."

"I'm so sorry. Can I ask what happened?"

Anan gave a reluctant nod. "We were in London; the year was 1810, give or take. King George III was still monarch, albeit I recall his son was just named Prince Regent. It was a chaotic time in England: the colonies had been successful for years and the nation wasn't the same. We suspected Lucifer was supporting Napoleon in his wars on the Iberian Peninsula. It was a brutal campaign where countless humans suffered. Michael, Uriel, and I tracked Abaddon and Bernael to London, concluding they were trying to draw England into the conflict by assassinating the prime minister, Spencer Perceval—a task they succeeded in a few years later—sowing their seeds of chaos as usual."

Anan sipped his water again. "After the assassination, we traveled to a specific neighborhood, White Chapel, where a series of killings occurred that were hallmarks of Bernael's trade. While investigating, we received information on the IOD's location from a supposed reliable source. That tip turned out to be a trap. They, along with more than one hundred humans, attacked the three of us. In the chaos, our group was separated. I was forced to choose between saving Michael or Uriel. I chose Michael and watched, powerless, as Abaddon slit Uriel's throat. We were lucky we didn't end up with that fate as well." He paused, taking a deep breath. "Abaddon took a trophy from Uriel that day: a ring that belongs to Michael's family. Michael still wants it back, and one day soon I hope to help him do that."

An awkward silence fell between the two.

Anan was the first to speak. "Well, that was heavy. Tell you what, we're boarding soon. I'm going to go for a quick walk and stretch my legs before we have to sit for seventeen hours in flight to Tokyo."

Anan grabbed his pack and started for the far end of the terminal.

Rebecca organized her carry-on, then lifted it to her shoulder. She was stepping to walk away when her admirer moved in front of her.

"Hi! I'm sorry to bother you. I'm about to get on a plane and before I go, I wanted to tell you that I'm sorry for staring; I'm usually more polite." His raised his eyebrows, waiting for a response. None came. "To be honest, I think you're a very attractive woman, and I got caught up in the moment, but it was rude. I apologize." The man nervously ran his fingers through his long, sandy-brown hair that framed his suntanned face, his gray eyes never leaving Rebecca's.

"Not a problem, it happens. And not to be rude to you, but I have to make a stop before I board. Take care; hope you have a good flight."

"I will, and you the same. If our paths cross again, I'll buy you a drink to make up for it. And in the off chance that happens, my name is Joshua." As he spoke, he extended his hand, his six-foot athletic frame closing the gap between them. "Again, my apologies."

Rebecca took his hand. "I'm Rebecca." She gave him a weak smile before walking away, hoping he wouldn't follow.

She strolled alone down the terminal walkway, stopping at a store for a magazine and a bottle of water. After a few minutes of people watching, she returned to her gate to find Anan standing in the mass of those waiting for the plane. "They're boarding us now. I don't know about you, but I prefer not to be one of the cattle. I'm just going to wait."

"For sure. I can fit this bag under my seat, so there's no rush for me," Rebecca agreed.

Almost the last on board, they took their seats opposite one another across the aisle. As the plane reached cruising elevation, Rebecca pulled out her tablet and began to read her documents. The flight attendants had just begun their service rounds and one placed a small bottle of red wine on her extended table.

Rebecca glanced up, surprised. "I'm sorry, but I didn't order this."

The attendant leaned in, whispering, "It's from the handsome gentleman in seat 32A. He said, and I quote, he 'owed it to you' and that you had a 'red wine person vibe.'" She beamed as she poured a small amount into Rebecca's glass. "I suspect he's interested in more than wine. Enjoy and good luck."

Rebecca turned around to see the man in seat 32A. There, reading a book, was her admirer from the gate. Joshua peeked up from his pages to give a casual wave. Rebecca raised her partially filled glass, giving a small toast to him in response.

"What's that about?" Anan asked.

"Just a stalker doing his best to irritate me. He promised to buy me a drink next time our paths crossed. I assumed he was on a different flight. Trust me, I can handle it."

Anan stood from his seat across the aisle and started a slow walk to the men's room. He glanced down as he passed the young man consumed in his book. Returning a few minutes later, he leaned over and whispered to Rebecca, "He appears innocent enough. But be careful: people would kill for what you're reading now. Also, I had trouble seeing his energy. That may be a coincidence, but then again, maybe it's not."

CHAPTER 9

September 18, 2014
Thursday
The Lost City of Atlantis

Michael, Gabriel, and Austin raced along the lone standing bridge and crossed to the central island. Maya periodically thrashed against her bindings on the stretcher. Austin pushed his already fast pace in response.

Once across the span, they headed inland along a winding road, maneuvering between dilapidated buildings. They walked up the smallest of the three hills that made up the central island. The landscape was similar in appearance to the second land ring with one key exception: the dense city structures were, for the most part, still standing. Michael pointed up to the largest of the mounds where a gargantuan white palace still stood. He spoke to Austin, "There are three connected hills on the central island. The tallest one houses the palace, government buildings, and Cleito's Sanctuary. It was my home when we lived here." He motioned to the second hill. "The middle district is where we need to get to. It houses the medical building where Gabriel practiced, Poseidon's Temple, the university, and our library. The area we're climbing now is housing, public baths, a few science offices, and gardens."

"It must've been something to see at its peak."

"It was amazing," Gabriel said. "How are you holding up, Austin? We still have a couple of hills in front of us."

"Keep pushing, I'll manage." Austin adjusted the straps on his shoulders, making the weight more comfortable, and continued forward.

Michael navigated the narrow streets with little effort as he picked his way between fallen debris and the ivy growth. It was obvious he knew the road well.

To Austin, the city reminded him of the small sea towns built on Italy's Amalfi coast, even with the same cobblestone streets.

They continued until the road they traveled broke into a public square. Erected on the far side of the open space was the largest temple Austin had ever seen. Structured much like the Parthenon, its faded white marble with majestic pillars stood cracked and covered with the ivy growth. Austin could still see the intricate carvings of horses, monsters, and gods on sections of its outside walls. The wooden components of its collapsed roof had long ago rotted away, leaving only the block marble shell intact. In front, three massive statues resembling Greek gods lay broken on the ground.

"This is Poseidon's Temple," Michael said. "It was the largest shrine we ever built. The statues represent three of the original Atlantans who arrived here on our ship. The humans of this city—really the world—worshipped us as gods, hence we're depicted in human form. We were all too happy to let them believe in that fable. It provided societal order."

Austin asked, "Who are they, those statues, did you know them?"

Michael pointed. "The two men are Dias and Poseidis, the woman is Hera. They were the original gods, the foundation for much of ancient man's myths. I didn't know them. Their flesh bodies passed before I arrived, and I have not encountered their transient energies."

"This place is amazing. The design, the construction," Austin said.

Gabriel agreed, "Our engineers were the best. We lacked no comfort. We had a diverse food supply, clean running water, innovative waste disposal, advanced medical care, no crime, no poverty. It was a sight to behold at its peak. Unfortunately, it was all wasted."

Austin turned to Gabriel, "At some point, one of you will have to tell me what happened here, why there was war."

"Yes, at some point, but not now."

They pushed a few more minutes before Michael stopped. He paused next to an old stone building with a rusted metal gate dangling in an alcove that protected a partially open ornate tarnished silver metal door. The solid portal appeared damaged, as if someone had reinforced it with stone to prevent it from being opened, only to have it destroyed from the outside.

"Catch your breath; something's off here. This door is not abandoned like the others," Michael said.

Forcing the door back, they peered into the open room, where an old rusted Luger pistol lay covered in dust on the floor. Two worn shell casings sat on the ground next to it.

Michael picked up and studied the gun, then confirmed the find to Gabriel and Austin. "Something to add to our puzzle—it's a Nazi weapon. It appears the owner may have fought back against someone . . . or something." Tossing the gun to the floor, he glanced around one last time. "Let's move. There's nothing else to see."

They made their way to the top of the second hill, entering a large fenced-in compound enclosing a cluster of white stone buildings. Austin was breathing hard; sweat dripped off his brow from his efforts to keep pace. The two Atlantans appeared fresh as if they had strolled and not just sprinted up two consecutive hills.

Each building was rectangular, standing three stories, with no windows. A sturdy glass-like door was the only way in or out. Each building connected to the neighboring structure through a single, solid hallway on the ground level, creating a giant courtyard between the buildings. Even after all these years, it appeared solid and bunker-like, albeit antiseptic in style.

After easing Maya and the gurney to the ground, Gabriel moved to the side of the door. He stared at the white stone before stepping forward to press a small space on the wall. A few seconds later, a red laser projected from the surface and passed over his face. The glass door clicked open at once. He turned to Michael, a grin across his face. "I knew it would still work."

Michael slapped his friend on the back. "I never doubted you; you were right, as usual."

"What is this place? And how after all these years do the electronics still work?" Austin asked.

"I'll explain as we walk." Gabriel said as they lifted the stretcher. "This was—is—the Science and Technology Compound. They're some of the oldest buildings on the island, built over twenty thousand years ago. The city grew around them. Its fortress-like appearance was an intentional design. Our work was secret, thus only accessible to certain Atlantans. No humans have walked these halls. You'll be the first one, to my knowledge."

"I'm honored."

"My lab was here." Gabriel motioned to his friend. "And Michael kept an office here. During the last days of Atlantis, we sealed it up tight to ensure our records, equipment, and work were preserved. We knew we couldn't take them with us and didn't know when we'd get back, if ever. All the electronics are powered by our ship's batteries, with a half-life of one hundred thousand years."

Michael held the door open while Austin and Gabriel carried Maya down the hall and into a darkened room. They stepped to a medical table where they laid her. Gabriel then tapped a black panel on a wall, which lit up with odd symbols, then punched a series of the keys. The rooms lit up, and a bank of what Austin believed to be computers came alive.

Gabriel opened a cabinet and started rummaging through some

small containers. He stopped, turning to them. "I'll be a little while. I've got more than a few things to do. Why don't you find a room with another computer in it and decipher those files from New Orleans?"

"Are you sure there's nothing we can do to help?" Michael asked.

"Not right now. I've got to take blood and analyze it, then synthesize an antidote. It'll take at least a couple of hours, and as you know, I work better alone. Also, it's time you can use to solve your problem."

"I don't want to leave her now if there's a chance she's not going to make it." Austin stepped over to Maya and picked up her hand.

Gabriel's face softened. "Austin, I can only guarantee one thing: I will do everything I can. If she takes a turn for the worst, I'll get you. That is a promise. Now go, you're wasting time."

Michael touched Austin's shoulder. "Come on. She's in good hands here, let's give him some space to work."

Austin gave a reluctant look at Maya, so helpless on the table, then he crossed the room to follow Michael out, leaving Gabriel to his work.

They took a main hallway to the back of the building, arriving at a door that led into the outside courtyard. Above the door was a sign with "*Etre Dis Enda Norte*" in large, bold letters. Ignoring the portal, Michael headed right, into the hall connecting the buildings.

Austin stopped by the exit door, a troubled feeling in his gut. "That's odd, I just had a déjà vu. What's out there?" he inquired.

"It's a large courtyard used by the scientists here. The sign is in our native language, says something to the effect of 'development area.' Why?"

Austin glanced around. "I don't know, just an odd feeling like I've seen this before, but not like in a picture, like I've been here."

Michael hesitated, studying Austin. "That is odd; I wonder why. I'm confident you're the first of your kind here." His eyes lit up as he continued, "You recall that a true déjà vu is a transient's strong past life experience bleeding into this life."

"Yes, I remember. But as you said, that's impossible here since no human has been inside this building." Austin shook his head. "It feels so real though."

"I think we should keep moving," Michael said.

They continued into the next building and started up a set of stone stairs. Michael paused at another black box on the wall. Touching its screen, it lit up in response. He tapped a sequence of keys that turned on the lights and opened the door in front of him. Entering the office area, they walked through a small sitting room and came to a desk that held a flat piece of glass situated upright. Michael pulled out the silver box he took to New Orleans then sat, staring forward at the glass, but saying nothing. The clear screen in front of him came alive, scrolling with data, flashing Atlantan symbols and words.

"Whoa, how are you doing that?"

Michael glanced up toward him. "I'm doing it telepathically. Similar to your voice command technology, we long ago developed the ability to communicate with our computers via thought. If you don't mind, I need to focus for a few minutes." He paused. "Here, this may help pass the time."

Once again, he concentrated, and the rear solid wall faded into a shaded glass. Austin could now see the gargantuan courtyard between the buildings. The large compound-like area was covered with a thick layer of the ivy vegetation and other fallen debris.

He glanced back to Michael's screen. The files flashed in rapid sequence, stopping on one in a different language. It opened, and a series of schematics came up, followed by a lengthy text in Atlantan writing.

Michael scanned the information. "Charles was right: this is an old Atlantan binary code. It appears to be information on Hy Brasil."

"Like the book we took from Sedona," Austin said. He recalled the information on the phantom island they found in the living room of the Sedona mansion, moments before he burst in to Bernael's secret chamber, stopping him from performing the astral fusion process on Maya.

"The same."

He scrolled through more files, until finding the second in the unusual format. Opening this document, it was different altogether, being a series of maps that Austin recognized as Giza, Egypt and the surrounding area to the Red Sea.

Michael studied them in silence, causing Austin to eventually ask, "What is it?"

"Appears this one provides information on the ancient city of Abydos. Not sure why yet, but I can imagine. Maybe the piece of the Star Crystal in his possession is there. Then again, it could be a new section." He paused. "The first document is a little more confusing. It's a combination of clues and riddles about Hy Brasil, but again it's not clear for what. Solving this will take more time than we have here. I'll save the files so we can analyze them on the foundation's system." Michael concentrated again. The file flashed off the screen as it cleared. He returned the silver box to his pocket.

Austin asked, "Since we have a little time before Gabriel comes up with a solution for Maya, can we talk about the civil war? Why did the Atlantans turn on each other?"

"You sure you want to know? It may change how you think about life, your transient energy, probably your very existence," Michael said.

Austin returned the Atlantan's stare. "Yes, I'm sure, regardless of where the information takes me."

"Okay, let's take a walk."

Michael stopped next to the door to open a hidden cabinet and removed a safe-like box. He lifted out a round, metallic marble etched with deep grooves and dropped it in his pocket. He continued, "I think Gabriel spoke with you in Guatemala on the origins of the universe, living energy, and transient energy. So let me start there."

Together they walked out of the office. "We don't know with certainty why or how, but at a point before time existed, the entire energy of the universe was a singularity, a mass so dense that words cannot describe it adequately. A second energy—some call it the Creator's energy, but different from the bulk of the singularity's—jostled the mass. These quantum fluctuations caused the singularity to explode. This is what scientists today call the Big Bang."

Austin asked, "I'm confused—you're distinguishing the energy of the singularity from the Creator's, you mean like God?"

"Yes and no. Yes, the universe's creator can and has been described as a deity or god. But also, no, because both energies were part of the same singularity, the Creator-energy was just different from the bulk of the other energy that made up the singularity."

Austin continued, "So, you're sure there are two types of energy?"

"We're positive; we've measured the subtle differences between the two. The vast bulk of elements in our universe is what you see here: the sun, the rocks, the creatures that live on Earth, all different forms of energy, which I think Gabriel called star matter. The second energy is the Creator's energy, otherwise known as transient energy, or some call it God-energy."

Michael paused on the stairwell while opening the door under the E.D.E.N. sign leading to the courtyard. "Gabriel took you through the evolution of star matter; it started as simple atoms, then molecules in gaseous forms. Then through various processes it formed complex molecules that led to the solids, liquids, plasmas, and this—" Michael pointed to the leaves of the ivy, "—the living energy you see around you. We know this as fact."

"Yes," Austin answered.

Michael walked through the overgrown courtyard with his

hands gently clasped behind his back—the picture of relaxation. Finding a worn stone bench, he cleared an area of the fallen debris before sitting. He motioned for Austin to join him. "Good, now for the difficult part. The piece of God-energy that jostled the singularity blew apart into billions of pieces in the Big Bang, scattering around the universe like pollen in the wind. As things settled in the cold, dark recesses of space, these pieces of God-energy that scattered fused into the various forms of living energy throughout the cosmos. Creatures—or better yet beings with souls—came to exist. And with it, evolved intelligence and consciousness was set in motion. Do you understand?"

"I think so. The God-energy integrated into living energy, and intelligent beings with souls were born. Like the Atlantans and humans."

Michael tilted his head, studying Austin. "Almost right. Our species on Atla evolved as such billions of years ago. The humans of Earth took a different path, which brings us back to the civil war. We've discussed Marou and his work with bioengineering."

"Yes, he domesticated the animals of the planet and now creates monsters for Lucifer. He sounds like a psychopath."

Michael's face grew serious. "That is correct. Unfortunately, he did more than just that. Marou experimented with various creatures of Earth to create work animals—slaves if you will. The Atlantans had limited technology and numbers to work with to set up the wormhole and build this city. So, Marou attempted to create a smarter, more capable domesticated animal that could do the manual labor.

Having evolved for survival, the animals of Earth were aggressive and untrainable, so he crafted a species to become smarter, less aggressive, and thus easier to control." He paused, studying Austin. "Human ancestors were a direct result of these experiments."

Austin's mind buzzed as he considered the ramifications of Michael's words. "So, human evolution had help; that's not so surprising or terrible."

"You did, but there's more. Have you ever wondered why humans are the only species that has evolved on Earth with consciousness and an advanced intelligence? For three and a half billion years, living energy has been present, and no animal has come even close to what you have become. Why, then, fifty thousand years ago during the Upper Paleolithic period, does an intelligent version of humans show up?" He leaned in. "Austin, it wasn't by chance, but by design."

"Go on," Austin said, a sudden heaviness in his chest.

"An Atlantan scientist named Prometheus worked with Marou and took pity on the slave race. He created the branch to modern humans by bioengineering Atlantan DNA into your hominoid ancestor. When he did this, he gifted your species transient energy: your path to consciousness and intelligence."

Austin stopped him. "Prometheus like the Greek myth?"

"It's no myth, Austin. Prometheus, the Atlantan, gifted man 'fire'—transient energy, or, if you will, the human soul. And for it, he was tortured and killed by Lucifer and Marou, sparking the civil war."

Humans were not the evolutionary wonder that Austin had

believed, he now realized, but a laboratory experiment from an alien civilization.

Michael interrupted his thoughts. "The first of your ancestors were created in this lab, right here. They were studied in this courtyard, in the garden of E.D.E.N." His voice trailed off.

"The biblical stories of Adam and Eve are true? Eden was real?"

"Yes and no. It was real in that Prometheus did name the first man-like creation Adam, but the story morphed over the ages to fit the times in which it was documented," Michael said.

Austin rubbed his temples, a throbbing pain building behind his left eye.

"You okay?" Michael asked.

"Yeah, fine, just a little headache. Sounds like you're telling me that for all of the religions where God is our Creator, it's basically all lies."

Michael leaned forward, a softness in his eyes. "No, they are not lies, they are the absolute truth." He paused, still holding his gaze. "Everything you see, everything you feel, everything you experience is all from the same process, the same being. Is a test-tube baby any less human than one of natural birth? Obviously, no. Whether you were created as-is, evolved from a different species, or a combination therein, we're all of divine origin. And, you have transient energy inside you, connecting you to the Creator. You must understand that, believe it, and live it."

Austin processed Michael's words. As strange as they sounded, they made sense.

"I understand why you don't share this story. If I'd heard this six months ago, I may have questioned your sanity, but after all I've seen and all you've taught me, I believe it." He ran his fingers through his hair. "Oh, and except for Maya and Rebecca, I'll keep it safe."

Michael clasped his friend's shoulder. "You've taken this well."

Austin took a deep breath before continuing. "What happened next? Why the war?"

Michael leaned back, stretching in the sun. "When Prometheus first created the new species, Atlantans met the news with both curiosity and outrage. Lucifer and his followers viewed humans as nothing more than unclean animals suitable for slave work then slaughter. Others, like me, viewed the new species as enlightened energy with a piece of our Creator. When I first arrived here, the Atlantans were engaged in this philosophical debate about what it meant to exist and what was life's meaning. I argued that killing the humans is murdering a piece of ourselves and our Creator. We are, after all, a related species." Michael's eyes followed as a leaf floated down in the gentle breeze. "We made the decision to let the humans live. To continue using them as work animals, but to provide food, medicine, and education to allow them to develop self-sufficiency. I think Lucifer was reluctant but somewhat approving of the decision; he liked being a god, being worshipped. And these humans were now smarter, thus more controllable slaves for his interests."

"That's not too surprising from what I know of him. What happened next?" Austin asked.

"The most amazing thing: your species evolved much faster than we expected. You learned quickly, not only intellectually, but spiritually as well. Soon, your population grew, and your cities teemed with wisdom and promise. But with that growth, your ability to create weapons also advanced, and you still were an aggressive species. About ninety-five hundred years ago, there was a human uprising that killed two Atlantans. This was the trigger for the war. Lucifer recognized there was a mortal risk to the small number of Atlantans that inhabited the planet, and all the reinforcements in the world wouldn't change that dynamic. He developed a plan to exterminate the entire human population before it became too large. To this end, his followers did things like unleash fires and floods of biblical magnitude, all in his effort to destroy man. Marou captured Prometheus, the Atlantan who, in their eyes, unleashed the plague on the Earth. He was put in chains and murdered by Lucifer.

"There was no middle ground at that point. Each Atlantan had to choose: follow Lucifer and his dark ways, or support the humans. I chose to not be part of the darkness. I believed in the sanctity of human life, of your transient energy. Half the Atlantans followed me."

Austin thought about the chaos that Michael endured, the losses he suffered. "And what happened during the war? How did the city get destroyed?"

Michael stood up. "We should check on Gabriel, then there is something I'll show you."

"Did the great flood actually happen?"

Michael walked down the stairs and turned into the main building. "Oh yes, quite real and very important to the evolution of man. It happened about 7400 BC on the Bosphorus Strait in Turkey. The Earth was in a warming period, oceans had risen, and the Mediterranean Sea was high. Lucifer demolished a key section of the strait, allowing the Mediterranean waters to backflow into the Black Sea, flooding about sixty thousand square miles and killing hundreds of thousands of innocent people; many were peasant women and children. The event was tragic in both scale and cruelty. It was, however, that flood which made Lucifer realize he alone couldn't eradicate humans from the Earth. There were too many, they were too widespread, and your intelligence was growing fast. He needed a different way. So, he altered his tactics. The IOD pursued the control and killing of the masses through brutal human dictators wielding the sword."

They walked into Gabriel's lab. Maya was sitting on the edge of the treatment bed, her face tired and worn, but very much alive. Austin rushed to her side. He reached out then pulled back as she focused on the floor again. "It's great seeing you sit up. How do you feel?"

"Alive, but like I've been run over by a bus."

Gabriel came out of the back room. "Good, you're back." He beamed at Maya. "She'll be fine; weak for a while, but she'll live to fight another demon."

Relief swept over Austin and he audibly exhaled, his first deep breath in days.

"What was the poison?" Michael asked.

"It was a mixture of two things. Given the necrosis around the wound, I suspected it was some form of spider toxin, and widow DNA first came to mind. What I didn't see was the scorpion venom, which explains her neurological symptoms. I was able to take her blood, isolate it, and analyze it. As luck would have it, we had already synthesized an antidote for both venoms, so it was just a question of getting the right dosage. I didn't want the cure to kill her either. Her response is amazing. We made the right call coming here."

Michael gave Maya a warm smile. "Welcome back to the living." Turning to Gabriel, he asked, "How long before she can travel?"

"Let's give her a few minutes."

Austin didn't care anymore. He stepped to her, caressing her back. "You had me worried."

"Everybody was worried," Michael said. "Your strength in fighting through this was nothing short of amazing."

Gabriel said, "Michael, there's one other thing you should know. Let's talk a moment in private."

Michael nodded when Maya spoke, "Gabriel, you can talk in front of Austin. No more secrets." She clasped Austin's free hand and looked up to give him a haggard smile.

"You sure?" Austin asked.

Gabriel gave a tentative look to Michael, who responded, "He knows, Gabriel; we sat in the courtyard."

"Okay then, no more secrets. You were right, upon looking at her blood, she is a demi," Gabriel said.

Austin asked, "What's a demi?"

Maya rubbed her thumb over his hand. "You may want to sit down for this."

Austin squeezed back. "I'm good. What's a demi, Gabriel?"

Michael answered, "You know how we discussed Prometheus and his bioengineered gift of transient energy to man. Well, there was another way the gift of Atlantan DNA was given to mankind—nature's way."

Austin again appeared confused.

Gabriel continued, "Remember the myth of Hercules, where Zeus took a human form and slept with the woman Alcmene? The result was the demigod Hercules: half man, half god. As we discussed before, there is always some truth to these myths. And in this case, Zeus was the Atlantan, Jupit, who took on his human form to sleep with the human woman, Alcmene. That's happened a lot over the centuries. When a pregnancy occurred, the baby that survived birth and wasn't killed due to deformities almost always had unusual abilities, like increased strength, better reflexes, or superior cognitive intelligence. Some of the greatest warriors and academics in human history were secretly demis, and their achievements helped move the human species forward in so many ways." He poured a clear liquid into a canister and placed it into his pack. "Think about it: there are so many accounts of warriors, like Hercules, Perseus, and Theseus, to name a few from the Greeks. They had similar traits—all demigod warriors that also killed the demons of their time. Coincidence?" Gabriel let the information sink in.

Austin's eyes were wide. "Maya is half Atlantan?"

Gabriel answered, "Not half. Recall that all modern humans share some Atlantan DNA. Meaning we're all related. Maya just has a different variation and more in key areas as part of hers came from natural selection, from breeding, rather than in the lab. Over generations, the percentage of her Atlantan DNA has been diluted, but you can still tell she is unique, and it runs strong in her. I noted something unusual the day she killed the Chupacabra and a couple of days later with her fighting instincts in the jungle. Her resistance to the demon venom pretty much confirmed our suspicions. No human could have survived that. It's what kept her alive."

Maya turned to Gabriel. "Do we know who my relative was? Tell me it wasn't that sadist Bernael."

"It's impossible to know who it is without further tests. You're about fifteen generations removed, and believe it or not, the mating of our two species was not that unusual."

"So, Maya is a demi, maybe a relative to Hercules himself—that's some family tree." Austin laughed, trying to lighten the mood.

Maya raised her eyebrows at the thought. "What does this mean for me? Do I need to do anything differently?"

Michael took a step closer to her and said gently, "What you have is a gift. It means nothing different for you. You are who you are and will be who you are. You may find you're stronger, smarter, quicker, and more connected to the spirit world than some, but not all. You're the same person you were yesterday, only with a better understanding of yourself." He turned toward Austin. "I would add that Austin is in the same boat. He now knows his transient energy is a gift from the Atlantans."

CHAPTER 10

September 18, 2014
Thursday
The Lost City of Atlantis

Michael pressed his fingertips to a spot on the surface of a white stone table. A long, metallic pedestal emerged from the table's center. The silver stand had octangular edges with a circular cup at its top.

"Maya, while you were being treated, I briefed Austin on the events that led to the civil war that destroyed Atlantis. I promised him I'd finish the story. If you don't mind, while you recover, I thought I'd play this. You'll both be interested in watching."

Michael reached in his pocket, and removed the metal ball he had taken from his office and placed it in the rod's open cup. Electric sparks crackled, engulfing the metal orb with a low hum. A moment later, a three-dimensional holographic picture projected just above the ball.

"What's that?" Maya asked.

Michael tapped the table, and the picture stopped moving. "It's an Atlantan storage device for memories and video. Think of it as an advanced DVD, only indestructible. It contains a video we compiled just prior to leaving the city—under duress as you'll see. We didn't know if or when we'd ever make it back, so we created a record for any Atlantans that may someday come searching for the colony."

"How do you capture memories?" Austin asked.

"Telepathically, similar to my earlier interaction with the computer. You focus on the memory, it uploads to the computer, then burns it into the ball. This provides a good glimpse of the chaos just before and after the plasma generator exploded. My lips won't sync with the voice, as I'm translating so you can understand it. We spoke a different language then." Michael tapped his finger on the table once more, and the video rolled.

The image revealed a bloody and tired Michael in Gray form standing in a room with nothing but a table behind him. He wore military-type clothing—a far cry from the jeans and T-shirt he wore today. Every few seconds the image would shake, reflecting the tremors that rocked the ground he stood on. His image from ninety-five hundred years ago spoke, "This is Captain 412, leader of the Planet 3521, Earth, Colony. Our group has fractured. We are in the midst of a weaponized battle for control of the city. This video is being made to document events that happened in the hopes of bringing the traitors to justice. As ranking officer of this outpost, I've ordered the arrest of Atlantan officers 666 and 672, along with crew member 914 for the kidnap and execution of medical team member 1055, as well as sedition."

Michael stopped the machine. "666 is Lucifer, 672 is Marou, 914 is Bernael, and 1055 is Prometheus. Also, in this upcoming part, you'll hear 928, that's Uriel."

He pressed the start button again. "We imprisoned the three crew members before 666's rogue followers attacked the city, facilitating their escape. In the onslaught, they have catastrophically damaged the plasma generator. The associated explosions have torn a rift along the seismic plate that supports the western half of the city. The resultant earthquakes are at present collapsing the area into the ocean. Lethal levels of radiation have been released; thus, we are forced to abandon Atlantis and its resources. To that end, our force field is in a temporary shutdown, while Officer 928 leads our effort to evacuate the surviving human citizens away from the city. In their incursion, 666's followers have slaughtered many fellow Atlantans who remained true to Atla law. After successfully driving the traitors back, we now turn our efforts to our evacuation. The current plan is to head for the Nile River Valley of North Africa in hopes of building a new colony there, eventually reestablishing contact with Atla. To that end, we must leave the majority of our vital equipment and technology, as we don't have the time nor resources to salvage it. Last, I have just learned 666's forces have disabled the interstellar teleportation device and have taken the Star Crystal with them. This caused the abrupt communication blackout with Atla and ensures reinforcements cannot arrive. We will undertake all efforts to retrieve the Star Crystal and bring 666 and his followers to justice."

There was a pause in the video as Michael's image flashed away. His voice could be heard as a series of pictures rolled. "The following is a compilation of images taken from video and memories that show the events that led up to this cataclysm. I leave this ball here in hopes assistance does come and justice prevails. 412, out."

What followed was image after image of the Immortals of Darkness lethally attacking the city and its people. It showed the brutal massacre of the humans, then Gabriel treating the multitude of victims. Anan was there with Michael and an unfamiliar man leading the fight to save Atlantis and its inhabitants.

Austin interrupted, "Hey, can you stop it there?"

Michael reached out, pressing the button on the table. The holographic image froze in place.

Austin approached the picture, staring at the unknown man. "Who is this?" He pointed as he spoke.

"That's Uriel. He was an engineer for the colony and an excellent soldier. He was the one tasked with coordinating the humans' evacuation. Why do you ask?" Michael said.

Austin tilted his head. "I don't know, he seemed familiar for a second. But on closer examination, I don't recognize him. I'm sorry, let's keep moving."

Gabriel shot an odd glance to Michael, who replied with a nod before pressing the start button.

The movie continued. A few images captured the fighting on the outer land rings. It moved to the IOD planting munitions near the plasma generator and its eventual destruction. A short video from high above detailed the explosions, the earthquakes, and the collapse of the land into the ocean. The video showed Lucifer, Marou, and Bernael walking from their prison area and being greeted with cheers by their rebel supporters. The last scene showed a fleet of white-sailed ships navigating out of the Atlantis harbor, a map of the African continent, then a list of the names of the traitors. The hologram faded. The room fell silent.

Austin felt a fiery anger toward the IOD raging inside of him. "They destroyed everything, for what? They're no better than murderers."

"What happened next?" Maya asked.

Gabriel answered, "For the humans, most made their way to present-day Egypt, others scattered around Europe. For the Atlantans, the Immortals of Light settled in the Nile River delta with our salvaged technology. We reorganized, settled, then started hunting the IODs that betrayed their oaths to Atla. The IOD moved into the shadows, hid the crystals, created demons, and in general made plans for the eradication of the human species. I'd be remiss if I didn't say, they also hunted us."

Michael rubbed his chin. "But there's always been something else with Lucifer, some other plan we don't understand yet. Frankly, I'm not sure he's figured it out yet either, but I suspect he's getting close."

"I'm sorry you had to endure all that. It had to be awful," Maya said.

Gabriel gave her a thoughtful look, before answering with a shrug. "It is what it is. It would be naive for anyone to think that life will only have positive events. There will always be good and, just as important, bad things that happen that are out of your control. One must take stock and enjoy the positives. And when the bad occurs, you just have to deal with it knowing that it will someday pass. I view every day as a new opportunity to strive for excellence, to help a less fortunate soul, or to make right something that went wrong. It's why we continue our search for the crystal after all these years: to right the many wrongs that Lucifer has unleashed on you humans."

"Bad things are going to happen; best to deal with them directly and always maintain a positive view of yourself and life," Michael said while moving toward his backpack. "So now we need to pack a few things here—some medicine, some equipment…."

Gabriel interrupted, "All set on the medicine. I packed what I needed. And, you'll be glad to know I could synthesize Bernael's three drugs. The resurrection drug was the most difficult."

"Excellent, my friend." Turning back to Maya, Michael continued. "We only need to grab some of my equipment and get off this island and back to Florida. Then Austin is on a chartered flight to Japan to help Anan. Gabriel and I are heading to Kazakhstan on an unrelated matter. And you, Maya, are heading back to Tucson for some rest and relaxation."

Maya straightened, then stood. "I'm going with Austin; I can rest and relax in Tokyo. And if I feel better, who knows, maybe I can help."

"That's not a good idea, you've been through a lot and need to heal," Michael said.

Gabriel put his hand on Michael's shoulder. "It's fine, she can travel."

Austin had seen that light in Maya's eyes before and knew her decision was nonnegotiable.

Gabriel continued, "As long as she promises to rest in Japan. Which she does, right Maya?"

She returned his question with a small shrug. "Yes, I promise, sleep and relaxation, maybe even a spa day. That's all."

Michael gave a skeptical smile. "You guys pack up. I need to run upstairs for a moment to get a few things." He reached over and grabbed the metal memory ball, stuffing it in his pocket.

While Maya laid down on the makeshift bed with her eyes closed, Austin helped Gabriel pack the medicine and equipment.

Once done, Gabriel approached Maya with a syringe and needle. "This won't hurt at all," he said.

Maya asked, "What is it?"

Gabriel cocked his head, "You're tired, and it's a long walk to the helicopter. It's a feel-good remedy that will ensure you have the energy to make it there."

Michael returned with his bag. The group was ready to depart. While walking out of the room, Gabriel reached into his pack, withdrawing the quart-sized metal canister he had previously stored. He held it up for Michael to see. "Guess what I made."

Michael took the container and removed the lid, sniffing the contents. He jerked away from the smell. "Is that what I think it is?"

Gabriel's grin was mischievous. "It is. But it's only for medicinal purposes!" He turned to Maya and Austin. "It's an Atlantan alcohol, pretty much pure alcohol. A little rough now, needs to set for a few days, but then will be mellow and tasty. I haven't had this in years." Gabriel laughed as he placed it into his sack.

They left the building. Gabriel stopped for his facial scan, allowing him to lock the facility once more. While they waited, Michael removed a thin, pen-like device and a small handheld gun from his pack. Handing Maya the pen, he said, "These are Atlantan weapons that only Atlantans can operate. In essence, it reads your DNA—a safeguard we developed, so they didn't fall into the wrong hands. I'm wondering if you can use them."

Maya grinned as she took the metal pen-like device; it was just like the one shown to her by Gabriel in Guatemala. She pointed it at a patch of the ivy growth. Nothing happened.

Gabriel spoke to her mind, "Use your thoughts to fire it. You must see it discharge in your mind's eye."

Maya refocused, pointing the laser again, concentrating. A blue light erupted from the tip of the pen and turned the green leaves to black ash. Her face lit up. "Wow, that's incredible!"

"It's yours. Keep it safe. And this is also yours. It's more brutish, but at times effective." Michael passed Maya the small hand weapon that resembled a gun with no trigger.

"What is it?" she asked.

"A high-energy electromagnetic pulse gun, otherwise known as an EMP."

Austin said, "Like the one Kukulkan used on Ixlu."

"Yes, just like that one," Michael nodded. "There are two flat buttons: one is your power level, and one is your fire. Just keep your finger over the fire button, and electromagnetic waves will pulse in sequence until you lift it off."

"It's faster than a bullet and at full power, its impact can be lethal to all creatures—humans, Atlantans, demons," Gabriel added.

Maya pointed the weapon at a statue a few yards away. She covered the fire button. A powerful red light discharged, shattering the statue's head while a crackling sound roared through the area.

She grinned in response. "I think I'm going to like this one."

Austin stepped to Maya. "May I see it?"

"Sure." She lowered the power level before handing him the weapon.

As he examined it, Gabriel spoke, "Go ahead, Austin, try it."

Austin pointed the weapon at the same statue. He eased down on the fire button; the gun remained silent. He pressed the trigger button again, harder this time. Still nothing.

"Sorry Austin, you can't fire it, you're not enough Atlantan," Gabriel said.

Austin handed the gun back to Maya. "Too bad; it's light and accurate," Maya said. She laughed a little, before adding, "Guess you won't be invited to the Atlantan family dinners."

"We should start for the helicopter," Michael said. "The next opening in the shield is in about two hours, and we have at least an hour walk with no stops." He glanced at her. "You sure you are up for a hike now?"

"Yeah, I'm ready. Not sure what Gabriel gave me, but I'm feeling 100 percent better."

Gabriel's eyes went wide. "Let's just leave it as 'Gabriel's feel-good medicine.'"

Michael laughed. "Good, then let's move. Dr. Feel-Good, you want to lead the way?"

They backtracked their steps past Poseidon's Temple. The walk was all new to Maya, and she was astounded by the size and beauty of the city. Gabriel gave her a running commentary on the island's history while Austin and Michael walked in silence.

They walked the narrow streets of the central city area when a clatter from a nearby residence startled the group. They stopped and peered through a small window. First Maya, then Gabriel entered the door with weapons raised. Austin and Michael followed close behind. Once inside, they could see rusted metal pans strewn on the floor.

Turning to her left, Maya took a small step toward a toddler-sized, silvery-green creature cowering behind a chair, staring at her with yellow eyes. She pointed her new weapon at it. "Guys, what's this thing?"

Gabriel answered first, "It's an adaro." He squatted down to one knee, studying the creature at eye level. "What are you doing up here, little guy? You're supposed to be in the water." He spoke in a soothing tone, making no quick motions.

The frightened creature responded to his voice, coming out from its hiding place, sliding closer to him, yellow eyes wide. A sound similar to a cat's purring resonated from its chest.

"I bet it's foraging for food," Austin whispered.

Cautious and slow, the adaro slid even closer to Gabriel, inching to an arm's length away. Its eyes narrowed as it chirped its happy song. Gabriel turned to whisper something to Austin but never got the chance.

Without warning, the creature launched at Gabriel, growling through its pointed, gnashing teeth. It made it only halfway when a crackling blast blew it into the back wall. The creature landed with a crash, dead before hitting the floor. Maya glanced to Gabriel with a grin. "I do like this gun." She paused. "You okay?"

"I'm fine, thank you. That's odd, they're not supposed to be aggressive creatures," Gabriel said.

"They were also water creatures," Michael said, "and now they're on land. This explains our earlier mysteries. I don't like this. Time to leave."

They left the building and hurried down the street. As the group rounded a corner, three adaros sat in the shadows, watching them, then three more, and soon three more after that. Each person slowed, making no quick movements while drawing their weapon. Michael and Gabriel held their pen lasers, Austin had his gun, and Maya stood firm with her newly acquired EMP blaster.

"How many shots do I have with this?" Maya asked.

Michael's answer was flat. "More than you can shoot."

"You sure? Because I can shoot a lot."

As they walked past the adaro groups, the largest of the pack made a ferocious charge at them. Even with no legs, it moved fast, pulling its weight with two thin but muscular arms. Austin fired, hitting it square in the chest. The bullet pounded the smaller creature back and away, killing it on impact. The echoing blast scattered the other adaros into temporary hiding.

Austin watched in surprise and horror as a group of creatures hurried from the shadows toward the dead animal. They frenzied on the carcass as a horde, ripping its flesh into several pieces and maiming one another for a taste of the fresh meal.

Michael screamed, "Run!"

The group sprinted down the street. As the buildings flew by, adaros by the dozen emerged to join in the chase. A few times a pack appeared in front of them, and the four travelers ran through their attackers firing, killing the unfortunate and scattering the rest. A few of the creatures managed to get through their defenses, ripping at their bodies with claws and teeth. Mauled by a large one, Gabriel grabbed the animal by the tail, slamming it into the ground, breaking its neck. Two more got to Austin; Michael was quick to pick one off, while Austin, out of bullets, decapitated the other with his knife. Maya was lethal, her new weapon light and accurate; she decimated the pack, picking them off one by one. But the masses kept coming, their sheer numbers overwhelming.

Austin long ago ran out of bullets. Now with only Demon Slayer, he was at the mercy of his friends for protection. They dashed through the central city to the bridge leading to the first circle of land. Once on the span, they turned, making a stand against the horde. Maya pulled her antimatter laser, and standing aligned with Gabriel and Michael, the three covered the bridge's entry with wide beams. The creatures howled in pain as they crashed into the lasers' threshold. Dozens were incinerated in an instant; the others instinctively retreated, many severely burned. As fast as the chaos had erupted, it all fell to an eerie quiet. The sound of silence echoed in Austin's ears until a sudden mass of adaros on both sides of the bridge launched themselves into the water, swimming toward the far ground.

Michael urged, "They're trying to surround us, move!"

They dashed across the bridge to the collapsed city on the first band of land. As they left the span, they could see hundreds of adaros exiting the water, scaling the walls into the rubble in front of them. The creatures tracking behind them on the bridge made another dash to attack. Once again, a few made it through their defenses. Austin made quick work of the beasts with his knife while the other three held the masses at bay. With the attackers beaten back once more, they sprinted through the stoned streets to the edge of the next bridge. Austin could just see the helicopter on the far bank. He could also see a group of adaros at the far end of the bridge they still had to cross. The creatures had them surrounded.

He turned around and a sea of the green animals stormed toward them, fighting each other to get to the human flesh. There was no choice: they had to get over the bridge.

Austin screamed, "Come on, we can't kill 'em all! Let's go!"

Michael, Maya, and Gabriel beat back the advancing horde with their lasers. Austin had already sprinted halfway across the bridge when he came to the collapsed gap. He didn't bother to tiptoe around it as they did coming in, but instead he hurdled over the opening at full speed. Over a dozen adaros were his reward as he landed with a roll. They attacked as one, all going for the open parts of his body. He used Demon Slayer to slice through the pack, one by one. A giant adaro latched onto his arm and pain seared through his torso as its teeth found flesh. A second creature's dagger-like claws found the base of his neck. On instinct, he wrenched the smaller one off his neck, slamming it headfirst into the larger animal, breaking its grip on his forearm. As the two creatures crashed away, Austin was on them, using the long knife to finish them both. Bloodied, he turned to see his sprinting friends jump the opening in the bridge. Behind them, a green wave dotted with hundreds of yellow eyes bore down. The creatures created a bridge of bodies to cover the gap in the bridge, allowing the masses to cross.

Maya screamed at Gabriel, "Throw the canister, now!"

Gabriel didn't hesitate; he knew her plan. Ripping the metal canister of Atlantan liquor out of his bag, he threw it high over the advancing adaros. Maya pulled her EMP weapon and blasted the airborne container just over the bridge's surface. The explosion was deafening, sending shrapnel and a fireball into the adaro masses. The already damaged bridge couldn't take the concussive force of the blast. One by one, a cascade of collapsing blocks dropped the burning adaros into the water, stranding the horde on the other side.

Austin watched in terror as thousands of the creatures launched into the water and swam toward the wall that protected the land on which they stood. Sprinting to the helicopter, Gabriel called over his shoulder, "Hold them as long as you can!"

Austin, Maya, and Michael stood on the wall carving, blasting, and burning anything that tried to escape onto the land. They heard the chopper blades wind up, then the steady whine of the engines moving to full throttle. Michael yelled, "Maya, go! Cover us when you get there!"

She spun around and sprinted the short distance to their only hope for escape. She slid behind the copter, taking position next to the passenger door while yelling, "Go! Go! Go!"

Austin and Michael sprinted for their lives as the animals streamed over the wall in deadly pursuit. With her friends' lives in jeopardy, Maya unleashed the full fury of her new weapon, blasting anything that moved. She was a trained assassin, and her mark was absolute. The creatures' cries were piercing as she executed them with deadly precision.

Once in the helicopter, Austin grabbed Maya's shoulder. "Let's go!"

Maya climbed in before returning to her charge, blasting at the creatures through the open door. Austin slammed the door shut. Even through her lethal barrage, a few of the relentless adaros made their way to the chopper and latched onto the landing gear. They were carried up as the copter rose, vainly attempting to claw their way into the cabin, tearing at doors and scratching at windows.

Gabriel had had enough. Airborne now, he rolled the copter back and forth with great aerial skill. One by one, the creatures lost grip, plummeting from the force of the motion to certain death. The group watched in morbid curiosity as a throng of the adaros swarmed the outer circle of land and feasted on the bodies of their dead.

Austin sighed with a breath of relief, "We made it."

Michael was calm. "Move it Gabriel—no time to waste. We have two minutes before the force field window opens. If we miss it, there's nowhere to go for three hours, and we don't have enough fuel to hover."

Gabriel turned to Michael, a gleam in his eye. "Watch this."

He pulled back hard on the controls, and the helicopter responded with freakish speed. Austin nearly lost his stomach again as they blasted higher into the sky. He heard the snap, indicating the force field had opened, giving them two minutes to get to the safe altitude. Those seconds were harrowing as they flew vertically, Gabriel keeping his arms locked back and up, as he pushed the machine to its ultimate limits. A loud hum began, and a yellowish light filled the cabin.

"We're in the zone now. Get us up, it's going to close on us!" Michael urged.

With a great heave, Gabriel pulled back with all his remaining strength. In a rare display of emotion, he shouted, "Come on!"

As the copter maxed out its climb, Austin and Maya held on with everything they had. A thunderous snap occurred just below them, rocking the craft back and forth, then silence.

Austin peered out his window. A turquoise sky radiated above them, blue ocean rolled below, and a ring of storm clouds rumbled in the distance. They'd made it out.

Michael slapped his friend on the shoulder. "You always did like to make a dramatic exit."

Gabriel pointed in front of him. "We're still not safe, we have to navigate the storm." He pushed the throttle forward, slowing the copter's ascent. Once level, they flew toward the dark clouds: the last obstacle blocking their escape to the mainland.

Maya saw blood dripping down Austin's neck and arm. "You're hurt. Gabriel, where is the medic kit?"

"In my pack. Clean the wounds first, then bind them. Adaro bites are painful but not poisonous."

Austin examined his other hand, where his fingers were also covered in his dried blood. Two sets of puncture marks in the shape of a jawline were clear in the skin. With all of the action earlier, he failed to feel the bite.

Maya tore open a pack of alcohol wipes. She handed Austin a handful. "Clean your arms, I'll do your neck."

Turbulence from the storm rocked the craft. Maya spread the wipes across Austin's wounds while he stemmed the bleeding from the punctures to his hand. The pleasure of her gentle touch was soon lost to the sting of the antiseptic and the bounce of the ride.

They rolled through the chaos when at last the turbulence subsided. As they emerged from the clouds, Austin noted the last vestiges of a fiery orange sun setting in the western sky. Maya unbuckled, leaving her seat to kneel next to him. She cleaned the remaining blood from his arm, her touch reassuring. And then, carefully, she bandaged the wounds.

Michael turned from the front seat to admire her work. "That's a professional triage job. You might give Gabriel a run for his money."

Maya moved to sit again, squeezing Austin's hand as she let it go. "Something helpful I learned in the service." She paused, glancing to the front seats. "Michael, why were we attacked like that?"

Austin added, "I thought the adaro were just a nuisance, not blood-thirsty killers."

Michael turned to face them. "I was just considering that question. My bet is the creatures have had no natural predators for some time. They've bred uncontrolled, overwhelming their food sources, so they now feed on each other. They saw us and thought: something different for dinner."

"That makes sense," Austin said. "I didn't see any animals beyond those little yellow-eyed blood suckers."

Gabriel interjected, "What about the skull and the old Luger? What do you make of that?"

Michael hesitated, thinking. "That's a little more difficult to say.

My guess is a Nazi-era German craft—in all likelihood a plane, as we didn't see boat wreckage or anything docked—made it through the force field during the open cycle. It crashed or was stranded there, and the survivors were eventually hunted down by the adaro. It would explain the skull, the gate, and the Luger."

Austin agreed, "I've read a number of crafts have disappeared in the Bermuda Triangle. So it makes sense those remains are a crew member from one of them."

They rode in a disturbed silence for the rest of the flight back.

CHAPTER 11

September 20, 2014
Saturday
Tokyo, Japan

The flight to Tokyo went smoothly. Once safely on the ground, Rebecca packed her belongings and departed the plane. She was walking a few feet behind Anan in the terminal when Joshua came running up. "Rebecca, Rebecca!"

She stopped and waited. "Hey Joshua, what a coincidence meeting you here. I thought you were going to Caracas." She hoped her sarcasm was evident. Deciding to be nice, she added, "And—thank you for the wine. I am a 'red' person."

"My pleasure. I'm a man of my word. I told you I'd buy you a drink next time I saw you." He stood tall with shoulders back, obviously brimming with confidence. "And no on Caracas. I hate crowds, so I was waiting at the quieter gate. I didn't realize you were coming to Tokyo too. Do you have any time to get together?"

She shook her head. "No, I definitely do not. My schedule is packed."

He handed her a piece of paper. "I understand. But, if things change, I'll be doing research at Mount Fuji through the weekend. I'll be back in Tokyo Sunday night. Here's my phone number. If you get back and want to have a drink, call me. I'll come to you, and it's my treat."

Anan walked up. "Everything well, Rebecca?"

"Yes, everything is fine." Turning to Joshua she said, "Thanks for the offer. But I won't be calling, I'm pretty booked." She tried to return the paper to him.

He pushed her hand back. "Just keep the number. You never know, things may change." He gave a curt nod of recognition to the Atlantan, then strolled away.

As they left the building, a black SUV pulled to the curb. Rebecca saw "Charles Denton" on a sign in the window. The driver stepped from the car, handing Anan the keys attached to a laminated card. He spoke English with a thick Japanese accent. "Here you are, sir. Everything is taken care of. When done, call the number on the card and tell them when you will be returning. Give us at least one hour, and we'll have somebody waiting to pick up the vehicle curbside when you arrive."

Anan replied in Japanese as the driver loaded the bags, "*Arigatōgozaimasu. Watashitachi wa sore o yaru dakedesu.*"

The man bowed before departing.

Rebecca climbed into the passenger seat. "Wow, that's some impressive Japanese. What did you tell him?"

"I said, 'Thank you sir. We'll do just that.' I've done most of my work in the East Asia rim. Guess you can say it's my region to patrol.

I've become adept in all the languages and most of the dialects over the years. It's one of the many benefits of being so old."

Rebecca peered out of the window, watching the line of cars streaming from the airport terminal. "That'll make it easier to navigate the culture." After a moment, she said, "Now that we're alone, can I ask you a few questions about what I read?"

"Sure, did you find something?"

"I'm still not positive. The paper summarizing the different stories investigated over the years was an interesting read. I can see how difficult it could be to separate fact from fiction, even harder when the fact can be so unusual. The other six documents describing the trips in search of the crystal were fascinating. I loved reading the commentary of people and places at the times and how they've changed from trip to trip."

Anan replied, "Yes, the human culture has evolved and adapted through the ages."

"There were two threads that were consistent from each story and trip. The first is the reference to a wind cave and ice. Even the Irish passage tomb that identified Qitaxa referenced both of these. So that has to be involved somehow."

"I agree. We've focused on a few in the area, including the Fugaku Wind Cave and the Narusawa-Hyoketsu Ice Cave on the outskirts of the forest. They are very old, stable lava tubes, thus have been areas of interest. I've been through them top to bottom, more than a few times. There is nothing in there." He turned, catching her eye. "With that said, they're tourist sites now, and we're staying close by.

If you're not too tired, we should take a walk through them so you can see for yourself. Who knows? I could have missed something."

She shook her head. "Unlikely you did. My inner voice says we're still missing a key piece of information. Something is bothering me in the materials I read, but I can't see it yet. Anyway, the second thing I noticed is the Sea of Trees has always been an 'evil' location. In every report, no matter how far back we go, there is a reference to the suicides in the forest. Is dark energy there? And could it be hiding the crystal's location?"

"That's an interesting question. No doubt, there is dark energy in the Sea of Trees, and it's been present for a very long time. There are some ancient souls wandering out there. You're sensitive to the energy world, so you'll feel their despair and sorrow when we're in the woods. As far as the dark energy hiding the crystal, anything is possible, I just don't know if it is probable. That's something we should reach out to Michael about to get his feedback."

They navigated their way through the city of Tokyo to the western shore of Lake Kawaguchi. Anan pulled into the Fuji View Hotel. After a short check-in, they dropped their bags and headed out for the Fugaku Wind Cave.

"This area has changed a lot over the last ten thousand years," Anan said. "Old Mount Fuji was smaller, more volatile. The mountain you see today formed over the last ten millennia through a series of eruptions and cooling periods. The Sea of Trees formed over a thousand years ago on what was a much older lava flow, which covered an even older forest. Bottom line is, there are old and new lava tubes that riddle the area. We know that if Lucifer's men hid the crystal here, they would have chosen a stable spot underground. Something that could house a demon. So, we've searched for old formations. The wind and ice caves fit that description."

"Michael also said his informant mentioned an ice temple. Does that mean anything to you?"

"Not at all; first I heard of it," Anan answered.

After the short drive, they pulled into the parking area of the Fugaku Wind Cave, where they were greeted by park rangers standing in the lot of the general store that managed the attractions. They paid the entrance fee to tour the cavern and were soon descending the stairs into the shadows.

"Wow, this is new and much easier. Before it became a tourist trap, the descent was actually difficult," Anan said.

As they entered the cave, the path became solid and flat. The area was dim but lit by a series of weak lights strung on the ceiling. Strategically placed spotlights illuminated the main attractions, the ice pillars and lava ponds. Of more interest to Rebecca were the stops to shine their flashlights into the darkened recesses in an attempt to find a hidden crawl way or drop hole to a deeper crevice. There was nothing. The cavern itself was only two hundred yards long—not a lot of area to inspect. It appeared to be sealed tight.

As they exited back into the sunlight, Rebecca spoke. "I didn't see anything remotely close to a secret entryway or an undiscovered area. This place just doesn't feel like what we're looking for. When we walked into the temple in India, I could sense it right away: I knew it was the correct location."

"It's good you've learned to trust your intuition. And I agree, there is nothing here that indicates this is the location of the crystal."

The two walked the short distance to the ice cave where they took a similar tour. Rebecca learned all about the storage of silkworm eggs in a bygone era, but nothing regarding an ice temple or the Star Crystal. It was late afternoon when they made the walk back to the car.

Anan sighed. "As you can see, another dead end." He paused as if contemplating something. "Hey, are you up for taking a short hike into the Aokigahara? I'm thinking it would be good for you to experience some of what you'll see and feel tomorrow."

Rebecca was about to answer when Anan glanced past her into the parking lot. His faced was rigid as he ordered, "Stay here."

She ignored this request and followed right behind.

Stomping forward, Anan slapped his hand on a man's shoulder, turning him around. "Why are you here, are you following us?"

Joshua appeared startled. "Who are you, and what are you talking about?" Seeing Rebecca behind Anan, he smiled and said, "Oh, I got it. Hi, Rebecca." He focused back on Anan's scowling face. "I'm sorry, I didn't know she was your girlfriend."

Anan's response was even more angry. "That's not the issue. Why are you following us?"

Joshua face went blank, appearing confused. "Following you?

I'm not following you, I'm working for the US government testing some new technology that maps lava tubes. NASA thinks it may be useful in mapping some areas on Mars. Not that it's your business."

Anan glared at the man.

Joshua rambled on. "They're hoping to get new insights to planet dynamics, potential water sources, maybe even alien life," he said, stumbling even more as Anan's stare became unbearable. He fumbled out his ID badge. "Ask her, I told her at the airport that I was working this weekend at Mount Fuji. It's my third time here. I gave her my number. I never once asked where she was going. It's a coincidence." His voice cracked with stress.

Anan glanced at Joshua's badge. It showed NASA in big, bold letters, with "Joshua Pendleton" in black print just above a picture of the young man. "It's a big coincidence, don't you think?"

Rebecca grabbed Anan's arm, giving a light pull. "Come on, we have to go." She glanced at Joshua. "Sorry for the misunderstanding. And again, good luck to you."

Joshua gave a somber reply, "No problem, Rebecca, best of luck to you."

After a harder tug from Rebecca, Anan moved toward the car. He watched, steely-eyed, as Joshua got into his SUV and pulled out of the lot. Finally, they entered their vehicle.

"Be wary of him, I still can't see his energy," Anan said.

"You've mentioned that before. Why can't you see it? What does that mean?" Rebecca said.

"It means one of three things. First, he could be a zombie with no transient energy." His stern eyes met hers. "Not likely though, he's too thoughtful with logic. So, he's either masking his energy, ensuring we can't see it, or last, he has a very, very weak transient. Meaning weak of spirit and susceptible to possession."

"How do you mask your transient?"

"This is similar to what happens with our transformation device. It is Atlantan technology, beyond human capability. Meaning, he may be working for the IOD."

"Any guesses which one it is?"

"I can't be sure, but always assume the worst."

After a few awkward moments where neither spoke, Anan's demeanor returned to his easy-going self. "I'm sorry, you've done nothing wrong. But know my inner voice is screaming that something is off about him—I don't trust him."

Rebecca raised one eyebrow. "For what it's worth, my inner voice is saying the same thing. With any luck, that's the last we see of him."

Anan pulled into an off-road parking lot carved into the base of the woods. Hardwood trees surrounded the area, encroaching to within feet of the car.

"We're here. How about we take a quick walk into the forest to find out what you feel?" Anan opened the door.

"Feel? Do you mean see?" she answered.

He shrugged. "Both."

They walked on a beaten path, winding between thick trees. As they descended deeper into the forest, the light dimmed, creating a mysterious ambiance to the area. The growth thickened with lush, old hardwood trees, their hulking branches intermeshing seamlessly to create a sun-filtering canopy. Spiny fern, fallen leaves, and a green moss littered the forest floor while covering the carcasses of rotting trees who had long ago crumbled.

They crossed a short hanging bridge made of wooden ties and old twisted ropes that spanned a small ravine. The ropes anchored on two high stone trusses that created a doorway effect into the forest. Even this late in the afternoon, a wet mist filled the air, producing a creepy appearance. When they crossed the threshold into the primary woods, a small white sign greeted all visitors.

They stopped, and Anan translated the eerie warning: "Please do not enter the forest alone. Evil awaits. For those who wish to enter but not exit, get help!"

Rebecca hesitated, staring into the darkness of the trees.

Anan turned to her. "You ready?"

"I think so."

"Stay close, we don't want to separate. Have you ever been on a vision quest?"

"I have not, but I've heard all about Austin's. Drinking the red and black liquors, lifting the filters in your mind to first see and then travel into the energy world. I can't wait to do it."

"Good." Anan winked before plunging forward.

Rebecca wondered what that was about, but chose to follow in silence.

They walked side by side into the mist. The deeper they hiked, the more disoriented she became and was soon questioning their entry location.

"You are tracking where we came in, right?" she whispered.

He first motioned to his lips for her silence, then pointed away from the direction they walked.

They entered an overgrown section of the woods dense with trees and brush. The entangled trunks and limbs formed a natural wall against would-be invaders. They squeezed through a narrow gap between two solid trees, entering a shadowed area.

Anan pointed to a human skull, lying intact on the ground a few feet away, the bones to its body covered in part by fallen leaves and forest debris. He then motioned to a faded picture of a young Japanese man tacked to a gnarled trunk, a weatherworn note attached beside it, the last image of and final words written by the lost soul. Sitting down, he crossed his legs in the lotus position, then gestured for Rebecca to join him. Once she was down, he held his hand to his ear communicating for her to listen, then moved his fingertips, gesturing for her to close her eyelids. He leaned forward with a gentle motion and clasped her two hands with his.

With her eyes closed, she focused on the sounds of the forest. A cool breeze hit her skin, causing her to shiver. There were no squeaks or squawks of animals, just the soft rustle of leaves and branches swaying in the light wind. She then heard something different. A low, wailing moan that interrupted the hypnotizing sounds of nature's music. It started as a thought in the back of her mind, but soon became audible and then all encompassing. The voices of the dead filled her mind with their sad and melodic song. Just then, she felt a soft pressure on her hand.

She opened her eyes to find Anan holding a small container filled with a red liquid. He motioned for her to drink it. Remaining silent, she nodded her understanding that it was the same liquor used in Austin's vision quest. She hesitated for a second, then complied, downing the drink in a single gulp. Anan leaned over again, his fingertips gently closing her eyes.

The liquor's effects were immediate. As she sat sightless, the songs of the dead returned in depth and volume. It was then she realized, the voices weren't singing, but were speaking. She listened, mesmerized in the moment. There were at least four different tones echoing through her mind. And then Anan's telepathic voice shattered the tranquility. "Remain still. Open your eyes slowly."

Rebecca again complied. The images around her changed. The background light was now muted, the bodies of the trees gray and dark. Inside the trunks of the trees she could see the energy of the forest. Most were dark green and vibrant. Some older or sickly ones were a faded green. The fallen ones were black. She glanced back to Anan who sat motionless next to her. Immersed deep within his gray torso was a brilliant purple glow that radiated through his arms and into her fingers; its intensity rippled as she watched. He let go of her hand. She could see his extended tendrils rising from his fingertips; she could feel the warmth and peace of his energy leave as his touch faded. Gazing down into her own body, she could see her radiant blue energy, powerful and bright, pulsating with life.

Anan again spoke in thought, "Focus up and around you."

Again, Rebecca did as requested and scanned the forest. Floating in the air were four small orbs of colored energy. A faded brown orb floated down near her head. She heard its sad but clear voice. Peering into the energy, a young woman's face materialized. It was the face of hopeless despair. Rebecca could feel her anguish, and she absorbed the woman's pain of losing her long-deceased child.

Rebecca opened her heart to the apparition. Sympathizing with her loss, she thought, *I'm sorry for your suffering. I wish I could mend your sadness.*

As the mist wafted in the air, its brown color lightened. Rebecca thought she saw a thin smile before the woman's face vanished back into the light. Rebecca could feel gratitude from the lost soul as it floated away, its anguished voice fading into the wind.

The other orbs drifted around them for some time, their sad stories emblazoned in Rebecca's mind. Each of these lost energies was confused and scared. She absorbed their pain as best she could, returning kindness and empathy with her thoughts. She knew their living energies were taken close by in the Suicide Forest, their transients managing to escape the reapers.

Without warning, Rebecca felt something different, something evil. A dark, powerful energy approached. The three remaining orbs hovering around her shot through the trees, away from the darkness. Anan's words echoed in her mind, "There is a vile energy close by; be very careful with your thoughts."

Rebecca answered, "How do I do that?"

"Focus on positive things." An urgency filled Anan's words.

A wickedness grew within Rebecca's soul. Fear and rage that she had never before experienced roiled, and then an unbearable sadness washed over her. She tried to refocus on her mother's touch, the warmth of her embrace, her gentle soul. As she fought this internal struggle, a larger shadowy orb wafted into their walled forest compound. It hovered near Anan for a moment before gliding toward Rebecca. The black energy materialized into a dark mist. Rebecca could see the raging eyes of an aged man within a face of evil. The darkness grew in her, and she heard its wicked voice. "Why are you here?"

Rebecca answered in thought. "Who are you, and why do you bring despair?"

The dark mist answered, "I am Neikan, the Whisperer of Aokigahara. I only reveal what you carry inside of you. I sense your pain, your anger, and can relieve your suffering. Trust me . . ." His weathered voice trailed off with a low wail.

Rebecca's reply was defiant. "You are the suffering. Leave me, I don't seek your help." Fearing the spirit, she rambled on. "We are here in pursuit of an ancient crystal, hidden somewhere in this forest, underground." As she spoke, she struggled to maintain her composure; the pain and sadness were all-encompassing in her soul.

The mist moved closer, surrounding her on all sides. "I know of this crystal you seek; I have seen it. I can see it is your heart's desire. Let me fulfill this need. I will tell you where it is. But first you must allow me to help you, to show you the path to rapture."

Rebecca took a deep breath. "I don't trust you, Neikan, I sense your treachery."

The agitated energy swirled around her, then spoke. "The item you seek is small, green, and powerful. It is not far from here, deep underground, protected by a dark creature. It has been resting there since the beginning of my time. Trust me, my friend."

Rebecca could hear Anan's voice screaming, "No!" as she silently acquiesced to Neikan's demand.

The swirling mist stopped. It wafted in the surrounding air, then unexpectedly shot deep into her body. A darkness took hold of her. The memories of the creature flooded her mind, overwhelming her emotions. She endured the screams of agony and suffering from the long ago butchering of women and children by his mortal hand. His bloody work flashed before her in an ocean of flames. Then it all turned quiet, and she stood in the forest, in the Sea of Trees. She watched as Neikan the coward plowed his knife into his own belly. His pain shot within her, doubling her over as she sat. And then a tranquility flooded through her—a rest she had never known.

Neikan spoke, "I feel your pain. Come to me, come to the rapture."

Rebecca's mind flashed to her childhood, and she watched as her younger sister lay in bed, death stalking her body. She watched in horror as her sister's eyes opened wide in fear. She could hear her final gasps for breath once more. Rebecca tried hiding from the memories; the fear and sadness were too much to bear again. At that critical moment, Neikan's soothing voice rang in her mind. "End your pain, embrace the rapture. Come to me child, find your peace."

She was ready to give in to Neikan's beckoning, ready to do whatever it took to end the pain, when a gentle spark entered her mind. She thought of Austin's laugh in the car ride to Sedona, and then remembered the comfort of Maya standing with her arm around her as she trembled with fear in Bernael's warehouse. She remembered the love of her mother's embrace as she watched her sister gasp her last breaths. The spark began a fire, and Rebecca remembered who she was and the choices she made. She embraced her sadness, then replaced it with love and kindness. She pitied the dark energy inside of her, and offered it hope instead of fear.

His evil was overcome. The gray mist shot out of her body, and she was at peace. On reflex, she opened her eyes to see the energy coalesce into an orb as it floated up and away into the haze of the trees.

Anan squeezed her hands. "Are you okay? That was incredible!"

"I'm fine, and I know where the Star Crystal is!"

CHAPTER 12

September 21, 2014
Sunday
Mount Fuji Area, Japan

Austin and Maya walked into the lobby of the Fuji View Hotel. Their private flight had been both comfortable and efficient. Austin had managed to sleep for a large part of the time in the air. Unfortunately, Maya was only able to doze intermittently. Recurring dreams of demons and Atlantans created peaks and valleys in her sleep and recovery. Austin thought she definitely needed some sleep and a real bed; Gabriel's feel-good medicine had run its course.

As they stood at the check-in counter, Rebecca crossed the floor toward them with a skip in her step, beaming. She couldn't hide her happiness at seeing Maya standing before her. She threw her arms around Maya and said, "How are you? I can't believe you are up on your feet! Much less here!"

Maya squeezed her friend tight, despite her fatigue. Austin appreciated Rebecca's upbeat disposition; it was always contagious.

"I'm okay. A little worn out at the moment, but on the mend for sure," Maya said.

Rebecca stepped to Austin, giving a quick, if not awkward hug.

"We tried to get her to stay in Tucson, but she wanted nothing to do with that plan," Austin said.

"And let you have all the fun? No way!" Maya said.

"How's the shoulder?" Rebecca asked.

Maya rotated her wounded arm, making a slight grimace. "It's getting there. Gabriel did a great job treating me. He gave me some meds and told me to rest a few days."

"Which is what you intend to do, right?" Austin said, raising his eyebrows.

"Of course, while you guys do all the hard work." She glanced around the room. "Where's Anan?"

"He'll be down any moment. Supposed to meet at 9:00 a.m. sharp," Rebecca said, glancing at her watch, "which is thirty seconds away." No sooner had Rebecca finished the statement than Anan entered the lobby.

He walked over, shaking their hands. "How was the flight in? Any troubles?"

Austin said, "Great, slept like a baby the whole way."

"Meaning he cried a lot while holding his blankie," Maya joked.

Austin smiled. Even though the joke was a bit more cutting than her usual jibe, he couldn't feel more grateful for Maya's recovery.

"How about you check in," Anan said, "and we debrief for a few minutes. We've got a few things to tell you, and I'd like to hear your story."

Austin and Maya finished checking in and took their bags to their rooms. After a quick clean-up, they joined Anan and Rebecca in the hotel restaurant, where they ordered green tea and discussed the past few days.

Austin and Maya related their Atlantis trip, including the flight in, their success in decoding the files, Maya's treatment, and their harrowing escape from the adaros. Austin judged it was not the right time to retell the human origins story with Rebecca. Best to leave that for a private chat with Maya and Rebecca—maybe even over a stiff drink, which for some reason seemed more appropriate to him. He also decided it was Maya's decision whether or not to share her Atlantan heritage. As he expected, she chose not to.

Anan leaned forward, his face glowing. "Sounds like a complete success. You treated Maya and decoded the document." He paused, then added, nostalgically, "It was an impressive place at its peak."

"Even in its present condition, it's an impressive place. I would have loved to have seen it during its prime, teeming with people," Maya said.

Rebecca sat, wide-eyed. "That sounds amazing—but also a little crazy. Tell me more about the adaro, what are they?"

Austin responded, "They're small, hybrid creatures created by Marou to keep the waterways clean, and coincidentally the source for mermaid myths. Literally half man, half fish, only not sweet like in the movies. Picture an ugly serial killer crossed with a bass.

Alone, they're at worst a nuisance, but in a pack of thousands, terrifying."

Rebecca shivered.

"Strange the adaro attacked. They were always shy creatures that stayed in the water," Anan said.

"I guess a few thousand years of evolution has changed that," Maya said. "They are the dominant species on the island and very nasty. Particularly when they're hungry, which seems like all the time."

"How about you two, what did you find?" Austin asked.

Anan gave an odd glance to Rebecca. "We have a lead to the crystal; still not 100 percent sure of its location, but it's a start."

Maya asked, "Why that look to Rebecca? What happened?"

Anan hesitated, a sheepish grin on his face. "Based on the research we had to date, we walked the two caves considered to be the likely locations." He turned to Rebecca. "I assume you would agree that those should be eliminated now."

"Definitely. No way the crystal is in the Fugaku Wind Cave or the Narusawa Ice Cave. They're both too small and have been too well traveled over the years," Rebecca answered.

"Okay, so where?" Austin asked.

Anan continued. "We hiked into the Sea of Trees yesterday to experience the free spirits of the Suicide Forest—"

"And that means what?" Maya interrupted.

"Meaning, I drank the red liquor and had a mini vision quest," Rebecca answered. "The filters in my mind cleared. I could see the lost souls, and not only could I understand them, but I communicated with them as well. There was such sadness, it was overwhelming."

Anan continued, "That's not all. We also encountered the Whisperer of Aokigahara."

"And, who is that?" Maya asked.

"He is the free spirit of a diamyo warlord from the tenth century," Anan explained. "He slaughtered thousands of innocents. But one day after he murdered his own family in a fire, he took his own life in those woods. He is the embodiment of evil energy. He somehow escaped the reaper, and now his spirit talks to those troubled souls who go there considering *jisatsu* . . . I'm sorry, suicide, in English." Anan studied their faces, ensuring they followed. "He whispers to them, persuading the weak to kill themselves, with a false promise of ending their pain. It's why there is such a high number of deaths in the Sea of Trees. I've never run into him, but have heard stories and even sensed his presence. Yesterday, he found us. More like, he found Rebecca. She allowed his dark energy to enter her body on the promise he would reveal the location of the crystal. It was a very careless—" he raised one eyebrow to Rebecca, "—and brave maneuver."

Maya said, "Are you okay? What happened?"

"Yeah, I'm fine." Rebecca shrugged. "I'm not really sure how it happened. His energy felt dark but also very reassuring—it surrounded me. It was like he could read the pain in my soul. He knew what I desired, and he understood my love for my younger sister. I agreed in a moment of weakness." She paused, returning their stares. "I was only trying to help. And what I experienced next changed everything. When he entered my body, I felt his anger. I witnessed him slaughtering women and children with no mercy. I watched through his eyes as his family died in the flames. And then, I knew the peace he had realized when he ended his own life. He showed me . . ." she trailed off.

Maya took her hand, squeezing it. "Showed you what?"

Rebecca's eyes welled with tears. "He replayed the death of my sister, exposing my loss. By doing so, he forced me to relive the guilt and pain I went through. It was unbearable; I wanted to die. For a moment, I wanted to kill myself."

Austin could feel his heart pounding in his chest. He prodded, "And then what happened?"

Rebecca turned to Austin. "And then I remembered who I was. I remembered hope, love, and courage. I saw your face laughing in Tucson." She turned to Maya. "And I remembered your strength that day in the warehouse. And then I felt the love of my mother. Everything became clear, like a lightbulb had turned on. I shouldn't have guilt over her death, I didn't cause it. No one did. She lived a good life, then died a natural death surrounded by loved ones. Not everyone is that lucky. Her life wasn't as long as most, but just as much a treasured existence. I resolved that I wanted to live, to make a difference, to love." She locked her focus on Maya. "I'm sure the Whisperer felt this. In a way, my love tormented him, causing him pain when he was expecting grief. I sensed his suffering as his energy left my body." She took a deep breath and looked around at the others. "In his pain, he also told me the Star Crystal is in the Mortara Wind Cave. Its entrance lies hidden in the forest. The crystal is deep underground in a drained lava cavern. He ended with: 'Beware, death awaits any who enter.' He said it's guarded; I'm assuming there's a demon."

"I'm so sorry about your sister, I didn't know—" Maya said.

"That's an incredible story. I have so many questions about the Whisperer, but I guess the most important one is how do we find this cave?" Austin asked.

Anan answered, "We're not sure yet. I've already searched the internet for it, with no luck. I was thinking we'd start at Fugaku Wind Cave; there's a chance the people working there know where it is. If that doesn't work, we'll have to develop plan B. I've already emailed Charles to determine if he has resources to locate it. He's not answered yet."

"I agree. Let's start there." Austin pushed back his chair, standing.

Rebecca reached out, touching Maya's hand. "Why don't you stay here and sleep while we go to check it out? We won't be gone long, and it seems like you could use the rest."

"That works for me—I do need to sleep. Just promise you won't enter the cave without me. If there's a demon, it's best if we're all there—strength in numbers and all," Maya said.

"Why would we ever do something like that?" Rebecca joked.

"Says the woman who just allowed an evil transient to possess her to get information," Maya said playfully.

The group laughed.

Austin pulled the cloth sack from his backpack and handed it to Anan. "Michael retrieved this from Atlantis. Said you'd know what it is and what to do with it."

Anan folded the cloth back, glanced at the package, then stuffed it into his pack. "I do, and thank you for its safe delivery."

Maya made her way upstairs while the others moved outside.

Once in the car, Anan asked, "How is Maya, really? She seems down, maybe a bit sad. Or is it she's just tired?"

Austin replied, "I think both. At times she seems different from the old Maya. But she's been through a lot over the last seven days and without a doubt needs to rest. I think the best thing we can do is let her sleep. I'm not saying exclude her, but only include if necessary."

Anan and Rebecca both answered, "Agreed."

They again made the short drive to the general store near the caves that managed the tourist sites. They walked inside in search of a tour guide that could answer their questions.

Anan pointed to a man at the counter. "Hey, I want to talk with you."

The man spun around. Joshua's face went pale when he saw Anan walking toward him.

CHAPTER 13

September 21, 2014
Sunday
Fugaku Wind Cave, Mount Fuji, Japan

Joshua rolled his eyes, exhaling an audible sigh. "Hey man, I'm only getting lunch and cigarettes to bring with me. I'm leaving. I didn't even know you were here." He took a step toward the exit.

Anan gave a friendly wave to the young man while following him out. "I'm sorry, we got off on the wrong foot yesterday. I'm glad we bumped into you because I wanted to apologize."

Austin leaned in close to Rebecca. "Any idea what's going on here?"

"It's a long story. I'll tell you later."

Anan held out his hand, a plastered smile on his otherwise rigid face. "I'm really sorry for yesterday. It's been a long couple of days for me. I acted like an idiot, which Rebecca was all too happy to point out."

Joshua took his hand, appearing surprised by the gesture.

"Apology accepted, no hard feelings." He reached into his shirt pocket and removed a cigarette while patting his jeans, then dug into his shirt again. "Do any of you have a light?"

Austin replied, "I do; it's in my backpack. Hold on."

As Austin went into the trunk, Anan continued, "Where are you off to?"

"I'm going over to Mount Omuru on the western side of Fuji. There is an undocumented set of lava tubes below the Motosu Wind Cave. It's large and remote, so provides an excellent opportunity to not only confirm the technology works, but to test its range."

"That's sounds awesome. Motosu is pretty isolated, so be careful. What tech are you testing?" Anan said.

Joshua's eyes darted away. "It's top secret, so I can't tell you the details, but in general terms, we're sending ground-penetrating waves in a three-hundred-sixty-degree spherical radius, then compiling the results. So, basically mapping lava tubes above, below, and to the sides of the equipment. The hope is when we land on Mars, we can shoot from the surface to map some subterranean areas. It may lead us to frozen water, and even cooler—microbial life."

"That's impressive. I had no idea NASA was working on that kind of stuff. Alien life—wouldn't that be crazy?" Anan removed an area map from his pocket and opened it. "I take it you've been out in the field here a few times, have you?"

"Yep," Joshua said, "this is my third trip to this area. I've done quite a bit of fieldwork here and even more prep work in the lab. I'd say I'm pretty familiar with the area."

Rebecca stepped closer to Joshua. "You wouldn't happen to have heard of the Mortara Wind Cave, have you?"

He hesitated a little, head tilted in surprise. "Believe it or not, I have. It's actually near where I am heading today. Why do you ask?"

Austin was back with the lighter, offering its flame to Joshua. "By the way, I'm Austin. We were told by friends we should check it out, but didn't know how to find it. The Fugaku cave here is less than exciting, if you know what I mean."

Joshua dragged the cigarette, exhaling the smoke. "Fugaku is a freaking joke; can't believe people pay money to see it. But, Mortara is a beast of a cave to get into, Motosu is much closer and safer. I'd recommend staying away from Mortara."

Austin pocketed the lighter. "What's so dangerous about it?"

Joshua shook his head. "Pretty much everything. Tight quarters, icy conditions, bad footing, not to mention it's way more remote. Legend has it that people disappeared in there, and now it's haunted. I could go on, but trust me, it's dangerous." He glanced up as if remembering something. "Although, there is a pretty cool natural ice block that has columns. The locals say it's a temple. Are you sure you want to go there?"

Rebecca stepped closer, wearing a flirtatious smile. "Yes, we're sure. Our friends told us if we do only one thing, we must see the ice temple. Although they didn't mention ghosts."

"We appreciate the warning. If we get in and it's too dangerous, we'll turn away. But if not, we get to see a real wind cave and not this tourist crap," Anan said.

"Plus, we can brag to our friends that we made it in," Austin added.

"Well, I guess. I'm heading up that way, it's about a mile farther in than Motosu. I'm happy to take you. In fact, I'll bring you in to the first level, then you're on your own." Joshua hesitated, glancing at Rebecca a second too long, revealing his interest was more than platonic. He added, "You know, on second thought, I may even be able to test my equipment there. We'll see what the conditions are like when we get in."

Rebecca gave a soft clap, "That sounds great. We'll follow you to the lot."

They jumped in their vehicles and made the short ride up Highway 71, soon pulling into a small parking area. While they unloaded their three small backpacks from the car, Joshua pulled out a larger pack, throwing it over his shoulders.

"Are you okay with that? I'm guessing it's pretty heavy. Austin and I have room, we can carry something for you," Anan said.

"I'll be okay, thanks" Joshua said, making sure Rebecca heard him. "I've carried this all over the world."

As they entered the forest, Rebecca stepped in close to Austin, whispering, "Quiet your mind as you walk. You can hear the voices of the lost transients that wander the forest. It's kind of creepy, but spiritual. I have a new appreciation for your adventure on the vision quest."

"It's a powerful experience to see the energies, not to mention hear the voices of the dead." He caught her eye, holding her gaze. "But do me a favor, please don't do that again. I couldn't stand losing you."

Rebecca's face blushed; it was almost as if they were back in the coffee shop, flirting over the counter. "You don't have to remind me." She paused before taking the chance. "You should know, I don't plan on losing you either," she said, clasping his hand as she spoke.

Austin enjoyed her gentle touch for a moment before smiling and letting her fingers slip away. The last thing he wanted was to spook Joshua from helping.

As they started up the well-worn path, the environment was green and lush. Moss covered everything, with giant ferns on the ground.

The farther they walked into the forest, the denser the tree growth became. The narrow path became jumbled and shifted often to avoid the morass of gnarled trunks blocking the way. They continued like this for almost an hour when Joshua stopped in front of a small wood-framed building. A placard with Japanese text was posted on its door. He didn't bother to read it. "This is the Motosu Wind Cave. If you find Mortara is too much, come back to explore this one. It's a little harder than Fugaku, goes in about a thousand yards. It doesn't have concrete sidewalks, handrails, or lighting, but still easily doable. Oh, and there's ice on the floor year-round, so be careful walking."

"That's good to know. We'll keep that in mind if Mortara doesn't work out," Anan said.

"How about we take a quick break," Austin suggested.

The group rested, sipping water and chatting while sitting on some larger rocks. Joshua asked Rebecca a constant ramble of questions while volunteering information about himself. Rebecca maintained her usual pleasant demeanor, taking it all in stride. Before long they repacked, and Joshua led them deeper into the forest.

The woods beyond Motosu were less congested, but wilder with fewer but larger trees and more broken rock.

Anan said, "The path seems cleaner here, and straighter. Is this what we can expect the rest of the way?"

"Yes, pretty much," Joshua said. "Although, another three-quarters of a mile or so and we head off path. It gets kind of rough for a little while, but the higher we climb in elevation, the less dense the trees. You'll see; we still have a ways to go."

Austin could discern a dark energy nearby, feeling the presence of lost souls and their low, wailing moans. But there was something else out there, something more evil than the transients—he could sense it.

Rebecca reached out, startling him. She whispered, "You okay? What is it?"

"I sense dark energy, something much worse than the free spirits around us. Stay sharp; we're not alone."

"I feel it too. This shadow is different from the Whisperer. Could it be a demon?"

Austin caught her eye. "That's my guess."

Joshua stopped and peered left toward an elevated section of the hill they were climbing. He scanned the path in front of them, then took a quick peek behind. "I think it's only a little farther. I'll know it when I see it."

He continued trekking up the mountain for a few more minutes when they came to a natural break in the path. The main trail headed north and continued its gradual climb. The smaller trail ran up a steeper section of the terrain, bisecting a line of young trees with gnarled branches intertwining just above their heads to create a spooky, tunnel-like enclosure.

"This is it. I remember the tunnel, it's eerie." Joshua pointed. "See the mist on the other side? I remember thinking there's a monster waiting in the fog."

"A monster, what kind?" Anan asked.

Joshua's eyes narrowed. "Not a real monster, there's no such thing. I was using my imagination." He paused, raising an eyebrow to Rebecca as if saying, "Where did you find this guy?" He continued walking. "Come on, it's not much farther."

They hiked through the tunnel of limbs, past some large moss-covered boulders, and into a small open area of the forest. They were high enough now to glimpse the full valley through the tangled boughs. The Sea of Trees sprawled below them in all its glory, a wave of green for miles and miles. Off in the distance, Austin could make out Saiko Lake, the resort area where he hoped Maya was sleeping in peace.

Joshua made an abrupt halt next to a hidden gash in the side of the hill.

"Mortara Wind Cave, as promised," he said.

The cave opening appeared a dusky gray with sun rays beaming into it. The small mouth was less than three feet wide and surrounded by dark rock overgrown with green moss. Small, leafy plants grew scattered around its edges.

Anan stepped to the opening; the chilly air flowing out of the murkiness blasted him in the face, forcing a slight recoil. Shining his flashlight into the entrance, he saw the crease pinched even further. "Appears tight down there, you sure we can make it in?"

"Yeah, I've been down once before. The mouth is narrow here, but it opens up a few feet in. I pretty much stayed in the first chamber as it gets icy the farther down you go. I didn't get to explore anything beyond the temple." Joshua paused, glancing to Rebecca. "With that said, we can scan it with the sonar today, see what else is hidden down there."

Austin peered into the darkness. "Let's do it."

Joshua switched on his flashlight before creeping down to the opening. He pushed his pack in first, then slithered his body through the small crevice and vanished from sight.

Austin grabbed Anan's arm, whispering, "I sense dark energy. You sure you're ready for this?"

"I sense it as well. But this is too good an opportunity to pass up. Even if we don't go beyond the first chamber, to get a map of the cave and its interconnections would be huge. We have to go in."

"What about Maya? We promised not to go in without her," Rebecca asked.

Anan looked at her. "Always the voice of reason." Then he shrugged. "We'll be fine. Sometimes you have to call an audible to take advantage of the situation presented. I'm pretty sure she'd do the same thing."

Austin nodded. "Besides, she shouldn't be going out in her condition."

Anan followed Joshua down. Rebecca crawled in next, with Austin bringing up the rear. When he got to the pinch point of the opening, he removed his pack and slid on his belly to squeeze through the narrow crack. It was a tight fit for Austin's broad frame, but it opened up just as quick.

Once through, Austin could see that Joshua was right: the chamber expanded up and out to a long tube, tall enough that he was comfortable standing upright. He checked his energy stone. It glowed yellow with a hint of red.

Joshua had already assembled a small floor lamp that lit up the coarse gray rock walls. The area's roof and sides were curved, creating a circular rock tunnel that ran deep into the mountain. A brisk breeze blew up toward them, its source hidden in the darkness below.

Joshua continued removing materials from his pack. "Careful, the floor becomes icy." He took out a tripod and started to assemble the equipment. "Not sure how much you know about lava tubes, but if you have questions, let me know."

Rebecca said, "I don't know a lot about volcanoes, much less lava tubes. How do these things form?"

Austin and Anan flashed their lights around, inspecting the area before treading deeper into the tunnel.

"He's right, the footing is bad, be careful," Austin said.

Anan stopped his progress. "Stay with them while I check things out. I don't trust him."

"Okay, but don't go too far; there is something dark down there."

Austin returned to the illuminated area. Joshua didn't acknowledge his presence as he prattled on, showing off to Rebecca. "Lava is released by the volcano in either uncontrolled free flows on the surface or in underground channels. These caves were remnants of underground channels where the outer layer of the flow crusted over, forming an insulating barrier for the inner molten rock. When the pressure subsided, the lava ran out, the tubes drained, and the outside crust remained. These are classic examples from Mount Fuji and pretty old—at least fifty thousand years old. They've been stable, not impacted by any of the more recent Fuji eruptions. Most of those lava flows were uncontrolled on the surface."

"Wow, that's fascinating," Rebecca said. "How many of these tubes are here, and how far down do they go?"

Joshua strutted as he finished assembling the equipment, almost giddy showing off his knowledge. "There are miles and miles of them in total. They crisscross all over to some exit point on the surface like this one. As far as depth, all I can say is they run deep, some to the center of the mountain. I've only been a few hundred yards down in this one—it gets pretty creepy pretty fast." He caught her eye. "With that said, I don't want you to worry, I'll stay close to you the entire time." He stopped talking to fasten two cables, then switched on his monitor. "There you go; all hooked up." He turned to her. "Do you think your very intimidating friend wants to see this?"

"Why don't you take Austin and I through it. I think it's best if we just let him wander," Rebecca said.

"That sounds perfect." Joshua held his stare a moment too long.

"The machine, Joshua, back to work," Rebecca scolded.

He glanced away, pretending to fiddle with the equipment. "I'm sorry, it's just that you are so . . ." His voice trailed off as Austin stepped in closer.

Rebecca pointed at the screen, "That's kind of you to say, but back to work."

"All right, message received . . . for now." Joshua focused back on the machine and pressed a button; the machine started to hum. "What I'm going to do is blast the area with high-frequency waves. The signal will penetrate the surrounding rock, and in a few seconds bounce back up. The amount of time it takes to return will dictate rock type and/or open space. This computer will take these echoes, compile them, and form a diagram of the surrounding tubes."

Rebecca said, "That's amazing. How far will it go?"

Joshua adjusted a knob, and the hum went higher. "That's one of the things we're trying to better understand—its maximum range. You guys ready?"

"Go for it," Austin urged.

He flipped the switch. The machine made loud, repeating clicking noises. "Come over here, watch the computer compilation, it'll map it out in front of us."

The two squeezed in to get a clear view of the screen. Joshua nestled in uncomfortably close to Rebecca, peering in over her shoulder. After a few seconds, a three-dimensional diagram started forming. The clicking processed for a few long minutes before shutting down on its own. The drawing continued, finishing well after the testing was complete.

"Wow, this is perfect. Check it out!" Joshua pointed at the screen as he talked, his voice peaking with excitement.

Anan walked back to them. "What do you have?"

"This tube," Joshua said, "slopes downward for about five hundred yards, then disappears out of range—that's a long run. Who knows what's below there?" He tilted his head to better see the screen. "You can see there's an intersecting tube about a hundred-fifty yards from here that runs down to this little cavern area." He paused, bringing his face closer to the screen. "That's odd. The cavern is formed like a lava pool drained from there. You can see all these connecting channels . . . although these are smaller than anything I've seen." He paused, studying the screen. "That's an unusual formation."

Anan studied the data. "Maybe we should go check it out. But first, I found the temple. Come on, it's not that far."

Austin examined the screen, making a mental imagine of the

tubes and their connections, just in case. "One second, Anan. Joshua, anything else to report?"

He shook his head while staring at the screen. "No, not really. I mean, the equipment range is farther than expected. But that area is unique in nature, and something we should check out." Joshua hesitated while he glanced up and around. "I've got a crazy question, do you guys hear anything, like a high-pitched noise? It's weird, but I've been hearing something like a screeching noise on and off all morning." He pulled at his ear. "I don't know, maybe I'm going crazy."

Rebecca raised an eyebrow at Austin. "No. Do you Austin?"

Austin replied, "No, I haven't heard anything, and that does sound weird. Be careful, it may be medical, like high blood pressure. You should have a doctor check that out." He whispered to Rebecca, "Let's get going; daylight is burning."

Joshua asked, "Do you mind if I tag along?"

Anan turned to him. Having gotten what they needed from Joshua's equipment, his courteous demeanor had changed and his tone was curt. "Don't you have more important work to do, like test the range of the equipment?"

"I do have more work, but I can take a half hour. I'd like to see the temple again. And who knows, maybe we head down to that little cavern area together. Do you mind?"

Anan clenched his jaw while he chose his words carefully. "Come along, but only to the temple. And keep up."

Joshua whispered to Austin, "Is he always this jolly?"

"Yes, and be careful, it's icy down here," Austin said.

They made slow and cautious progress downward. The farther below surface they traveled, the more ice they encountered. Austin shivered from the noticeable drop in temperature, and saw vapor as he exhaled. The floor was made up of broken rock encased in an intermittent layer of dirt and ice. They could slide their feet on the ice until they hit the next rock, then stepped over it with care. Although chancy at times, the tube ran straight and wide.

They continued this way until they came to an expanded area of the tube, where the ceiling was much higher, as if the lava had pushed up and out. On the far wall, a trickle of water dripping from the vaulted upper recesses had formed a huge icefall, reminiscent of columns, that covered the underlying rock from ceiling to floor. Toward the bottom of this formation, the columns merged to create a flat, uniform square which bore a striking resemblance to the floor structure of a temple. Austin moved his flashlight over the ice block, exposing a mix of deep-blue and white ice. It was nature's art: both delicate and beautiful.

"This is amazing. How long would you guess it's been here?" Austin asked.

"Mother Earth took a long time creating this. The temperature rarely gets above freezing here, so I'm guessing centuries, probably since the last eruption ended," Joshua answered.

Rebecca whispered to Austin, "That's what I was missing earlier. The reports I read on the plane never mentioned an ice cave. It only mentions ice, and I, along with everyone else, assumed it was a cave. This has got to be the place."

Anan answered in a hushed tone, "I can feel a dark presence. My bet is a demon, but I can't rule out a powerful dark spirit. Either way, let's keep moving; we're at risk." Anan spoke louder for Joshua to hear, "This is cool Joshua, but we're going to head down farther. I think this is where we say our goodbyes."

"What? No way, I'm going with you." Joshua stopped, glancing to Anan. After seeing his expression, he continued, "And you can't stop me."

Anan stared at him for a moment longer before assuming a threatening tone. "I can stop you, if I choose to."

Austin held his palm up to Anan, motioning for him to calm down.

Anan's jaw unclenched while his shoulders relaxed, clearly deciding to take a more conciliatory approach. "Joshua, it's nothing personal. This place is dangerous and even more so where we're heading. I don't want to see you get hurt."

Joshua shot back, "You know, you're not as tough as you think, and you don't scare me. I brought you down here, and to be honest, I don't need you to go with me. I've been in more caves than you'll ever be. It's you who should be worried, not me."

Anan's voice was firm. "Hey Joshua, I didn't mean to be a jerk. But there's something dangerous here, I can sense it—things you're not aware of."

Joshua stared back, then without a word started toward the shaft in direct challenge to Anan's direction. "Well, you are a jerk," he said, moving forward.

It was clear to Austin that Anan recognized how this would play out, thus he adjusted the strategy. "Wait, if you insist on going, stay between us at all times."

Joshua appeared triumphant as he strutted past Rebecca. His sarcasm was abundantly clear as he added, "Thanks Dad, but I think I can lead the way. Better watch your cane as you come down."

Austin thought Anan's blood might boil. Both fists were clenched as Joshua strolled past him.

"Let's hope he's that confident when we face the demon," Austin whispered to Rebecca.

She nodded, her face rigid with concern.

The group wound their way down the passage. The ground was still icy, but became easier to walk on the deeper they traveled. Austin noticed a subtle change in the air from the frigid blasts around the ice to a sulfur-infused warmth coming from the bowels of the mountain.

They reached the smaller intersecting tube. Anan shined his light into its blackness. The upper area showed a steeper descent with a narrower tunnel. The warm air rising from the darkness smelled like rotten eggs. Anan's eyes were like daggers at Joshua. "Are you positive you want to do this? You have nothing to prove."

"I'm going down; feel free to follow me." Joshua's response was laced with venom.

Austin watched as Joshua stepped into the tunnel feet first, sliding on his backside. He used his boots to check the grip of the rock floor. Holding his flashlight out, he crept down the stone tunnel, inching his way forward. They watched as his light faded away.

Anan whispered, "Austin, check your energy stone."

Austin pulled the crystal from his shirt; it glowed a faint red.

"Stay close, the demon could be anywhere," Anan continued.

Anan followed Joshua, Rebecca soon after him, and Austin came last. Step by step, they moved downward. Their lights radiated out, illuminating the gray rock close to them before fading into the darkness. The air thickened, and Austin was breathing heavily now, sweat trickled down his face. A déjà vu flashed in his mind. He saw himself trekking along a similar rocky path masked in shadows when a winged monster attacked under a crack of lightning. He winced from the unwanted memory, shaking his head to clear his mind. The thoughts faded as he focused on breathing and the shapely image of Rebecca's backside illuminated by his flashlight. He was startled into the present by the sound of rocks tumbling and Joshua's shrieking. The three followers froze.

"Joshua? Are you okay? Where are you?" Anan hissed.

"Joshua, answer!" Rebecca added.

His weak voice called up, "I'm okay . . . I think." They breathed a collective sigh of relief. "I've reached the cavern floor. Watch your footing; it's steeper and slippery toward the bottom."

Anan shined his light so it illuminated his own livid face, "It'll be a miracle if he didn't wake the demon. I'll go first, Rebecca next, Austin last. Wait until I call for you. Stay down on your back, keep your center of gravity low. Most of all, take your time, and be quiet." He sat down and inched forward. He reclined his muscular torso until he was almost lying on his back. He edged down the path this way before he whispered up, "It's clear, Rebecca, and only about fifteen yards. Take it slow."

Rebecca repeated Anan's flashlight move and illuminated her own face. "I'll see you down there." She leaned in, pecking Austin's cheek. "Be safe."

She grasped the flashlight at her side, creeping down using both feet and hands on the tunnel walls to hold her body from sliding. Austin watched her light travel down the tunnel until it was out of sight. A second beam was prompt in replacing it.

It was Anan, lighting the way. He whispered again, "Your turn, Austin."

Austin mimicked Rebecca's method of descent, wondering how they would later ascend the steep grade. It was challenging with his larger frame, but he quickly found himself on a level area. He eased out of the tunnel and into a main cavern. His three companions stood only feet away, their backs to the wall, flashing their beams in a systematic attempt to identify the next step.

Anan rubbed his hand on the header for the tunnel he just exited "See this? It's smooth, man-made with inscriptions."

Austin shot his beam at it. "I've seen this type of thing before—"

Joshua's voice interrupted, sounding agitated, "You're kidding me—you guys didn't hear that? There are voices speaking to me. They're crying out for help!"

Rebecca put her hand on his shoulder, her voice soothing, "Shhh, calm down, you're safe. The mind plays tricks on us in times of stress. Try to relax, we'll be out of here soon."

He rotated away, flashing his beam indiscriminately. "I'm not crazy; there's someone else here." He hissed defiantly.

Ignoring his claims, the others started exploring the cavern. When flashed upward, their beams faded into the darkness, failing to expose the elevated ceiling high above them. On both sides, rounded walls of dark rock rose around them, creating an oval shape to the room. A few small tunnels connected into the area. Austin couldn't identify if these headed up or down, but he knew their impenetrable darkness made them ideal hiding spots for a demon. He stopped and listened for subtle noises from the shadows, but only heard Joshua's labored breathing and the muffled footsteps of his companions. Checking his energy stone, it still glowed a faded red.

A warm wave of stifling, foul, sulfuric air rolled over them, signaling the direction they were heading toward held the source of the heat. They were soon comfortable enough with their immediate surrounding to continue moving through the cavern. Anan led the way; every stride taken was measured and precise, ensuring each step was not their last.

Joshua whispered, "What is this place?" He froze where he was standing, holding his flashlight aloft. His eyes were locked into the darkness ahead of him.

Anan replied, "Seems like there's lava still close—"

Austin touched Anan's arm, abruptly silencing his friend. He pointed ahead toward a faint green glow in the darkness.

"Turn off your flashlights," Anan urged.

They complied without question, each standing motionless while their eyes adjusted to the darkness. The subtle iridescent glow grew in intensity. Austin immediately recognized the beacon in the darkness: the green radiance of the Star Crystal.

Austin whispered, "I see it."

"Can somebody tell me what that is?" Joshua asked.

Austin answered, "It's why we're here." He relit his beam before shining it toward Joshua. "We'll explain the details later. Right now, we have to figure out how to retrieve it."

A silent moment later Joshua hissed toward Anan, "So, the chance run-in at the shop, your apology, was all for effect to get me to guide you down here?"

"No, my words weren't for effect. I meant it," Anan admonished. "We only wanted directions here, you insisted on coming the whole way. Remember saying, 'You can't stop me'? This is why we didn't want you to come; it's dangerous."

Joshua continued in a more agitated tone, "How about you, Rebecca, were you acting too?"

Rebecca lit her beam. "We're here. Let's worry about hurt feelings later. Our focus is getting to the crystal and then getting out—alive. Something else is down here, I sense it."

Austin didn't bother with the bickering, having already started crossing the open space. He paused every few feet to study the ground in front of him. His light would only illuminate a short area, so he'd take a few steps, stop, and once convinced the ground was safe, move again. The rest followed his path as he navigated the rock floor.

He was soon standing outside a circular pattern of white stone on the floor, yards from a pedestal that held the yellow quartz bowl containing the crystal. Austin recognized the general design at once, having seen something similar in the pyramid in Guatemala.

Rebecca recognized it as well. "I'm sure there's a trap. It's the same scenario. The circle will either collapse on the way in, or the way out. The pedestal is counterweighted. Once the yellow quartz bowl is removed, something will happen."

"We need to find our way across. Suggestions?" Anan asked.

Austin answered, "I'll go." He took off his pack and opened it. Removing a length of thin rope, he looped it around his chest, nestling it below his arms before tying it tight. Once secure, he handed the other end to Anan. "Keep it taut. This should hold as long as you don't let me drop."

Rebecca added, "Be fast; remember the roof collapse in India."

Austin grinned at her, a surge of adrenaline kicking in. "I appreciate that comforting reminder."

An audible wailing echoed through the chamber and sent shivers down Austin's spine.

Joshua became more agitated and spoke in a hushed, urgent tone, "You guys heard that, you had to! What the hell is down here?"

"Yes, we heard it. Relax, they're voices of lost spirits. They're harmless if you leave them alone. Now, please, just stay out of the way." Austin's frustration with Joshua had peaked; they didn't have time for this. He attached Demon Slayer to his belt.

Once Anan secured his end of the rope, Rebecca and Joshua held the flashlights. Austin moved to the circle's edge and looked toward the pedestal that was five yards from where he stood. Anan handed him a small cylindrical container made of a light weight metal. "Use this for the crystal. We don't need the bowl. Also, be careful; there's been acid in some retrieved."

Austin took the container and slipped it in his pocket. He took a deep breath and stepped into the circle with his right foot. The ground held firm. He moved his left foot inside; no change. He took one small step, then froze as a cracking noise radiated through the floor. The rope around his chest pulled tight as Anan dutifully retrieved the slack. He took another careful step forward. Again, the subtle breaking occurred, but the floor held firm. Sweat ran from his brow, the stench of sulfur causing his eyes to tear. Inch by tedious inch, he slid his way over the first circle into the safe area next to the pedestal.

"I'm here," he called.

Austin shined his light on the stand holding the Star Crystal. The setup was similar to the one in Guatemala: a single, smooth pedestal; a square, flat table; and a translucent yellow quartz bowl with a green glow emanating from its core. He inspected the quartz container. On the lower right side, a large crack was evident; any liquid held by the bowl had long ago spilled out. That was good—one less obstacle.

He reached into his pocket and removed Anan's container.

"I'm going to go for it on three. Be ready, especially you, Anan. This floor is going to drop." He paused, took a deep breath, then called in a loud voice, "One . . . two . . . three!"

In one fluid motion, he lifted the bowl's top, scooped the crystal into the container and began sprinting for his friends. His dash was as quick as he'd ever moved, but still not fast enough. Two steps into his retreat, everything in the circle collapsed. He pushed off, desperate in his leap for the edge, but came up far short. As he fell, the rope around his torso cracked tight and pulled him forward, slamming him hard into the pit wall. The crushing thud knocked the breath from him, but the Star Crystal was still firmly in his grasp. Something above gave, and he fell deeper into the pit. He started clawing at the rock wall, desperate for something to grab. There was nothing.

His drop continued until the cord jerked tight around his chest. A bolt of pain shot through his body, and a sound squeaked from his lungs as the air was squeezed out.

For the moment, the rope held firm. He could feel his heart pounding as his life dangled from the thin cord. Glancing down, he saw an orange glow deep below, its vapor burning his nostrils. Changing his focus to above, he could just discern his friends scrambling, Anan's voice screaming, "Help me! The rope's slipping, pull the rope! Pull the rope!"

Austin felt a glimmer of hope when a piercing tug on his back signaled a slow, painful ascent. Like clockwork, grunts and groans echoed from above, the cable pulled, and he rose. Right below the edge, he felt a yank as a single arm grabbed his shirt, pulling him out of the darkness.

It was Joshua, who rolled to his back, body shaking, gasping for air. He screamed into the air, "Oh my God, you're a freaking lunatic! You almost died!"

Rebecca knelt next to Austin, grasping his hand. "Are you hurt?"

"I'm fine, but give me a minute." He lay on the cold, stone floor, taking heavy breaths, his pulse racing.

"Shhh," Anan whispered.

A tremor ran through the cavern. Boulders dislodged from above and tumbled into the pit.

"The roof is coming down! Get up!" Rebecca urged.

Jumping to their feet, they grabbed their packs and sprinted to the tunnel that led them in.

Halfway across the cavern, a small rockslide cascaded down the walls, shaking the ground around them. To Austin's surprise, the trembling stopped, and the bulk of the roof held. They stood next to the entryway, shining their beams toward the pit. The cavern's darkness consumed the light; without the glow of the crystal, there was only an impenetrable black.

Austin tucked the prize into his pack. As he closed it, Joshua cried out while swinging at the air, "Stop it! Leave me alone!" He turned to Rebecca, whimpering, "Help me, Rebecca, please help me!"

Rebecca stepped to him, shining her light in his face, gently touching his arm. His eyes were wild with fear, his face contorted with anguish. "Joshua, calm down! We can help but you have to listen to my voice. Listen to my voice!"

Tears fell as he pushed her away. "I'm tired, I can't do this. I can't pretend anymore." His voice elevated to a wail. "I'm coming to you! I'm doing it now! Make the pain stop!"

"Austin, he's possessed. Grab him!" Anan yelled.

Austin jumped on Joshua's back as Anan attempted to wrestle his arms down. Seemingly filled with adrenaline, Joshua broke Anan's grip then flipped Austin over his shoulder. He landed with a jarring thud.

The possessed man pushed Anan to the ground and put his boot in the Atlantan's ribs to keep him there, then stepped toward Rebecca. Flashing his beam onto his own deranged face, he snarled in the grotesque voice of Neikan, "His soul is mine. Leave now, or I'll return for your other friends!"

Joshua dropped the flashlight and dashed into the darkness. The echo of his screams reverberated as he plunged into the black pit. At that moment, the remaining rock ceiling came down, boulders crashing everywhere. The dust cloud from the rock fall hit like gale-force winds, stinging their skin. Sand blasted against the rock wall. Everything fell silent again.

Rebecca moved to run after him. Austin just managed to seize her from behind, squeezing her tight as she struggled to escape. "He's gone, you're not going to save him."

"We don't know that he's dead. We can't leave him here!" she cried.

Anan stepped in, cradling her face with his weathered hands. "Rebecca, listen to me. We'll search for him, but not now. There's a demon here. We look for Joshua, we all die."

Austin froze—the stench of decaying flesh was near. He released Rebecca. "The demon's close, I can smell it."

Pulling his energy stone from his shirt, a dark crimson radiated from within the crystal. Austin shined his light around the base of the cavern wall. There were at least five tunnels that connected into the main area—any of which could hold the monster. He listened; a faint clicking like claws on rock echoed in the darkness.

Anan reached into his pack and removed the gift Austin had brought him from Atlantis. It appeared to be a small handgun. Rebecca and Austin reached into their packs, unholstering their own weapons.

Anan whispered urgently, "We need to get up the tunnel and out into the open. The demon will have the advantage down here. Austin, you're first, I'll go last. No lights." He turned to Rebecca. "We'll come back for Joshua's body, but right now if you want to live, we have to run!"

Rebecca's lip started trembling. She nodded, and started toward the tunnel out.

Austin dove into the black hole. Using his hands to grip the rocky path, he scrambled up the steep incline. He sensed Rebecca right behind him, and that pushed him to move faster. They made it up the first part of the lava tube, and Austin bent down to help Anan out of the narrow section. He stooped while studying his energy stone once more. There was no change: the creature was still close.

They made better time to the intersection with the main tube just below the temple. Austin ignored Anan's warning and flashed his light on, shining it both up and down the corridor before stepping into the larger tunnel-like cave. The reek of death filled his senses, and he knew the creature stalked them from the shadows.

Seeing nothing within the radius of his beam, he pulled Rebecca's hand, guiding her into the main tunnel, and Anan eased out behind her. They took two steps up the slippery incline toward the ice temple and the cave entrance, then the beast attacked, raging from the darkness below. Austin heard the scrape of claws on rock and dropped to a knee, firing his gun. His first shot must have hit the mark as the charging beast shrieked in pain. Anan drew the new weapon.

The creature howled a bloodcurdling scream; then a firebolt exploded from its mouth, the blast heading straight for them. Anan stood firmly in front, pressing the trigger to the device. Nothing visible happened, only a small whine screamed in Austin's ears. The flames hit an invisible barrier and were deflected into the walls of the cave, the gun's force field now evident. The dragon's deadly breath let up, and Anan lowered the shield, "Now Austin, fire!"

Austin unleashed his entire cartridge in a matter of seconds. He knew the rounds hit their mark as the gun blasts' echoes inter-mingled with the creature's screeches of pain. A moment later, the screams stopped. All he could hear was a snake-like slithering echoing in the darkness.

"Move, now!" Anan shouted.

Rebecca flicked on her light. The three sprinted past the ice temple and up the tube. Austin slipped on the ice, crashing to the ground. Anan reached down and grabbed him by the shirt, lifting him up while urging, "Get up, get up! Keep moving!"

They ran a few yards farther when once more, Austin was overwhelmed by the scent of the creature. He checked his stone—blood-red. Slowing down, he turned. "Anan, it's back."

Austin loaded a fresh cartridge. Rebecca stood motionless, her gun raised. Anan again stood in front, pointing his new weapon down the shaft. They stared into blackness, hearing only the slithering of the monster, feeling its malevolent presence. Once more, it stalked them, staying just out of sight. A sinister hiss echoed around them. A rock tumbled from behind.

Rebecca yelled, "There!"

They spun, rotating just in time to see the beast scream and breathe a new blast of fire. Anan just managed to get the force field up, protecting them from the worst of the discharge. Rebecca recoiled from the heat singeing her face, dropping to one knee.

When the fire blast ended, Anan screamed, "Hit it!"

Rebecca and Austin emptied their cartridges, unsure if they hit anything. The demon appeared to have learned from the first encounter. Once it attacked, the creature darted back into the darkness, vanishing from the fight.

"Move, move!" Anan commanded.

They again raced toward the entrance. They had no choice but to slow their escape as the conditions deteriorated and the trek became treacherous. Seconds seemed like an eternity as Austin pushed the lead. A few steps later, he saw the ambient glow of sunlight from the crease that was the cave's entrance.

"The exit!" he shouted.

Without warning, the creature attacked again from behind, only this time with no screech or blast. Its hulking frame rushed forward, slamming into them while swinging an armored tail. The vicious blow cracked Anan into the side wall, crumpling him to the floor and knocking the force field weapon away. The demon attacked him in a frenzy, seeking human flesh.

Anan battled back, holding the creature's fanged jaws away from his chest. Austin raised his gun, he squeezed the trigger again and again. It clicked in response; his ammunition was drained. He drew Demon Slayer and prepared to charge, when Rebecca pounded the demon's torso with bullet after bullet, a painful wail resonating in response to the lethal onslaught. The beast retreated, squealing in pain, and escaped down the tunnel toward the safety of the protecting shadows.

Austin caught a better glimpse of the demon in the shaded light. It traveled on four clawed feet with a thick reddish body, muscled with armored back scales. It had two curved horns protecting its large crocodilian skull that supported a powerful jaw lined with razor-sharp teeth. Its eyes were primitive and black, embodying the evil it exuded.

Rebecca helped Anan up, then swiveled to Austin, "I'm almost out of ammo, just one more bullet. We need to get out of here."

"Grab his weapon and give me yours. I'll help him," Austin said.

Rebecca did as requested, while Austin slid under Anan's arm. They limped their way past Joshua's equipment and through the final length of the cave to the narrow opening. As Anan worked his way outside, Austin guarded their rear, armed with the single bullet and Demon Slayer. Austin glanced back to see his companions safely outside, waiting for his exit.

A crash came from the tunnel below. He turned to see the creature in full charge, its screech pulsating forward. Raising the gun, he fired the last bullet into the creature's skull. The impact sent the dragon crashing into Joshua's standing equipment. The delay gave Austin just enough time to squeeze through the narrow crack as the jaws of the beast snapped at his feet. With one fluid move, he leapt to the rocks above the mouth of the cave. The demon squeezed its armored head out of the opening, screaming in preparation for its incendiary blast. Austin grabbed its horn with his left hand and pulled the skull up with all his strength. Reaching down with his right, he plunged Demon Slayer deep into its exposed neck, slicing its throat to the bone. The creature squealed and writhed in pain, then let out a silent scream as it gasped for life, blood and fuel pouring everywhere.

Austin searched his pocket, and finding his lighter, he sparked it, tossing the flame into the splatter draining from the creature. The dragon fluids ignited into a fireball, engulfing the demon in flames. It flailed as its body roasted.

Austin leapt from his perch to the safety of the ground. In three quick steps, he made it to Rebecca.

She launched herself at him, wrapping her arms around his neck, squeezing him tight. "I thought I'd lost you!"

"I'm good," he said, pulling her close.

"Thank God for that." She guided his head down and kissed his lips, holding him.

Lost in the embrace, Austin finally moved. "Are you hurt?" He whispered, feeling confused by mixed emotions of arousal and guilt.

"A little fried from the blast, but otherwise fine. I'm not so sure about Anan."

Anan leaned heavily on a tree, trying to stand and wincing in pain. "I'm good, or I'll be good. We need to leave before somebody comes to investigate the fire."

He limped forward to the remains of the still-roasting creature. The reek of burnt flesh and acidic alcohol filled the area, and a cloud of black smoke wafted high in the sky. Removing his pen laser, he pointed it at the demon, and an intense blue light fired from its tip. The blackened body shuddered as the laser penetrated into the carcass, glowing orange for a moment, then crumbling. The bones, the flesh, the energy, all disintegrated into a pile of black ash.

"We don't want anybody stumbling into this; demon energy lingers. And sooner or later somebody would have found those bones," Anan said.

Austin grabbed Rebecca's hand, pulling her away. "Let's get out of here."

CHAPTER 14

September 21, 2014
Sunday
Fuji View Hotel, Mount Fuji, Japan

Maya woke to the ringing of the hotel phone beside her bed. "Hello?"

She heard a click, then a dial tone.

"Jerk," she whispered under her breath as she cradled the handset. She lay still for a moment considering her next move before peeking at the clock; it was close to four p.m. Although she had slept all day, her body still felt worn. She rolled deeper into the soft sheets, wondering where Austin was. The mental image of him triggered her to relive their adventures in Atlantis. Despite the dangers they had encountered, the thought of being near him brought a smile to her face.

She stood and stretched, rotating her damaged right shoulder in a circular motion. The wound was healing well, but still sore and somewhat weak.

After cleaning up, she decided to get some fresh air and take a walk around the grounds. The exercise would be good, plus, it would pass the time while she waited for the others to return from the scouting mission. An image flashed in her mind: Rebecca working side by side with Austin in the field. In her heart, she knew those two belonged together, and that she was destined for something else—she could feel it. Although she tried to convince herself it was right, the thought was painful.

When she opened the door to leave, she surprised a woman who was fighting with the door handle to the hotel room next to hers—Austin's door. "Can I help you?" Maya asked.

The young woman's long dark hair covered her face. She stopped what she was doing. "Mind your own business. I'm trying to get in my room."

Maya took a menacing step toward her. "This *is* my business. That's not your room, it's my friend's."

The woman stopped fiddling to glance up at the door's number. "Oh. No wonder I can't open it, I'm in the room one floor down. That's my mistake." She turned away from Maya, blocking the full view of her face before scurrying off.

Maya stepped to the door to jiggle the handle. Still secure, it appeared no damage was done. She proceeded down the same hallway and took the stairs to the lobby below.

She approached the front desk attendant. "Good afternoon, I have a weird question for you. Do you have a young woman about my height, with long dark hair, in room 225? I found her trying to get into my friend's room in 325. She claims she was on the wrong floor, I just want to make sure that was it."

The man's face went taught. "Oh my, I don't think so. But let me check."

He clicked on the computer keyboard while watching the screen then shook his head. "No. Nobody is in that room. We have a pretty light booking right now." He clicked the keyboard again. "In fact, nobody is even in that block of rooms on the second floor. Maybe she's in another suite. But her description doesn't ring a bell." He paused, not able to hide the concern in his eyes. "We'll keep a watch out for her." He motioned for the security guard to come over.

"Thank you, it's probably just a harmless mistake," she said, with a hint of skepticism in her voice.

Maya stepped toward the large glass entrance of the lobby, and glimpsed the mysterious lady outside, walking at the far end of the parking lot by a group of cars. Maya hurried her pace, attempting to catch the would-be intruder.

Rushing through the sliding front door, she entered the carport for arriving guests, and continued across the pavement and into the parking lot. Almost in a run, she lost sight of the woman while passing behind some leaf-covered trees in the infancy of their autumn turn. When she arrived at the first car, there was no visible trace: the black-haired woman had disappeared.

She scanned the lot, peering into the vehicles while walking the long line of cars parked side by side. With no luck, she walked onto the manicured lawn toward a wall of green-leaf shrubs. Stepping through the plush grass, she followed a small path that split the hedges to a series of flower beds.

Upon entering the gardens, the last vestiges of seasonal butterflies were flitting from flower to flower, their delicate dance peaceful. Maya enjoyed the simple moment, temporarily forgetting the task at hand. Her hunt became a casual stroll as she followed the path and turned the corner into an aromatic section. She considered giving up the pursuit altogether to just enjoy the park when it opened to a secluded grassy area with a wooden bench centered in the green space. The dark-haired woman sat alone, her head lowered, hiding her facial features and hands folded on her lap.

Maya approached the woman with caution. "What did you want in my friend's room? You're not a guest of the hotel."

The woman raised her head and locked her eyes on Maya's. "What, no small talk?" She gave a wicked sneer. "I can do that. You're right, Amaya, I'm not staying at the hotel. But you're also wrong. I wasn't there to get into his room, I was there to lead you out here."

Maya could now see the woman's face. She was not much older than Maya, fit, attractive, with jet-black hair and light-blue eyes— an unusual combination. Maya had never seen her before. "How do you know my name, and why would you want me out here?"

The woman responded, "We know a lot about you. But for today, I just wanted to have a private conversation."

"About?" Maya didn't bother to hide her anger.

"How about the past, the present, and the future?" As the woman said this, three men in dark suits entered the garden from behind Maya. They encircled her, just out of arm's reach. The largest of the men stood next to her unknown antagonist.

"I'm not sure who you are, but I am sure I'm not interested in anything you have to say. I'd pull your boys back, or things may not end so well for them," Maya said.

The woman looked past Maya, giving a short nod to her thugs. Without warning, the first of the men attacked from behind. The onslaught came quick; he swung his fist at her head. Maya ducked under the attempted blow, and in one move swept his legs. The assailant fell hard to his back. With savage accuracy, Maya's heel found her attacker's neck. The blow crippled the man; he thrashed while doubled over, struggling for his next breath.

Her other two assailants wasted no time. The closest grabbed her from behind in a bear hug, while the second stepped in to throw a roundhouse at her head. Maya reacted, jerking her body forward, ducking under the blow. Her dodge pulled the assailant on her back forward, placing him square in the path of the incoming strike. The punch caught his jaw clean, crushing him back while breaking his grip on Maya. Freed, she faced the larger man in front of her. He feigned a punch, then made the costly mistake of rushing her. Side-stepping his advance, she threw her right knee into his midsection. An audible "hmmph!" followed as the air expelled from his lungs. For a fraction of a second, he stooped over, immobilized. Maya took advantage of the opportunity. She jammed her foot down on the inside of his bent right knee. An audible snap ensued, followed by his screams of agony as he collapsed to the ground.

Maya sensed the presence of another and ducked just in time as a blow from the second attacker sailed over her head. The brown-haired man stood facing her, just feet away, his face a mask of rage. He stepped in, throwing a straight punch. Maya blocked it, countering with a blow to his chest before stepping back out of reach. The man touched his sternum where the blow landed, a surprised grin emerging on his face. She could see this was a game to him. He spun, throwing a kick high at her head. Maya saw it coming. Ducking low, she stepped in with a straight-leg kick to his groin. The man crumpled like a ragdoll, cupping his midsection. A corresponding scream of agony came as he fell to the ground.

As the three injured attackers writhed on the ground, the dark-haired woman stood from her seat on the bench. She clapped. "Impressive. I was told you were a talented fighter."

Maya breathed heavy, her injured arm hanging by her side. "You've got thirty seconds to tell me what this is about."

"Or, what? You're going to put me down too?" She stepped toward Maya. "You'll leave only if I let you."

Maya prepared herself, but the woman attacked with precision, speed, and power, forcing Maya to defend. It wasn't the same brutish assault carried out by her male conspirators, but an elegant style of martial arts. The woman threw multiple strikes in quick succession. It was all Maya could do to block the targeted blows. The last punch thrown got through, landing square on Maya's jaw.

She stepped back, a biting sting in her chin, a metallic taste seeping in her mouth. First blood was drawn.

The woman gave a playful grin before gesturing for Maya to continue. She was all too happy to oblige. Instigating the next assault, Maya went for the woman's head in a blazing flurry of punches. When the woman stepped back, overwhelmed by the sheer force of the charge, Maya spun, landing a backhand fist direct to her face. The vicious crack sent the assailant sprawling on her back, a dazed look in her eye. Down for a moment, the black-haired woman shook her head, clearing the cobwebs, then sprang back to her feet. She dabbed the blood on her lower lip, then licked her finger with a devilish grin.

Maya readied herself—this was going to end now. Her assailant appeared like-minded, returning fire with fury, spinning, kicking, and punching through Maya's injured defenses, blasting her with multiple strikes. The last blow hammered Maya down to her hands and knees on the grass, a dull pain and agonizing gray filling her mind.

The assailant leapt to Maya's back, locking her in a choke hold until she stopped struggling and was flat on the ground. With a knee on her spine, the woman grabbed Maya's long, black hair, pulling her semi-conscious face off the ground.

She hissed in Maya's ear, "My name is Ojater. Remember it. Fear it!" She slapped Maya's face, ensuring she was fully aware. "Now, focus, while I cover the past, the present, and the future."

Ojater reached into a tiny sheathe in her boot and removed a small razor blade. She made a slice high on Maya's cheekbone. She squirmed from the burn of the blade, blood spilling down her face.

"That's for the past—you killed my friend, my mentor, Bernael. Now, every time you gaze in the mirror, you'll think of his death."

Maya twisted, trying to break Ojater's grip.

In response, Ojater strengthened her pull on Maya's hair while pressing down harder with her knee. "For the present, we know you're going after the Star Crystal here. Good luck with that dragon. Tell your friend Michael we're aware of his plans, and we'll be waiting for him in the end."

Ojater reversed the pressure, now forcing Maya's bloody head down into the grass. She moved her mouth close to her ear, whispering, "Last but not least, for the future. Know that the next time I see him, I will kill your little boyfriend for what he did to Bernael and Lilith. After you watch him die, I'm coming for you." She pressed Maya's head down hard, burying it in the grass.

Ojater stood up and gave one last kick to Maya's ribs. "Stay down. If you get up, I will kill you here and now." She pulled out a gun, cocking it for effect, then turned away from her beaten victim to admonish her injured thugs. "Get up, you idiots."

Maya lay motionless on the ground, rage bubbling inside. She turned her blood-smeared head to get one last glimpse at her assailants as they limped away.

"Till we meet again, Ojater."

CHAPTER 15

September 21, 2014
Sunday
Fuji View Hotel, Mount Fuji, Japan

Austin knocked on Maya's door. He waited a few seconds before rapping harder. Hearing no answer or movement inside, he pounded on it. As he waited for a response, Anan walked up.

"She's not in there?" Anan asked.

"Doesn't seem so. I thought she was sleeping, but maybe she's out."

The elevator down the hall opened. Maya stepped out, holding a bloody towel to her face, with Rebecca holding an arm around her shoulder. "I found her walking in the parking lot. She's hurt."

Austin's pulse quickened. "What happened?"

Maya removed the bloody towel, revealing the one-inch slice wound high on her cheek. The blood had started to dry, leaving the cut dark and soiled. "Let's get into my room. I'll tell you there." She unlocked her door and entered the suite, going straight to the mirror in the bathroom. The others followed.

Anan moved in behind her. "Let me see."

Maya removed the towel again, showing the bloody cut.

"You've been marked by Ojater," Anan said, matter-of-factly.

Austin's mouth dropped open. "What? Who's Ojater, and why did she mark her?"

Anan exited the bathroom, partially closing the door behind him. "Let me clean Maya up, see if I can triage this to minimize the scarring. We can discuss what happened on the way to the airport. We need to leave ASAP." He glanced to Austin. "Call Charles, make sure the plane is ready to roll. We'll be there in two hours." He handed Rebecca his room key. "Here's my key. Make sure everything is packed and ready to go. We leave the hotel in thirty minutes. Knowing Ojater is here makes our departure a lot scarier."

Anan turned and walked back into the bathroom. Rebecca was already out of the room when Austin raised his phone to call his uncle. He knew it was early morning back in Arizona, but was sure Charles would pick up.

"Hello Austin." His uncle's jovial voice greeted him.

"Charles, need your help here. We've been successful on the mission. However, Maya was attacked by someone named Ojater. Anan is cleaning the wound now."

"Oh dear, is Maya okay? And Ojater's there?" Charles's voice changed. "And you say success on the mission already, that's unbelievable!"

"It's not serious; she'll recover. Uncle Charles, who's Ojater?" Austin asked.

"We can talk when you're on the plane. It's on standby at the airport now; I'll make sure the flight plan is filed and it's ready to go by the time you arrive." Charles urged, "And take care of Maya!"

As Austin hung up the phone, he smelled burning flesh.

When Maya stepped out of the bathroom, her cheek was swollen and discolored, but much improved. The wound had been cleaned and cauterized, leaving only a small black line on her cheek.

Following her out, Anan spoke. "Not bad, scarring will be minimal. Keep it covered with this." He handed Maya a small tube.

Maya's response was cool. "Thanks, but a little scar is fine. I want to remember that bitch."

Rebecca walked into the room. "Ready to go." She paused, studying Maya's face. "Wow, that's 100 percent better. What did you do?"

"He cleaned it, then used his pen laser to cauterize it. It was the oddest feeling," Maya answered.

Anan interrupted, "We have to go. Let's talk about it in the car."

They were walking through the main lobby when Austin spotted a man in a dark suit observing them. The man tried to act casual while raising his wristwatch up close to his face, appearing to say something into it. It was clear Anan had seen him as well. He put one arm around Rebecca's shoulder, pushing her along while providing cover against a potential assault. They rushed their way into the parking lot and were approaching their car when a black SUV screeched to a stop yards in front of them. Four large men stepped out of the vehicle and drew handguns, while a black

Mercedes squealed in behind them. Austin didn't recognize the tall woman with black hair and sunglasses when she exited the back door of the vehicle.

Anan greeted her as she stood to face them. "Ojater, I heard you were here. Just repaired some of your handiwork."

"Save it, Anan, I'm not interested in catching up. Give me the crystal, and I'll spare you."

"That's not going to happen. Are you really going to shoot up the parking lot, given all the potential witnesses?" Anan responded.

Ojater smirked. "Do you really want to test me?" She raised her hand to the four men, and they responded by targeting their handguns at Austin and his friends.

Austin and Rebecca raised their hands in response, while Maya raised her EMP weapon.

Maya didn't wait for their counter. She squeezed the trigger button four times in quick succession. An electric hum resonated as the thugs were blasted in the chest with a flash of light. The blows knocked each one back into the side of the black SUV, their bodies smoldering as they lay motionless on the ground.

Maya shifted, training the weapon on Ojater and her driver. "You, out of the car, now."

The man stumbled out of the vehicle, glaring at Maya for a few seconds before putting his hands above his head, confirming he held no weapon. Austin stepped over to remove a handgun from the holster under the driver's coat and tossed it away, safely out of reach.

Weapon raised and a scowl on her face, Maya walked over to Ojater. When standing arm's length from her, Maya pointed the gun to Ojater's head. "You should have killed me when you had the chance."

Ojater couldn't mask her surprise. Her eyes were wide with shock, or maybe rage. "That's impossible. You're firing an Atlantan weapon."

"Yes, I am. Isn't that curious?" Maya said.

Ojater recomposed herself and responded with a challenge to Maya. "Your day is coming, Amaya Luna, and I'll be there when it happens." She turned to stare at Austin. "And I'll be there for you as well, pretty boy."

Maya swung the weapon, pistol whipping the Atlantan's face. Ojater crashed to the ground, blood running from a rip in her temple.

Maya stepped back and blasted a shot into the rear of the black Mercedes. The car exploded in a fireball, wild flames and billowing smoke dancing in front of them.

She bent down close to Ojater. "If you so much as touch a hair on his head, I'll rip your heart out."

For a split second, a shade of fear filled Ojater's eyes.

Austin put his arm on Maya's shoulder. "We have to go. The police are on the way."

Maya stepped forward, then turned back to Ojater. "What did you tell me? Stay down or I'll kill you here and now."

Anan shouted as police sirens blared in the distance, "Move, now!" He jumped into the driver's seat of their assailants' black

SUV. His three companions grabbed their bags and dashed in just after him. Once the doors slammed, Austin peeked in his pack, confirming the crystal remained safe inside.

Anan hit the accelerator, and the car responded by lurching ahead. They raced out of the parking lot and onto the surface streets, weaving through traffic. Anan pushed the car to its limit as he turned onto the ramp to the Chuo Expressway. He merged into the heavy traffic when a black Mercedes squeezed in just behind. Austin recognized the driver as the man from the hotel lobby. The chase car sped forward, ramming their vehicle with a violent shudder and a loud crunching noise on impact. Anan kept the car on the road.

Maya started to unholster her weapon when Anan calmly said, "I've got this."

Flooring the accelerator, the engine raced while he swerved in and out of the staggered traffic. At one point, he maneuvered into the breakdown lane to avoid a few slower vehicles before speeding back into the marked lanes. The Mercedes fell back for the moment, trapped behind a silver SUV blocking the passing lane. Anan watched in his rearview mirror. Even though there was a safe gap between him and his pursuer, he took his foot off the pedal, slowing the vehicle down, allowing the assailant to catch up.

"What are you doing?" Maya stressed.

"Trust me."

The Mercedes blew pass the obstructing vehicle and hurtled toward them in a clear attempt to ram them one more time. Just before impact, Anan spun the wheel while slamming the brakes, and the car spun wide in a circle. The Mercedes raced past the whirling SUV, missing its mark. Anan righted their vehicle behind the chase car, the hunted becoming the hunter.

Anan gunned the accelerator one more time, and the SUV responded by crashing into the trunk of the Mercedes. Pressing forward and locked in contact, he forced the Mercedes toward a bridge buttress. At the last moment, Anan hit the brake pedal and spun the wheel left. Once more, the SUV bolted to the open highway. But it was too late for their assailant. The black car hit the base of the bridge and launched up and over into the ravine below. They had just crossed the span when a fireball exploded into the air, a billow of black smoke following. Anan never looked back, keeping his focus on the road in front of them.

"I never doubted you," Maya said.

They traveled in silence until they arrived at the airport. The knot in Austin's stomach loosened when he saw the terminals in the distance. He turned around one last time, scanning the road behind them, anxiously awaiting another chase vehicle, but none came. Once safely on the grounds, they abandoned the SUV in a cluster of cars parked in the garage, then rushed to the private plane on the tarmac. Austin felt a wave of relief as the door slammed closed, and the pilot called out instructions.

Maya was ready for answers. "What did she mean give her the crystal? Tell me you retrieved another piece of the Star Crystal! You said that you wouldn't go in without me!"

Anan reclined his chair, resting with his eyes closed as the plane taxied. "I'm sorry, Maya, but we got lucky. We had a chance to follow a guy who was mapping lava tubes in the cave." He opened his eyes, focusing on her. "He led us in, but didn't make it out. We were fortunate to get the crystal."

"Agreed, we were lucky to get in, and even luckier to get out," Austin added.

"We're safe now; we need to call Charles about Joshua. Have him notify NASA. Somebody has to get his body," Rebecca blurted out, her voice on edge.

Maya stared at Austin, her eyes penetrating. "What the hell happened?"

Austin grabbed Rebecca's hand. "I'll call once we're off the ground. We'll get somebody down there." He turned to Maya. "We have a long flight. I'll fill you in about the crystal, but first, what's the deal with Ojater? Who is she, and why is she after you?"

Anan sat up. "Ojater is Lucifer's sadistic daughter. And if she's here, the IOD are dead serious about stopping us." Anan leaned forward, locking eyes with Maya. "You're either lucky to be alive or a very good fighter."

Maya's response was a matter of fact. "It was mercy. She could have killed me if she'd wanted. She chose not to, opting instead to give me a message to carry back. Said to tell Michael they're aware of our plans. She also threatened to kill Austin—then me—the next time we meet. Guess that strategy didn't work out for her." Maya glanced to Austin, lips pursed. "Sorry, but she knows we were the ones that killed Bernael, and as crazy as it sounds, she was fond of that serial killer."

Austin frowned. "No doubt they're aware of our plans, how else would they know we're here? I suspected they would at some point come after us for Bernael's death." He paused, shaking his head. "For every action there is a reaction, and revenge is a powerful motivator." He asked Maya, "Is that why you shot first and asked questions later in the parking lot?"

She met his stare. "No, not at all. I just sensed they were going to fire. Having just dealt with Ojater one on one, I wasn't taking any chances." She glanced out of the plane's window, fist clenched. "With that said, I'm tired of giving others the advantage. 'Drop your weapons or I'll shoot.' Bullshit. They'll kill you in a heartbeat."

Anan leaned over. Touching her arm, his energy clearly calmed her. He offered a gentle reply, "It's tempting to meet brutality with brutality, but it's a heavy responsibility to be judge, jury, and executioner. You become them when you do. I know you recognize that; it's why you didn't kill Ojater in the parking lot. Gabriel told me you have a clean conscience and pure energy. Don't lose that."

Maya considered his words. "I won't, but it's so frustrating! We play by different rules."

"What did Ojater mean when she said it's impossible for you to fire that Atlantan weapon?" Rebecca asked.

Maya pulled out the EMP gun for Rebecca to see. "This was a gift from Michael. It can only be fired by an Atlantan. Let that sink in."

As the aircraft's wheels lifted off the ground, Austin picked up the onboard phone and dialed Charles. He glanced up to add, "We learned a lot about Maya's family tree in Atlantis."

CHAPTER 16

September 21, 2014
Sunday
Astana, Kazakhstan

Michael peered through his binoculars and studied the abandoned warehouse. Seeing nothing of interest, he surveyed the city area around it, noting two men staggering side by side on the neighboring street. Late-night revelers, who apparently had one too many. He watched as they strolled past a lady of the evening, and one of the drunks made an obscene gesture in her direction. The woman became agitated, flipping them off before hurrying on her way.

"How reliable is the source for this?" Michael whispered.

Gabriel gave a small shrug. "It's as solid as these things can be. I would swear my life on the doctor; he had good energy, wanted to do the right thing. And a friend I trust put him in contact." He paused, looking at the darkened parking lot, watching for movement. "The guy was positive the deal would go down tonight.

With that said, something may have happened or changed last minute." He shrugged. "We're here, the night's already wasted; let's give it a few more minutes."

"No problem, a little while longer won't hurt."

Michael raised the glasses again and watched as a dark-colored car turned the corner and cruised down the street. It slowed in front of the entrance of the warehouse but rolled past, out of view.

"Ah, too bad, I thought that may have been them." Gabriel sounded disheartened.

The two sat in a tense silence when a second set of headlights came around the same corner, prowling the street.

Michael raised his glasses. "You may be right after all, that's the same vehicle circling the block."

This time, the sedan turned left and pulled into the shadows of the old brick building they monitored. The driver stepped out of his door to open the metal fence gate situated in front of an old wooden guardhouse, the barbed protection against intruders entering the parking lot. He climbed back in his car, switched off the headlights, then slow-rolled to the darkest part of the lot. The driver parked, and the car sat isolated in the shadows for a few seconds before he flashed the vehicle's headlights.

Gabriel remarked, "This has got to be it. Let's head down."

Michael checked his shoulder holster. The pistol in it was loaded and ready; he hoped it wouldn't be required.

Gabriel led the way through a darkened alley. They crept down a short side street and arrived just behind the warehouse. As they traversed the path, a second vehicle paused by the guardhouse before continuing through the gate and into the lot. The two Atlantans crouched in the shadows behind a stone wall on the property line—an ideal spot to observe the transaction.

The arriving SUV parked twenty yards away from the sedan. Two men exited the SUV, the taller passenger holding a blue backpack. Both appeared cautious, waiting next to their vehicle.

Three men got out of the sedan, all inconspicuous in appearance, except the passenger from the backseat, who held a hardened suitcase. The trio strode forward side by side, stopping halfway between the cars. The black SUV's occupants followed suit until the two groups stood feet apart.

Gabriel telepathically said to Michael, "That's our informant, the doctor, the one with the case."

"Yes, but it's odd, no IOD are present," Michael responded in thought.

The man with the hardened case spoke English with a Russian accent, "Do you have the money?"

The tall man with the backpack answered, "We do," as he unzipped the main compartment, revealing neatly packaged bundles of cash. "Show us the material."

The Russian opened the hardened case. "The material, as requested."

From his position, Michael couldn't identify the contents, but from the buyer's reaction, he assumed it contained the illicit goods promised.

The driver from the SUV stepped forward with a small box. He held it close to the hardened case. A low ticking noise followed at once. He gestured a thumbs-up in affirmation to the man holding the backpack. The taller man acknowledged the test by tossing the packaged money on the ground, then stepped forward to grasp the suitcase.

As he reached out, the third man from the sedan pulled an automatic pistol and fired, spraying two short rounds into the torsos of the would-be buyers, the blasts nearly cutting the men in half. Two of the three sellers laughed as the buyers' corpses hit the ground. The shooter stepped forward, firing a few gratuitous rounds into their heads, an unnecessary coup de grâce.

With the executions over, he reached to grab the backpack. With no warning, a series of muffled pops accompanied by flashes came from the shadows of the warehouse. The two laughing men were dead before they hit the ground, only the man holding the suitcase remained standing. Panicking, he spun around, then twisted again, frantically searching the darkness for the shooter.

Michael saw the muzzle flashes and knew the killers were hidden, in position for just such an event. He closed his eyes, opening his other senses: a dark energy was near.

"An organized plan and a deadly shot. Our old comrades may be here after all," Gabriel whispered.

"My thoughts exactly," Michael answered.

A moment later, two figures emerged from a door in the warehouse, one shouting in Russian at the terrified man holding the hardened case, "Put the suitcase down and your hands up!"

The Russian did as ordered while shouting, "Please, I'm not armed. I'm only the delivery man. Please!"

Abaddon and another figure walked out from the shadows. Abaddon stepped forward, speaking English. "Who else is here? And where are they?"

The confused man was shaking. "What . . . what are you talking about? There is nobody but me, Doctor Plonakov. I brought the material, just as promised. I didn't know they would do this. You have to believe me!"

"We need to help him," Gabriel whispered while creeping forward, still hidden by the wall.

Michael grabbed his arm. "I'm sorry, my friend, but if we rush in there, we'll be next. I fear it's too late for him. I sense Abaddon is going to act."

As if on cue, Abaddon stepped closer so the man would know who he was dealing with. "That suitcase is ours."

Plonakov stepped back and shielded his eyes. "No, I don't want to see your face. I don't want to know who you are. Keep the money, keep the material."

"It's too late for that, Doctor," Abaddon said. He glanced to his associate standing in the shadows, who made a small gesture with his hand, signaling his approval. Taking a bottle out of his pocket, Abaddon stepped in close and doused Dr. Plonakov with a clear liquid, then stepped back just as fast.

The doctor panicked. "What is this? What are you doing? I told you, keep the money, I haven't seen your face!"

Abaddon pulled out a cigarette lighter and sparked the flame. "It doesn't matter if you know me or not. You betrayed us; the penalty is death for your living energy." He tossed the burning lighter on Plonakov. Intense blue flames erupted high into the air, consuming the doctor in an unmerciful flash. The dying man screamed in agony, running to nowhere until he collapsed to the ground, his flesh roasting as the flames rose higher. A few agonizing moments later, his cries became whimpers before all went silent.

Michael glared, fury welling inside him as the black reaper collected the good man's transient.

Abaddon and his unidentified companion stood, not speaking, comfortable in the viewing of Dr. Plonakov's mortal demise. With the flames subsiding and the screams long stopped, Abaddon picked up both the suitcase and backpack, then started the walk back to the warehouse's darkened recesses. His companion, finally bored of the spectacle, followed to their safe haven.

In the blackness of the warehouse bay, a car engine started, its headlights flashed on, and the muted sound of tires slowly traveling over crushed rock resonated across the lot.

As the car inched forward, Michael motioned to Gabriel—it was time for action. The two separated. Gabriel stayed in the shadows and made his way to the guardhouse at the fence gate, the choke point to any who wished to leave the lot. Michael watched his friend throw a punch at a shadowy assailant before vanishing from his line of sight. He turned from Gabriel and crept toward Dr.

Plonakov's still running car. Crouching low, Michael eased into the driver's seat, holding for Gabriel's signal. He didn't wait long.

Abaddon's car exited the warehouse, rolling toward the open gate. It stopped for a second, as though the occupants were taking one last glimpse of the full scope of the destruction they just wreaked, then continued their slow glide to the parking lot exit.

As they passed the guardhouse and moved toward the street, Michael saw Gabriel's black silhouette roll a small device under the rear wheels of the car. It bounced once before a low-profile explosion sent smoke and sparks everywhere. The rear axle of the car snapped as its trunk and rear seats burned white hot from the phosphorus flames.

At that moment, Michael accelerated through the parking lot. Once in the street, he turned the other direction, then backed to where Gabriel stood over the disabled car. In position, Michael stepped out of his vehicle, gun in hand.

Abaddon and his unknown passenger had no alternative but to run from the smoking chassis. Gabriel was waiting there to greet them as the doors opened and the two stepped out, coughing. Aiming the gun at the men, Gabriel commanded, "I'll take the suitcase."

Abaddon reached for his pistol. Gabriel sent one silenced round whizzing by his head.

"Give me a reason to kill you, please." Gabriel's eyes locked on the enemy, and there was no mistaking the loathing within. It was clear to Michael: Gabriel wasn't bluffing.

Abaddon also recognized his danger and decided to comply by raising his hands high in the air. His companion raised one hand while holding the suitcase in the other. Michael still couldn't identify the mystery guest.

"Now, very slowly, take your weapon out and toss it over there," Gabriel ordered.

Abaddon reached in with two fingers and grabbed the large .44-caliber handgun, throwing it into a grassy strip a few feet away.

Gabriel motioned for the second man to come forward. As he stepped out of the shadows, Michael could see the black hair and groomed goatee of Lucifer. "I need to relieve you of that suitcase. I have no interest in the money."

Lucifer placed the case on the pavement and made a small gesture with his hand.

Gabriel laughed. "Subtle. But if you're signaling for help, I've already taken care of the clown in the guard shack."

Lucifer glared at Gabriel before turning his ire to Michael. He hissed, "What are you going to do, arrest us? Throw us in jail?"

Michael answered, "That's pretty much exactly what I'm going to do. Only, there will be no police, just a jury of your peers. You'll face Atla law and sentencing. And who knows, if you tell me where your disciples are, maybe you'll even avoid the noose."

"Gabriel, if he moves an eyelash, shoot him." Michael holstered his gun and popped the trunk to the running car. He grabbed the suitcase and tossed it into the well before slamming the lid shut.

"That would be my pleasure." Gabriel cocked the gun's hammer.

Michael stepped past Lucifer, turning his attention to Abaddon. He took a small step and threw his full body into a punch that landed flush on the Atlantan's jaw. "That's for Uriel!"

Abaddon toppled back, hitting the ground hard.

Michael rushed in, slamming a solid foot into Abaddon's ribs. "And that's for New Orleans!"

Abaddon took the blow with a "hmmph," but seemed determined to fight. Blood oozing from his mouth, he rolled to his side and tried to get to his feet. He hissed, "For what it's worth, I enjoyed killing Uriel more than most. My only regret is I didn't get his transient." Rising to his full height, he added, "Who knows, maybe someday, I'll get another shot at it."

Michael's face went taught; his eyes narrowed. He motioned to Abaddon's hand. "I'm taking that ring!"

Gabriel stepped forward, pointing the gun at Abaddon's head. He reached in his pocket, and removed a set of zip cuffs, tossing it to the renegade Atlantan. "Put those on and no sudden moves. I'd hate to rob the hangman."

At that instant, the first explosion tore through the empty warehouse, a fireball bursting through the roof. The detonation was followed by three successive blasts. The concussive energy blew the four men off their feet. Gabriel's weapon flew out of his hands.

Although quick in recovery, he wasn't fast enough. Abaddon rolled to the gun and grabbed it. Before he could aim it, Gabriel threw a wild punch that rocked Abaddon's head, hammering him down again. He kicked the gun from Abaddon's hand, then sprinted to Michael's running vehicle.

Lucifer threw a punch that connected with Michael's face, following with a short elbow to his chest. Michael blocked the third blow. Then he spun and delivered a straight-legged kick into Lucifer's sternum, driving him down and away. Michael hesitated, considering his next move, then glimpsed Abaddon picking up the pistol. Gun! his inner voice screamed.

Taking three steps, he jumped into the sedan as Gabriel slammed the passenger door. Michael thumped the accelerator, and they screeched away from the chaos of the burning warehouse.

As he watched in the rearview mirror, a bullet exploded the back window. Michael stared at Abaddon, who was grasping the gun in his right hand while holding up his left, highlighting the ring he stole years ago from a dying Uriel.

After squealing around the corner and out of sight, Michael slammed his fist on the steering wheel. "Dammit, we had him. We could have stopped the madness tonight!"

"It was C4 on a delayed timer—I could smell it. I'm guessing set to cover their earlier misdeeds long after they were gone." Shaking his head, Gabriel added philosophically, "We did have them, but lost our advantage with the explosion. Abaddon had the gun, and he doesn't miss easy shots. Better to live and fight another day. Besides, we have the case and that's what we came for."

"We do. Time to find out what's so important that Lucifer himself would show up to retrieve it," Michael said.

"Lucifer and Abaddon both—it must be a valuable commodity,"

Gabriel added.

The roads were empty as they drove to a deserted parking garage—the perfect place to leave the car. As they stepped out, they heard a symphony of sirens from the rush of emergency response vehicles that were converging on the burning warehouse.

"From the sounds of it, they've found the bodies around the wreckage," Gabriel said.

"That should keep the authorities busy for a while."

Michael popped the trunk and removed the case. After unlatching its fasteners, he opened the hardened bag. Embedded in the foam interior was a metal canister. Michael recognized the marking on its surface as the international symbol for plutonium.

He glanced in disbelief at Gabriel. "What the hell is Lucifer up to?"

CHAPTER 17

September 23, 2014
Tuesday
Tucson, Arizona

Austin walked into the reception area of his uncle's law offices, coffee cup in hand. As usual, Connie, Charles's executive assistant and office manager, was there to greet him.

She walked over, offering him a light hug. "Welcome back, world traveler. How many miles did you log these last few weeks?"

"Let's see, India, Japan, and the Caribbean, carry the one . . . I guess too many to count." He smiled. "It's great to be home. I slept so well in my own bed last night."

"I'm glad you're back safe. Here's hoping you get to stay for a little while." Her hand gestured him in. "Let's get you in to see Charles. He has something he wants to discuss prior to the others getting here. You have your coffee; can I get you anything else?"

"No thank you, I'm good."

Austin glanced into the meeting room to find nine places set;

there would be a large group today. He continued down the hall, entering his uncle's office.

Charles was on his cell phone. He waved Austin in, gesturing that he should sit. "Okay, okay, I've got it. I'll do a little research and get back with you as soon as I can." He paused while listening to the voice on the other end of the line. "Got it, thank you. We'll talk soon." Charles ended the call.

"Hey! You finally made it home. How are you feeling?"

"I'm well, a little tired, but I've had worse. Like Guatemala." Austin suspected his sleep-deprived eyes and worn-out smile ran counter to his optimistic response.

"I figured you would be. Bet you woke up wondering what continent you were on this morning," Charles chuckled.

Austin was too tired to join in.

Charles continued in a more serious tone, "Thanks for coming in early, I wanted to talk with you before the others arrived."

"Not a problem, what's up?"

"As you've probably observed, things are heating up around here. We'll get into more details at the meeting, but we've just got another piece of the crystal, which makes two in under six months. To put that into perspective, the last piece was retrieved in 1947, and the one before that, hundreds of years ago. It's unprecedented. And I'm sure you've noted that Ojater's attack on Maya was personal, and from what she said, you're also a target."

"Yes, I'm not too surprised they're after me, knowing who they are, but it's still worrisome. Makes me wonder how far they'll take this revenge business. Will they come after you? Is Mom in danger?"

Charles held up his hands, signaling his uncertainty.

"In short, we're all in danger. I would guess you and Maya are presently at the top of their list, given Sedona. Rebecca may be up there as well, just can't be sure. Make no mistake, there are no limits on what they'll do to achieve their goals, and revenge is one they enjoy." The phone rang, interrupting him. He glanced at the number, but chose to ignore it. "You kind of beat me to the punch here. I wanted to talk with you to let you know that I've asked your mother to go into hiding—or better yet, an extended vacation."

Austin felt a wave of concern. "That seems wise. Was there an actual threat or is it just precautionary?"

"Precautionary for sure, knowing Lucifer and Abaddon will use any method possible to extract what they want. It's not beyond them to kidnap her or worse in an effort to get to you or me. And while I'm confident you and Maya can handle yourselves in the face of an assault, your mother cannot. Michael and I both felt it was the right thing to do."

"Makes sense. How did she take the news?"

Charles shrugged. "Well. This wasn't the first time we've done this; it happened once before when your father was still alive, so she knew the drill."

"Where is she, or can you tell me? And is there anything I can do to help?"

"Nothing for you to do, just call, be there for her. I can tell you she's in the United States at a very comfortable resort under an assumed name for as long as needed. Oh, and we've given her a burner phone. We'll give you her new number after the meeting. When you call her, don't ask where she is, for her safety."

Austin hesitated, feeling guilt for putting his mom at risk. He knew his work was important and was glad Charles was thinking about her. He trusted that his uncle knew what was best.

The door opened. Maya walked in and sat down next to him in the open chair.

"Hi guys, Connie said to come back to see you. Everything okay?" Maya's eye had darkened but the swelling was down, and the wound appeared to be healing well.

"Nothing too urgent. I was just telling Austin that his mother is on an extended vacation for her own safety. And I wanted to see how you were doing? Between India and Ojater, you've had a rough couple of weeks."

Maya glanced to Austin, meeting his eye. "That's a good choice for your mom. Safer, lets you focus on what you need to."

"Agreed," Austin replied. "And how are you?"

Maya hesitated, then gave a shrug. "I'm okay. Shoulder is getting stronger every day, and Anan did a great job with my cheek. The way it's healing, I think it'll only be a small scar."

"That's all good, but those are your physical wounds. How'd you sleep last night?" Austin probed.

"What are you, my doctor?" she shot back, her tone icy.

"Well, I am a PhD." He paused, his eyes holding hers. "I'm serious. I only ask because I'm worried. I watched you sleeping on the planes and in Atlanta. You seem to be having a lot of animated dreams, like you're fighting . . ."

Her brow furrowed. She started to speak but then stopped. When she spoke again, her tone was soft, like her old self, "I know you're worried, and I don't want you to be. I'm good. And, I slept fine, no fights in my dreams. Although, I did wake up a few times last night with odd dreams of Atlantis." She paused, looking past him while in thought. "It was weird, more like a déjà vu than a dream, and not about the adaro. I was actually living in Atlantis, and Lucifer was with me. It was some crazy stuff, but no violence." She shrugged, smiling at Austin. "Anyway, I'll manage through them. I have in the past. And thank you, Dr. Denton, for caring."

Charles studied her, the creases in his face reflecting concern. "We'll find out everything that's happened with Gabriel and Michael today, but I'm going to insist you're both here for a few days, at least to catch up on sleep. You look tired." Charles glanced at his watch. "Let's head to the conference room. Everyone should be here shortly." As he stood, he reached in his desk and removed a small wooden box.

They went down the hall to find Rebecca and Victoria Meyers, the foundation's board member, in the conference room, deep in discussion. Rebecca's hands floated back and forth in animated fashion describing the spider demon in India. Victoria followed each word and hand gesture, fully engaged, interjecting questions whenever the opportunity arose. Austin noted the museum curator appeared to have aged since that fateful night in Sedona when she was on Bernael's arm.

Rebecca stopped mid-story to greet them. "Oh, hey all. I was just telling Victoria about the demon encounter in India." She leaned over to Maya, giving her a hug. "How are you?"

Maya gave a weary shrug in response. "I'm good I guess, thanks for asking."

Rebecca added, "The cheek is much better, it's healing well."

Victoria stepped over, shaking Austin's hand while rubbing his arm with a little too much vigor. "Heard a little about your trip. Between Atlantis and Japan, it sounds unbelievable. Are you recovered yet?"

"Could use some sleep, but otherwise all good. We were a little lucky in Japan, thanks in large part to Rebecca, but I guess we'll be covering that in a few minutes. And how about yourself? I haven't seen you since Sedona. How's the Field Museum?"

Her face lit up with the question. "Busy! We're adding to our portfolio every day. We're building a section on Easter Island now. Definitely keeps me hopping."

The door opened and Anan, Gabriel, and Michael entered the room. Jonathon Brand, the foundation's financial director and Maya's Sedona date, followed last. Jonathon slid into the open chair next to Maya. The financial wizard was quick to engage her in quiet conversation that ended with both laughing out loud and him touching her arm as she leaned in closer, her face beaming. Austin shifted in his chair, an uncomfortable feeling welling in his chest.

Charles sat down and raised a hand, requesting quiet. "Let's begin. To start, we have Tom Warner on the speaker phone. He's traveling, thus couldn't join us."

Charles continued, "Let's get right to it. We've had a whirlwind of activity the last few weeks, including retrieving our fourth piece of the Star Crystal. I wanted to bring everyone together to discuss the events, including a few security concerns we have."

Tom interrupted from the phone. "Wish I could be there to see the crystal. Superb work, everyone."

"Thanks Tom. I'll take a picture and send it to you on a secure line," Charles replied.

As he spoke, he pulled out the wooden box taken earlier from his desk, opened it, and removed the Star Crystal in the same clear container used for the Guatemalan piece.

Passing it to Victoria, she said, "Beautiful. It's such a deep green with perfect symmetry."

She handed it to Jonathon. As the artifact made its way around the table, Jonathon spoke. "There is no yellow quartz containment for this. I understand Austin made the call not to grab it?"

"I did," Austin said. "It was broken; all liquid had drained out long ago. Plus, we suspected the roof would come down, so time was of the essence. I decided it was faster to grab only the crystal itself and run."

"It was a good call, the floor collapsed at once. He only made it out of the circle because we had help," Anan added.

"Help? What do you mean?" Victoria asked.

Charles interrupted, "Anan, why don't you describe the events of the day? Rebecca, Austin, please add anything he misses."

"I'll start when Rebecca and I first arrived, summarizing from there," Anan began. He told the story of Rebecca's chance airport meeting with Joshua, including his difficulty reading the man's energy. He covered their visit to the tourist-oriented wind and ice caves, highlighting his confrontation with Joshua. He described in great detail the visit to the Suicide Forest and Rebecca's encounter with Neikan, the Whisperer.

Jonathon interrupted Anan, and asked Rebecca, "What was it like when his energy entered yours?"

Rebecca considered the question. "It was painful at first, both physically and emotionally. He dredged up my most heartbreaking memories. But then, I think I was stronger than he expected. I remembered who I was, and the pain passed. I can't be sure, but it felt like I unloaded my grief onto him. He left soon after, but kept his word, and told me where the Star Crystal was." Rebecca's voice trailed off as she finished.

"That was a very dangerous thing to do," Michael said, "to invite a spirit—a known evil spirit—into your energy like that. Now is not the time or place, but we should speak about the dangers of this. Gabriel or I will give you some insight later. And yes, you may have unloaded your pain on him. It's a testament to your inner strength that you were able to do that." Michael's tone was firm—borderline fatherly.

"I understand now that I shouldn't have encouraged it," Rebecca replied. "I was terrified while it was happening. And thank you, I appreciate any information you can share. It'll prepare me for any future encounters."

Anan continued, with Rebecca and Austin chiming in to describe the trip to the ice cave.

Charles interrupted him. "About Joshua, we have friends at high levels within NASA. Given all he has done to advance their space programs, Michael is a trusted friend. As a favor to him, they searched all of NASA, its contractors, and subcontractors. And while there is a project similar to what you've described, there is no one named Joshua Pendleton within the agency or its contractors, much less associated with the project. He's a ghost."

"Then who is he?" Rebecca asked.

"That's one of many questions to answer," Michael responded. "There are others, like how did he know you'd be at the airport? Where you were going? And why even help you locate the crystal?" He paused, shaking his head. "This and Ojater being there worries me. We may find that, in the end, it was fortuitous the Whisperer possessed him. Who knows what they had planned for you?"

"Could this still be fallout from Mack's betrayal in Sedona?" Victoria asked.

"I wouldn't discount it, but from what we know now, we can't be sure it is," Charles replied.

The room fell silent. Anan was the first to speak. "This all makes sense. I mentioned earlier I couldn't observe his energy, which was odd. But also, when his body was possessed, he said, 'I can't do this anymore. I can't pretend.' I'm realizing it now—he was admitting his betrayal."

"You're right, he did say that. And that guilt is something Neikan could force out of you," Rebecca added.

"We'll keep digging, including monitoring if anyone associated with NASA goes missing. He was aware of their project, so there's a connection. Maybe he works in the organization but made up his name." Charles paused, scanning the faces around the table. "There are a few other leads, such as the airport manifest, that we'll follow up on as well. But Austin, why don't you wrap up, time is getting short."

"The only thing left to tell is our escape from the demon. It attacked a few times, tried to incinerate and then beat us to death. Anan saved us twice using the force field gun to block its fire blasts. And, it was pretty insane when Rebecca unloaded her clip point-blank as the creature attacked Anan. After we escaped out of the tunnels, I was lucky to kill it."

Rebecca jumped in. "I think Austin is underplaying the whole thing. At one point, it slammed Anan into the wall, trying to finish him. When we got out of the cave, Austin sliced the demon's throat with his knife. At that point, we had run out of other offensive weapons. It was terrifying—anything but routine."

Austin watched Maya as she listened to the story again. She clenched her fist as Rebecca finished.

Gabriel said, "So, while you three were battling a dragon, Maya was battling her own demon. Tell us about your run-in with Ojater."

Maya scanned the faces around the table. "Sure. I think you're all aware I was less than 100 percent after India and Atlantis. These three promised they were just going to scout the area and would not enter the cave without me." She overemphasized the word "promised" while glaring at Austin. Then she told her story of Ojater's ruse to lure her outside, culminating in the fight in the gardens.

"Any idea why Ojater targeted you, or why she only wounded you? From all I've learned, her specialty is a precision death," Victoria asked.

"That's a good question. I'm not sure why. I was alone and an easy target. Without a doubt, she wanted to send a message. To let us know they were aware of our plans to retrieve the crystal." She paused. "Although, I suspect she hadn't learned these three had already retrieved it. But, why even tell us they're aware we're going for it? It doesn't make sense." Maya hesitated again. "When she cut me, she told me to remember Bernael every time I see the scar. But again, why not kill me? She had the advantage."

"Why didn't you kill her when you had the advantage?" Michael asked.

Maya considered the question. "There was no reason to. It would have been murder versus self-defense, and I'm not a cold-blooded killer."

"I suspect that's your answer," Michael replied. "While Ojater is cold-blooded and not above murder, she has a code of honor. She'll kill you in battle or for a cause, but not just for fun, unlike Bernael and Lucifer who butcher people because they like it. She also has a flair for the dramatic, hence the marking of your face. She enjoys being in your head."

"That may have changed when Maya marked her back," Anan

said. "I'm sure she won't hesitate to keep the advantage the next time you meet. Make no mistake, she's a vengeful Atlantan."

An unsettled feeling washed over Austin. He unclenched his jaw to ask, "Who is Ojater, and how does she fit in with Lucifer?"

"She's the daughter of Lilith and Lucifer, and his most trusted associate," Gabriel answered. "She's a trained killer, the first choice for his delicate but dirty assignments. It sounds like she hates you and Maya for killing Bernael and sending her mother's transient to the reaper that day."

"That's how they operate: they search for a weakness and use it," Charles said. "Like ensuring Maya was alone. We need to be vigilant twenty-four-seven. We're all at risk. Also know that we've taken precautions for the specific threat to Austin." Charles glanced around the room while his words sank in. "If there's nothing else about the Japan trip, Michael, why don't you take us through Kazakhstan? Everyone should hear your story."

"Gabriel received a tip that an important IOD person would be purchasing black market nuclear material," Michael said. "Our gut was Abaddon was on the move; something that perilous wouldn't be left to anyone else. I decided we'd both go. If it was Abaddon, it might be a great chance to capture him."

"Our informant was a senior scientist for a Russian uranium firm. He was confident that he was the second guy contacted for weapons-grade plutonium. The first guy, Dr. Petrov, disappeared without a trace," Gabriel added.

Michael continued, "We arrived at the designated drop point

well in advance, and watched as the exchange turned bad. Our informant, along with four other men, died at the scene. The only ones left standing were Abaddon and Lucifer."

"Lucifer?" Tom's voice asked from the speakerphone.

"That's right, Lucifer. It's unusual for them to be on an assignment together." He glanced around the table. "We intercepted their delivery, making a narrow escape under fire. Once we opened the case, we found plutonium, enough to build a very large bomb."

Jonathon leaned back in his chair. "What would Lucifer want with plutonium?"

Michael rubbed his jaw, "We're not sure, and that worries me. An acquisition of this magnitude is both costly and dangerous. There are some ruthless players in the market and a lot of undercover government spooks. You can't be certain who you're dealing with."

"We're asking questions to trusted senior officials around the world now. So far, the missing plutonium wasn't on anyone's radar, no rumors or hearsay, meaning it was done in complete secrecy. We're lucky our friend was the contact. Sadly, he paid the ultimate price for it," Gabriel said.

"I'm sorry about your loss. It took courage to take on what he did," Austin said.

"What about the plutonium, what did you do with it?" Rebecca asked.

"It's safe in the hands of the right US officials," Michael said. "Unfortunately, we missed our chance to get Lucifer and Abaddon. They've vanished."

Charles said, "The Star Crystal will be stored with the other pieces—Michael and Gabriel will take care of that. We'll continue our search for Joshua, and we're pursuing information on the plutonium. Anything else?"

Maya asked Michael, "I have a question. The retrieval of the Japan crystal has me wondering: we now have four pieces, what happens if we get all six?"

"What do you mean?" Michael asked.

"I mean, let's say we get lucky and find all six. What will you do? The crystal is restored, the wormhole opened, then what? You go home, or maybe reinforcements come? What is the plan?"

Michael glanced to Gabriel. "It'd be a nice problem to have. All I can say is we'd start by communicating the events to Atla, then figure out what the next step is in coordination with them."

"We're still a long way away from having all six pieces," Gabriel said.

Michael took a reflexive shift in his seat, looking suddenly uncomfortable in his chair.

Charles asked, "What about the files taken from New Orleans, were you able to access them in Atlantis?"

Michael's face relaxed. "We did and have analyzed them— though not thoroughly as yet. One is an ancient scroll on the island of Hy Brasil. It describes how to find the place with some other obscure information. From what I read, it's a riddle inside of a larger puzzle. There are vague descriptions of places not identified by name, so we need to understand the text, then figure out what it's referencing. I'm hoping this group can assist with that."

"Of course. We'll get right on it," Charles said.

Michael continued, "The second document describes the underground city of Abydos, located south of Giza, somewhere in the desert. I'm familiar with the stories, as it was built soon after the collapse of Atlantis. It stood for thousands of years with a reputation for dark secrets where evil things thrived. Legend has it the IOD built it, so I never took the chance on visiting. It disappeared into the desert a few thousand years ago, during the same time the IOL was focusing our efforts on building the great pyramids. My bet is it's a candidate for either the last hidden section of the crystal or the holding spot for Lucifer's piece. Either way, I suggest a few of us head there to investigate."

"I'll go," Austin said, but his uncle cut in.

"Before anyone else volunteers to go, let's take a breath. We're all a little beaten up and could use a few days of rest. I suggest we spend the rest of the week researching Hy Brasil and Abydos. Find out what we have on it and what we don't. Then organize a well-conceived plan of attack, including who will go, based on what we find. As far as I can tell, there is nothing so time sensitive here that it can't wait a few days."

Michael built on that thought. "While I agree, and I don't want to rush headlong into something, the stakes are high, and people's lives are at risk. We should move with urgency as Lucifer won't wait. My guess is we'll only get one chance, so let's prepare a smart plan over the next few days, then head out."

Tom's voice echoed through the speaker, "Guys, I've got to sign off. We're landing and I have to run. Nice work by the team. Let me know how I can help in the plans going forward. Charles, call me later to discuss."

"Will do." Charles said before hanging up the line "Everybody, go rest, relax, and take care of personal obligations. If you don't have any, then go out for a nice dinner, maybe enjoy a good glass of wine. But let's convene here first thing tomorrow. We'll split into teams to do the research. I suggest Rebecca and Anan take Hy Brasil. Maya and Austin take Abydos." He turned to Michael and added, "I realize you and Gabriel are already traveling with the crystal."

"That's it for today, we'll see everybody tomorrow."

Austin watched as Jonathon left a lingering kiss on Maya's cheek and said goodbye, to which she replied, "I'll see you later." Austin quickly looked away.

Maya stepped down the first set of stairs when Rebecca called out, "Maya. Hey, just wanted to check your plans tonight." Austin walked up behind them. "Any interest in meeting for a pizza and a few beers?"

"Unfortunately, I can't," Maya said, "I'm already meeting Jonathon for dinner. But you two should go, sounds fun."

"You sure? You can invite him. It'll be good to catch up," Austin added.

"Thanks guys, but I'll have to get a rain check. I'll see you both tomorrow." Maya turned to Austin and with a half-smile said, "And you better be fresh, we have a lot of work to do."

September 26, 2014
Friday
Tucson, Arizona

Gabriel entered the conference room where Maya was sitting next to Austin, researching Abydos. They had spent the last couple of days looking for clues on the ancient desert city. At present, both had their heads down, reading text off the computer screen, with large maps of Egypt open next to them. Despite being near her, Austin felt a separation growing between them.

Maya's sparkling eyes flashed up. "Gabriel, you're back! How was the trip?"

Austin leaned over to shake his hand. "Welcome back. How'd everything go hiding the crystal?"

Rebecca strolled in, a coffee cup steaming in her hand.

"No issues at all. The piece is safe with the other ones." Gabriel paused, removing his jacket. "It's odd seeing it come together. For so long we've only had two sections, now we're up to four with a lead on the fifth. Who knows, if we can find Lucifer, maybe even the sixth." He glanced to Maya. "I have a feeling this long journey is almost over for us."

"I hope for all of the IOL's sake it is. I can't imagine what you've been through," Maya said.

Gabriel beamed his warm smile, his eyes radiating their purplish hue. "Thank you. This may sound crazy, but the events here are not that unprecedented for our species. We are explorers; settling a new world is never easy, nor simple. There is always risk to life in some form or fashion. What's unusual for us on Earth is our lives are so long compared to yours. It's the change that gets to me. I grow attached to individuals and always have to say goodbye too soon. I need to keep reminding myself that all of our journeys are one long energy transformation and rebirth. Although our mortal lives are longer than yours, the process is still the same." He paused. "If anything, we need to appreciate the time we have together. Think about the probability that our unique energies would interact with one another at this exact time and this specific spot in the universe. The chance of that occurrence is infinitesimal; it makes me wonder if it wasn't ordained."

"I've thought about that—a lot. The chances of our species' existence alone are remote, coupled with our individual time here being so short." Rebecca spoke quickly, sounding like she'd ingested too much caffeine. "I feel the need to squeeze in everything I can into each day." She sipped her coffee. "What blows my mind is seeing so many people not living life. Instead, they have their noses glued to their cell phones, obsessed with how many likes or emoji faces they get in a post." She shook her head. "Living via electronics is not for me. I'd rather a hot cup of coffee, a good friend, and a thoughtful topic." She raised her mug as she finished.

"In the spirit of making the most of our days, we've got a lot to do. Let's brief Gabriel on what we found," Austin said.

Gabriel agreed, "Yes, tell me of Abydos. What did you find out from the document?"

Maya glanced back to Austin. "Would you like me to start?"

"I insist."

She peeked down at her notes. "First, we went line by line through the translated document. Although a lot of it we don't understand, Michael was right, it does describe the location and the city's characteristics. Turns out it wasn't all underground but built into the walls of what sounds like a very narrow canyon or maybe a gorge. Sections of the city had a view of the sky, meaning it was probably built into the canyon's hillside. When approaching from a distance, the area is flat terrain with limited natural markers to guide you to it. In a way, it had a natural protection. We can't be sure if after all these years something is still there. The city could be covered with sand, collapsed by erosion, destroyed by war, or maybe even an earthquake."

"The document details the location as 'toward the morning sun of Giza, half the journey to the great water in Deshret,'" Austin said. "We've identified Deshret as the ancient name for Egypt's Red Land, or the desert, and the great water has to be the Red Sea. It also says there was a single trade road in; but merchants would take it and never come back. The document doesn't say what happened to them, only that dark energy protected the city."

"The dark energy is IOD-related, for sure," Gabriel replied.

Maya continued. "It also gives a clue. There were four linked oases that fed the city with water. Given the city was built into the hillside, it was likely fed water from the surface down. It all sounds sophisticated, like Atlantan design." She glanced up to Gabriel. "You wouldn't by chance remember the oases, would you?"

Gabriel laughed. "Sorry, I never went to the city, too dangerous given its reputation as an IOD center. Not to mention I don't remember what I had for breakfast, much less a five-thousand-year-old oasis." He glanced at the map on the desk. "So, does this lead us to any specific locations?"

Maya answered, "Yes and no. We've scoured the maps and while we can't find an oasis, we've identified three likely areas. We're going through satellite photos now, trying to find something that may indicate a lost city."

Austin touched the computer mouse, lighting up the screen. The three potential sites came up.

Gabriel bent down. "I'm wondering . . ." Gabriel said as he rubbed his chin. "Will you pull up Egypt's planetary grid lines?"

Maya typed a few strokes on the keyboard. She brought up a map showing a grid of lines over Egypt. "What are they?" she asked.

Gabriel answered, "Overlay those to the potential sites. While you do that, I'll explain." He paused, watching Maya go to work.

"Earth is one large, electrically charged ball. A good example is the Aurora Borealis. Have you seen those brilliant lights?"

"I have, just once though," Austin said.

"Sure, the northern lights," Rebecca nodded.

"These northern lights occur when the solar winds reflect off the Earth's magnetic field. This highlights the unseen energy grid protecting, or better yet, filtering the energy that is bombarding the Earth every moment of every day. This includes solar flares, cosmic winds, and even the Universal Energy Stream."

"I've seen that twice: once in Sedona and again at the Well of Souls," Austin said.

"That's right, you have." Gabriel glanced to Rebecca. "Are you following me so far?"

"Yes, the Earth has a giant magnetic force field that protects it by filtering the energy bombarding it every day."

Gabriel clasped her shoulder. "Wow, that's a much better summary. And yes, the magnetic grid protecting the Earth is like a blanket that covers the entire planet, but it isn't uniform. Given the rotation of the Earth, the makeup of its core, and the masses of land versus water, the magnetic grid forms channels of stronger energy that crisscross the world. These channels are planetary grid lines, or PG lines. They can be used—and were used by ancient man and Atlantans—to communicate with one another here on Earth. The great engineer—and demi, I might add—Nikola Tesla even experimented using these lines for a wireless power grid." Gabriel winked at Maya. "Given we could only salvage a limited amount of technology from Atlantis during those early days, the Atlantan founders of Abydos may have located the city on one of these grid lines to maximize the use of the Earth's natural energy field."

Maya completed the overlay. "Wow—this third site is on one of Egypt's PG lines. In fact, a main line."

"Good, then that's where we start. Now we search for any other clues that a missing city could be there," Gabriel said.

"Tesla was demi?" Austin asked.

"Yes, he was. A lot of the luminaries of their day were demis: Einstein, da Vinci, Ghandi to name a few. All were brilliant and well ahead of their time because they were better evolved and used more and different parts of their brains. They were more evolved due to a higher ratio of pure Atlantan DNA."

Maya said, "On that note, I'm surprised to find I can read some Atlantan writing." She winked at him. "Must be in the genes."

Gabriel's eyes narrowed, head tilted to the side. "That is surprising."

"Maya told me about her ancestry," Rebecca said. "I always suspected she was special."

Focusing back on her computer screen, Maya said, "Is it a coincidence that the grid lines flow directly over the Giza Pyramids?"

"It is not a coincidence," Gabriel said. "When we built the pyramids, we chose that precise location for the energy properties there. It's an intersection point between a major PG line and the Universal Energy Stream."

"The IOL built the pyramids?" Rebecca asked.

"We did. Their construction was one of our greatest achievements," Gabriel said proudly. "We developed a communication device to reach Atla using only the tools available to us here on Earth five thousand years ago."

Austin was confused. "Communication device? I thought the pyramids were burial tombs."

"Let me explain. Post-Atlantis destruction, Michael and a few of us Atlantans wandered at first, but ultimately settled in Egypt's Nile Delta. There were many favorable attributes there, such as food, water, and materials for housing—things we required for survival. With most of our technology destroyed or abandoned in Atlantis, the wormhole closed, and the Star Crystal hidden, our group realized we were alone. And more importantly, there was no way to contact Atla to ask for help, like sending troops or supplies. That was, until one of our more brilliant engineers, Uriel, figured out we *could* contact home. But, in order to do so, we would have to build a structure—and it would have to be enormous—in the right location with the right materials. Knowing time was not an issue, that's what we did. We first identified Giza as the best location. Its spot as an energy vortex and a main grid of the PG lines would be ideal for harnessing the natural energy vibrations from the Earth and channeling them through the machine we'd build to focus them, so that they would reach Atla as low-energy radio waves."

"Like a signal?" Austin asked.

"Yes, like a signal. Our brothers and sisters in Alta monitor the sky. They knew we were on Earth and lost contact. We needed to send them a flare," Gabriel answered.

"That makes sense, but how would you differentiate your signal from the ambient background noise using just rock and water? I mean, a signal traveling through space could be anything," Maya asked.

"Correct, a very astute question. First, you hit them with a constant signal, one they would recognize as new. Then, you send higher energy bursts, the nonrandom type, so they can see it's created. If possible, you even use an embedded code."

"Like SOS in Morse code," Rebecca said.

Gabriel turned to face her. "Yes. The natural attenuation of the Earth's magnetic, electrical, and gravitational fields through the pyramid provided the constant low-frequency signal desired. We designed the King's and Queen's Chambers in the Great Pyramid such that when hydrochloric acid was mixed with hydrated zinc inside the pyramid, massive quantities of artificial high-energy signals were generated." He raised his right hand, index finger pointing to emphasize his words. "In essence, the Pyramid of Khufu is a big battery that creates radio signal bursts until the zinc runs out."

Rebecca eyes grew wide with amazement. "That's freaking brilliant!"

He continued, nodding. "We ran it for hundreds of years, trying to encode a help message. In theory it works, but in practice we're still not sure how successful it was because no answer has been received." He looked at Austin. "Oh, on your original question, some smaller pyramids are burial sites, but not the Great Pyramid of Giza. No tombs have been found there and none will be, at least not from that era."

"Wow, that is quite the tale. But how did you do it?" Austin said.

"If you study the details, the answer to the question of this being an organic project accomplished by ancient man with limited technology becomes crystal clear. Over two and a half million stones were moved from up to five hundred miles away. The multi-ton blocks were cut and built with such precision that the interlock of the limestone cover fit so perfectly, a piece of paper couldn't fit between the blocks. The platform that supports the seven-million-ton weight is less than two feet thick and still level today, despite that kind of pressure resting on it for five thousand years. Oh, and the square base is within an inch of being perfect. And that is just the tip of the iceberg—the amazing beauty is in its details."

"Well, how did you do it? I mean, just lifting the stones must've been a Herculean task," Maya asked.

Gabriel's eyes lit up. "We used a combination of salvaged Atlantis technology, ingenious engineering, and the brute strength of a gargantuan non-slave labor force. Some heavy lifting and precision stone cuts were done with advanced Atlantis technology, things like lasers and anti-gravitational lifts. But much was done with just good engineering and planning. We had to provide food, transportation, and equipment infrastructure to support hundreds of thousands of workers for over a hundred years." Gabriel took a breath. "Listen, I could go on and on about the location, the mathematical precision, or the short time in which the three Giza pyramids were built, but I'll conclude by saying that they are laid out to be in perfect alignment with the stars of Orion—this is not a coincidence. It was to send a message to any who searched for us."

"That is amazing—it makes perfect sense. You were stuck here with lots of time," Rebecca said.

"Tell us more about Uriel. What happened to him?" Maya asked.

"He was Michael's nephew," Rebecca said, "killed by Abaddon in the early eighteen hundreds. He slit Uriel's throat and took the family ring that Michael really wants back." She glanced to Gabriel. "I'm sorry, I asked Anan that question on the way to Japan."

Gabriel shrugged. "Oh no, that is an excellent summary. I wasn't aware Anan had shared that. I'll only add that Uriel was a brilliant engineer, a great soldier, and a loyal friend. His passing hurt us all a lot, in particular, Michael."

Maya focused her attention on the three sites on the screen. "We'll do the research on these sites and see if we can confirm anything on the one that overlays the PG lines. Charles wants to talk tomorrow afternoon. I think we're close."

"We're not as far along on Hy Brasil," Rebecca said. "There's not as much information. But we've gone through the document and have a few leads that we're following. I don't think Anan and I are ready. So, let me pull everything together tonight, and I'll update you tomorrow."

"Okay, if you don't need anything more from me, I'll take my leave of you to see what Charles and Michael are up to," Gabriel said.

Rebecca moved right behind him. "I've got to go as well. Need to get ready for tomorrow, plus I have a couple of errands to do." She turned to Austin. "See you in the morning for coffee?"

"Sure, that sound great, how about eight o'clock?"

"Perfect, pick me up!" she called.

Austin said to Maya, "You want to head out, maybe grab dinner?"

Her face tightened, belying her friendly tone, "I've got a weird feeling on that third site, but a good one." She paused. "I'm going pass on dinner. I have a lot of stuff still to catch up on."

"I understand." Austin's inner voice told him something else was at play. He glanced away, hesitated for a tense moment, then said, "Can I ask you something?"

"Of course."

"Is everything good between us? I'm worried that you're avoiding me. It seems that lately you're always too busy or something else is going on. If I did anything to anger you, it wasn't intentional." Austin's gentle voice trailed off.

Maya's eyes locked on his as she answered stiffly, "Everything is fine, you did nothing wrong. Things change over time, that's all."

"What does that mean?"

"Meaning, you and Rebecca make a great couple, and I've got Jonathon."

"Hey, Rebecca and I are not a couple, we're friends, that's all,"

Austin said, feeling defensive. "I think I've been pretty transparent about how I feel about you. You're the one pushing me away. And why is that? I mean, if it's Jonathon, just say so. If he's the one, I'm really happy for you. But something tells me he's not."

"It's not Jonathon, and I don't want to get into this."

"Why not?"

"Just trust me, you are better off with her in a thousand ways. She can give you a life that I can't."

Austin put his hand on hers. "I thought in Atlantis you said no more secrets." He paused, waiting for a response. She didn't bite, so he continued. "Okay, I won't push it right now." He brushed her hand. "If you ever want to talk about us, I'm here."

Her eyes met his, and with her lips pursed, she said, "I know, but now is not the time."

CHAPTER 19

September 27, 2014
Saturday Morning
Tucson, Arizona

Austin sipped his coffee while Rebecca stood reading a text message on her phone. They were standing outside his Uncle Charles's law office. "Everything good?" he asked.

"Oh yeah, everything is fine. It's my old roommate. Kayla wants to meet for dinner tonight."

"How's she doing, now that you moved to your own place?"

"Good. She misses hanging out, and doesn't like living alone, but I understand she'll be getting a new roommate soon, so that'll pass. We're trying to meet once a week for dinner or drinks to catch up and stay connected."

Austin opened the door to his uncle's office building and held it for her. "I've been recently reminded that time changes all things." He was still bothered by Maya's statement last night. "I sat in the coffee shop earlier this week and thought of the days you were the barista. I remembered how much I enjoyed being there, seeing you, having all of our crazy conversations."

"I know, at the time you don't realize how special it is. If you could only bottle those moments and save them, then reopen them when you need to adjust your mood."

He chuckled, "You know, in many ways, that's what memories are, both good and bad—mood adjusters. I thought about your crazy Bigfoot conspiracy theories. They brought a smile to my face."

She rolled her eyes. "Conspiracy theories? I thought Gabriel put that all to rest. Bigfoot lives in the mountains east of Portland and is part alien," she said, entering the elevator. "Speaking of good memories, how's Maya doing? She appears different since that sting in India. I can't be sure as I didn't know her well before Sedona, but it seems like she's gotten quieter, more withdrawn."

Austin nodded. "I've noticed a difference since the fundraiser. There's no doubt when she does engage, she seems more on edge. Between Guatemala, Sedona, India, and Japan, she's had a tough run of luck. I'm guessing it's just wearing on her." He shook his head. "I tried to talk with her, to see how she's feeling. But she only shares what she wants, which is never much."

Rebecca opened the door to the office, holding it for Austin. "Best to not push it. She'll talk if and when she's ready."

They walked into the conference room. Maya was sitting, deep in conversation with Gabriel and Anan. She was looking less drawn, and her cheek was almost healed.

"Morning, another beautiful day," Anan said.

"Everybody have good energy today?" Austin asked. "We have a lot to do." Austin and Rebecca took seats at the conference table.

Rebecca pointed to Gabriel, "Speaking of energy . . . Don't forget, Michael said either he or you would brief me on transient energy and the risks of Neikan's free spirit entering my body."

"Yes, yes, we must do that. Do you have a few minutes now? I'm happy to take you through it," Gabriel asked.

"I think so. We still have a few things to run down on Hy Brasil, but we're not meeting with Charles until two o'clock this afternoon." Rebecca glanced to Anan, looking for feedback.

Anan frowned. "I'm not sure we're going to find much more ever. We have the time for sure."

"Then let's begin with the basics. You're familiar with transient energy and living energy," Gabriel started.

Rebecca nodded.

"And you are familiar with auras?" he continued.

"Kind of?"

"Okay, that's where we'll start. An aura is our body's energy that radiates, and the color reflects the balance of our physical and spiritual life, meaning it reveals the health of mind, body, and soul."

Maya asked, "And how does it do that? I mean, why are colors associated with it?"

Gabriel considered the question for a moment. "Think in terms of energy versus the physical. We are energy: our bodies are living energy, and our souls are transient energy. And being energy, like most, we emit a field around us called radiant energy, which is based on our combined physical and spiritual tuning. This radiant energy is frequency-based waves, similar to light. And like light waves, each energy frequency reflects a color when observed. Recall what happens when you shine white light through a prism, or see a rainbow after a heavy rain. When you do this, you're breaking white light into the individual waves. Broken apart, they show their true colors, which tie to their frequency."

"So, our bodies are power plants that give off energy that radiates like light waves and the color you emit depends on the wave frequency that your body generates?" Austin asked, hoping he summarized correctly.

"Yes, exactly, and your body's tuning is not just based on physical tuning like what you eat and how much exercise you get, but spiritual tuning as well. Both your actions and thoughts affect the spiritual tuning," Gabriel said.

Rebecca said, "I'm not sure I'm following. How does thought affect your body's tuning, and even more so your transient energy?"

Gabriel stood. "Let me give you an example on where your thoughts impact your physical health. Emotional stress is a good one. Consider the extreme case of a loved one's death. In that situation, nothing physical happens to you, but your mind is consumed by sorrow, which manifests itself in a physical way by not allowing your body to rest, thus wearing you down, causing you to lose efficiency. It's a clear illustration of where your thoughts have a direct impact on your body's tuning. And because your physical body is connected to your transient through the seven chakra points, this flows to and impacts your transient energy."

Anan said, "Extend that logic to your everyday life. Every action you take requires a conscious decision. If you think negative thoughts or take negative actions, over time your transient and living energy will feel that stress, eventually reflecting it. Meaning, the radiant energy your body emits also reflects it, which is the catalyst for people projecting different colored auras."

"A good action, much like a good meal, provides positive emotional feedback, fine tuning your energy production machine, which generates the associated radiant energy. As you know, the Rule of Energy Attraction is that like energies will draw one another together—good karma, if you will," Gabriel said.

"Always remember," Anan said, "that if you're ever stressed out, meditation relaxes the body, puts your organs and mind at rest, allowing a more efficient operation of your physical self. This means lower blood pressure and better-aligned brain waves that create a more restful sleep—a more efficient production of energy. All of this stuff changes the frequency of your aura. Our knowledge of this is one reason we, the IOL Atlantans, have purple energy."

Rebecca replied, "Okay, I got that. Going back to Michael's concern about Neikan's energy within mine, what could have happened there?"

"Oh yes," Gabriel said. "Two things can happen when two different transients occupy the same living energy. First, the stronger of the transient energies will, in time, control the living energy. This is demonic possession and what almost happened to

Maya with Lilith. Thank goodness Maya had the stronger transient and won the battle." Gabriel nodded, smiling at Maya. "The second thing that can happen is the energies become enmeshed, meaning a part of one transient fuses into the other."

"On my vision quest, an evil spirit passed through my transient. Michael warned me of that," Austin said.

"And good that he did. If a piece of his energy fused into yours, that evil would stay with you until it was extracted by force," Anan added.

"Can it be extracted? Michael didn't mention that," Austin asked, feeling surprised.

"Yes, it can be done, but it's very, very dangerous. It's not a good idea to mess around with a person's soul." Gabriel turned back to Rebecca. "In your case, you risked Neikan's energy possessing you, or worse, fusing with your transient. Either situation is bad. My bet is he sensed your strength of spirit, your love, if you will, and that made it uncomfortable. He chose to depart as there are easier victims."

Maya asked, "Gabriel, how would you know if Rebecca's and Neikan's transients enmeshed?"

Gabriel's eyes narrowed. "There would be a change of behavior. Over time, different traits or characteristics emerge." He chuckled as he finished, "Why do you ask, is she becoming homicidal?"

A strained look crossed Maya's face as she tried to smile. "Not yet, but better to be safe and all."

Rebecca laughed, adding, "I think I got it, thanks for the information. I'll ensure it doesn't happen again, at least not on a voluntary basis."

"Glad I could help. With that done, I need to check on some things. I'll see you all later for the debrief," Gabriel said. He left the room.

Anan and Rebecca moved to work in a separate office.

Austin was doing a meticulous review of a super-magnified satellite image when Maya commented, "I'm not sure we're going to find anything else. I mean, the landscape has shifted so much. How can you identify a lost road or an old oasis?"

Austin sighed. "Agreed, it's like a needle in a haystack. I'm going to finish reviewing this map then take a break."

"Can I ask you something?" Maya asked.

"Sure, what's up?"

"What did you think about Michael's answer to my question, about what the plan is if we get all six pieces?"

Austin had a bad feeling about where this was going. "Hard to say for sure. On the one hand, his answer seems reasonable. I mean, who knows what's happened on Atla in the last nine thousand years? Meaning Michael really will call and figure out what can be done. But . . ." He paused.

"But what?" she asked.

"My gut says he's not telling us something. He seemed uncomfortable with the question. How about you?"

"Exactly my read. I mean, over nine thousand years after the events, you don't know what you're going to do? You would think they'd have it meticulously planned. I'm not buying it. Plus, I agree, his body language told me he's hiding something."

"Yep, that's a valid point," he said, avoiding eye contact.

Maya nudged him on the shoulder. "What is it Austin? Something's bothering you." She tilted her head to the side. "You're an easy read."

"That obvious?" He hesitated, knowing her instinct was right. He considered whether now was the time to tell her of Mack's dying plea. "There is something I haven't shared with you. I've been wrestling with it since Sedona."

"That doesn't sound good."

"It's not." Austin thought of General Mackey and how he kidnapped Maya in Sedona in order for Bernael to transfer Lilith's transient into Maya's body. He leaned forward, his voice just above a whisper. "Back at Bernael's mansion, Mack was shot, literally dying, and he didn't want me to save him. Just before he passed out, he confessed regret for his crimes with Lucifer. Do you remember that story?"

"Yes, how could I forget that. Why?"

"Well, he also told me something else. He warned me not to open the wormhole. That we were on the wrong team. If it opens, an Atlantan invasion force will cross, and billions of humans will die. It's why he did Lucifer's dirty work for so long; he was trying to save humanity."

Maya's mouth dropped open. "That's a pretty huge piece of the story. Did you believe him? I mean, what were you going to do with that information?"

"Mack believed it. But, whether it's the truth, I can't be sure." He leaned back, considering the question. "My thought was to uncover Michael's plans before all six crystals are found. You're the only person I've told, and I don't think it's wise to share it any further." The sense of relief from sharing the burden of a secret welled inside, so he continued. "If Mack's wrong, there's no harm done by quietly investigating it. But if Mack is right, Michael wouldn't tell us an invasion force is coming. His lack of an answer at the group meeting Tuesday kind of confirms that. I figured time is our friend here. We're still two pieces away, with lots of time to research the question, and if needed, develop a plan to stop it. Whether it's Michael, Gabriel, or Anan, somebody will eventually tip their hand. Your question on what happens when we get all six may, in the end, be the catalyst to answers."

"I guess you're right," Maya said. "I didn't realize it was such a loaded question."

"Michael's always been honest with me, and I know he has good energy. So, I'm going to give him the benefit of the doubt and assume he's telling the truth. But I'll keep pushing it."

Maya gave him a skeptical look. "While I agree about Michael's energy, I also think he plays things close to the vest. Think about the revelations at Atlantis. He was hiding that for a long time. What's to say he's not doing so again here? I think if we get close to another crystal, we need to drive this hard. We can't risk an invasion of Earth."

"You mean *when* we get close to another crystal." Austin motioned to his computer screen.

"Got it, back to work. What are you researching again?" she asked.

"They describe the city as being built in a gash in the ground. Given it's a desert, it's reasonable to assume that the area has eroded over time, versus being covered. So, I'm scanning eroded rifts, trying to find any openings in the hillside. I'm focusing in the area of the PG lines."

Maya stood up and stepped over, putting her hand on Austin's shoulder. She bent down close to get a better view of his screen, bringing her body tight to his. Austin glanced up to her, enjoying this closeness, the smell of her perfume, the gentle touch of her hand. It had been too long since they'd sat in quiet comfort, side by side.

"See, like this area here," he said, "this shadow seems like it could open into the hillside. I just can't be sure."

Maya tilted her head while pointing to the screen. "What is this line? It looks almost etched into the soil and stands out against the dry terrain."

There were multiple fingerlings of an eroded landscape caused by the region's infrequent rain. He recentered the photo and zoomed in to the maximum pixel size, when he saw what Maya saw: a faint straight line connected to another straight line forming a triangular top. He zoomed out, scanning the landscape square by square until he found a second triangular shape a short distance away, and then a third. Even more amazing, they appeared symmetrical.

"No way!" he blurted out.

"What is it?" she asked.

"Hold on." He hit a button on his keyboard, and the printer nearby hummed in response. He left the room, returning with a wooden ruler. Setting the paper on the table, he grabbed his pen. Then using the straight edge, he connected the lines. It made up three of the five points to a star.

Maya saw it at once. "Oh my God, it's the Star Crystal carved into the desert!"

Austin glanced up at her. "Have you ever heard of the Nazca lines in Peru?" he asked.

Maya raised an eyebrow. "Yes. Giant animals carved into the high desert."

"Well, experts speculate the ancient Peruvian tribes etched the figures into the desert to communicate with the gods. What if their gods were the Atlantans? Their wormhole and the staging area were nearby, and they had flying ships. And most of all, what if this was etched into the desert of Egypt to communicate with those same gods flying those same ships? Maybe even to tell them the location of the city?"

Maya beamed while touching his arm with her hand. "Or maybe where to land? I think you're right. And what better way than to use an image of the Star Crystal."

In his excitement, Austin stood and stepped toward her, hesitating just a second as he gazed into her beautiful brown eyes, wanting to pull her in, to feel her in his arms.

In his moment of indecision, she stepped away. "We need to show this to Gabriel."

CHAPTER 20

September 27, 2014
Saturday Afternoon
Tucson, Arizona

Austin entered the conference room and joined the group. Once situated, Charles said, "Let's begin with Abydos. What do we know, and what don't we know?"

Maya glanced to Austin and said, "Go ahead, you lead. I'll interject sarcastic comments as you forget stuff."

The group laughed.

Austin chuckled; it was good to see her smile. "What are we talking about again?" he joked while glancing down to his notes before turning serious. "We did three major things with a lot of detailed research in support. From Michael's document from New Orleans, we got a general description of the area we are searching for. The most meaningful were: one, the city is east of Giza; two, it's in the Deshret, which is the Red Land; and third, it's in a gash in the ground. It wasn't a lot to go on."

Austin hit a button on his computer, and a map of the region popped up on a large flat screen on the wall of the conference room. "We scanned aerial maps and came back with these three sizable areas based on those general descriptions. You'll see each of the locations is between Giza and the Red Sea, in the red desert with both mountainous terrain and valleys."

"That's harsh country; trying to get to those sites will be tough. Were you able to narrow it down?" Michael said, studying the map.

"Yes, we think so. Gabriel had the next idea," Maya answered.

"We were talking about the construction of the pyramids," Gabriel said, "when I realized they may have located the city on or near a major PG line to take advantage of the power and communication benefits of the grid."

Austin hit another button, and the PG lines overlaid the regional map. One of the major lines crossed over the southernmost site.

Charles drummed the table, unable to mask his excitement. "That is excellent work. You suspect this is the site?"

Austin turned to Maya. "Yes, we were confident, but couldn't be positive until Maya found the last clue."

"He's being modest, we found the last clue together. Austin was searching for entryways into the cliffs when we noticed something."

Austin zoomed in on the southernmost location while Maya continued. She stood, walked to the screen and pointed. "Can you see it?"

Everybody stared at the flat screen.

"Appears to be three angles carved into the desert rock," Anan said.

"Correct. And when you connect the angles, you get this." Austin hit the computer keyboard one last time. A star overlay the area, its shape fitting the three angles to perfection.

"Much like the Nazca lines," Maya said, "they carved the Star Crystal into rock as a message to approaching aircraft, communicating they were at the location. It might even be the landing pad. Given the topography of the area, it would have been visible from the air. Only the 'gods' could see it." Maya held up her hands, making air quotes for all to see.

Charles stood and stepped closer to the screen. "That's pretty compelling; I expect you're right. What do you think, Michael, is it enough to send a research team out?"

Michael furrowed his brow. "I agree it makes sense. Use of the carvings was smart and careful during that tenuous time. What is your proposed plan?"

Austin hesitated for just a moment, not intending to discuss the next phase so soon. He expected more questions and discussion.

Maya jumped in. "Gabriel, Austin, and I fly to Cairo. We drive a four-wheel drive SUV into the desert, bringing food and supplies for a week, including climbing and caving gear. This place is built into cliffs, so whether we need to go up or down, we'll have to climb. And once on the cliffs, who knows how far into the hillside it goes. If we can't find the Star Crystal in a few days, we exit and regroup. Water will be key: we'll have to carry in what we need to drink."

"If the crystal is there, it's likely guarded by a demon, an ancient one at that, so we'll definitely be bringing large caliber guns and armor piercing ammo," Gabriel added.

Austin glanced to Rebecca. Her jaw appeared clenched, her face tense. He wasn't sure if it was the risk of the job, or the fact Maya didn't include her on the team. His thoughts were interrupted by Michael. "It's a solid plan, but let's hear what's going on with Hy Brasil before we finalize anything."

Anan said, "We've had some success with the document, but we still don't understand a lot more than we did. Rebecca, why don't you go through what we've found so far."

Rebecca stepped up. "Sure, not a problem." She flipped some paper in front of her. "We dissected the document line by line, then followed that up with research on the specific insights we found. We also did general research. Let's start with the document Michael retrieved." She paused while pulling it up on the screen. "This represents an old history of Ireland and Hy Brasil that locates the island southwest of the Emerald Isle, but does not provide any distances, longitude or latitude coordinates. Other literature indicates sightings by humans as far back as one thousand years. Meaning we can assume it's sailing distance from Ireland using boats constructed during that era, which had a limited range. This helps some, but not a lot." She sipped her coffee. "We've scanned years of satellite photos of the ocean off western Ireland, unfortunately with no luck."

"We assumed locating it would be difficult," Michael said. "We recognize from the Sedona documents that Lucifer has been studying this for some time and still doesn't seem to have found it. It also sounds like this doesn't answer the question of why he's searching."

"We were able to lift a few things that may help on both of your questions," Anan said. "It describes the island as being shrouded in mist and protected by rocky shoals, making navigation to it difficult. But the weirdest piece we translated is that the island becomes visible on the eleventh day of October in the Shemitah year. Otherwise, it sounds like it's naturally hidden unless you sail into it by chance."

"Sorry, I'm not familiar with that—Shemitah?" Austin asked.

"In ancient Israel, they planted crops on seven-year cycles. There were six years of crops and on the seventh, the Shemitah year, the fields were left alone to recover."

"October 11, a very random day. Can we figure out when the Shemitah year is?" Maya said.

"Yes, we've done that. We calculate this year starting on September 24 is the Shemitah. Meaning if the island shows itself, it'll do so on this coming October 11," Anan replied.

"Just a few weeks, so we don't have a lot of time. Since this document was drafted using the Jewish calendar, it's been drafted within the last 5700 years, which means the author of the document is either an Atlantan who survived the civil war, or it's a human that knows the full story of your presence here."

"This might explain the increase in activity we've seen from Lucifer and the IOD—he's gearing up for something to happen on October 11. If he misses it, he'll have to wait another seven years," Michael said.

Rebecca added, "One more thing. In 1674, a captain, John Nisbet, claims he stumbled on the island while sailing from France. He confirmed shipwrecks littered its rocky coast. He also reported they sent a search party onto the island, and the crew had a wonderful day on the island in the company of large black rabbits and a mysterious magician who lived alone in a castle. It sounds made up, but during the last few months, I've learned not to discount any legends, no matter how crazy they sound."

Charles asked, "How about the why—have you gotten any idea on why Lucifer is searching for the island?"

"We have nothing conclusive. But two possibilities. One is almost religious; the passage said the path to Jehovah is through Hy Brasil. Seems an obvious reference to God, but whether it's a spiritual journey or an actual journey, there's no indication."

Michael's face tightened.

"What is it, Michael?" Austin asked.

He glanced down at his papers, responding with an obvious white lie, "Nothing right now. Keep going."

"The second line was even more cryptic," Anan said. "It said the secret to the island's location is protected by the heroes of Amaru. We're assuming they mean the Door of Amaru, which obviously housed the Star Crystal securing the base of the wormhole. I've scanned a large chunk of our history—there were no heroes who fought or worked there. Just the IOD butchers who took the Star Crystal after sacrificing our guards."

Gabriel rubbed his chin, appearing thoughtful. "They may be

the heroes. It depends on which side of the war the author of the document was on. In the eyes of Lucifer and the IOD, the Atlantans who ripped the crystals out to hide them were the heroes."

"That's a good theory, so let's assume they are the heroes," Maya said. "Do you know who they are and where they could be? Maybe that will tell us how they're protecting the secret."

"We're confident the Atlantans who stole the crystal were also the ones who hid the broken pieces around the world, helping to unleash the demons on humans. We only have a guess to their identities. Legend has it that Lucifer sacrificed them, so their secrets would go to the grave," Michael answered.

"But how does a dead man protect the secrets of Hy Brasil? Could it be they were guarding something while they were alive?" Rebecca asked.

"That's possible, or maybe the secret is buried with them in the grave," Maya said.

"I like that theory, but where would the IOD entomb them? And wouldn't Lucifer know the location?" Austin asked.

"Not necessarily, things were chaotic during those times," Gabriel said. "There were a lot of deaths, most of them murders. People were spies, some double spies. I suspect Lucifer didn't kill the Atlantans himself, I don't even think he was there. I'm guessing whoever drafted this document was there and saw the burial. Lucifer may know nothing about it." He paused. "Still leaves the question of where."

Michael said, "I'm betting it's the passage tomb in Ireland, where we found the unusual hieroglyphs that led us to Qitaxa. It was always odd, we never found bodies in the tomb, just the etchings. It all makes sense. They hid the crystals around the world on various continents and subcontinents. Then came together one last time to be sacrificed, leaving a trail of clues at their tomb for the crystals, and eventually one that includes information on Hy Brasil. But why?"

"Could they hide a crystal at the passage tomb?" Austin questioned.

"It's possible, but this feels different." Michael leaned back, contemplating the riddle. "The only way we'll answer this is by going to Ireland." He gave a cautious scan around the table. "I recommend Gabriel, Austin, and Maya go to Abydos. They did the work and understand the information best. This frees Anan, Rebecca, and me to go to Ireland." He finished and turned to Charles. "What do you think?"

"I agree," said Charles. "I don't like these missions so close together but as you said, Lucifer is on the move and October 11 is right around the corner. Connie and I will make the travel arrangements. We'll need no more than three days to get things coordinated." He paused, shaking his head. "I'm still skeptical of Hy Brasil. If it's real, where is it and how is it hidden? Most important, how do you get there?" Peering around the table, he added, "I'll coordinate some time for you at the Trinity Library in Dublin. If any place has history or folklore on it, it'll be there."

"All good questions we'll need to answer," Gabriel said.

"Remember that the island of Atlantis has laid hidden for almost ten thousand years, so it's not unprecedented."

"Yes, good point." Charles gave a heavy exhale. "Does anybody have concerns about the trip? Are you physically ready to go?" Charles glanced to Maya as he spoke.

She was the first to respond. "Never better. I'm good to go."

The rest of the group responded with "yes" or "good."

Rebecca was the last to confirm her reluctant approval with a "fine."

Charles continued, "Good, then it's a plan. I'll get you travel details as soon as I have them. Plan on leaving midweek, most likely Tuesday. Thank you all for your excellent work."

When out of earshot of the others, Maya asked, "Rebecca, you okay? It appeared you wanted to say something when Charles spoke over you."

Rebecca's eyes went wide, clear she was surprised by the observation. "You saw that?"

"Yeah, she saw it and so did I," Austin added.

"What is it?" Maya asked.

Rebecca stepped closer to them. "I hate to say this, but I have a weird feeling about your trip. Like you shouldn't go—or maybe I should be there. I didn't pursue it as I can't articulate why, but the feeling is there. Plus, I'm not sure it would have changed Michael's mind."

Maya put her arm around her friend. "Always, always trust that inner voice. I can't say it would have changed anything, but speak up, they need to hear you. You should know that while there, I'll do everything I can to watch out for Austin. As tough as that can be." She glanced at him, smirking.

"And I'll make sure Maya comes home safe as well," Austin added.

CHAPTER 21

September 30, 2014
Tuesday
London, England

Marou entered the front door and stepped down a worn set of stairs, his associate close behind. They walked into the windowless candlelit basement room with equally dreary furnishings: a solitary wooden table, four faded chairs, and a matted throw carpet that had seen much cleaner days. The room's musty air held the stale reek of incense and clove cigarettes.

Marou glanced around the room. Seeing nothing but a single discolored door, he recognized his destination. As he moved forward, a rustling sound came from behind the door. A deadbolt turned, followed by hinges creaking open. A small, mousy man in disheveled clothes and stinking of alcohol emerged.

"May I help you, gentlemen?"

Marou responded, "We're here for Elijah."

Panic flooded the drunken man's ashen face. "There is no one here by that name, only I, Master Curio, the All-Seeing Eye, psychic, seer, and clairvoyant extraordinaire. I cross to the other side to communicate with the spirits of loved ones." The small man gave an awkward bow.

The Atlantan took a step forward and jerked the mousy man's wrist up and pressed the large silver bracelet adorning it. Master Curio started his transformation. In moments, he was in his Gray form.

Marou let go and addressed the diminutive Atlantan. "Elijah, it's been too long."

Elijah tapped his bracelet again, the transformation back to human form taking only seconds. "What do you want, Marou? And who is he?" Elijah pointed at Marou's traveling companion.

"He's of no concern to you." Marou gave a dismissive wave toward his associate. "Is this what you've become? A carnival act operating in a moldy basement on the bad side of town?"

"I'm happy. It pays the bills, keeps me in liquor and cigarettes, and I don't have to kill anybody." Elijah stared at his old companion. "Speaking of which, how is your psychotic boss?"

Marou's associate stepped toward Elijah. As he did, the candlelight exposed the open sores of a healing burn across his face. Marou put his arm out, stopping the man's menacing advance. "Lucifer is fine. He sends his regards with a message. He needs your help."

"Sorry, I left that business a long time ago," Elijah said.

Marou's tone edged to lethal. "Don't misunderstand, Master

Curio, he's not *requesting*. But if you like, I'll give him that message. I'm sure he'd enjoy coming here to convince you in person."

Elijah's eyes flashed with fear. "Of course not, it never is a request, always a demand." He glanced away, then looked back at his old colleague and his associate. "What does he want?"

Marou smirked. "Much better." He walked over to a small table and picked up the crystal ball that sat in its center, turning it in his hand while staring at its core. "He requests two things. First, he asks that you use your special skill to send a message to a transient that was reaped."

"He knows I can do that. I contact the dead for a living now. And?" Elijah shot back.

Marou raised his focus from the ball and into the eyes of Elijah. "He wishes you to retrieve that specific transient energy from the Well of Souls."

"That's impossible," Elijah scoffed. "It's never been done. Lucifer is insane to even try it." He hesitated, fear creeping back into his eyes. He whispered in an urgent tone, "Marou, consider the havoc that could be inflicted if he has the ability to choose a specific energy to retrieve. He could bring back the most evil transients in the history of the species."

Marou stepped forward again, this time to wrap his free hand around the small man's neck. He applied a slow, steady squeeze. Elijah coughed, choking in response. Marou said, "I like where your head is at. But that's not his intent, he only wants Lilith back for a short time. Can you do that?"

Elijah struggled, nodding his answer. Marou released some pressure but kept his iron grip.

Elijah squealed, "We'll need her energy vibration to extract her. I'll have to do some work to figure out the exact process. A removal is only theoretical. With the reapers, there is no room for error." He paused, getting his full voice back. "And you realize if she's freed, she can't get back into the Well on her own, she'll wander the energy world as a free spirit."

Marou's penetrating stare never wavered. "Yes, we assumed that. Can you do it?" He applied more pressure to reinforce the message before letting up so the small man could respond.

Elijah's words choked out, "Yes, I think so. I can try."

Marou released him.

Elijah massaged his stinging neck. "The difficult part is getting her energy vibration, unless of course you had the wisdom to measure it before."

"We did not."

Elijah continued, "That'll make it difficult . . . but, I think there is a way I can get her out. What's the message for her?"

Marou's words were very precise, "Tell her exactly this: Our time is now, the plans are almost complete. She must leave the Well of Souls."

"Got it. Our time is now, the plans are almost complete. She must leave the Well of Souls." Elijah paused. "What's happening, what is Lucifer up to?"

"I wouldn't tell you even if I knew." Marou paused and stared into the crystal ball, seemingly mesmerized by its center. "Elijah, if you want to stay alive, deliver the message and get her transient out. I'll be back in a week to get an update." As he finished, he launched the crystal into the front wall, shattering it into a thousand shards.

Elijah stared back, emotionless, unmoved by the action. "Tell Lucifer if I do this, I'm out. He leaves me alone—and for good this time."

Marou motioned to his associate to leave before following him to the base of the stairs. He turned, studying his old friend's tired face, "Do this and I'm sure he will. And Elijah, don't try to run. We're watching you, and I'd hate to introduce you to my newest demon pet."

He reached into his pocket and removed a miniature box. Pressing its silver button, a small flap opened. A wasp-sized insect flew out and hovered for a second before flitting over to Elijah. The micro-demon landed on his ear before crawling inside.

Elijah stood frozen in fear, not daring to move as the animal nestled in.

Delighted, Marou watched his old friend's paralysis, then gave a short whistle. The creature responded, taking flight from its hiding spot, it buzzed the air direct to Marou, and landed in the small container. He pressed its flap shut.

Marou gave a wink to Elijah before striding up the stairs and out of the house.

The two men continued down the street to a dark sedan with blacked-out windows. His scarred companion entered the front passenger seat while Marou slipped into the back, sliding in next to Abaddon, who was busy typing a text.

"What did he say?" Abaddon asked.

"He thought it could be done and will start work at once on the solution. Said the process is only theoretical, he needs to figure out how to get her energy vibration." He paused. "I'm not Bernael, I understand some of what he is doing, but not all. I believed him; said I'd return in one week to check on progress."

Abaddon studied his face, "Will he run?"

"Unlikely. It took a little convincing, but he got the message that we'd find him."

"What else?"

"He also said this was it. We leave him alone, no more working for Lucifer."

"Ha," Abaddon peered out of the car window and watched a lone dog walker on the street. "Naive idiot. He should know that when you make a deal with Lucifer, it's for life."

"Are you off to Egypt now?" Marou inquired.

"Yes, Ojater and I have a date with Gabriel and his two human friends at old Abydos." Abaddon continued, "Are you ready for Ireland?"

Marou returned a devilish grin, "Yes, I look forward to seeing Michael again. It's been many years." He leaned forward and patted the shoulder of his associate in the front seat. "And I suspect Joshua is looking forward to his reunion with Ms. Davis."

Joshua turned his gruesome face. "I can't wait to show her my scar."

CHAPTER 22

September 30, 2014
Tuesday
London, England

Elijah climbed the stairs and locked the front door; there'd be no more visitors tonight. He flipped off the small neon sign, the street beacon that guided those desperate enough to search for his services. Once the shades were closed, he returned to the basement and proceeded through the wooden door into the back room. He relocked the deadbolt, ensuring his isolation, then poured a half tumbler of vodka. After downing it in one gulp, he brought a cigarette to his lips, inhaling while holding a flame to its tip. A moment later, his exhale sent a cloud of wispy smoke wafting through the room.

He toked his addiction while considering his options. He could try to run, but with limited resources and a penchant for honest work, he would at some point have to find a job. Which meant it would only be a matter of time before they found him, and then who knows how they'd torture him. Lucifer was, if anything, vengeful. Plus, he believed Marou; he was being followed and the idea of meeting one of the fiend's creatures was equally troubling. He was all too familiar with the sadist's deadly craft. Running wasn't a good choice.

The second alternative was that he could do as requested and perform Lucifer's request without knowing the endgame. This was always dangerous; Lucifer's tasks never ended well. He was sure the humans would suffer, maybe even the remaining Atlantans, and almost certainly him.

His third option was to play the game, buying time while seeing if he could recruit help. Michael or Gabriel would be his best choice. He didn't know their location, but thought he could find them, vaguely recalling some foundation in Arizona. At the least, they could offer some protection, maybe even a place to hide. He was sure they would jump at the opportunity to find Lucifer.

Option three was his best, and really only, chance.

First: buy time. He put out his cigarette then stepped to the narrow cot set in the back of the room. He sat upright on the makeshift bed, filled a shot glass with a black liquor and downed it. Lying back on the smoke-infused mattress, he closed his eyes.

The black liquid began its work at once. His blue transient rose above his body, hovering while gazing upon his human form. He noted his face appeared worn and tired; a condition caused by too many drinks in an attempt to drown the memories of too many dark deeds. His mind flashed to the old days, when they first came to this planet, recalling the hope and optimism he had. Those emotions were crushed long ago—like all the people he cared for—a casualty of the war.

Time to move. His energy accelerated; the psychedelic colors blew by as the sound of the howling wind filled his senses. He traveled for a few moments before halting in the usual spot to gaze outward, never tiring of the view. The sky above shone with billions of specs of starlight, the Universal Energy Stream roared before him, and the Well of Souls radiated out in the distance, flashes of lightning illuminating the rainbow of colors within. He had performed this routine many times for the hopeless, contacting the transient of a deceased loved one, requesting their momentary presence to send a message, possibly receive one in return, all for a small price of course.

He waited, arms out, absorbing the white energy of the Well, basking in its brilliance, enjoying its love while feeling less broken. As he scanned the stars above, a shadowy mist approached, its white eyes glowing with danger. It swooped low and near, circling around him.

Using his telepathic ability to communicate, Elijah spoke a garble of clicks and squeals, the reaper's language. "Hello again my friend, it's good to see you." He held out his hand, and a burst of his blue energy shot into the black mist.

The creature didn't speak back, its black smoky body fluttered happily in response, circling closer than before, seeming to enjoy the energy surge.

"I need your help once more. There is a red transient present in the dark area of the Well. I need to speak with her. Her name in life was Lilith, an Atlantan with a powerful energy."

Once more the reaper dove toward Elijah before bolting into the darkened side of the Well. Elijah studied the large cloud-like object, waiting for the creature's response.

He didn't wait long. The reaper came screaming out of the energy mass, its black nebulous body surrounding a dark-red orb. It cruised directly to Elijah's energy, stopping feet away. The black mist dematerialized away from the crimson energy, leaving it floating in front of Elijah's transient. The reaper wafted up, hovering nearby while the red orb dissipated into a hazy figure of a woman. As it coalesced, Elijah heard a clear message, "I am Lilith, who are you and what do you want?"

"Lilith it's me, Elijah. I come with a message from Lucifer."

The red mist swirled like the wind in a tornado. "What message does my master send?"

"That your time is now, plans are almost complete. You must soon leave the Well of Souls."

A wailing cry came in answer. "Please, take me now, the pain is unbearable, my sorrow all-consuming." Her transient started toward him.

"Lilith, stop!" he screamed.

The reaper floated down toward her red energy, an unnatural screech pulsating from the black mist.

"Don't move, the reaper will consume your energy, returning

you. There is no escaping it, not now, not yet."

Lilith arrested her progress, but the Well's keeper still appeared agitated, hovering nearby, keeping its careful view and proximity.

Elijah spoke to the reaper in its unusual language. "I'm sorry, my friend, this is her first time here, she will return with you in one moment. I thank you for your patience." He lowered his head in respect to the creature.

The black mist gave no verbal answer but withdrew a short distance, signaling its temporary approval.

Elijah spoke once more to Lilith, "I need to know your energy vibration to get you out. Was it ever measured or photographed?"

"Long ago it was measured in Atlantis. I fear it is long lost. But there may be another way."

"Go on." A sense of hope welled in him.

"Before my reaping, I possessed a woman named Amaya Luna during Bernael's resurrection process. She was traveling with a man named Austin. I heard him say Michael and Gabriel were on their way. My transient energy enmeshed with hers. Find her transient and you can measure my energy vibration."

Elijah considered the situation. "When I find Michael or Gabriel, I'll find Amaya and within her, your energy. That—that is perfect!" The reaper drifted down. "I'm sorry Lilith, but our time is up. I'll return as soon as possible. Be ready."

As the reaper enveloped her energy, she shrieked one word, "Nooo!"

The black mist growled as it darted away. Elijah hovered,

mesmerized as the creature plunged back into the Well of Souls. He took one last scan of his surreal surroundings before flashing back to his basement home, the light and roaring wind escorting him during the journey.

He opened his eyes. His body felt rested and for the first time in a while, his mind calm. He needed to find Michael and Gabriel, then maybe this madness would be over, forever.

CHAPTER 23

September 30, 2014
Tuesday
Tucson, Arizona

Maya sat in the back seat of Austin's car on the way to the airport, listening to him talk to his mother on the phone.

"Yes, will do, Mom, I'll be safe. And same for you, just keep a careful eye open when you're out and about." Austin listened, phone pressed against his ear. "Yes, Maya will be with me. Yes, I'll tell her and Rebecca you say hello and to be safe." He paused, "Yep, I love you too, Mom. I promise I'll visit when I get back. Take care, bye."

Austin glanced to Rebecca next to him, then Maya in the rearview mirror. "Sorry about that, but I wanted to check in with her before we left. I was a little concerned about her going into hiding. She says hello to you both."

Maya smiled. Austin was lucky to know a mother's love, a caring that many people take for granted until it's too late. Something she had never known but always wished for. She appreciated the thoughtful message directed to her.

"She okay?" Rebecca asked.

"Yeah, I think she's fine, although maybe a little scared. Said she wanted to hear my voice before I left. I think assignments make her nervous—understandably so."

Austin put the car in park then turned off the engine. Maya felt the bothersome sensation of being a third wheel. He faced Rebecca before turning around to her. "You two ready to go? It's going to be a long night."

"Not really," Rebecca answered with a frown. "I hate these east-bound flights, you get there midmorning, then fight all day to stay awake. I really hope I can sleep on the plane."

Maya remained silent, opening the door as her response.

Austin stepped out, popped the trunk hatch, and pulled out three backpacks. Two were more heavily laden, the smaller one was far less packed—he handed that bag to Rebecca. Maya and Austin shouldered their packs.

As they walked to the terminal, Rebecca turned to her, "Everything okay, Maya? You've been quiet."

Maya debated how much to share. "I'm fine, thanks. A little anxious about getting in the air; these overnight flights also make me antsy." Maya forced a smile. "How about you? Excited for shamrocks and leprechauns?"

Rebecca shrugged, "Mmmm, wish I was going with you guys, but oh well. I understand Ireland is nice this time of year."

"Yeah, nice, cold, and windy," Austin chuckled.

They walked into the private terminal of the Tucson airport, and after a cursory security check, they went straight through the back door to the tarmac where two private jets were positioned side by side. Each had its doorway down and luggage compartment open. Michael and Gabriel stood nearby. Charles and Anan were exiting the closest plane. Dusk was setting in, the afternoon shadows growing long.

Charles greeted the three of them. "Oh good, you're here." He reached into his pack. "I've got something for you, Maya. I came across this from a friend in the defense world and thought you may need it." He walked over, handing her a small binocular-like device.

"What is it?" she asked.

"That is an energy spectrometer, or ESpec. It identifies the energy of people or things from a distance. Think of it as an energy stone on steroids."

She took the device. "Cool, thank you! And how does it work?"

Charles responded, "Just hold it up and look through it, like binoculars. The only downside is you have to have a line of sight for it to be effective. Unlike energy stones which can pick up any energy radiating around you."

Maya brought the ESpec up to her eyes and peered at Austin. All she saw was a magnified version of him. "I don't see Austin's energy."

Charles added, "You need to turn it on. Switch is on the left side."

Maya did as instructed before staring through the lenses again.

This time, centered in his gray torso was Austin's bright blueish-yellow aura. Maya noted his energy had darkened toward the purple of Gabriel and Michael, his spiritual development progressing well. She read the upper right portion of the viewer, where the meter showed Wavelength (447.0065), Frequency (672.1218).

Maya replied, "This is great. Assume the wavelength and frequency reflect the light's tone?"

Charles motioned to Maya. "Correct. Now, try pressing the control switch on the right side."

She again focused on Austin, pressing down on the small rectangular button. She heard a click just before a picture filled her frame of vision. The photo lasted for a few seconds before vanishing to the storage card in the device.

"It also has a camera function. Just in case you need to document someone's energy. It's like taking a fingerprint: each person's energy is unique. Austin has his energy stone, and now you have this," Charles said.

While Maya fiddled with the ESpec, Charles stepped over to Rebecca. "I have something for you too." He pulled out and handed her a military knife with a six-inch blade, one side serrated, the opposite a razor edge. "I hope you only have to use this as a tool and not in self-defense. But a good knife is a prudent thing to have while in the field."

"Thank you." She pulled the knife from the sheath, feeling its weight, then examined the blade before shoving it back in. "It's rugged! Appreciate it, I'll keep it with me."

Michael interjected, "Charles, we have to go. Flight plan has us out in fifteen minutes."

At that moment, the pilot of the plane stuck her head out. "All aboard, wheels up in fifteen."

Charles acknowledged the woman with a wave before turning back to Michael. "Don't forget, the Trinity Library is expecting you."

"Now," he said to the crowd, "we'll meet everybody back here in no more than a week. Be safe, call our number if you need anything. Somebody will be available twenty-four-seven. And please check in daily if you can. Keep the message short."

Maya watched as Rebecca slipped over to Austin. She appeared troubled as she locked her arms around his neck, squeezing him hard. After releasing him, she whispered loud enough for Maya to hear, "Be careful, and I want details about the pyramids when you get back." Stepping away, she gave a flirtatious wave. "Take pictures!"

Austin waved back. "You be safe as well. Good luck finding the secret to Hy Brasil. And try to enjoy the Emerald Isle!"

Rebecca turned to Maya and Gabriel and waved, mouthing the words, "Be safe."

Maya reciprocated with a short wave. "I will, and you too."

Gabriel raised an eyebrow at Maya as the group heading to Ireland closed the plane door. "She's a nice person—fun to be around and very intelligent."

Maya met his eye, giving him a strained look. "Are you in my head now?"

He shrugged. "No, but I can sense your tension. I'm guessing it has to do with her." He paused, giving a short nod to Austin. "And him."

Maya realized she was biting her lower lip; she released the pressure. "I don't know what it is. Seems like I'm always angry now, similar to the old days during military missions. I'm on edge, and it's all the time." She sighed. "And to be honest, I'm not sure what I want anymore."

Gabriel's eyes lit up. His hand touched her lower back; she could feel his positive energy radiating from his fingertips. "Have faith, my friend. I've learned things happen for a reason. In the end, it'll all work out. I promise."

Believing him, she said calmly, "I know. Thank you for reminding me."

Austin removed a book from his backpack, then tossed the pack into the luggage well. "Ready to go."

"Let's move, the pilot is waiting for us," Gabriel said.

Gabriel sat across the aisle from Maya while Austin sat in the single seat in front of him. A few minutes later, they were speeding down the runway. They felt the familiar shake of the plane as they rose off the ground. Gabriel pulled out a pile of papers. "Did you have time to go through Michael's notes on Abydos?"

"Yes, it was a good read, very informative," Maya answered.

"He seems worried this may be a trap," Austin added.

"As am I. Was it luck Michael got the documents in New Orleans, or a plan? The whole betrayal with Mack has cast a shadow on a lot of things. It's as though the IOD has been one step in front of us the whole time," Gabriel said.

"I agree, we were lucky in Qitaxa," Maya said. "If Austin hadn't woken to stop the IOD from planting that tracker in El Remete, we'd all be dead and rotting in the jungle now. Not to mention, if he's just a few minutes later in the Chupacabra's den, I might not be having this conversation."

"We were fortunate, but you two were also smart and tough. You created your own luck in Guatemala and Sedona," Gabriel said.

"I agree with that, Maya's shooting in the jungle and in Bernael's warehouse saved both of our lives. That wasn't luck," Austin added.

At first Maya was uncomfortable with the mention of those memories, but then a surge of power welled within her. It had felt good to be judge, jury, and executioner.

Gabriel seemed to notice. He asked, "The other day you asked a question about our plans if and when we get the six crystal pieces. Why did you ask that?"

Maya's eyes darted to Austin. "I don't know. It just dawned on me that we were getting close, and I wondered what would happen." She paused. "I guess a part of me is worried you'll be leaving us."

"The thought has crossed my mind as well," Austin said. "I'm glad she asked."

Gabriel hesitated before speaking, studying Maya's face. "It's a fair question, one that we can't fully answer. The only thing I can say is Atla will send help, but we're not sure in what form."

"I can understand that. It has been so long; a lot could have happened." Maya pursed her lips.

"All will be well when that beautiful day arises," Gabriel said. "Can I play with your new toy?"

"Sure, here you go." Maya handed him the ESpec.

He raised it, viewing her energy. "Ah, I can see the real you." He pressed the button on the side. Maya heard the click of the picture being taken.

He handed the device back to her. "Your energy's image was just captured for eternity."

Maya peered in the viewer, her aura framed in its center. She studied it, noticing an almost imperceptible crimson haze at the center of her torso surrounded by radiant blue. She blinked a few times, then dismissed it. The lighting in the plane must be bad.

Austin interrupted her thoughts. "When you're done, can I see the pictures?"

"Of course." Maya reached across the aisle, handing him the machine.

"This is awesome. Your aura is such a deep blue, almost indigo," he replied.

"Yes, her energy is radiant. Press the button again to toggle through the two pictures. You'll find your aura in there," Gabriel said.

Austin did as instructed. His yellowish-blue energy came into focus. After a moment examining it, he said, "Guess I still need to work on my spiritual side."

"I see progress there. Can you make out the blue hues?" Maya said.

"It's a journey, Austin, and Maya's right, you're trending in the right direction," Gabriel added.

Austin handed the ESpec back to her. "Well, I hope someday to be as balanced as you and Michael are." He yawned as he finished. "But right after I get a little shut-eye." He reclined his chair, moving his head back while covering himself with a blanket.

Maya joked, "We'll keep the party noise down back here." Austin gave a thumbs-up as he closed his eyes.

Maya reached behind her seat and turned off the cabin lights.

Gabriel turned on his small reading light and began thumbing through his papers. Maya took out her book and turned on her own light.

They flew in calm skies for over an hour when Gabriel whispered, "Do you want to talk?"

Maya shrugged, recognizing there was no use pretending she wasn't thinking about Austin. She knew Gabriel could sense her heartache. She peeked over at Austin. Eyes twitching, he was deep in sleep.

"Where should we start?" she asked.

Gabriel answered, "Let's start with an easy one. Why don't you tell him how you feel?"

Maya turned to him, eyes throwing daggers, "That's not an easy one and you know it."

Gabriel gave a soft laugh. "Now you know how I feel when you ask questions." He paused. "Okay, then let's start with a hard one. Why don't you tell him how you feel?"

She glanced away, a feeling of vulnerability washing through her; it was foreign and uncomfortable. "Because part of me—I mean, all of me—doesn't believe it will help."

"Why not?"

"Because in my heart, I truly want him to be happy. And he's better off with her. You said it, she's smart, pretty, and nice, with no baggage. She can offer him a different life than I can. A better life."

Gabriel hesitated before answering. "Shouldn't *he* determine what makes him happy and not you? It is his life, after all."

"In a normal situation, I'd say yes. But not when you're dealing with a relationship and me. You know enough of my history in the Army, things have a way of dying around me," Maya said.

Gabriel considered her words. "All of the people and things that died due to you deserved that fate. They were evil—masquerading as human. I've seen your energy many times. It's pure; you did mankind a service with your actions, and you need to own that and believe it in your heart." He stared deep into her eyes. "You said Rebecca can offer him a different life than you, how so?"

It was Maya's turn to reflect, the pain of facing her innermost demons all too real. "To be perfectly honest, can you imagine us as a couple walking into a PTA meeting at school with our little Junior? 'Hi, I'm Dr. Austin Denton, this is little Tommy, and this is my wife, Maya. She has seventeen confirmed kills as Special Ops in Iraq, can handle an AR-15, and butcher a wild pig in just minutes.'" She glanced away, her eyes stinging. "I'm sorry, but I can't see that life for him . . . with me."

Gabriel gave another soft laugh. "That's funny." He studied her, as if seeing through her fears to the person she was. "I now understand your baggage." He sat up to better see her teary eyes, and took her hand. She found the gesture comforting, feeling the sincerity in his words. "I can see you attending a PTA meeting. And I see you as a great wife and a great mother. To be honest, I can imagine you doing anything you want." He paused. "Maya, your past does not define your future—it does not define who you are. Your past only defines who you were. It's you, Maya, who is preventing you from being happy. Follow your heart. If you want to be an astronaut, go be one. If you want to have a relationship with Austin, to know what it is like to love and be loved, then go do it. And work as hard on that as you did to excel as a soldier." His eyes were reassuring. "Understand, there is no guarantee how it'll work out in the long term, there's always the risk of being hurt. But in my opinion, the only real failure would be not going after what your soul desires." He glanced to Austin. "I suspect he'd welcome your change of heart." He let go of her hand, and leaning back as he finished, he gave a subtle laugh. "Not that I read his mind or anything."

Maya gave a shy smile in response. She reached over, taking his hand once more, embracing its positive energy flow. She breathed in the moment, feeling almost normal for the first time since Sedona. "Thank you, Gabriel. You're a good person and I know you're right. Guess I need to reflect on what I want in life."

She pulled away and turned off her reading light. And for the first time in a long time, the demons cleared from her mind. She drifted off to sleep in peace.

CHAPTER 24

October 2, 2014
Thursday
Slieve Bloom Mountains, Ireland

The Land Rover bounced along the narrow, two-lane country road. Anan drove while Michael studied a local map on his tablet. Nestled in the backseat, Rebecca thought about their day at the Trinity College Library in Dublin researching information on Hy Brasil and the heroes of Amaru. Beyond a few benign references buried in dusty, arcane texts, there was little new information found. Michael and Anan had stepped out for a brief meeting with a government contact but had also come up empty. After a hearty meal and a good night's sleep, they were now on the trip to the passage tomb in central Ireland.

They'd been driving on the Irish roads for almost two harrowing hours. Old Irish cart paths were paved long ago into the streets they now traveled. The narrow and sunken roads were lined by stone walls, acting as indestructible guard rails. The locals drove with both passion and speed, making the trip feel close to lethal at least a few times.

Rebecca hoped they were getting close to their destination.

"Take a left up here; the road is kind of hidden and I think it gets tight," Michael said.

As usual, he was correct. The two-lane road soon turned to a dirt path, climbing deep into the western side of the Slieve Bloom Mountains. They continued on, through rolling pastures and groupings of hardwood trees.

They passed a mostly collapsed castle. "We're getting close, that's the shell of the old Ballydunn Castle," Rebecca said. "It was built in the thirteenth century. I read speculation that people built the castle near the passage tomb, as they thought the site was a mystical energy source."

Anan peeked in the rearview mirror, catching Rebecca's eye. "I read the same thing. Wouldn't surprise me. The passage tomb predates the castle by thousands of years. I'm sure the castle residents thought the gods built it and wanted their protection."

"Have you been here before?" Rebecca asked.

"I have not. I've spent most of the last few years in China and Japan; this is a fairly recent find," Anan answered.

"I have," Michael said, "although it was just after the place was discovered. I'm told it's been cleaned up and repaired where needed. Also, we added security systems to ensure only the right people have access. The information in the hieroglyphs is unique and dangerous."

"What kind of security do we need to get through to get in?" Anan asked.

"No guards, but Charles has installed some high-tech gates and fences. Since we discovered the site last year, we've worked hard to keep the area secret, protecting it from vandals and treasure hunters. We're fortunate that it's so remote."

"Why is it so remote? Why build a tomb way out here?" Rebecca asked.

"All I have is a theory." Michael shifted in his seat to see her better. "I think when constructed thousands of years ago, the area was isolated; only a few primitive humans were on the entire island. And if this place is what I think it is, meaning Atlantan in origin, getting here wasn't a huge issue for us. We had—I mean have—flying craft. It would have been easy for the IOD to hop over from anywhere, bury whatever secrets they had, and get out."

"That makes sense. So, you have flying craft? Do you still use them?" Rebecca asked.

"We still have them, but don't use them much. A few need repairs, and with human technology advancing, it's far more difficult to keep them hidden in the air from radar. Thus, we take conventional travel unless there is some kind of emergency."

Anan slowed the car and rolled to a stop at the stone-lined end of the road. "We made it. It's on foot from here."

They exited the vehicle, shouldering their light packs. Given the nature of the trip and the ease of travel in, most of their tools and supplies would stay in the car, to be retrieved only if needed.

Rebecca holstered her gun, then belted the knife sheath. Michael and Anan kept their laser weapons secure in their front pouches.

Michael stepped forward. "This way, single file behind me, so we don't trigger alarms or defenses."

Rebecca zipped her coat tight, giving her some protection against the biting wind.

They hiked a circuitous route along a large wall of natural boulders, backtracking toward Ballydunn Castle. They had walked almost thirty minutes when they came to their first "No Trespassing" sign, hung on a barbed wire fence. Michael walked to the reinforced gate, flipped a hidden switch on its backside, then inserted a key into the thick, solid metal lock.

"Step one, disarm the gate alarm before opening the titanium lock." He gave an untypical grin to Rebecca.

They entered the protected area and Michael closed and locked the gate behind them. They walked a few more minutes along a small dirt path before they came to an even higher, sturdier fence that included razor coils at the top.

Rebecca commented, "Wow, I've seen maximum security prisons with less threatening barriers."

Anan laughed. "What happens if we trigger an alarm?"

"I don't want to find out, but sirens are supposed to go off and pressure sensitive stun grenades buried in the ground become armed. If I know Charles's overzealous planning, probably tranquilizer darts and an oversized anvil falls on you," Michael joked. He placed his hand on a solar-powered scanning plate. "Seriously though, we have an early warning camera system and a security company on call with helicopters for emergencies." The plate glowed while reading his palm. The loud popping of the lock ensued, confirming success.

They continued up a short mound. When they reached the top, the grassed land dropped gently into a small bowl-like area which then elevated into a larger hill beyond. In the middle of that rise, a rectangular doorway lined by white stone blocks indicated the entrance to the tomb. In front of the door, three large stones stood vertically, half-buried in the ground, like sentinels guarding the front gate. Each boulder was adorned with ornate etchings that formed a series of grooved circular designs in each.

"These are the entrance stones, intended as a warning to any who approached to stay away. This was a sacred place," Michael said.

"This area has really been cleaned up since the old photos that I saw were taken. It was when the tomb was first rediscovered and was pretty overgrown. It's practically manicured now," Rebecca replied.

Michael walked past the carved sentinels to the stone-lined entryway. It had been modified from its original design, with a solid metal door now blocking the path in. He approached the door. This time, he positioned his right eye in front of a retina scanner. The laser flashed, resulting in the lock popping.

"We're in. Just a reminder to be aware. I don't expect any issues, but . . ."

The midday sun peaked overhead, reflecting only a short way

down the entry corridor. Rebecca followed Michael through the shadows into darkness. Searching in her pack, she removed the flashlight and turned it on. The wide passage was framed with tall rectangular stones on each side. Its floor was covered in round river stones, then packed down with dirt. The ceiling was a polished rock slab that connected the two sidewall stones over their heads. It was obvious: repairs had been completed when reopening the chamber.

"The design of the passage tomb was such that on the winter solstice, sunlight would radiate up this corridor and into the inner chamber. We could use a little of that light now." Anan spoke in a low tone.

"Agreed, if only for warmth." Rebecca paused, studying the rock walls. "I read this tomb was even larger than Newgrange. Do you think this was the model Newgrange followed?" Rebecca whispered.

In the shadows, she could see Michael glance back as he inched forward. "This predates the Newgrange passage tomb by a few thousand years. I'm betting it was the prototype. But how they acquired the design is beyond me. The only man-made disturbance we saw to this tomb was done by the people who built the castle, and that was well after Newgrange's construction."

They paced slowly through the angled passageway. Anan kept a close watch on their back. Once they entered into the main chamber, Michael stopped. Rebecca and Anan squeezed by him on either side, flashing their lights around the room.

Circular in design, the walls were block stone built up to create a domed structure. The floor was hard-packed dirt. On the wall opposite the entry passageway, a polished metallic disk was mounted to the rock. Anan shined his flashlight into it. The beam reflected onto a flat stone embedded in the center of the chamber's floor. Rebecca stepped in farther, passing Michael.

"What are these?" She shined her light on six oblong stones set into the ground circling the center rock. Each boulder was carved with hieroglyphs, top to bottom.

"Those etchings are the glyphs that led us to Guatemala," Michael explained. "We've been able to decipher three of them, the one leading us to the crystal in Qitaxa; the Roswell cave; and the one from the Minotaur's Labyrinth on Crete. We're speculating the other three are Japan, India, and Abydos. It seems the IOD scattered the various pieces of the Star Crystal around the world and hid them in remote places. Since we've retrieved the Qitaxa, Roswell, and Crete pieces, we've confirmed the descriptions are accurate. We believe two of these would indicate Japan and India. The sixth piece is the only question mark. It's unfortunate we haven't been able to translate all of the glyphs."

"We should know soon enough if Abydos is the location of the last piece," Anan said.

The three spread out through the room. "Any guesses as to what we're searching for?" Rebecca asked.

"No," Michael said. "Look for anything that may give us a hint of a tomb, Hy Brasil, or the Heroes of Amaru."

They walked the entire room, first covering walls and ceiling, then moving to the floor. Nothing jumped out as unusual or as a clue.

"Let's walk through it once more. I feel like we're missing something," Michael said.

While the two Atlantans tapped wall rocks and peered around the metal disk, Rebecca focused on the floor's center stone. Embedded flat into the ground, its circular surface was milled smooth with white stone blocks forming a tight edge around it, giving it a manhole cover appearance.

She stepped across the room to the chamber's entrance, once more shooting her light on the wall's metallic disk. Again, the beam reflected to highlight the center stone. She studied the center rock's surface, rubbing her fingertips across the smooth top. It was there, albeit ever so subtle, she felt a circular ridge invisible in the light but revealed by her touch. She moved to her knees, lowering her face inches from the stone and bringing her light to an equal distance.

"Hey guys, I think I've got something. Anan said on the winter solstice the sun would shine into this chamber. Wouldn't the sunlight have hit the mirror on the wall and highlighted this center stone?"

Michael stepped over, squatting down, adding his light to hers. Anan followed. With their combined beams, a faint, jagged circle carved in the rock face was just evident.

"What are you thinking?" Anan asked.

Rebecca answered, "It's an irregular circular shape. I'm thinking it's a diagram of an island."

Michael flashed his light up, illuminating his own features. His eyes were wide with recognition. "That is a brilliant thought. Help me with the stone."

Rebecca pulled her knife and began scraping years of packed dirt from between the edge of the center stone and the surrounding ring. Anan and Michael joined in. Once clear, Rebecca placed the hardened knife blade between the two rocks but struggled to pry the center piece up.

Michael made a polite offer. "May I try?"

"Please, be my guest."

Michael centered his weight then leaned into his pull. The stone shifted before prying up. He slid the blade deeper under the rock face.

Anan flashed a grin at Rebecca. "You must have loosened it for him."

"Yeah, I'm sure I did," she chuckled.

With a little more work, they managed to get their fingers under the milled rock, allowing them to roll it out of the retaining blocks like a sewer lid. When done, they peered into a black hole that opened into a lower room. A blast of musty air wafted up to them.

"I don't remember reading anything about a subchamber here," Rebecca said.

"There was none found," Michael declared.

Anan stooped, placing his light inside the hole. He peered into its darkness, rotating his beam around to view all sides. "Definitely seems like a new find; doesn't appear anyone has been down there."

He paused, studying the area. "Tough to gauge the drop, but I'm guessing only ten to twelve feet."

Michael reached into his pack. Pulling out a thin coil of rope, he tied it around the base of the closest hieroglyph marker. "I'll go down first. Rebecca next, and Anan, you're last. Wait for my signal before you come down." He peered into the darkness below, concern heavy on his brow. "I sense an evil energy present, so weapons ready."

"I sense it, but it doesn't feel like a demon," Rebecca added.

Anan gave a wink. "You really are a quick study."

Rebecca sheathed her knife, then fed the first bullet into her gun. Michael stuffed his flashlight into his back pocket before grabbing the rope. He shimmied down, sliding carefully into the black hole. A few seconds later the rope fell slack when he had reached the subchamber floor. Rebecca and Anan watched through the hole. Michael's flashlight rotated in a complete circle. After a few anxious seconds, he called up, "It's clear."

"Your turn, you got it?" Anan asked.

"No problem, I've been climbing my whole life."

She clutched the rope, sliding feet first into the short tube that quickly opened into the larger chamber. Making easy work of her descent into the lower room, she hit the floor in half the time it took Michael.

Rebecca called up, "Clear."

Repeating the process, Anan shimmied down the rope.

The three stood back-to-back, studying their surroundings.

The room was smaller, but constructed similarly to the hall above with one notable difference. On the floor, placed in a symmetric pattern, lay seven rectangular stone boxes, each about six feet long. Three lay on each side of the room, with the largest, most ornate one centered in the middle, creating a separating barrier between the two groups.

Rebecca stumbled as she touched the closest stone box. "What—what are these?" she asked, knowing the answer in her heart.

"I think these are what's left of the Heroes of Amaru," Michael responded.

Anan stepped to the nearest coffin. "Michael, it's our language. This reads, 'Phenex.'"

Michael had already swiped the covering dust of the nearest casket; he was reading similar text. "This says, 'Sytri.'"

"Did you know them?" Rebecca asked.

"They were Atlantans, followers of Lucifer. And yes, we knew them well." Michael's voice was cold, showing no emotion for these lost Atlantans.

"These were the brutal seven who ripped out the crystal, slaughtered their own kind, then hid the pieces around the world." Anan heaved to push the stone lid off the coffin. It held firm for a second but finally ground open in begrudging fashion, reluctant to reveal its long-hidden secrets.

In the casket's base lay the cloaked, dull white bones of a human-like skeleton, untouched and unmoved for thousands of years. Rebecca crouched lower, shining her light, exposing the skull. It was larger, with a fuller forehead than a human's—typical of an Atlantan. She was surprised the skull was not near the neck but situated as if being held by the hands of the skeleton.

"What do you make of this?"

"Decapitated," Michael answered. "An honorable death. The seven were aware they would be sacrificed and probably agreed to die that way in a mistaken belief it strengthened their transient energy for the next life. It doesn't."

"We found the heroes, now what are they guarding?" Anan asked.

"I'm not sure," Michael said. "Check the engravings on the tombs, maybe there's a clue on it."

Anan and Michael examined the lids and sides of the closest caskets.

Rebecca motioned to the center tomb. "This one is in the center. Is he somebody important? And if he is, would he be guarding the secret?"

"This would be Azazel, their leader," Michael said.

Lighting the coffin lid, he read the chiseled inscription. From his reaction, he saw nothing obvious. Bending down, he strained to remove the cover. It resisted for a moment, then gave. He continued to push until the lid toppled off, exposing the entire casket's contents. Similar to Phenex's casket, an Atlantan skeleton lay intact except for the head, which again sat on its midsection. Rebecca at once saw two notable differences from the first casket. First, there were the decayed remnants of an ornamental robe still visible, its fibers faded into a powdery dust. Second, there was a small stone tablet nestled on its right arm.

Michael reached in to remove the square rock, examining its front before turning it sideways to brush away centuries of dirt. Once cleaned, he lit the tablet with his beam. There were four squares of equal size etched into the block with some remnants of a color or dye.

The upper left square showed a map of what appeared to be Ireland and off to the southwest, a second, much smaller island. The upper right square depicted a castle behind a sunset. In front of the castle, there seemed to be a small, stone well. The lower left square wasn't clear, illustrating what was either a ladder or some lettering from an old forgotten language. The last quadrant shown a circular cloud painted with rainbows.

Michael flipped the tablet over. The back side was chiseled with lettering Rebecca could not identify.

"What does it mean?" she asked.

"I'm not sure. It's clear the first square is a map. I'm betting that's the location of Hy Brasil in relation to Ireland. The other three squares, I don't know. Michael turned the tablet over again. "This side is a passage in our old language: *Fulfilling our task, we found the Path, the secret now travels with our transients.*" He paused. "'The Path'? What that means, I can only guess."

Anan added, "Azazel was close to Lucifer, maybe 'the Path' was the plan to hide the crystal or release the demon horde."

Rebecca pulled out her cell phone. "Do you mind if I photograph it? This way I can study it without having to handle it."

Michael's brow furrowed as he considered the question. "I'm going to say okay, with one strict condition: Be very careful with the pictures. No one else sees them; this information must be controlled. We don't yet know what the puzzle means, and more importantly, we're sure Lucifer will kill for the information."

"I understand. Once home, I'll upload them to a safe device, then destroy these."

Michael placed the square flat on the ground, then lit it up with his flashlight. Rebecca snapped six photos. The first was the entire tablet, and then a close-up of each square, finishing with one of the flip side. She checked each picture before stuffing the phone back in her pocket. When done, Michael wrapped the stone in a cloth and placed it in his pack.

"We'll study this in a lab," Michael said.

Anan moved to the next undisturbed casket. Pushing its lid off, it broke as it fell.

Rebecca asked, "What are you doing?"

"Being prudent. We need to be sure this is the only clue. We should check the others and confirm there's nothing else here."

"Got it," Rebecca said.

Each person strained to remove an unopened lid, Anan doing the last tomb as well. They found nothing else unusual, only dry bones covered with a musty stench of death.

As they finished searching the graves, Rebecca considered how each Atlantan buried here had volunteered to sacrifice their living energy for the information they held. The Heroes of Amaru were murdered in ritualistic fashion, placed in the coffin, then sealed in this tomb for what they thought was eternity, all for the sake of Lucifer, his cause, and the promise of strength to their transients. It was, by definition, insane.

"I suspect that's it; there are no doors or secret alcoves," Michael said. "To be safe, we'll have a team come back to scour the site under better lighting. Let's get out of here."

Making their way to the rope, Anan said, "Rebecca first, I'll help you up. Michael second, and I'll do the climb."

Rebecca grabbed the cord, starting the short climb out, while Anan lifted her by the legs, pushing her feet up and helping her exit. She pulled herself up and through with ease.

Once out, she turned to offer Michael help up. She heard a shuffle from behind, then a hand locked across her mouth, stifling her breath. Her gun was ripped from its holster and clattered to the ground. She started a muffled scream when a knife was placed to her neck, silencing her.

As she struggled for freedom, a familiar voice hissed in her ear, "Remember me, you lying bitch?"

Restrained and unable to see her attacker, she struggled and was unable to warn Michael as he climbed up the rope. Someone grabbed him, dragging him away from the hole. As Anan climbed out, it was clear he knew something was amiss. He pulled himself out of the shadowy hole and took to a fighting stance. A light flashed on, and Marou stood with a gun to Michael's head.

"Calm down, Anan, you don't want to get Michael killed," he ordered.

The hardened Atlantan gritted his teeth, "I'm calm. Put down the gun, we can talk." He took a quick step toward Marou.

Boom!

The gunshot ripped through the chamber, exploding into the sidewall.

Anan froze. Rebecca feared the worst, and was relieved to see that Michael was still standing.

Marou threatened him, "That was your only warning. The next one won't miss." He pushed Michael toward Anan and pointed the gun at both.

"Are you okay, Rebecca?" Michael asked.

Marou made a motion with his head, and her captor released his grip on her mouth. "I'm fine," she said shakily.

As she finished, the raspy voice whispered in her ear, "Not for long."

Marou continued, "There's somebody here who wants to have a private word." He reached into his coat pocket. Removing a small box, he pressed the silver button on top. The front lid opened. A large flying insect emerged and took flight. It flew straight to Michael, hovering for a moment before blasting a stinger out of its abdomen. Michael swatted, missing the creature as the needle embedded in his neck. He collapsed at once, limbs convulsing spastically.

The wasp flew quickly and shot a stinger toward Anan, who unsuccessfully tried to block the injection with his pack. The stinger rooted in Anan's neck. As he hit the ground, the bug returned to the box in its master's hand.

Marou shut the lid and slipped the device safely away. He grabbed Michael by the shirt and dragged him a few feet across the floor, placing him in a sitting position against a hieroglyph stone. He repeated the process for Anan.

Rebecca's attacker spun her around and slammed her against the stone wall, an audible "hmmph" coming from her chest as a sharp pain seared through her back. She had her first glimpse of his contorted face and didn't recognize the man.

Grinding his body against hers, he thrust his pelvis repeatedly while crushing her neck with his vise-like grip. Releasing some of the force, the attacker moved his free hand down, groping her upper thighs. She tried pushing, then punching him, but his hold was locked in, and her senses were beginning to fade. Then he stopped. His eyes locked on her face, and his hand released the pressure of his asphyxiating grip. "Do you even know who I am?"

Trembling with fear, she shook her head and sputtered, "N-no."

He raised his light, flashing it onto his injured face. "How about now?"

Rebecca gasped as Joshua's scarred features came into focus. She trembled, "No . . . you were dead . . . the Whisperer had you. We heard you fall, then the demon attacked."

"Not dead, only possessed! I fell into a lava tunnel where I got this pretty scar. The Whisperer left me when I was unconscious. Like you had left me for dead," he hissed.

Rebecca mouthed, "I'm sorry," but the words couldn't come as Joshua retightened his clasp.

Holding her pinned to the wall, one hand on her throat, he leaned in and licked her lips. "You like that, don't you!"

Despite her fear, Rebecca sensed a new malevolent energy in the chamber. Joshua halted his assault as a man entered. Tall with black hair in a dark suit, the man paused near them.

Lucifer's black eyes penetrated into her soul. "I remember your face from my warehouse in Sedona. You killed my servant, my friend."

He took a casual step away, continuing deeper into the room, stopping only to observe the layout of the tomb. He walked toward the two Atlantans paralyzed on the floor, lying limp against the stone.

As he approached, he spoke calmly to Marou. "Is it safe?"

"Oh yes, my new creature worked to perfection. They'll be like this for quite a while."

Lucifer said, "And they can understand me?"

"Yes, they're fully conscious, but immobile."

"Good, thank you." Lucifer continued over, settling close to Michael, squatting down to look his old commander in the eyes. "Once again we meet. I'm sorry about this. For all of our differences, we do have a history, and I hate to see you in pain." He reached over, gently straightening Michael's body to a more comfortable position. "Did you find the information to locate Hy Brasil?"

Marou answered, "I haven't checked his pack. But they discovered a subchamber; they were exiting when we came in."

Lucifer continued, "Interesting, let's see what you have in these bags." He stepped to Anan's first, opening it. Finding only a rope, a knife, his flashlight, and some water, he tossed the bag into the black hole, landing with a crack on the subchamber's floor. He moved to Michael's next and unzipped the main pocket. He pulled out the heavy cloth-wrapped tablet. Removing the material, he commanded, "Light."

Marou scurried over, shining his flashlight at the exposed square stone. Lucifer studied it for a few moments, giving no visible reaction. He spoke at last, "This is it. Excellent." He bent down again to eye level with Michael. "Thank you for doing the hard work. I was never any good at these stupid puzzles." Lucifer paused, lifting Michael's slumped head up so he could see him. "Your actions in Kazakhstan caused me some problems; it was fortunate that we could solve them." He let Michael's head drop. "I want you to know, our little game of cat and mouse is almost over. I should just kill you and your little attack dog now." He glared at Anan. "But where is the fun in that? Let's give you some time to suffer while thinking about your own mortality." Lucifer turned to Marou. "Throw them into the subchamber, and make sure they can't get out."

As Lucifer finished his order, Joshua renewed his attack on Rebecca. Releasing her arm but not her throat, his left hand groped her breasts. He pressed his lips to hers in a mock kiss, but instead bit her lip. Pulling back, he tore at the skin.

Rebecca felt a sharp pain followed by the acidic taste of blood. With her hand freed, she slipped her knife from the sheath, thrusting it at his thigh toward the groin. The serrated blade found flesh.

Joshua howled in pain as the blade bit hard. Jumping back, he released her throat, his eyes burning with hate.

Gasping for breath, she held the knife high in front of her, flashing it back and forth, her hope swelling as blood oozed through her assailant's pants.

Enraged, he stepped in. Throwing a spinning kick, his heel blasted into her face. The stunning blow collapsed her like a rag doll, her knife clattering to the ground. Things went gray.

Lucifer stepped near the two combatants. "Throw her in the pit too."

Joshua protested, "No! I want her, I'm not done playing yet!"

Still dazed, Rebecca managed a kick as Joshua grabbed her arm, yanking her across the ground toward the entrance.

Lucifer stopped in his tracks and stared at the young man. His voice still calm but menacing, "Put her in the pit, or I will skin you before cutting your body up into little pieces while you're kept alive." His cold black eyes left no doubt to his resolve.

Joshua glanced down, his hands trembling, "I'm sorry, Master, it's just she did this to me. I need revenge."

"And you'll have it when she's in the pit." Lucifer's voice was cold.

Rebecca watched as Marou pushed Michael through the hole; he hit the floor with a thud. He repeated the process for Anan.

Joshua gave one final kick to Rebecca's ribs. A bolt of pain shot through her body, her breath exploding out.

"You're lucky, bitch, what I had planned for you was far worse than this."

Dragging her across the floor, he pushed her legs, then her body through the hole and into the darkness below. She hit the ground hard, jarring her bones from head to toe. The only thread of good fortune was her legs hit first, absorbing the worst of the impact.

Marou put his head over the hole. "If you haven't guessed yet, we've disabled the alarms. There is no help coming."

Unseen in the background, she heard Joshua's voice, "Think about me while you're alone in the dark, bitch!"

Moving as fast as possible, she strained under the limited light to shift Michael, then Anan to a lying position, their breathing labored and weak. She heard the men above struggle to lift the center stone to its intended position. As they slid the rock into place, light to the lower room faded to shadows until the cover slammed into its final resting spot. Then, as it had for so many years, complete darkness ruled over the crypt.

CHAPTER 25

October 2, 2014
Thursday
Giza, Egypt

Maya was greeted on the Giza tarmac by sunny skies and a seventy-degree temperature. She felt rested and was in high spirits. "Wow, it's beautiful out."

"Sure beats wind-blasted Ireland," Austin answered.

They walked to the luggage compartment and removed the packs. Austin checked his phone. "Is it really Thursday here?"

Gabriel glanced at his watch. "Let's see, we left Tucson Tuesday evening, total travel time for flight and stops was twenty-four hours, meaning we arrived here Wednesday evening Tucson time. Adding nine hours for time zone changes makes it eight o'clock local time, Thursday morning."

"Thanks. These overnight trips always mess with my head."

"It does the same for me. I thought it was even worse when traveling to India, longer in the air and a bigger time change."

Maya smiled at Austin, who responded in kind, seeming to note the change in her.

They walked with their bags to the parking area where they found a sand-colored Humvee, with all the bells and whistles, waiting for them.

Gabriel couldn't hide his enthusiasm. "Nice, I've always wanted to drive one of these! Charles took good care of us."

They made a quick pass around the vehicle. Maya noticed the large black tires were new, its knobby grips jutting out, the matching spare mounted on the hatch door. On the front bumper, an industrial winch with a huge coil of metal wire hung securely beneath a silver brush guard. The truck had its hard top on, but Maya could tell it was easy to remove. It was a vehicle that appeared capable of navigating through the harshest terrain and back again. When she opened the rear door, she found three large containers of gasoline, two cases of bottled water, a large box of packaged food, and climbing gear strapped securely down.

"Wow, we could spend a couple weeks out here with these supplies," she said.

"Let's get moving; the faster we get there, the faster we get out," Austin replied.

Gabriel said, "I figure we have about three and a half hours to get to the location, depending on terrain. If we run into a bunch of washes that we have to navigate around, it'll be longer. Either way, I expect we'll be at the coordinates by midday or so. And, I've built in a little time so we can drive by the Giza site to view the pyramids. They're thirty minutes from here and on the way. Thought you'd want to assess our old work firsthand."

"I was hoping you'd say that. I'd definitely like to see them and if possible, the Sphinx as well," Austin said.

"I want to remind you both of our pit stop in Tikal," Maya warned, "where Mr. Smith was following us. So, while I also want to take in the pyramids, it's not at the risk of being tracked or attacked."

"Always the voice of reason, Maya. We won't tour the site, we'll just see it from afar. Nobody will pick us up there. If someone is following us, they're doing it now and the stop may even expose them," Gabriel replied.

Gabriel took the driver's seat. On Austin's insistence, Maya took the front passenger seat while he climbed into the spacious back.

Gabriel pressed the ignition, and the throaty engine roared to life. "As a heads-up, there are a lot of bad characters in this part of the world, so have your weapons loaded. But, if we're pulled over by the police, let me do the talking."

"Should we worry?" Austin asked.

"Not really, 99 percent of the local police are solid citizens, but that other 1 percent sees a car like this and thinks: easy payoff."

"And what will you do?" Austin pressed.

"I'll pay them off. We don't need entanglements now."

"Gabriel, I did a little research on the way over," Austin said. "There are the three major pyramids on the site, but also three smaller ones. Were they built by the Atlantans too?"

"The three small ones sit at the base of Menkaure's pyramid.

They're called the Pyramids of the Queens, built about forty-five hundred years ago, after Khufu and Khafre. They are the tombs of Khufu's wives and sisters and are not Atlantan-built, but an attempt by Menkaure to rise to a divine level. The Atlantans had already built the larger pyramid that bears his name and thought if he added three more, they would be even more grand than Khufu." He gave a soft laugh, shaking his head. "The egos of the pharaohs were enormous; they considered themselves actual gods."

Gabriel pulled off the main road onto an isolated side street. He drove parallel to the pyramid complex until he shifted into four-wheel drive to cruise off-road. He drove for a few minutes across the sandy ground before skidding to a stop.

"This is close enough. Anybody comes near, we'll have plenty of notice," Gabriel said.

They stood by the front grille to view the jewel of the Atlantans sprawling before them.

"Khufu is the largest and first built; that is the communication tower. Our main mission here was to build that beautiful behemoth, then send a message home. Khafre and Menkaure were built afterward, intentionally positioned to reflect Orion's belt. If the Atlantans were searching for us, they would calculate where the beacon was emitting from and find those three lined up, hopefully recognizing it as a sure signal for help from us." Gabriel pointed as he spoke.

"And what of the Sphinx?" Maya asked. "It's small compared to the pyramids."

Gabriel caught Maya's eye. "A warning to any human who considered war. Half man, half lion, sound familiar?"

"Like some type of demon," Austin said.

"Correct. The message was clear: Atlantans were here, the creators of demons," Gabriel said.

"Pictures can't do it justice. The size is what's really amazing. Hard to believe it was all accomplished with hand tools and back sweat," Maya said. Her right hand dropped, slipping in Austin's left and clasping it tight. She flashed him a smile before glancing back at the landscape.

Austin moved closer to her, rubbing his thumb across her hand in response. She was enjoying the first intimate contact with him since Sedona. Austin seemed to enjoy it too.

"This is nothing. You should have seen them with their polished limestone caps. The centerpiece of this entire valley was packed with ornate temples, bustling people everywhere. It was a magnificent site to behold." Gabriel beamed.

A silver SUV rolled by on the surface road behind them, its pace slower than normal. Gabriel turned to track it, fixated on its progress. He followed the car's movement, stepping to a point a few feet behind their vehicle, ensuring the driver had no bad intent. It continued past them, straight along the isolated road, eventually vanishing from sight.

During their few seconds alone, Maya whispered, "I've been thinking of you a lot. I'm sorry about being so distant; these last few months have been tough for me." She gazed into his eyes.

"When all this is done, I'd like to spend time together, just you and me, alone. I've got so much inside I want to share with you." She touched his face, then added, "No more secrets, I promise." She squeezed his hand before standing on her toes to kiss his cheek.

His eyes lit up. "No more secrets, that sounds good."

Gabriel turned back to them. "Time to get moving. We can discuss any more questions you have in the car."

"Anything to be concerned about?" Maya asked.

"I don't think so, but let's be extra safe. Plus, the earlier we're out, the higher the probability we get there with some meaningful daylight left."

Gabriel navigated with ease onto Highway 75 toward Ain Sokhna, the city of Cairo sprawling in front of them.

As they crossed the Nile River, he reflected, "The whole valley has changed so much. Try to imagine this area littered with mud huts and limestone temples. Wooden boats traveling to and from the Mediterranean packed the river. And now, observe the metropolis before you. The human evolution has been amazing."

"How do you process it all?" Maya asked. "I mean, things change in our lifetime, but it's incremental. You've seen twenty thousand years of development, from prehistoric man living in caves around a fire, to a landing on the moon. It must seem surreal."

Gabriel changed lanes, accelerating past a car. "At times, it is. But you learn that change is the one true constant in life that no one escapes. You can either adapt or be left behind. For Michael and me, we've tried to guide that change to create a better world."

"I wish more people worked toward that goal," Austin said.

Gabriel navigated a patch of heavy Cairo traffic.

"King Tut, the boy king, did you know him?" Maya asked.

"I did. And there's a unique story about him, one that you'll appreciate."

Austin leaned forward in his rear seat. "Ancient gossip, I like it."

"Tut's head was misshapen, elongated. His eyes were different. Scientists published these facts a few months ago after they scanned his mummy."

"That's right, I read that. They speculated a deformity due to inbreeding," Maya said.

"It wasn't inbreeding, he was a demi. His skull and eyes reflected the mix of Atlantan and human DNA." Gabriel paused while his words sunk in. "In most cases, the babies that exhibited Atlantan traits, such as bigger heads, were killed upon birth as freaks or harbingers of bad luck. The only demis that lived were those who appeared human-like. Tut was different, he was a prince of divine birth. The pharaoh refused to slaughter him. He's evidence of Atlantan-human children."

"Wow, the boy king was a demi," Maya said. Somehow this fact made her feel more normal, knowing others had faced the same reality and lived a happy life. "I read he was also frail."

Gabriel gave a short nod. "He was—he suffered from malaria and a few other ailments. But he was a good person. I was sad to hear when he passed and still hope to meet his transient energy again. Who knows, you may as well."

The car fell silent as they drove down the highway.

"We're getting close to our turnoff," Gabriel said. Austin, reach in my bag, top pocket—grab the GPS locater."

He did as requested. "What are you going to do?"

"I used high-def satellite maps to route a path through the desert to get us to Abydos. Essentially, moving through frame by frame studying the landscape to avoid washes or hills that were not drivable. I then input the composite of coordinates into this machine. Should help us avoid getting lost, or worse, stuck."

Maya mounted the locater onto the dash and turned it on. A voice with a British accent spoke to them at once. "Turn right in one mile."

Gabriel followed the directions to a tee. The four-lane highway turned into a two-lane back road, and then to a barely passable dirt road. When that ended, Gabriel popped the car into four-wheel drive and took it off-road, straight into the red desert.

Progress was slow and methodical now. The farther into the desert they drove, the harsher the landscape became, transforming into a Mars-like surface with no life evident. The ground was rocky on sunbaked clay with areas of red wind-blown sand piles. Eons of erosion were the primary force in crafting what they saw. The dryness of the environment created the ideal conditions such that over the centuries, when the rains hit, the dry soil washed down and out to the Red Sea.

Two hours into the drive, he spoke to no one in particular. "Interesting."

Rolling the Humvee to a stop, Gabriel jumped out, his two companions following just behind.

Austin asked, "What's up?"

Gabriel appeared concerned. "The GPS indicates we're getting close: take a look at that." He pointed off to the east where at the peak of a hill, a set of tire ruts scarred the landscape.

"What are the odds of a truck being out here?" Austin asked.

"My thoughts exactly," Gabriel answered.

"Low probability. Let's not take any chances." Maya removed her EMP gun, moving the energy level to the maximum power setting.

Austin followed her lead, chambering the first round of his Sig.

They returned to the car and continued their drive for a few more minutes when the GPS lit up, announcing, "You have arrived."

Gabriel's eyebrows raised, confusion on his face. "Arrived? How can that be? We're in the middle of nowhere."

Austin stepped out. With his binoculars he began scanning the horizon in front and to the sides. Maya looked in all directions as well. Nothing to see but the endless terrain of red rock and sand.

He climbed back in. "We're in a small bowl here. Keep going straight to the top, but slowly."

Gabriel revved the engine and put the SUV into gear, rolling forward for a few hundred yards, up an almost imperceptible rise. As it reached the crest, Gabriel braked. Now visible in front of them, a narrow canyon-like gash fractured the ground, splitting the rolling hillside in half. The valley was narrow, no more than two hundred yards wide, and ran a jagged path as far as Maya could see.

"The document's description was correct: unless you're standing right on this canyon, the illusion is that it's flat ground," Austin said.

Maya stepped out of the vehicle and peered through the binoculars to the west. Scanning the red soil, she saw the partial remains of the geoglyph that replicated the Star Crystal. Rapping on the Humvee's window, she called, "This is it, bring it closer to the ledge."

Gabriel complied, driving the car near the rocky edge of the weatherworn cliff.

Maya walked over and peered over its jagged side. With the binoculars, she looked over the floor of the canyon wash and scanned the inhospitable land, but found only natural formations. Peering at the other side, she thought there were small black openings burrowing into the cliffside, but the shadows were too dark to be sure.

With no firm conclusion, she returned to the Humvee. The two men had already removed their packs and were attaching the harnesses required for their descent.

Maya did the same. "It's a good drop. I can't be sure how deep, but definitely doable. I assume it's early enough that we can go down tonight, right?"

Gabriel peeked up at the sun still high in the sky. "Yes, we have more than a few hours of daylight. We can rappel down easily and do some reconnaissance at a minimum." As he finished, he pulled out his phone and started texting. He spoke while typing, "Found the site, descending now."

A buzz came back at once, he read it to the others. "Your uncle says good luck and to be safe."

"It's amazing we can reach out halfway across the world in a matter of seconds," Austin said as he finished belting his harness.

"Standing in the middle of a desert," Maya added.

As Maya strapped her equipment tight, Austin said, "How about you lower me down? Once I find a way in, you can position the car and throw down the rope. Then you two can descend."

"Sounds good. I couldn't make out anything on the cliffs below us. I have no idea how we align to any doorways or openings. You probably have to descend to the canyon floor and do some searching. Once you find the main entrance, we'll move the car then hoist you up to where you have to get to."

Gabriel handed Austin a walkie-talkie. "Use this."

Austin took the radio and clipped it to his belt. "Thanks." He snapped the hook of the car winch to his harness. Gabriel attached the end of the climbing rope to the bumper and threw the rest of the coil on the hood. Maya stepped in, rechecking his connections, tugging on each one. Once he was secure, she wrapped her arms around his neck, pulling his head down to her. She gave a tender kiss to his lips, holding it for a long moment.

Maya finished, "You're carrying, right?"

"Always. And Demon Slayer."

"Good, be careful."

Austin touched her cheek. "I will."

Gabriel started the winch motor, uncoiling the wire, allowing Austin to plunge over the cliff's edge.

Maya walked to the ledge and watched his descent.

Feeding the wire out, Gabriel stepped closer, but remained more than a few feet back. He peeked over the side and spoke in his gentle way. "It seems you've thought about your future and what you want." He glanced up at Maya, his eyes had their purplish hue.

She smiled back. "I did. Thank you for last night. It was the first time in a long while I slept well."

"That's good. No one deserves peace of mind more than you," Gabriel said.

The moment was interrupted by a screech from the radio. Austin's voice came through. "It's getting dark here, the light is dropping. Just turned on my flashlight. I'm seeing some openings in the cliff face; they may be doors or windows. They're small and symmetrical, as if designed, but not like a main entrance." Static came again before Austin's voice continued. "I'm also seeing remnants of an outside walkway system. A few areas are built into the rock, others appear like a frame was attached to it. It's pretty broken up."

Gabriel raised the radio. "Got it. How is your speed? Too fast?"

Austin responded, "No, speed is fine." The radio crackle fell silent for a few seconds but returned in abrupt fashion. "Hold, hold."

Gabriel hit the stop button on the winch. "I've got you down fifty yards on the wire."

Austin responded, "I'm on an old walkway now; it's narrow, no more than a yard wide. And I think I found the main door. It's about thirty yards to my left. I'm going to try to get over there. Can you give me a little slack?"

Maya peered over the side, leaning as far as she dared, gauging if she could detect anything. She studied the cliff face; no movement was evident. "I can't see him, Gabriel."

Gabriel let out a little more line. Thirty seconds later, a loud crash thundered from below, followed by the line snapping tight.

Maya screamed, "Austin!"

They waited on edge for the answer. Gabriel hit the stop button, the winch halting at once. "Talk to us, Austin, everything okay?"

Static greeted them in response. Maya cupped her mouth, calling, "Austin!" Turning to Gabriel, she ordered, "Take him up."

Before he could act, Austin's voice rang through the radio. "I'm all set, the walkway collapsed. I fell, but the wire caught me. Sorry for the delayed response, I needed my hands to get situated before calling. I'm back on the walkway now." There was a pause. "Whew, that was a little hairy."

Maya breathed easier.

Austin said, "This is the place. I'm situated on a stone platform about twenty yards above the wash. I'm guessing I walked a little more than that. Move the vehicle to your right so the wire is vertical, then drop the rope."

Gabriel complied and moved the car while Maya guided the wire. Once on the correct line, they lowered the rope until Austin confirmed, "I got it."

Gabriel raised the winch while Maya clipped her climbing harness to the rope. Right before starting her descent, she asked Gabriel, "You ready for another adventure?"

"Repelling down to a lost city in search of a powerful crystal with a demon likely in wait? Just another day at the office," he answered with a grin.

Maya gave a wink and a smile before starting the uneasy descent. Never looking down, she focused on the cliff in front of her and the rope as she repelled until she reached the platform. Gabriel followed soon thereafter. Once situated, the three congregated at the main entrance to the cliff city of Abydos. After removing their harnesses, they each scouted around. Austin was right, the entrance was constructed well above the floor of the canyon. Wide steps from the entrance descended down toward the canyon floor, but faded into the shadows. The facade was quarried granite surrounded by ornate carvings in the limestone rock. These appeared to be humans toiling under the Grays' whips, with demon-like gargoyles staring over them all.

Gabriel shined his light across the chiseled stonework. "This was actual life under Lucifer and the IOD. They enjoyed being feared by humans."

"Scary," Austin said. "I can't even imagine the hell those people lived through. But let's keep moving. Faster in, faster out, remember?"

Gabriel followed right behind. "Agreed."

They continued through the open-air main entrance. Any

remains of a door had long ago been removed or rotted. The first room was modest in size but royal in decor. Small vestiges of colored tile and intricate carved scenes littered the walls. The floor was a polished stone that had a liberal covering of dirt and debris that had blown in during the centuries of abandonment. Maya walked to one side of the entry chamber as Austin walked to the other. A tall, open portal stood to her right. She stepped to it, flashing her light around the room. It was larger, even more beautiful. At the back of the chamber near the edge of her beam, she saw an opening to another room.

She navigated back along the far wall to rejoin Austin and Gabriel. "There's another chamber off this one and seems like more of the same."

"Same over there. Which begs the question, how big is this place, and where would they hide the Star Crystal?" Austin asked.

Gabriel mopped his forehead with a handkerchief and flashed his light to the back of the entry room. It ended in shadows. He strolled toward the darkness, stopping after a few steps. "I sense something. An evil energy is here—a very old, dark energy."

Maya walked over. Standing beside him, she closed her eyes, tuning her mind to the surrounding darkness. "You're right, I feel it too."

She continued to the back of the main room, stopping just short of a stone rail protecting a vertical drop. Austin and Gabriel followed, flashing their lights back and forth, illuminating the unknown. They could just make out the large square opening that rose in the darkness above them but also dropped to an abyss below. As they closed in, they recognized the opening as a vertical shaft with smooth limestone walls holding a decrepit spiral stairway. Its steps were precariously constructed along the wall edges, appearing to be attached by a few unstable bolts drilled into the rock.

Austin asked, "What is this?"

Gabriel highlighted the stairs with his beam. "It's the transportation center to the city. They didn't have an elevator, so they created this shaft and ran a stairway through it to connect all the floors and rooms. The design is skillful."

"That's logical. The question now is, do we go up or down?" Austin asked.

Maya again closed her eyes, tuning in to the energy in the room. "It feels like the dark energy is down. And if history is any indicator, that's where we need to go."

"That's my sense too; the crystal is always guarded by a demon," Gabriel replied.

"I was afraid of that." Austin pulled Demon Slayer from its sheath, checking the blade before sliding it back in. He then took the energy stone from his shirt, its yellow-blue hue reflecting only their energies. "We're alone," he added.

They entered the stairwell and began descending into the darkness. Built like the outside walkway encountered by Austin, parts of the path were built into the wall, the rest attached.

Well into their slow and careful descent, Gabriel halted. "There's a gap in the path, I'm guessing five to six feet, and I can't be sure what's beyond that."

Austin stepped forward, searching the darkened walls with his beam. "Let me go first. I think I can climb over, there seems to be enough handholds." He removed a small coil of rope from his pack, tied it around his chest, and gave the other end to Gabriel. "This worked in Japan. Tie it around your chest, keep it taut, and brace yourself. If I fall, you'll need to catch me." He turned to Maya. "Be ready to pull."

Gabriel did as asked, wedging himself as best he could on the stairs.

Maya stood near the edge, grasping the rope. "Be careful."

When ready, Austin shimmied onto the limestone wall, searching for foot and handholds. Once secure, he edged onto the vertical face of the shaft. Taking his time, he climbed methodically, testing every hold before applying his full weight. Halfway across, he instructed, "Note where I'm going, so you can follow."

In a few tense minutes, he was safe on the other side. He adjusted the rope, shining his light back. "The stairs are fine here, very stable. We can move forward. Maya, your turn—loop the rope around your chest. I'll hold this end, Gabriel the other."

They repeated the process with Maya. She was nimble and quick over the chasm. Once safely across, she slipped out of the noose holding her.

Austin took his end, wrapped it around his chest one more time, then secured himself on the stairs. "Your turn, Gabriel, we got you."

The Atlantan was more hesitant. "I don't like this."

"There's no choice, you've got to do it," Austin urged.

Gabriel muttered something Maya couldn't understand as he climbed on the wall face. His process was uneven and slow. He had progressed halfway when his hand slipped from a hold. Lurching sideways, he began sliding down the cliff. "Pull the rope! Pull the rope!" he yelled.

Austin was way ahead of him. Stepping back on the stairs, he yanked the line tight. Maya joined in. Muscles screaming, she strained with everything she had.

Gabriel started an uncontrolled slide. With few options, he pushed off the wall, propelling himself toward the lower stairs.

With his momentum shifted, Austin pulled once more, and he fell backward while the rope tightened.

Maya launched up to the edge to find Gabriel hanging over the side, his hands locked in a death grip on the top stair. She reached over, grabbing the Atlantan's shirt. "On three together guys, pull like you mean it. One, two, three!"

They all heaved in unison. Gabriel slid onto the last stair and collapsed onto the safety of the hard path. He lay still, face down, sweat rolling down his temples.

Maya stepped over. "You okay, Superman?" she joked.

After taking a moment to collect himself, Gabriel rolled over to a sitting position. "I think I am. Thank you both." He wiped the sweat from his brow.

Maya squatted down, putting her hand on his shoulder. "You sure you're okay?" Her gentle eyes locked on his. "That was really scary." She paused, letting the words sink in. "You battle demons, fly helicopters, heal wounded friends, and fight like a Navy Seal. I didn't think there was anything you couldn't do. I admit, I'm kinda surprised."

He rolled his eyes. "I appreciate the sentiment, but you'd be even more surprised at how many things I can screw up."

"If you're not hurt, we need to keep moving," Austin said. "And I like the name Superman, that may stick." He winked at his friend.

Gabriel stood. "Yes, yes, I'm fine. Let's go."

The remaining journey down the stairs was without incident. There were spots where they had to jump small collapses or lean against the wall to squeeze by. Considering the age of the structure, they made fast progress, slowing only to ensure their solitude.

On occasion, Gabriel would pause to listen at the doorways to the black rooms connecting into the central shaft, in the end always motioning them to continue down.

When they hit the bottom floor, Maya said, "Austin, your energy stone is glowing."

He pulled the crystal out; a deep crimson red radiated through it. "That's demon energy, and from its color, I'd say a strong one."

Austin and Maya unholstered their guns, and Gabriel removed his laser.

Covered by shadows, they crept toward the one visible door.

The air was hot, dry, and dusty compared to the fresh breeze above. A considerable amount of sand from centuries of accumulation covered the floor, making walking arduous. Austin led them through a stone portal into a walled hallway. With his light out front, they moved cautiously to the unknown evil that waited in the darkness.

"Watch out for rooms opening off this passage," Gabriel said.

The subterranean corridor ran deep into the cliff, and the farther they traveled in, the more stifling the air became. Maya was questioning their choice of paths when she spotted flickering shadows on the walls ahead.

Austin stopped, whispering, "There seems to be a light in front of us." He turned off his beam.

Gabriel wiped his brow. "I agree, but it's too inconsistent to be a lamp."

"Lights off, silent travel, weapons ready," Maya whispered.

The amber glow intensified as they continued down the corridor, keeping its rhythmic dance across the surrounding stone. They crept onward until Austin reached the end of the passageway. Maya and Gabriel stood back while Austin peeked his head out and peered toward the source of the light. He stared for a moment before retreating to the safety of the shadows with his friends.

"The light is from burning torches; they're placed on the walls around a huge room. Someone else is here." His voice was low.

Gabriel's eyes narrowed. "This is a trap. We should leave."

Maya said, "We're here now, we need to find out if the crystal is here. We're at risk if we stay or go. I say we play this out. Gabriel?"

A metal-on-metal grinding noise clanged from the shadows around them, and a thick iron gate thudded close just behind them.

Their path for escape through the tunnel was now blocked. Austin leapt over and grabbed the iron blockade at its base, straining to move it. Gabriel and Maya jumped in, pulling with all they had. The metal wouldn't budge.

Austin stopped, exasperated. "No way we're moving that thing."

"It appears the decision was made for us," Maya said.

Gabriel gave an audible exhale, eyes locked on theirs. "Only one way to go. I'm in first, stay close behind, guns ready: this is going to get ugly."

Maya held her EMP gun firm. Her pulse calm, she was ready for the fight. "Bring it."

With his weapon raised, Gabriel inched into a vast cavern. Austin and Maya followed.

The cavernous room was limestone, top to bottom, with no doors or windows on the ground level. Torches were burning in equal distance along each of the four walls, lighting the place like an afternoon sunset. Halfway up the sidewalls, long benches were chiseled into rock, with rows of these seats rising high up the wall. The floor in which they walked was deep sand. On the far end, a balcony carved into the rock sat precariously above the ground, its two ornate chairs overlooking the pit they now stood in. A light glowed from its recesses.

A booming voice came forward, "Gabriel, welcome to our city. I'm guessing you've never been here before."

Gabriel stopped, clear he recognized the voice. "Abaddon, I suspected this was your doing."

Ojater stepped forward on the balcony. "And I see you've brought friends. Amaya and—Austin isn't it? Welcome to our little home." Her voice dripped with sarcasm.

Maya's jaw clenched, she hissed, "Bitch."

"I'm glad I ran into you again," Abaddon addressed Gabriel. "Our last visit was too . . . short." Abaddon reached into his pocket. "As you know, I'm more of a man of action than words. So, let me get right to the point. First, we already retrieved the crystal." He held up a glowing container in his right hand. "It was difficult to get, guarded by a nasty sand demon. You remember those, don't you?"

"We're not interested in anything you have to say," Gabriel said.

"But the second thing is the fun one," Abaddon continued. "You see, you're standing in what was our old battle pit. We had so many sacrifices here in front of the frenzied mob. And today, after over five thousand years, this pit once again contains one pissed-off sand demon and now three sacrifices." Abaddon gave a booming laugh. "I'm sorry, but Ojater and I will have to stand in for the mob." As he finished, he pointed his gun down and fired three shots into the sand by their feet.

The ground shuddered, then began shaking, and sand rolled over their shoes. Something below was stirred and was now rising to the surface. The three friends edged to the pit's walls just as the sand started to lift off the floor.

With a raging shriek, a giant scorpion-like creature emerged from the floor between them. Double their height and equal in length, the creature's hard exoskeleton connected two giant claws with its hooked tail, a large, black stinger at the end. Its deformed mouth held jagged, spiked teeth that reeked of the corpses it devoured. A knobby head held a group of black bulbous eyes that sat protected by a row of horns. Fully emerged from its slumber, it roared again, snapping a claw with lightning speed, almost decapitating Austin in the process.

As if an unspoken command was given, the three friends surrounded the demon and unleashed hell on the beast. Austin unloaded his full clip of armor-piercing bullets. Maya hammered it with blast after blast from her EMP gun, while Gabriel's antimatter laser fried its right side. The demon howled in pain, shaking from the onslaught. It then responded with equal ferocity, whipping around and crushing Gabriel with a crack of its tail, the blow knocking him on his back. A wild slash with its bony claw connected with Maya, stunning her down to the ground and neutralizing the gun. The monster turned last for Austin and his pistol.

Maya watched from the ground as Austin popped a new cartridge in. He raised his weapon again while Maya shouted, "Go for the eyes!"

Blasting another cartridge into the beast, he picked off a group of the black bulbous orbs. The creature wailed with pain before rushing the prey. With supernatural speed, it closed the gap. The creature enveloped him under its legs and abdomen, knocking his gun free in the process. Time after time, the demon slammed its black stinger into the sand, just missing Austin's head or torso as

Austin rolled over and over in search of a safe harbor that was nowhere to be found.

Maya heard Ojater's screams of delight over the roar of the animal. Turning toward the balcony, she went to a knee and aimed the EMP at Ojater and Abaddon, then lowered it an inch, setting her sight on the target. She fired three blasts, all shots hitting the rock just below the balcony. Ojater's cackles grew louder at what she perceived was a misfire, but when the brittle limestone rock crumbled away, her cackles changed to cries of anguish. The balcony collapsed into the pit, tumbling her and Abaddon down with it.

Maya turned her attention back to the beast. Austin was still on the ground, fighting its brutal assault with Demon Slayer now, slashing at the creature's legs while twisting for his life. She charged from behind, firing round after round of the EMP into its back. The demon screeched with pain as its bony tail fractured at its base, listing to one side.

It spun in response, once more assailing Maya, gnashing its claws in a frenzy. A glancing blow brushed her arm but still had the power to send her flying. The creature attacked, trying to spear her with its damaged tail, jabbing the sand around her. Maya watched as Austin jumped onto the beast's back. Straddling its body, he lunged forward, driving Demon Slayer deep into the base of its skull. The creature screeched, then shuddered before spinning out of control, throwing Austin and his knife into the sand. Frothing at the mouth, it spasmed, then collapsed into a quivering heap. In a twist of fate, death now stalked the demon.

Maya rose, glancing left to see Gabriel brawling with Abaddon. Gabriel held the upper hand and was pounding Abaddon to the ground. Blow after blow rained onto Abaddon's body, as years of pent-up anger were released in a primitive, brutal moment.

With Gabriel safe, she turned back to find a bruised Ojater holding Austin's fallen gun. The Atlantan pointed it at Austin as the creature lay twitching beside him. Austin stood in defiance, his blood-splattered face staring with cruel intent at the woman.

Ojater shouted to Maya, "I told you the next time I saw you, I'd kill your pretty boyfriend. Well, it is the next time!" She squeezed the trigger.

Maya was faster. Raising her EMP, she fired once. The blast clipped Ojater's arm, knocking her sideways and directing her bullet into the fallen creature. As if in collaborative response, the demon reacted, raising its broken tail and spearing Austin through the back of his shoulder. The black, shiny stinger popped out of his chest by the collarbone before being pulled back by the creature. Shock lined his face as he collapsed to his knees, then slumped to the ground.

"Austin!" Maya screamed.

In a moment of chaos, all is forgotten but the highest priority. Maya ran to her friend, ignoring Ojater and the beast. She lifted his head and placed it in her lap, holding him close. She was helpless as he convulsed through this fight for his life. The scorpion's poison raged through his body. The veins in his temple bulged; his breathing became rapid and shallow.

"Hold on Austin, I'm here," she urged.

She laid his head down and knelt beside him. Reaching down, she pumped his heart twice, three times—she couldn't be sure. Her mouth locked to his. Breathing out, she filled his lungs with the hope of life. She did it again. He coughed in response, a flicker of life rekindling in his eye. Foam and a black liquid dripped from his mouth. She tried it again, only this time, the flicker faded.

Black blood continued to ooze from his gaping mouth. His fingers reached for her. They ran through her black hair to her cheek, to her lips. He gazed into her eyes one lasting moment and whispered, "I love you." His eyes turned glassy and hollow as his chest exhaled one last time.

Maya watched in disbelief as the blue-yellow mist emerged from his body. It was Austin's face. He appeared happy, at peace. It wafted for a moment, hovering just above them both, when a black shadow materialized. She heard the growl, and he was gone.

She pulled his body into hers, holding him even tighter. Through tears she whispered, "Don't you leave me. I love you."

A beaten Gabriel strode to her side, his medical bag in hand. He pulled out his supplies and began working. Maya laid Austin's head down. She kissed his forehead, then rose. Speaking, her words were controlled rage. "He's gone, Gabriel, I saw his transient."

Wiping the tears rolling down her cheeks, her face turned cold and she transformed from victim to hunter. "Where is she? I'm going to kill her."

CHAPTER 26

October 2, 2014
Thursday
Abydos, Egypt

Pain seared through Austin's shoulder. He glanced down to see the tip of the demon's stinger protruding below his collarbone, then it was gone. His chest tightened, and the sharp, stabbing pain spread quickly, becoming unbearable. He tried to scream but nothing came out. He needed air—if only he could inhale, everything would be okay. *Breathe, breathe,* he thought.

Once more, he tried to inhale, but his chest became taut, his lungs wouldn't pump. Life-giving air surrounded him, but none could save him. The agony radiated through his body and he still . . . couldn't . . . breathe . . . His legs gave way, and he dropped to his knees.

I've got to get up, I've got to save Maya. Why can't I breathe?

He tried standing, yet another shock raged through his body and his legs wouldn't respond. *What is happening, why can't I move? Is this it, am I going to die?* The questions raced through his mind. As his adrenaline kicked in, his heart raced, the survival instinct still strong.

With no prompting, Maya was there. She would help. He embraced her touch. He was lying on the ground now. She pounded on his chest, then breathed for him. Air at last. She tried again, but he could feel her slipping away. She cradled his head, holding him. It felt so good to be close to her—her gentle touch, the smell of her hair, her beautiful smile. *Stop crying, Maya, it's all okay.*

He tried to tell her what he wished he'd said a thousand times before: "I love you."

He wasn't sure the words made it out. He hoped she knew his heart and could feel his energy.

The agony subsided as his vision faded to gray. A twitch radiated in his back, and then he felt seven distinct pops, up his spine and the last in the top of his head. Something was different now; a calm flowed through him as his sight returned. The gray cleared, and he began floating above the chaos. He saw his body on the ground with Maya still holding his head, weeping. She whispered something but her words fell empty on his dying shell. He tried to comfort her, tried to speak, but she didn't seem to understand. *Maya, Maya, it's okay. I'm fine.* He tried smiling at her one last time.

He realized he had seen this view once before at the vision quest with Michael. He knew his transient had departed his expiring living energy. So, this is the end. The process was strange, but fear was not a part of it.

He hovered above his dying body for a moment, then saw Gabriel in the distance, running to his side, a bag in his hand.

A white light opened above him. What was it? He hesitated. Was this good? Should he enter the light, or should he run away from it? The glow exuded a warmth. It seemed right; a familiar voice called his name. The choice was made for him as a black shadow enveloped his being. The mist's gentle motion comforted him before guiding him toward the glow. The wind rushed loud, psychedelic colors flew by, all outside the safety of his black protector. He soared straight into the radiance greeted by a roll of thunder and a flash of lightning.

A blinding glare washed over him, its warmth and security providing the hope he craved during this transition. When the light cleared and his vision returned, he stood outside the main ballroom at the Red Rock Valley Resort in Sedona. Maya stood in front of him. Beautiful in her black dress, she reached up to kiss him. Their lips touched, her love consuming him.

The picture blurred, dissipated, then reformed. Austin recognized the coffee shop in Tucson. Rebecca handed him a mug before sitting down next to him. Her hair was tied back, her gentle face radiant and beautiful, the delicate red rose on her arm shining bright. She stood up, placing her hand in Austin's. She held it for a moment, squeezing as if she'd never hold it again, then gave him that innocent smile before vanishing. He reached out, *Don't go, please Rebecca, I miss you.*

The mist clouded his vision again, then cleared. Austin was

waiting outside a classroom; he recognized his lab at the university at once. He stood in the hallway and watched a young woman with black hair and mocha skin appear from around the corner. He remembered this day; it was the first day he'd seen Amaya Luna. He grinned at her as she walked by. He said, "Hello." She gave a shy smile back, then glanced away before disappearing down the hallway.

He turned to see his living room as a child. The Christmas decorations were hanging in festive fashion around the room—a merry little tree sat in the corner, a pile of presents wrapped underneath. In walked his mother, then Uncle Charles, his father following last. His father walked up and gave him a bear hug. Austin hadn't seen him in so many years. He nestled in his strong embrace, taking in the fragrance of his cologne, the love exuded, the comfort provided. He moved to his mom. She reached out, touching his hair, sliding her hand down to caress his face. She pulled him in tight, saying, "I love you, my only son." Uncle Charles approached last. He hugged Austin, then stepped back, smiling, hands lingering on his shoulders. The three faded away.

An EMP blast flew by his head. He crouched down even lower behind a white marble wall. Michael knelt next to him, Gabriel a few feet away. Anan stood above the wall, firing and screaming, "Get down, get down!" He dove to the ground, ducking low behind the protective rocks. "Incoming!"

The ground trembled in violent response as the explosion rocked the nearby housing. A fireball rose in front of them, the resultant heat wave rolling over the wall, singeing Austin's face.

Michael turned to Austin. "We've got this; Lucifer and his followers are faltering. We'll press our attack from here." Michael placed his hand firmly on his shoulder. "Uriel, I need you to evacuate as much of the city as possible." Michael paused, staring him in the eye. "I'll get the force field. Take every boat that can sail, and get the humans out. It's urgent, Uriel, they can't withstand the radiation we can."

"I understand," Austin replied as the Atlantan leader faded into a mist.

He closed his eyes, the puzzle complete. The visions vanished. When he opened his eyes, he lay in an open field, yellow flowers littering the landscape. He had no perception of space or time, he only existed at peace in the rapture.

CHAPTER 27

October 2, 2014
Thursday
Tucson, Arizona

Connie stepped into Charles's office. "Any word from the teams?"

He shook his head, still studying his computer screen. "No, and I'm getting worried. I received word from Gabriel as they started their descent into Abydos, but nothing after. I also heard from Michael on their drive in to the passage tomb; it's very unusual they wouldn't connect back. I've checked the gates and alarms; everything seems to be normal, just no word."

"You know as many times as we've coordinated trips like these, you'd think we'd get used to the silence. Unfortunately, it doesn't get easier." She glanced down, casually scanning the sheets of paper in her hands.

"No doubt about that."

"To change the subject, do you have a minute I can talk with you about something?"

It was rare for Connie to request such a discussion. "Sure. You okay?"

She continued, "After Mack's betrayal . . . for lack of a better term—"

Charles interrupted, "No, no, that's the exact right term. Go ahead."

"As we've discussed before, on routine I scan some printed summaries of the company's emails and text messages to see if there are any unusual addresses, phone numbers, or anything that jumps out as odd." She paused, a sick expression filling her face.

"That's prudent you do those checks. After Mack, we can't be too safe," Charles replied.

"Well, I think there is something you need to see. I noticed a pattern of text messages that were being sent at two in the morning and then deleted at 2:02 a.m. Using one of our police contacts, I ran the number they were being sent to. It's a burner phone."

Charles's brow furrowed. "Go on," he said, a gnawing anxiety forming in his belly.

She reluctantly continued, "I pulled the actual text messages from the phone company. There were a few things sent in August, most of it benign, appears they were starting their contact. But the ones in September were the most concerning. Here are a few key ones."

She set down four pieces of paper. Charles put on his glasses to read them.

Message 1: September 12, 2014; 2:00 a.m.; G.Au.R.Am. West Bengal, India; 09/14/14; L23.327 L87.615

Message 2: September 19, 2014, 2:00 a.m.; An.Au.R.Am. Mt. Fuji, Japan; Fuji View Hotel; 09/20/14

Message 3: September 28, 2014, 2:00 a.m.; M.An.R. Slieve Bloom Mountains, Ireland; 10/02/14; L53.081 L-7.603

Message 4: September 28, 2014, 2:00 a.m.; G.Au.Am. Abydos, Egypt; 10/02/14; L29.587 L31.913

"I'm not 100 percent about the two Ls at the end, but best guess is they're longitude and latitude coordinates," Connie finished.

Charles stared, incredulous. "That's exactly what they are." He paused while taking it all in. "This is crazy. They're telling someone at the other end of the line the exact date and location of where we'll be, and who will be there. Who sent these messages?"

Connie again hesitated before answering firmly, "I'm sorry Charles, but they came from Maya's phone."

CHAPTER 28

October 2, 2014
Thursday
Abydos, Egypt

Maya paced back and forth, her rage boiling over. She pulled the EMP and blasted the lifeless remains of the sand demon. The overkill did not alleviate the pain of her grief. Through tears she gave a primal scream, "Ojaterrrr!" The word echoed through the cavern.

Gabriel stepped to her, pulling her close, holding her while she cried. "Maya, listen to my voice. Ojater is gone, and I need your help, now!" He stepped back, grasping her arms with his hands, his face grave. "I'm going to save Austin."

Her eyes narrowed in disbelief. "What do you mean save him?"

"Please trust me right now." He pointed down to Austin's ravaged body. Stepping to his fallen friend, he knelt, handing Maya a cloth. "Bind this into the wound; it'll stop the bleeding."

She was confused. "What bleeding? He's dead." But she did as requested anyway, opening Austin's shirt and stuffing the dressing into both sides of the puncture wound before taping it down.

Gabriel's hands danced in a flurry, moving over Austin's body and ensuring his friend was ready for the procedure. He reached into his bag and withdrew a syringe filled with a blue liquid. "The bleeding that will occur when I start his heart with Bernael's resurrection drug." He jammed the needle deep into Austin's chest, shooting the life-giving substance into his torso. He thrust down on his heart three times before breathing air into his lungs. Reaching into his bag again, he removed a second syringe.

Maya asked, "What's that?"

Gabriel glanced up, "This is the next generation antivenom we developed in Atlantis. It should address the sand demon's poison." Finishing his statement, he jammed the second needle into his dead friend's heart.

Austin's body arched, then collapsed, then raised one more time before falling again, landing with a spasm. His body gasped for breath; black blood choked out from his mouth.

Gabriel lifted his jaw, clearing his blocked airway. After a few spastic tremors, his breathing became rhythmic.

Gabriel put his ear on his friend's chest and listened to his heartbeat. His eyes lit up. "His body will live."

"What difference does it make? His transient is gone, I saw it reaped," Maya cried.

Gabriel's eyes glowed. "First, we save his living energy, then we resurrect his transient. I'm not sure how, but I think I know somebody who does. Meaning, we need to get him out of here, fast."

Gabriel reached in his pack one more time. "And guess what I took from Abaddon?" He held up the fifth piece of the Star Crystal.

Maya stared at the glowing green jewel. "How . . . How did you get it?"

Gabriel returned a small shrug. "I had the better of our discussion and took it. Ojater stopped me from killing him while you cared for Austin. She kicked me off of him, then helped the bastard escape. They were both wounded, her arm from your blast, and he was bleeding badly. She was so intent on his rescue that I don't think she realized I had taken it. I let them go, recognizing I had the crystal and more importantly, Austin needed our help."

Maya stared at him, a tinge of hope welling inside. "You really are Superman." She wiped some sand from Austin's face. "Let's get him out of here."

CHAPTER 29

October 3, 2014
Friday
Atlantic Ocean, Southwest of Dingle, Ireland

Heavy waves bobbed the fishing trawler in conjunction with a howling wind, pitching the vessel up and down, then back and forth. The rough seas didn't appear to bother the seasoned captain nor his two focused customers. Their attention was fixed on the horizon, scanning the waters for any sign of land.

Staring through his binoculars, Marou answered the buzzing satellite phone in a hushed tone. His conversation was short. "Got it, I'll let him know." He ended the call.

Turning to his taller associate, he spoke, "Sir, success in Africa. There were fireworks, but everything went according to plan. They'll meet us at the usual spot in two days."

The silent passenger nodded his approval.

Captain Malley lowered his binoculars. "I'm telling you lad, there's nothing out here. Are you sure we're in the right area?"

The taller client's gaze stayed on the rolling waters. "Let's move a half mile south," he said.

The captain engaged the engine forward, steering into the incoming waves. The ship responded, chugging ahead. "It's your money. I'm going to say it again: this isn't a good day, the swells are too high. Unless you literally stumble on this mythical land mass, it's impossible to pick it up on the horizon." He paused. "How big did you say the island was?"

"We don't know," Marou snapped back, lowering his glasses and glaring at the seaman. "Did you forget our deal? No questions and you forget everything you see today. Failure to do so will become an occupational hazard."

Malley returned his stare to the ocean in front of him. "Whatever you say, you two are the bosses today." The Captain reached down and opened a cabinet. He removed a small bottle of whiskey and presented it to them.

Marou gave a slight shake of his head. Lucifer made no acknowledgement, instead focusing ahead through the trawler's window.

After an awkward moment, the captain twisted off the cap and sipped the brown liquor with a small grimace. "That'll warm your soul," he added.

The trio continued plodding through the steep rises and falls of the angry sea. Marou was about to suggest their return to port when Lucifer pointed to the horizon. "There! What's that mist?"

The captain picked up his binoculars and peered through them. He responded, "Mmmm, maybe a storm, although it's low on the water. Shite, that is odd." He paused, refocusing the glasses. "I guess I can't be sure. I've not seen that before."

"Take us there," Lucifer ordered.

The captain spun the vessel's wheel, steering the boat west. "Aye lad, but you best hold on, the sea's getting rougher."

Cross waves pounded the hull, creating a huge sway with each crest then drop. The headwinds had also picked up and now wailed over their secure encasement, drowning out the engine's steady growl.

The seasoned captain checked his coordinates.

Marou read them over his shoulder, 51.6559 and -12.0717.

The captain returned his gaze to the mist, which was now visible to the naked eye. "That's crazy—I been in this area a hundred times, I've not seen anything like that before."

The craft chugged forward for a few difficult moments before coming into an area of calmer waters.

Marou brought the binoculars up and thought he saw a rocky cliff but was having difficulty keeping his focus as they swayed back and forth.

Lucifer said, "I've got it, I can see cliffs and green land. That's it, we found it." His voice reflected an unusual hint of excitement.

He had no sooner finished when the depth-finder alarm started screaming from the dash. The captain studied the boat's sonar map, which now illustrated rock shoals and a shadowy mass just below their hull. He turned the wheel, steering toward deeper water, all the while watching the gauge. "There appears to be a sunken ship just below us, resting on the floor."

Marou watched as he turned his attention back to the surface, peering into the ocean. Malley pointed to the mussel-encrusted shoals peaking above the water line, the razor-sharp rocks bidding for the ship's bottom. "There's the danger."

He spun the wheel harder, steering farther east. Once clear, he looked down to focus on the map. "Lads, we can't go in farther, not today. I have no way of navigating these rocks and don't have the fuel for an exploratory. We need nautical maps, otherwise we risk sinking the boat."

Malley glanced up one more time, turning to his left to view the mist on the horizon. To his clear surprise, the cloud had vanished, and an ocean of blue water was rolling in its place. "What the hell happened? The fog lifted?"

Lucifer didn't lower his binoculars, continuing his gaze at the location the phantom island should have been. "What are your coordinates now?"

Malley read them off. "51.6218, -12.1045."

Lucifer continued, "And that's due west." It was a statement, not a question.

The captain made a gruff reply of, "Aye."

Marou removed a paper map from his jacket pocket and wrote down the coordinates of their current location.

Once complete, he leaned in to the captain. "Great work, you did it. Now let's celebrate!"

He pulled a small flask from his inner pocket, twisting the top open. He started to bring the liquor to his lips, then stopped, offering it to Malley. "You got us here, you should have the first sip. It's a unique Irish whiskey." He paused as the captain took it. "Remember the deal, forget the coordinates, forget our faces. If you ever speak of this trip or try to return here, it'll be the last voyage of your life."

The captain grinned, revealing his brown stained teeth. He gave a subtle toasting motion before taking a big draft from the container, appearing comfortable holding the flask. "For the amount of money you paid me, I won't remember anything."

"Take another, you've earned it," Marou said.

Malley gladly raised the whiskey again in a toast, taking another shot of the harsh liquor before handing the flask back to Marou.

He motioned to Lucifer. "What about your serious friend? He needs to lighten up, celebrate a little . . ."

His last word slurred, seeming difficult to get out.

Marou twisted the cap shut, keeping a close watch on the captain's deteriorating condition.

Malley's hands began shaking, eyes bulging while his face turned red. A white foam oozed from the corner of his mouth. He stumbled going forward, catching himself against the railing for a futile second before collapsing on the deck. His body twitched for a moment, then ceased all movement. A black shadow growled through the cabin, then vanished.

"He was right, he won't remember a thing." Marou touched the man with his boot's toe, confirming the death of his living energy.

He studied the horizon again, searching for the vanished island. "We've located Hy Brasil, what's next?"

With his eyes still fixed on the water, Lucifer gave orders. "Get that vermin overboard and take us back to the harbor. We need to check on Elijah's progress, then finish the bomb that will destroy the Well of Souls."

Acknowledgments

Thank you for reading *The Immortals of Light: The Rapture*. It took a lot of work and a lot of help from others to get it done. To that end, I'd like to thank editors Betsy Thorpe and Katherine Bartis and book graphics and designer Diana Wade. Thank you to beta readers Greg Boudreaux, Amanda Sullivan, and Christina Hiller for their editorial contributions. And thank you to Erica Benefield for her social media help.

Special thanks to my family for the unwavering support and specifically, Veronica, my partner in life and the best marketer a writer could hope for.